STAR TREK®
MIRROR UNIVERSE
GLASS EMPIRES

STAR TREK®
MIRROR UNIVERSE
GLASS EMPIRES

Mike Sussman with
Dayton Ward & Kevin Dilmore
David Mack
Greg Cox

Based on *Star Trek* and
Star Trek: The Next Generation®
created by Gene Roddenberry
and
Star Trek: Enterprise®
created by Rick Berman & Brannon Braga

POCKET BOOKS
New York   London   Toronto   Sydney

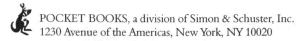
POCKET BOOKS, a division of Simon & Schuster, Inc.
1230 Avenue of the Americas, New York, NY 10020

Library of Congress Cataloging-in-Publication Data

Star Trek : mirror universe, glass empires.—Pocket Books trade pbk. ed.
    p. cm.
    "Based on Star trek and Star trek : the next generation created by Gene Roddenberry and Star trek : enterprise created by Rick Berman & Brannon Braga.
    "Star trek fiction original"—T.p. verso.
    Contents: Age of the empress / Dayton Ward & Kevin Dilmore ; story by Mike Sussman—The sorrows of empire / David Mack—The worst of both worlds / Greg Cox.
    1. Science fiction, American. 2. Star Trek fiction. 3. Interplanetary voyages—Fiction. 4. Space ships—Fiction. I. Roddenberry, Gene. II. Berman, Rick. III. Braga, Brannon. IV. Star trek (Television program). V. Star trek, the next generation (Television program). VI. Enterprise (Television program: 2001)

PS648.S3S6588 2007
813'.0876208—dc22

                            2006051740

ISBN-13: 978-1-4165-2459-5
ISBN-10:   1-4165-2459-2

This Pocket Books trade paperback edition February 2007

10 9 8 7 6 5 4 3 2 1

Age of the Empress

Dayton Ward & Kevin Dilmore
Story by Mike Sussman

For Jerome Bixby,
who gave us that first tantalizing peek through the mirror.

And for James Blish, who made Star Trek *come alive in print*
for two young readers all those years ago.

Prologue

Hoshi Sato twisted the turbolift control grip. "Bridge."

The grav-plating adjusted as the turbolift ascended, and Hoshi could not resist an inward smile, pleased to feel the faint but unmistakable rush of upward acceleration as though traveling in an elevator on a planet with Earth-normal gravity. It was a familiar, even comforting sensation. The engineers who designed this ship obviously had paid attention to even the most minute detail. On her *Enterprise,* a turbolift passenger would feel absolutely no shift in g-forces as the car traveled, but the builders of this vessel realized there was something disconcerting about a lift that never seemed to be moving. Hoshi could almost hear Maximilian complain about the waste of time and resources required to program a turbolift's gravity plating to mimic an Earth-bound elevator. Her former captain had never been one for subtlety.

But to Hoshi, it was *artistry*.

That she was preoccupied with something so trivial, only moments after making love to Jonathan Archer and murdering him in his quarters struck her as—she wasn't sure what to make of it. She decided it was a sign of confidence.

As the lift slowed, nearing the top of the primary hull, Hoshi realized there was a problem she had not yet addressed. That it had not occurred to her before now gave her pause, and she wondered if she had made a grave miscalculation, one that she might very well pay for with her life.

The "problem" was Charles Tucker III.

With Archer dead, Reed incapacitated, and T'Pol in the brig, there was only one senior officer left to oppose her. Hoshi knew she had the support of Sergeant Mayweather and the surviving *Enterprise* MACOs, but Commander Tucker could yet prove to be a thorn in her side. She would need his expertise if the ship sustained damage during the battle she was sure was about to unfold. Would Tucker follow her orders? The lift doors were only moments from opening when another scenario flitted through her mind. . . .

What if Mayweather has been working with Tucker all along?

It would be the perfect setup—Hoshi eliminates Jonathan Archer, leaving Tucker in command of the most powerful vessel in the quadrant. He might be waiting for her on the bridge right now, ready to spring his trap. She imagined the lift doors opening to reveal the engineer perched confidently in the captain's chair, swiveling to face her with that leering, deformed smile of his. That's when she would feel the sharp pain of Mayweather's pulse rifle slamming against her skull. . . .

The doors opened. The center seat was empty.

Hoshi stepped onto the bridge of the *U.S.S. Defiant*. Mayweather and the MACO corporal followed her out of the lift, maintaining a respectful distance. Neither man had said a word during the brief journey from Archer's quarters. All around her, the various stations were manned by her colleagues, survivors of the ill-fated Imperial flagship, *Enterprise*. And what of this vessel's original crew? According to Phlox, they had killed each other in a fit of madness—a century in the future, in an entirely different reality.

Let's hope we have better luck, Hoshi mused as she strode with confidence toward the front of the bridge, knowing that her body language would be speaking volumes even as the crew sized her up.

"Open a channel to Fleet Admiral Gardner," she said as she moved past Crewman Newbill at the communications station.

"Channel open," the young woman replied.

An image of Earth rotated lazily on the bottom third of the

viewscreen as Hoshi moved to stand before the helm and navigation stations at the front of the bridge's command well. She placed her arms atop the free-standing console, leaning back and attempting to affect an air of calm and composure. "This is the *Starship Defiant*," she said with as much command presence as she could muster. "If you don't surrender immediately, we'll begin targeting your cities. Respond!"

Nothing. On the viewscreen, Earth continued to turn.

Hoshi's pulse quickened, but she showed no outward sign of anxiety. She knew chaos would be erupting at headquarters as they monitored *Defiant*'s approach. A minor delay was to be expected. She casually turned away from the viewer, apparently unconcerned as to whether Starfleet responded or not. Hoshi could feel the eyes of the bridge crew boring into her back.

Finally, the image of the Earth warbled out and she turned to see the grizzled visage of Fleet Admiral William Gardner filling the screen. The admiral's expression was one of utter rage. Understandable, Hoshi decided, as it was doubtful a lowly Starfleet communications officer had ever spoken to him in such a tone before.

"Where's Archer?" Gardner barked. *"Who the hell are you?"*

Hoshi's eyes narrowed as she gave Gardner the most withering look she could muster. It was the same expression her mother had used on her father on numerous occasions.

"You're speaking with *Empress* Sato. Prepare to receive instructions."

Hoshi thought she heard someone gasp behind her. The admiral and everyone on the bridge realized at that moment that Jonathan Archer was dead.

Gardner seethed, as though wishing he could reach through the viewer and throttle her. *"I won't give this order again. Stand down your weapons or I'll blast your ship to kingdom come."* His threat made little sense. *Defiant* was well outside the range of any ground-based phase cannons.

Behind her right shoulder, the navigator reacted to an urgent chirping at his console. A human male, whose name Hoshi could not remember. "Lieutenant— I . . . I mean, *Empress*—seven ships are closing on our position."

Hoshi had already guessed the answer before she formed the question. "From *where*?"

"They were hiding, Your Majesty. Behind the Moon."

"Show me."

On the viewer, Gardner blinked off, replaced with a view of black space, empty save for the distant silver points of light arcing toward them from around the crescent moon.

Hoshi was impressed. Archer had calculated—correctly—that the fleet would take another day to reach Earth at maximum warp, but like human beings, starships could often be called upon to exceed their design parameters when the need arose. The captains of those ships must have burned out every warp coil in their nacelles to make it home ahead of *Defiant*. Such initiative and resolve were traits to be admired—assuming those officers survived the day.

"Tactical," Hoshi said. The viewscreen switched over to a schematic overlay, showing the seven starships moving toward their position.

"Four *NX*-class battleships, a pair of destroyers"—the navigator hesitated for only a moment—"and the *Imperator.*"

A four-nacelled dreadnaught, *I.S.S. Imperator* was a killing machine, originally designated as the Terran flagship, until the Emperor decided it was too big and too ugly to carry that distinction. The first vessel of its class, the rebels had made certain *Imperator* was also the last. Knowing that the tide would turn against them if more dreadnaughts were commissioned, they had launched a massive attack on the Antares shipyards where the vessel had been constructed. The rebel losses were significant, but they had achieved their goal: *Imperator* would be one of a kind.

"They're hailing," Crewman Newbill reported from the communications station.

"Put them on," Hoshi ordered.

The lantern jaw of Fleet Captain A. G. Robinson filled the viewscreen. Hoshi had never been aboard *Imperator*, but from what she could see over Robinson's shoulder, its bridge was far larger than *Defiant*'s.

"*Hoshi?*" If anything, Robinson appeared even more surprised to see her than the admiral had been. Hoshi remembered a time when it appeared Robinson would be given command of the NX-01. In order to secure a position aboard his ship, she "befriended" the up-and-coming officer. But when it was clear Maximilian would give up his admiral's bars and assume command of *Enterprise,* Hoshi ended the dalliance with Robinson. He took it better than most. Truthfully, she had to admit she liked him. He had done well for himself in the intervening years; *Imperator* was nearly as prestigious a command as *Enterprise*.

"A.G. You're looking well."

Robinson addressed her as if trying to talk someone off a ledge. "*Hoshi, listen to me very carefully. If we're going to win this war, we need that ship. It would be a waste to destroy it.*"

She didn't appreciate the tone. "Skip the idle threats. You've scanned us, and you know what *Defiant* can do."

Leaning forward in his chair, Robinson said, "*You can't take on an entire battle group with* one *starship. I don't care what century it's from.*"

Hoshi didn't react outwardly, but she was surprised that news of *Defiant*'s origins had already reached him. She wondered what Robinson and Starfleet had been told about the starship and the Federation universe it came from.

"If you want to put down this rebellion, I suggest you stay out of my way."

"*I can't do that, Hoshi.*"

The Empress had hoped Robinson would ally himself with her, an action that might have convinced the other ship commanders to follow his lead. "It was good seeing you one last time, A.G.," she said with a touch of regret. "End transmission."

Robinson dissolved; *Imperator* and the rest of the battle group were moving fast toward them. Hoshi moved casually to the center seat and settled in—the leather felt cool against her exposed lower back. She nodded to Mayweather, who assumed the combined helm/tactical post. "Sergeant, take us into low orbit over San Francisco. Four hundred kilometers."

Several decks below in the brig, T'Pol felt the first blasts dissipate against *Defiant*'s deflector shields. Phlox, dozing in the bunk, bolted upright at the commotion.

"It's begun," T'Pol said simply. She had felt the ship drop out of warp a few minutes earlier, presumably near Earth. Starfleet had known of the *Defiant*'s approach, and the Admiralty would doubtless have formulated some kind of desperate strategy with whatever ships they could assemble. T'Pol was certain that Starfleet would not prove much of a challenge.

"The next few days should prove most interesting," Phlox said with more than a touch of sarcasm. "Do you think we'll be executed before or after Archer's coronation?" Vulcans had little use for rhetorical questions, and T'Pol saw no reason to respond to the one Phlox had posed. She understood the source of the doctor's despair—they had gambled and lost.

It was clear to her how the next few days would unfold. Like other Terran emperors before him, Archer would designate a new imperial capital in the nation-state of his birth. His coronation would follow soon after—possibly in one of the many North American palaces built by George the Second in the early twenty-first century. Then, T'Pol and Phlox would be put on trial for their mutinous actions against "Emperor Jonathan." Terran forms of execution were excruciating, and lasted for several days; T'Pol's mental disciplines would likely spare her most of the discomfort. She found herself more concerned for Phlox, who would likely die a horrible death, his suffering transmitted live to Denobula for his people to see. It pained her to know that would be the last image Phlox's wives and children would see of him.

Having risen from his bunk, Phlox now paced the width of their small cell, his movements drawing the attention of the guard standing on the other side of the force field. "We shouldn't underestimate Admiral Gardner," he said, his tone one of stubborn—if misguided—hope. "If he has enough ships, there's a chance we'll be rescued."

"Unlikely," T'Pol said, barely hiding her disdain.

Phlox halted his pacing, turning to face her. "Vulcans!" He spat out the single word like a curse. "I was a fool to listen to you and Soval. 'Concubines,' indeed!"

T'Pol recalled how she and Soval, her late friend from the now-destroyed *Avenger,* had lured the Denobulan into joining their mutiny with tales of the women and riches that would be bestowed upon him by a grateful Emperor. To her it was a ridiculous proposal, but at the time, Phlox had been tantalized by the possibilities.

The doctor stepped closer to her, an expression of menace twisting his features as he hissed through gritted teeth. "I should've turned both of you in when I had the chance!"

T'Pol returned an icy glare of her own. "I suggest you move away from me, Doctor." Obviously unwilling to test her, Phlox complied, though he held his aggressive stance for an additional moment before returning to his bunk. He dropped heavily down onto it, releasing a sigh of frustration.

T'Pol closed her eyes and gripped the edges of her own cot as the *Defiant* shook again in the face of another salvo of enemy weapons fire.

"Can I help you, sir?"

Opening her eyes at the sound of the guard's voice, T'Pol turned to see a Starfleet ensign approaching the guard. Tall and thin and with a head of close-cropped black hair, his dark blue uniform sported the blue stripes of the science division.

"Ensign Willingham," Phlox whispered. "What would he be doing down here at a time like this?"

"Be silent, Doctor," T'Pol replied, her own voice low. She felt her muscles tensing in anticipation of what the next moments might bring.

Outside the cell, Willingham offered the MACO a data padd, a small, rectangular electronic device. "I'm to take the prisoners to the hangar deck for execution," he said.

The guard did not move. "I only accept orders from Sergeant Mayweather."

"These orders are from the *captain,*" Willingham countered, his voice firm. "Unless you want to join these two in front of a firing squad, I suggest you stand aside." Willingham again offered the data padd to the guard, and this time T'Pol could see the MACO's expression change as he considered his options.

Finally, he took the device and touched a control to activate the small display. Arcs of electricity erupted from the padd, the MACO's fist clenching tight as every muscle on the right side of his body contracted.

Willingham reached for the guard, finding the pressure points at the base of his neck. The MACO jerked once more before his body went limp, and the ensign gently lowered him to the deck.

"What's happening?" Phlox asked, his tone one of confusion and shock. T'Pol ignored him, her attention instead focused on Willingham as the man reached for the control pad set outside the door to her cell. The force field flickered off.

"My apologies for the delay, Commander," Willingham said.

Nodding, T'Pol replied, "You've spent too much time among humans, Staal. Apologies are not logical." She turned to see Phlox regarding her from where he still sat at the edge of his bunk, his mouth open in surprise. Then his brow furrowed and she saw comprehension in his eyes.

"Wonderful," Phlox said. "Another Vulcan."

The doctor knew that it was not uncommon for Vulcans or other non-Terrans to have their appearance surgically altered before joining Starfleet. *Species reassignment* was often the quickest path to advancement—it was no secret that human officers have a distinct advantage over their alien colleagues. Once the rebellion became an established threat, Imperial Intelligence launched a witch hunt to find these imposters, believing that many of them were rebel operatives. Staal had avoided detection from everyone except his immediate superior—T'Pol. She had been aware of his true heritage for more than a year—she briefly considered surrendering him to Starfleet, but instead chose to look the other way, believing that one day Staal could be useful to her.

An accurate assessment, she mused as she stepped out of the cell and bent over the unconscious MACO. "You've secured a transport?"

"A long-range shuttlecraft," Staal replied, nodding as he returned his attention to the corridor outside the brig. "The shuttlebay should be unguarded."

T'Pol reached down to retrieve the unconscious guard's dagger and phase pistol. "We cannot leave yet. There is something I must acquire first."

"Commander," Staal protested, "there's very little time."

T'Pol was in no mood to argue with her rescuer. "You're with me, Ensign." She turned to Phlox. "Doctor?"

"Will someone please tell me what the hell is going on?" the Denobulan asked, stepping from the cell.

T'Pol ignored him, instead setting off down the corridor with Staal behind her, both of them with phase pistols at the ready. Phlox gave an exasperated look to no one in particular and decided to follow them.

The bridge shuddered under the force of yet another salvo. *Defiant*'s shields were repelling the attack, but Hoshi knew they were steadily weakening. She caught herself tapping the armrest with her index finger and clenched her fist tight, forcing herself to stop.

"Mister Mayweather," she said with a trace of impatience.

Hunched over his targeting scanner, the sergeant did not look away as he replied, "We'll be over the target in forty-five seconds."

"Two battleships are taking position, dead ahead," reported the navigator.

Behind her, Newbill called out from the communications station, "I'm intercepting a signal from Admiral Gardner." The crewman hesitated before adding, "He's ordering a *suicide run.*"

Her eyes widening, Hoshi was forced to admit that the audacious strategy was a sound one. *Imperator* was disabled, severely damaged but still intact. *Defiant* had reduced two of the *NX*-class battleships to vapor and debris, but their sister ships—*Broadsword* and *Khan's Wrath*—could do real damage if either ship collided with the Federation vessel. With this rate of attrition, Hoshi realized that her Starfleet might soon be comprised of a single ship.

A new alarm echoed throughout *Defiant's* bridge, a sound Hoshi did not recognize. "Collision alert!" the navigator shouted. "It's the *Broadsword,* one hundred eighty kilometers and closing at full impulse."

"Target them," Hoshi ordered, gripping the armrests of her chair.

"Evasive maneuvers?" Mayweather asked.

"Negative. Present minimum aspect and divert emergency power to forward shields."

On the viewscreen, the magnification factor automatically adjusted downward as *Broadsword* hurtled directly toward them. Lights flickered across the bridge, and Hoshi was sure she heard the drain on the starship's impulse engines as *Defiant* launched a furious barrage at the oncoming battleship. Explosions rippled across its hull, chunks of the vessel tearing away and spinning into the void, but *Broadsword* maintained its collision course.

"Impact in ten seconds," Mayweather reported, his voice tight.

"Continuous fire, all weapons!" Hoshi ordered.

Everyone on the bridge watched as out in space, the massive onslaught of *Defiant's* weapons finally overloaded *Broadsword's* polarized hull plating, tearing through the vessel's superstructure. Its warp reactor went critical and the battleship was instantly transformed into several million molten chunks of duranium and plastiform, a hailstorm of superheated debris that smashed against *Defiant's* forward screens. On the bridge, the crew struggled to remain in their seats as the ship lurched in response to the maelstrom.

With the muzzle of her phase pistol pressed against the base of his neck, T'Pol watched as Commander Charles Tucker entered the final sequence of commands in the small desktop computer interface. As he worked, she glanced out the small window looking out from the environmental systems control room. Below in main engineering the members of Tucker's team scurried about the massive chamber, their attention focused on maintaining the ship's systems as the battle was being waged.

Only moments before, Tucker had informed T'Pol of what had transpired on the bridge nearly twenty decks above them— word of the change in command had traveled at warp speed through *Defiant*'s intraship comm system. If anything, the news that Hoshi Sato had claimed the throne made T'Pol's flight from this ship even more urgent—the new Empress would probably shoot the Vulcan herself.

Another phase cannon blast rocked the *Defiant,* and T'Pol steadied herself against the bulkhead. Tucker looked up in response to the newest assault, shaking his head in mounting aggravation. "I need to be out there," he said, growling every word.

Then she heard the telltale string of beeps signifying that the computer had completed its task. Tucker removed the data card from its slot and offered it to her without turning from the workstation.

"Sato's going to kill me when she finds out I gave you these schematics," he said as T'Pol reached for the proffered data card and slipped it into a pocket on her uniform.

Two days ago, T'Pol had discreetly downloaded *Defiant*'s schematics onto a similar card—imprinted with detailed schematics of the vessel's warp and power systems, weapon yields, shield strength. It was her intention to turn the specs over to the rebels, giving them the means to defend themselves against this futuristic technology, and perhaps replicate it for themselves. T'Pol should have anticipated that Captain Archer's ever-resourceful comm officer would be monitoring her station on the bridge—T'Pol was arrested shortly thereafter.

"I have every confidence that an engineer of your skill can erase any evidence of your illegal access to the ship's computer," she replied. "Or, I could simply kill you now. It would be more merciful than anything the new Empress might devise."

Ignoring the weapon aimed at him, Tucker turned his head so that he could look at her, his expression a mix of confusion and anger made all the menacing by the way his drooping right eye narrowed as he regarded her. It was but one aspect of the man's features—marred by discolored, swollen scar tissue along the right side of his face—that bore mute testimony to the physical damage inflicted upon his body. The disfigurement was but one consequence of his exposure to delta radiation after years spent working in the poorly shielded engineering spaces of various Imperial starships.

"Who are you working for now?" he asked, his mouth curling into a snarl. "You're a rebel! Why don't you admit it?"

"You are wrong," T'Pol answered, her words low and sharp as she stepped back from him. It was not a lie, at least not yet, as she had no guarantee that any resistance cell—assuming she could find one—would admit her to their ranks. Her mother, T'Les, had joined the rebellion years earlier, but T'Pol had not been in contact with her since that time. Indeed, her service to Starfleet and the Empire would be seen as a threat to any rebels she might locate. They would be almost as likely to shoot her on sight.

Still, I must try.

An obstinate smile formed on Tucker's misshapen face. "You think Hoshi's going to let you fly away with the keys to her kingdom? When she learns you've stolen those specs, our beloved Empress will send every ship in the fleet after you."

She regarded him evenly. "Then it would be best if I left no witnesses."

Tucker laughed. "After all we've been through, you're gonna kill me?"

T'Pol had to admit that she held some lingering emotional attachment to the engineer. He had helped her through a difficult period—her most recent *Pon farr*. But the price she had paid was steep—she had developed a telepathic bond with this Terran, something she had not believed to be possible. He now haunted her during her nightly meditations; sometimes she could see him in her mind while in the middle of a duty shift. Tucker had admitted experiencing similar visions, but she convinced him they were merely waking dreams, or a delusion. She did not tell him that she shared this "delusion"—and that when she saw him in her mind's eye, his face and body were whole, unmarred by radiation scars.

She was forced to accept that some deeply buried part of her was *in love* with this human.

T'Pol had been uncharacteristically emotional—even vulnerable—during this last *Pon farr*. For reasons she did not entirely understand, she had decided to confide in Tucker, making him aware of the existence of certain Vulcan psionic techniques. Few off-worlders had ever learned of Vulcan telepathic abilites—to her everlasting regret, in a moment of intimacy, she had even chosen to *meld* with this human.

It was something of an unspoken agreement among all Vulcans to keep their mental abilities a closely guarded secret, particularly from Terrans. History was rife with examples of telepathic species persecuted by those who feared their abilities—humans as a whole may be powerful, but they were also paranoid. T'Pol had been fortunate—to her knowledge, Tucker had not told anyone of her secret.

She realized this was an opportunity to cover her escape and correct an indiscretion—or as Terrans are wont to say: "Killing two birds with one stone." Eliminate Tucker, and her secret dies with him.

T'Pol's grip tightened on the phase pistol, and the derisive smirk faded from Tucker's face—would she kill him after all?

Her thumb moving across the phase pistol's power setting,

T'Pol pressed the firing stud and the energy blast struck Tucker square in the chest. As he went limp, she reached out and caught his unconscious form before he could fall to the floor. Pushing him back in his chair, she studied his partially disfigured face, relaxed and vulnerable.

She could not kill him, but neither could she leave the ship without first seeing to it that he could not betray her, willingly or as a consequence of whatever prolonged, excruciating interrogation he was sure to suffer. T'Pol was certain the Empress needed him alive, at least in the near term. His currently unmatched knowledge of the *Defiant* and its advanced systems ensured his survival.

With a final glance through the control room's small window to ensure she remained unobserved, T'Pol holstered her phase pistol and leaned closer to Tucker. The fingers of her right hand reached out until their tips found the *katra* points on his face. Even through the blanket of unconsciousness, she felt the engineer's mind rouse at her touch.

"My mind to your mind," she whispered.

T'Pol found Staal and Phlox outside the triangular access way leading to *Defiant*'s hangar deck, a MACO crumpled on the ground nearby. Through the open double doors T'Pol could see a muscular, warp-powered shuttlecraft rising on the elevator pad— the markings of its hull identified it as the *McCool*, NCC-1764/4.

Phlox was kneeling at the side of the dead MACO, the soldier's neck twisted grotesquely. "You *had* to kill him," he dryly noted to Staal. "Another crime to add to our resume."

"I've overridden security lockouts on the hangar doors," Staal said to T'Pol as the shuttle elevator locked into position. "It won't be long before the bridge discovers my tampering."

"Prepare for departure," she replied. Staal walked briskly toward the craft. T'Pol turned to Phlox, still bent over the MACO—he was showing uncharacteristic concern for this dead Terran.

"There's nothing you can do for him, Phlox. We must leave."

Shaking his head, the Denobulan didn't meet her gaze. "I'm not going."

"You'll be executed," T'Pol replied, not without a trace of concern.

"If I run, the Empire will seek revenge against my family. I won't let them pay for my mistakes."

They had all heard the stories of how Imperial Intelligence used torture against relatives in order to find insurgents and traitors. Disappointed, T'Pol accepted his decision.

"I understand." She raised her hand, fingers splayed in salute. "Live long and prosper, Phlox."

"Good luck."

She touched a panel, and the access doors began to close, the doctor's expression one of determination and uncertainty. It would certainly be her last view of him—the one person she had truly called friend during her tenure aboard *Enterprise*.

T'Pol was certain he would be dead within a matter of days, perhaps sooner.

Multiple recoils reverberated through the hull, and Hoshi felt the vibrations under her feet as *Defiant* unleashed another barrage.

"Torpedoes away," Mayweather reported.

On the viewscreen she could see an aerial view of the placid, picturesque Horseshoe Bay. Hoshi watched as deadly blossoms silently appeared one by one across the landscape. She was pleased to see that Mayweather had spared the northern section of the Golden Gate; it would have been a shame to see harm come to the historic bridge. The eruptions ceased, leaving a haze of destruction hanging over what had been Starfleet Headquarters. If Hoshi did not know better, she might have thought the buildings were merely obscured by a thickening cloud layer.

"Get me the fleet captain," she ordered.

Robinson's image replaced the scene of destruction, his hair matted down by sweat. *Imperator*'s bridge seemed the worse for battle; a damaged console sparked behind the captain, black fumes filled the air.

"There's been a shakeup at Starfleet Command," Hoshi said, adopting a deliberately casual air. "Gardner and his senior staff have been relieved."

"I saw it," came the bitter reply.

Leaning forward in the command chair, Hoshi said, "I need someone with experience to take over—someone I can trust to put Starfleet back together and end this war. Know any good candidates?"

Robinson said nothing, his brow creasing as he comprehended her meaning.

"I'm promoting you to Starfleet chief of staff," she said after a moment. "Congratulations, *Fleet Admiral.* That is, assuming you want the job."

She watched as Robinson glanced about his shattered bridge, carefully considering his next words. His crew had stopped work mid-motion, watching their captain's next actions very closely. Finally, he rose from his command chair, appearing weary as he snapped to attention and placed the closed fist of his right hand over his heart before extending the arm in salute.

"Long live Empress Sato."

On the viewscreen, Hoshi saw *Imperator's* bridge crew trade nervous looks before apparently deciding to follow their leader's example.

"Long live the Empress!" came the chorus of pledges. Around her, Hoshi watched as—under the fierce scrutiny of Sergeant Mayweather—*Defiant's* remaining bridge crew joined in the salute.

The reign of Empress Sato had begun.

1

S erenity.
It was the only thing Her Imperial Majesty, Sato I, required of the *oikeniwa* surrounding Kyoto Palace. The tranquility offered by the meticulously maintained arrangement of ponds and gardens allowed her a brief respite from the demands of ruling the Terran Empire. The residence of Japan's imperial family between the fourteenth and nineteenth centuries, the palace had served as a tourist attraction since the end of the second world war. Hoshi had visited the grounds many times, having spent much of her childhood in Kyoto. Upon her return to Earth six months ago, the palace had naturally become her chosen home. It amused her that the city of her birth was now the center of the universe.

Hoshi watched the sun rise above the horizon, illuminating the lake beyond her veranda. She observed this simple morning ritual whenever possible, enjoying the few moments of solitude before turning her attentions to the issues of the day. It was one of the few indulgences she granted herself, but it also was her favorite, since she could enjoy it without interruption.

Most of the time, at least.

"Your Majesty," a voice, deep and masculine, said from behind her. So lost in thought was Hoshi that she had failed to hear the approach of the man, an oversight that might prove fatal anywhere else but here. In this place, however, she was perfectly safe.

Turning in her seat, Hoshi looked up to see Solomon Carpenter, her personal bodyguard, standing several paces away near the entrance to her bedchamber. In keeping with her directives, the bodyguard was dressed in dark trousers with the cuffs tucked into polished boots that came up to his knees, and a vest that left bare his muscled chest and arms. Around his waist he wore a wide leather belt, strapped to which was a dagger in its sheath as well as one of the phaser weapons taken from *Defiant*'s armory.

Just one of the many treasures to be found aboard that wondrous vessel.

"What is it?" she asked, already knowing the answer. Given the schedule for today, there was only one reason Carpenter would come to her at this time of the morning.

"I apologize for the intrusion, Your Majesty," the guard replied, "the general has arrived."

"Show him in." Hoshi rose from her seat, pulling the folds of her blue silk kimono tighter around her trim form. While she knew this meeting was necessary, it was one she had been anticipating with more than a bit of dread. After all, the next few minutes might well decide the future of the Terran Empire.

The Empress smoothed the wrinkles from her robe, realizing as she heard the sound of approaching footsteps that the motion made her appear nervous or tentative or—worst of all—weak. Momentarily irritated with herself for the lapse, Hoshi clasped her hands behind her back, drawing herself to her full height as Carpenter reappeared from inside the villa, followed closely by three Andorians.

All of the new arrivals were dressed in identical black leather uniforms, with varying numbers of small silver rectangles affixed to either side of their collars. Two of the Andorians, obviously subordinates, each carried a rectangular box perhaps one meter in length. The leader of the group would have been easy to identify even if Hoshi did not know him; his status was evident by the numerous medals pinned to his uniform. His left eye was a pale, dead orb, and he was missing his right antenna. Other, smaller scars adorned his face, the most visible signs of a long and distinguished military career.

"General Shran," Hoshi said, offering a polite nod.

Thy'lek Shran bowed at the waist, his hands locked at his

sides. "Your Majesty," he said. "I bring you greetings on behalf of the people of Andoria." As he straightened his posture, Shran indicated his two escorts and the containers they carried. "I also wish to present to you gifts which are but a taste of the spoils collected from our recent occupation of the planet Beta III." Shaking his head, the general released a sigh. "It is almost criminally inappropriate to call it a conquest, given their utter lack of resistance. They are little more than sheep."

Hoshi waved in the direction of the general's party, dismissing them and their gifts. As the other guard removed the Andorians, she turned to Shran. "General, walk with me."

The Empress and the general made their way toward the narrow wooden bridge leading from the palace out into the gardens, with Carpenter following but maintaining a discreet distance to afford them some privacy. Hoshi walked slowly, her arms folded across her chest, saying nothing as they crossed the footbridge and entered the inner perimeter of the *oikeniwa*.

"Leadership suits you, Your Majesty," Shran said after a moment. "You have weathered the obstacles facing you with great poise and dexterity."

It was a shameless compliment, even by the general's standards. Shran was being uncharacteristically deferential this morning, and with good reason, Hoshi knew.

"The ease with which you acquired the loyalty of Starfleet and the late Emperor's followers was simply—"

Maybe I should have him killed and spare myself any more of this.

"General," Hoshi said. "Shut up."

"Yes, Your Majesty."

An uncomfortable silence hung in the air. "I need your counsel," Hoshi finally said as they walked together along the narrow path winding through the garden. "This war is deadlocked—we're making no progress. Starfleet is still recovering from the losses we suffered at Tau Ceti. So far, we've been lucky—the rebels seem to be reluctant to launch a major offensive against Earth."

"I imagine you have the *Defiant* to thank for that," Shran replied.

It was true that the rebels—a loosely organized coalition of Vulcans, Andorians, Orions, Tellarites, and several other species conquered by the Empire over the years—had aborted their planned attack on Earth, thanks to the timely arrival of the starship from the future and, incredibly enough, a parallel reality.

The sudden appearance of *Defiant* in orbit above Earth had been enough to send the rebels scurrying for cover, bolstering the flagging morale of imperial forces. Hoshi knew the effect was only temporary—the rebels would eventually redouble their efforts and launch an all-out offensive. The Empress needed something more than a tactical advantage.

She needed a victory that everyone believed to be *inevitable.*

To that end, Hoshi had taken steps to ensure that knowledge of *Defiant*'s true origin in a parallel reality remained suppressed. As far as her subjects were concerned, *Defiant* was from the future of *this* universe—a future in which the Empire had not only defeated the rebellion, but thrived well into the next century. In the months since her ascension to the throne, she had used the imperial media to disseminate these revelations of "future history," allegedly garnered from the vessel's historical database.

As news spread on every subspace channel, a renewed optimism swept across the imperial territories. Skeptics need look no further than *Defiant* itself—definitive proof of the Empire's eventual triumph. Word eventually filtered back through operatives in the field that the rebels, too, were believing the story. Some had already abandoned their cause; many more were considering their options.

She had broken their spirit; now she would crush them.

"The rebels are using the pause to rebuild their forces," Hoshi said after a moment. "When they strike, we may not be able to drive them off, even with *Defiant.*"

Shran nodded. "Of course, you have considered a counteroffensive?"

"I can't order an attack if I don't know where they're hiding. We've been searching for their fleet for months." Hoshi could send *Defiant* and its advanced sensor array to hunt for the rebel fleet, but the moment the starship left orbit, Earth would be open to attack, something she was not prepared to risk—at least, not yet.

"The rebels will not hide forever," Shran said. "Earth is too tempting a target, even with *Defiant* as its protector." He bowed slightly. "How may the Andorian Guard be of service?"

Stopping her leisurely stroll through the *oikeniwa,* Hoshi turned to face the general. "You could stop supporting the rebels."

Shran's shocked expression was almost comical to behold. "Your Majesty, I . . ."

Hoshi's eyes narrowed as she glared at Shran. "Elements of the Guard have been providing aid and supplies to resistance cells for months. The rebels would never have been able to acquire seven decommissioned vessels from one of your most well-protected surplus depots without assistance. Those ships—and the tactical assistance you *personally* provided—may have made the difference in our defeat at Tau Ceti."

Shran said nothing for several seconds, during which Hoshi heard nothing save the sounds of rippling water and the call of some exotic bird she could not see. Regarding the general, she noted that his expression was no longer that of denial. Instead, Hoshi saw guilt and even a hint of fear in his one good eye. Stepping closer, she folded her arms across her chest. "Save us both the embarrassment of denying any of this, General." She noticed Carpenter moving up behind Shran, his hand drifting to the handle of the phaser on his belt. A subtle shake of her head halted him in his tracks, but the bodyguard maintained his alert stance behind the Andorian.

To his credit, Shran said, "I will not deny it, Your Majesty, but you must understand that I was acting in defense of my own people. The former Emperor saw Andoria as nothing more than a subject world to be pressed to the ground under his boot. He considered us no better than Orions or Tellarites, despite the fact that we helped build this Empire. Even the Vulcans did not show our level of devotion!"

"Is that your rationale for *treason*?"

Shran remained silent, and Hoshi caught him glancing over his shoulder to where Carpenter stood at the ready. The general's body language spoke volumes, as he no doubt considered his chances of overcoming her loyal protector.

"Relax, General," Hoshi said, amused by his evident anxiety. "I wouldn't think of ruining our stroll with an execution. You're more valuable to me alive." She stabbed a slender finger at his chest. "But don't think me a fool; your betrayal is not something I'll forget."

"I beg forgiveness, Your Majesty," Shran said meekly. "I will do whatever is necessary to make amends."

"Good." Hoshi resumed walking, and the general followed. "If I'm to win this war, I need resources I don't currently have. Starfleet isn't ready, which means I must look elsewhere. Pledge the allegiance of the Guard to me. Take command of Starfleet and hunt down the rebels. Help me, and I will reward *all* of your people."

Obviously unprepared for the opportunity being laid at his feet, Shran appeared genuinely humbled. "Your Majesty, this is most unexpected. I must confess some confusion. Why would you present such a generous offer after my betrayal?"

"Because history must unfold as it was written—as it *will be written*."

She watched as Shran considered her words carefully, his eyes finally widening in realization. "The historical database from *Defiant*. It foretold your act of mercy. . . ."

"Much more than that," Hoshi replied as she moved closer to him, her voice barely more than a whisper. "In addition to my lengthy and compassionate reign, there was the rather surprising and intriguing revelation that you and I will *marry*."

It required physical effort to maintain her composure as Hoshi watched the color drain from Shran's face. *"Marry?"* he repeated.

She nodded. *"And* I will bear you a son."

It was all a lie, of course. Hoshi had no more idea what the future held for Shran than she did for herself. Even the fate of the Andorian in the other universe had not been listed in *Defiant's* memory banks, owing to his withdrawal from public life after the end of his military career.

Hoshi pressed her case: "Once we are joined, your people will enjoy rights and privileges so far known only to Terrans. A new order will emerge. Andoria will stand beside Earth as a partner—an *equal.*"

Shran looked away for several seconds, and Hoshi watched as he considered everything he had heard. He would be a poor tactician if he was not evaluating all possible angles to the proposition she had made.

While she admitted to finding him strangely attractive personally, in reality Shran was a means to an end. A military strategist of unmatched ability, he would not stand by and wait for the inevitable attack as A. G. Robinson seemed prepared to do. Shran would take the fight to the rebels. His influence over the Andorian insurgents would prove invaluable. When they learned of their new status, they would desert in massive numbers, leaving the other rebels no option but surrender.

Returning his gaze to hers, Shran regarded her with a neutral expression. "I honestly do not know what to say, Your Majesty."

Hoshi was unable to resist the smile teasing the corners of her mouth. "It's very simple, Shran. You can become my consort and the supreme commander of Starfleet, or be executed for treason."

A nervous laugh brought a glint even to his lifeless eye. "Your negotiation skills are unrivaled, Empress." Then, with her trusted bodyguard standing as sole witness, the general stooped to one knee and held out his right hand.

"The people of Andoria would be humbly pleased beyond measure if you joined me in the bond of matrimony."

Hoshi smiled as she felt his hand tighten around hers, seeing both uncertainty and determination in his remaining eye. What the general did here now was for the sake of the Andorian people. His loyalty to the Empire might be suspect, but his fidelity to his home planet was inviolable. It was one of Shran's greatest strengths.

That devotion would also be his downfall.

2

The intruders were good. T'Pol did not hear them until an instant before she opened her eyes and saw the *lirpa* blade in front of her face.

Tossing aside the blanket that insulated her from the desert's chilly night air, she used it to entangle her assailant's weapon as she rolled to her left and scrambled to her feet, kicking over the small portable lamp situated between her and Staal. The wavering light illuminated the shadowy figure facing off against her; the man who twirled the *lirpa* in a circular motion and freed it from the blanket as he raised it for another attack.

In her peripheral vision T'Pol saw Staal facing off against another of the intruders, easily sidestepping his opponent's attack with a maneuver she recognized from her own defense training. He moved first left then right, catching the other Vulcan with the feint before closing the distance between them. Staal's right hand found the juncture of the intruder's neck and shoulder and applied the appropriate pressure, and his attacker fell unconscious to the cave floor.

His companion turned at the sound, giving T'Pol the opening she needed, and she lunged forward. He recovered, swinging the *lirpa* again, but now she had maneuvered inside the blade's arc. Grabbing the polished wood of the weapon's long handle with her left hand, T'Pol lashed out with the heel of her other hand, catching her opponent just beneath his chin. There was a satisfying grunt of surprise and pain and she felt his grip loosen on the *lirpa*. It was all the advantage T'Pol needed as she reached for the dagger secured to her left hip.

"*Kroyka!*"

So loud and emphatic was the command, echoing in the narrow confines of the small cave, that T'Pol froze in the act of pulling her dagger from its sheath. Looking toward the source of the directive, she saw that two other intruders—both Vulcans—now flanked Staal, who also had been roused from sleep. Each of the figures wielded what T'Pol recognized as Starfleet-issue phase pistols, no doubt obtained from one of the several arms shipments that Vulcan ships had seized in recent months. One of the figures turned toward her, aiming his weapon at her head.

"Do not move," a female voice said from somewhere to T'Pol's left, and she turned to see a Vulcan woman step from the shadows, the dim light from the portable lamp illuminating her figure and her features. Dressed in simple woven clothing that approximated the hues of desert sand, and with the bulk of her dark hair concealed beneath a light-colored tudung, the woman all but melded into the cave's surrounding rock.

Her eyes narrowing in recognition, T'Pol bowed in greeting to her. "T'Pau."

The woman nodded. "Indeed. You know who I am?"

"From visual records taken during your tenure as a minister at the sanctuary on P'Jem," T'Pol replied, her eyes shifting as her original attacker moved into her line of vision, still brandishing his *lirpa*. The ancient ceremonial weapon seemed like a toy in the muscled Vulcan's hands.

"You are known to us as well." T'Pol was surprised to hear the resonant voice of the Vulcan who had attacked her. "Commander T'Pol of the Terran Starfleet. A traitor to her own kind." His eyes narrowed. "It is no mystery why your mother renounced you."

"Sevor," T'Pau said, her tone one of clear warning.

At the mention of her mother, T'Pol took a step forward, only to stop when Sevor lifted his *lirpa* blade to her throat. Ignoring the obvious threat, she glared at T'Pau. "Where is my mother?"

"T'Les is dead," T'Pau said simply.

Despite years of training and discipline, T'Pol flinched at the pain as she absorbed the news. It had been several years since she had last seen T'Les, her mother having resigned her position on the faculty of the Vulcan Science Academy and disappearing from public life. T'Les had been an outspoken proponent of the teachings of Surak, a philosopher who had extolled the virtues of peace and harmony not only for Vulcans but also for every other species. The rumors that she had joined the rebellion had been difficult for T'Pol to hear. They also had provided no small measure of difficulty for her as her Starfleet superiors began to question her loyalty. To his credit, Captain Forrest had been one of the few humans who had never doubted her integrity. Nevertheless, the shame over her mother's actions against the Empire had haunted her for years.

None of that seemed to matter now.

Struggling to maintain her stoic demeanor and ignore the sudden feeling that the walls of the cave were closing in around her, T'Pol asked, "How?"

"She was killed when Starfleet attacked the Zakal Sanctuary," T'Pau replied. "An entire cell was wiped out, along with a large cache of weapons and supplies. As you can see, we are in constant danger of discovery and execution. We must therefore always be on our guard."

Raising his *lirpa* blade once more to her throat, Sevor added, "We know that spies supplied Starfleet with information about the cell's location, but the identities of the traitors remain a mystery." T'Pol felt the point of the blade touch her skin as he said, "Perhaps that is no longer the case."

"Silence," T'Pau said before ordering Sevor to step back and lower his weapon. Though she spoke in normal tones, there was no mistaking the commanding presence that belied the woman's petite stature. Whether it was as a once-respected minister or as a resistance leader, T'Pau bore the weight of her responsibilities with an ease normally found in someone of greater age and wisdom.

"How did you find us?" T'Pol asked, keeping her anger at Sevor in check. The Vulcan warrior stood at the edge of her peripheral vision, ready to strike at an instant.

T'Pau did not provide an immediate answer, pausing instead to glance about the interior of the small cave in which T'Pol and Staal had sought temporary respite as night fell. They had chosen this cave because of its small opening, hoping to deter any of the wandering *sehlats* from venturing inside in search of shelter or an easy meal.

Unfortunately, the cave entrance was still large enough to admit other types of predators.

"Your movements have been tracked since your arrival on Vulcan," T'Pau finally replied. "I almost ordered your execution then, but I decided to wait. Perhaps you were here to meet with other traitors."

T'Pol did her best to hide her anxiety at this revelation—if T'Pau was being truthful, then it was possible the rebels were already in possession of their shuttlecraft—*and* the *Defiant* schematics.

Though it was logical to assume that T'Pau and her resistance cell were hiding somewhere on Vulcan, it had taken *months* for T'Pol and Staal to transverse the 16.5 light-years in the stolen shuttle. The small vessel was far more advanced than the sublight shuttlepods carried aboard *NX*-class battlecruisers, but its maximum velocity was limited to warp four, and that speed could only be sustained for a few days at a time. To complicate matters, the renegades were forced to plot a circuitous course to the 40-Eridani system, in order to avoid imperial patrol routes.

T'Pol believed the shuttlecraft would prove useful in her dealings with the rebels—aside from its miniaturized warp drive, the vessel also contained a cache of personal sidearms. T'Pol had touched down in a canyon on the easternmost side of the Forge—as she had surmised, the geomagnetic instabilities that disabled most forms of technology in this region had no effect whatsoever on the Federation shuttle. Although it was safe from government patrols, she now realized the rebels may have resources of which she has been unaware.

"We were looking for you," Staal said before T'Pol could offer a reply. "An informant told us that a rebel cell was using the catacombs beneath the T'Karath Sanctuary as a base of operations. We have information of interest to the rebellion."

Holding his position to her right, the stout end of his *lirpa* resting on the cave's dirt floor, Sevor turned to Staal. "You have nothing of value to us, human."

"Do not let my appearance fool you," Staal said. "I am not human." He held up his left forearm, and T'Pol noted the small, thin gash just below his wrist that now dripped a line of dark green blood. His attacker's blade had come closer than she had first thought, after all.

"Perhaps you failed to note his fighting skills, Sevor," T'Pau said. "Have you ever seen a human demonstrate such proficiency with a *lirpa*? He has also mastered the nerve pinch, another skill Terrans lack." Indicating her surgically altered companion, she added, "This is Staal, a member of the resistance cell that once operated out of ShiKahr." Looking to T'Pol, she added, "That is, until the cell was eradicated by Vulcan security forces loyal to the Empire." To Staal, she said, "Of course, that massacre occurred while you were embedded among the Terrans. For a time, it was believed that you had turned against us."

T'Pol did her best to hide her surprise at this revelation—the apologetic look in Staal's eyes told her all she needed to know.

He had been a rebel spy all along.

Staal cooly countered. "Regardless of what you know about me, there is much you do not know about T'Pol. She was imprisoned by the humans for betraying the Empire, for sabotaging their new warship, and nearly destroying it."

T'Pol watched as the former minister's eyes widened—if only slightly—as she listened to Staal. T'Pau turned back to face her; there was no mistaking her piqued interest. "Fascinating, if irrelevant. The war is over."

"I do not understand," T'Pol said.

Stepping away from her, T'Pau folded her arms across her chest as she began to pace the cave's perimeter. "The warship from the future has added an element to the war which we cannot overcome." She eyed T'Pol again. "The new empress has made no secret of her plans to use *Defiant* to destroy us. Imperial broadcasts are flooding subspace, telling how the Terran Empire will flourish well into the next century, conquering worlds throughout the galaxy with ships just like the one she plans to send against us."

"From what I have heard," T'Pol replied, "you would *never* accept defeat so easily."

T'Pau shook her head. "It is simple logic. Our spies within the Empire have confirmed the information contained within the *Defiant*'s memory banks—history records the Empire's victory. Vulcan, Tellar, Andoria, the Orions, and numerous other worlds are doomed." Her pacing brought her back to stand before T'Pol once again. "The war is lost, but we may yet survive. We will leave Vulcan, leave the quadrant if necessary, traveling far beyond Earth's influence, and begin anew. Perhaps, one day we will be able to challenge the Empire's tyranny."

Interesting, T'Pol decided. While she had heard of the Empire's ongoing propaganda campaign, she still was surprised to learn just how effective the disinformation efforts had been. As she listened to the resignation in T'Pau's voice, T'Pol also heard the reluctance to admit defeat, to scurry away into some dark corner of space. The once-proud Vulcan minister obviously was not satisfied with the actions she must take, but had accepted them as necessary for preserving the lives of thousands of followers who had pledged allegiance to the pursuit of freedom.

The needs of the many—as always—outweighed the needs of the few.

"Sato is lying," Staal said. "The future she describes for the Empire is fiction." T'Pol watched as her companion looked to her, his gaze locking with her own. "Tell her the truth."

"The *Defiant is* from the future," T'Pol told her, "but it is not from *our* future. The vessel traveled here from a parallel reality—a universe where the Empire never existed. The Empress is a scheming opportunist and a liar—the outcome of this war is no more known to her than it is to us."

The diminutive Vulcan woman absorbed this, intrigued, but not entirely convinced. "The Empire is still in possession of that vessel. We cannot defeat it."

T'Pol reached into her clothing—Sevor readied his *lirpa,* believing she may be moving for a hidden weapon. The former minister raised her hand, and Sevor lowered his blade.

T'Pol removed the data card from her clothing—the same card she had forced Tucker to hand over many months ago. "With this, you will be able to destroy *Defiant*—and defeat the Empire."

The once-respected minister looked at her again. T'Pol saw renewed determination in her eyes. "I must know the truth," she said. Stepping closer, she held up her right hand. "There can be no doubt."

"I understand," T'Pol said.

She felt the warmth of the woman's fingers as they pressed to the *katra* points on her face. Almost instantly, T'Pol was aware of the initial tentative probing of another mind, seeking out her own.

"My mind to your mind," T'Pau said, her voice low. "My thoughts to your thoughts."

Soon, T'Pol knew, the truth would be known.

Then the war would begin anew.

3

"In every conceivable manner, this ship is extraordinary."

Shran's voice echoed in *Defiant*'s spacious engineering section, which to Hoshi seemed to pulse with the very energy being channeled through the starship's massive warp engines. As she moved deeper into the cavernous chamber, nodding to various members of the engineering staff who had come to attention and rendered salutes as she walked past, the Empress once again found herself in awe of the restrained fury at the heart of this starship.

"With her at the forefront of the fleet," said Travis Mayweather, who walked beside Hoshi, "the rebels won't stand a chance."

The Empress regarded the tall, dark-skinned man who to her looked most dashing in his tailored Starfleet uniform replete with captain's insignia. "Captain, is your vessel ready for battle?"

"At your command, Your Majesty," Mayweather replied, his confidence reigned in just enough to avoid appearing arrogant. "*Defiant* and her crew pledge eternal loyalty to the Empire."

Stopping her slow stroll across the floor of the engineering room, Hoshi turned to face the young captain, her right eyebrow rising as she smiled. "Do you include yourself in that pledge, Captain?"

There was a momentary flash of irritation in Mayweather's eyes, but he suppressed it with surprising speed, offering a succinct nod. "With my life, Your Majesty."

Hoshi knew that the former MACO sergeant—for a time, at least—had felt betrayed by her recent decision to take Shran as her husband. No doubt he also was disappointed by the loss of the benefits and pleasures that had come during what he likely considered an all too brief tenure as her consort. Still, his ego was soothed to some degree by her decision to give him command of *Defiant*. He answered solely to her rather than the Admiralty, and Hoshi figured she had no reason to worry about Mayweather's allegiance, for the moment.

Her attention was drawn to Shran as the Andorian stepped toward one of the room's few bulkheads that was not packed with all manner of status monitors or instrumentation. Instead, the wall panel was adorned with a depiction of the planet Earth impaled on the double-edged blade of a sword—the symbol of the Terran Empire—rendered in a monochromatic dark blue that contrasted sharply with the pale gray surface of the bulkhead.

"This vessel is a wondrous testament to the Empire's continued dominance in the decades to come," Shran said as he rubbed his hand lightly over the wall panel and the symbol emblazoned upon it.

Hoshi smiled in response to the general's all but poetic observation. Among the first secret orders the Empress had given was for the imperial crest to be applied to all interior doors, as well as prominent locations throughout the ship. She also had ordered the modification of the vessel's exterior markings so that they more closely resembled those of ships currently in service to Starfleet.

One of the more complicated matters was *Defiant*'s historical database. She had seen first-hand how its revelations could turn loyal Starfleet officers against the Empire. If the knowledge it contained were to become public—if the species of *this* universe learned of the "peaceful Federation" that existed, or *will* exist, in the parallel reality—the Terran Empire would be finished. Hoshi took the only action a responsible leader could take—she secured an archival copy for herself, then used a tapeworm algorithm of her own design to erase the original database, leaving absolutely no traces of it in the ship's library computer.

"Your Majesty," a voice said from somewhere behind and above her. Hoshi turned to see Commander Charles Tucker, *Defiant*'s chief engineer, standing atop a service platform leading toward one of the section's smaller systems control rooms. "I wasn't told you were coming aboard. I would've prepared a proper reception."

As he spoke the words, which dripped with the engineer's usual sarcasm, Hoshi noted the passing look of irritation he offered to his captain.

"Your staff should be ready for inspection at all times, Commander," Mayweather said, his own voice tight. "Besides, I don't recall any requirement to alert you to the comings and goings of the Empress, or myself, for that matter."

Keeping her own expression neutral, Hoshi knew that the two men had never been friends, but she trusted *Defiant*'s captain to resolve the situation. If he could not, then she was certain that someone else would assume Mayweather's responsibilities.

Something tells me that eventuality may come sooner rather than later.

Making his way down a narrow service ladder set between two banks of consoles, Tucker stepped onto the main engineering deck and stood before Hoshi, snapping to attention and offering a formal salute. "Welcome aboard, Your Majesty. How may I be of service?"

Instead of Hoshi replying, it was Shran who stepped forward. "What is the ship's status, Commander?"

Tucker glanced toward the Empress with momentary uncertainty before answering, "As ready as I can make her, General." Returning his attention to Hoshi, he added, "We've repaired all of the damage she took during the battle with the fleet. Our diagnostics picked up a minor molecular phase variance early on, but it faded during the course of the repairs." Shrugging, the engineer added, "I figure it must've been some kind of transitional residue from coming through that rift the Tholians created."

"It's had no measurable effect, Your Majesty," Mayweather said. "All systems are fully operational."

"Naturally, I'd like more time to study everything," Tucker continued. "I'm still not comfortable with my knowledge of the power distribution systems, the shield generators, and about two dozen things I could rattle off the top of my head." For a moment, the engineer sounded the way Hoshi had remembered him on *Enterprise,* cynical yet casual in his demeanor, his mood almost always lightening when discussion of his ship's innards came to the forefront of conversation. Then, as if realizing just how much had changed since then, the commander cleared his throat and bowed his head. "I'm sorry, Your Majesty. I forgot my place."

"Indeed, Commander," Shran snapped, his one functioning antenna curving until it pointed toward Tucker. "See that you avoid such lapses in the future."

Eyeing her husband with a tolerant smile, Hoshi said to Tucker, "You always were passionate about your work, Commander. There's no need to apologize for that." She knew that Charles Tucker possessed one of the few engineering minds capable of understanding and—eventually—duplicating *Defiant's* advanced systems. He was useful, but would he remain loyal? The Empress resolved to never turn her back on the man even for a microsecond.

Hearing the distinctive pneumatic hiss of doors opening behind her, she turned to see three new arrivals enter the engineering section. The ship's chief of security, Major Malcolm Reed, was at the front of the trio, which also consisted of Doctor Phlox as well as Hoshi's science adviser, Professor Arik Soong.

After first nodding in greeting to Phlox, whom she had appointed her personal physician, Hoshi shifted her eyes to Reed, imagining she felt a cool chill on her exposed skin as she beheld the security chief. Though he had recovered from the injuries he suffered in his fight months ago with the Gorn, a black patch covered his left eye. That side of his face and head remained scarred and darkened from burned tissue, to the point that the major now wore a dull metal plate shaped to the contours of his ravaged face, designed to conceal the disfigurement.

"Captain," Reed said as he saluted first Hoshi and Shran and then Mayweather, "Professor Soong asked to see the Empress."

"Your Majesty," Soong said, holding his hands out toward her as he approached. Dressed in a brown leather jacket over a dark shirt and slacks, Soong was a thin wiry man in his fifties who appeared somewhat older due to his gray hair, which he wore long and secured in a ponytail that lay draped over his right shoulder. A pair of wire-framed glasses with blue, mirrored lenses sat perched atop his nose, and he gazed over them at her. "It is so good to see you again."

Making a mental note to have the exasperating professor executed the instant his usefulness proved to be at an end, Hoshi allowed him to take her hands in his own as she nodded in greeting. "Professor. I trust your inspection has gone well."

Soong nodded toward Phlox. "Thanks to the good doctor's comprehensive tour. I could spend the rest of my life crawling through this vessel. The technology is simply incredible." He held his arms up and to either side of his body as though to indicate the engine room and presumably the rest of the ship, his smile widening. "The *Defiant* is the tip of the spear that will pierce the heart of the rebellion."

An eccentric man, to say the least, Arik Soong always had possessed something of a flair for the dramatic. One of the few members of the previous Emperor's inner circle whom she had not replaced, Soong had been retained solely for his unmatched intellect, which she knew would be needed if she was to realize her plan of replicating *Defiant*'s technology and using it to arm the rest of Starfleet in like fashion.

Once that was accomplished, the professor naturally would share the fates of his fellow former advisers.

Tucker reacted violently at the sight of Phlox. "What the hell's he doing in my engine room?" he asked, his tone hard as he pointed to the doctor. "Why is he still *alive*?"

"He's here at my direction," Hoshi replied, allowing a hint of warning to lace her words. "Like you, he lives or dies at my command, and that's all the explanation you require."

She understood Tucker's anger. Phlox's sabotage had left *Defiant* vunerable to attack by the mutinous crew on the *Avenger* while it was under attack by rebel forces. When interrogated afterward about the incident, the doctor had pleaded his innocence, claiming that T'Pol had subjected him to drugs from his own dispensary—compounds he himself had created and which were most effective in rendering patients susceptible to suggestion—inducing him to carry out his acts of sabotage against his will. It was an assertion he had maintained even after being subjected to three days of near-continuous torture. A medical scan revealed traces of the illicit compounds in the Denobulan's system, though of course there were those who offered the theory that the doctor could easily have injected himself with the drugs. In the end, sufficient grounds had been offered for Hoshi to exonerate Phlox of any culpability in the affair. That was a fortuitous resolution, as she had always harbored a fondness for the physician.

Properly humbled by her stinging rebuke, Tucker nodded. "I meant no disrespect, Your Majesty." There still was an edge in his voice as he continued to eye the doctor. "I'm just worried about . . . security issues."

"Your concern is touching," Reed said from where he stood next to Phlox, making no effort to mask the scowl clouding his mangled features, "but I can deal with those issues well enough, thank you."

Tucker glared at the major. "Nice job keeping T'Pol from making off with one of our shuttles, by the way. You can bet the Vulcans have already torn that thing apart by now."

"That's enough," Mayweather snapped. To Reed, he said, "I'm sure you have other duties to perform, Major. See to them."

Hoshi watched the major bristle as he absorbed the dressing down from his former subordinate. Nodding stiffly, Reed said, "Aye, sir," saluting before turning on his heel and marching out of the engineering room.

Despite the long recovery from his injuries, there was no mistaking the lingering desire for power and advancement that had always driven Malcolm Reed. He had been loyal to Jonathan Archer, at least in so far as it furthered his own agenda, and the Empress had seriously considered executing him after seizing the throne. Mayweather, curiously, had instead requested the tactical officer be spared before assigning him to *Defiant* as the starship's security chief. To think that Reed would ignore the unparalleled opportunity such a promotion offered would likely prove a fatal mistake for the young captain.

As long as the *Defiant*'s captain remained loyal, Hoshi cared little who occupied the center seat.

"All of this advanced technology will be for naught," Soong said, "if we don't apply it to our primary goal of crushing the rebellion." He turned to face the Empress. "Your Majesty, the longer we wait to take advantage of the opportunity this vessel represents, the more likely your enemies will find some means of defending against it. We must act now, for the preservation of the Empire."

"If you start tearing this ship apart, I'm not sure I can put everything back together," Tucker said, his mouth curling into a sneer. "It's taken me this long just to figure out the basics."

Without turning away from Hoshi, Soong adjusted his glasses. "Then perhaps it's time better minds were set to the task."

"And what if the rebels decide to attack?" Mayweather asked, folding his arms across his chest. "How powerful will *Defiant* be with its weapons scattered across the deck? Will you be leading the charge to repel the boarding parties, Professor?"

"There is much more at risk than *one* ship," Hoshi said, her tone of voice serving to remind her entourage who would be making the decisions on this day. "Earth itself would be defenseless."

She heard the sound of a throat clearing to her right, and turned to see Shran regarding her with a small, wistful smile. "Your Majesty," he said as he clasped his arms behind his back, "surely there is some way Professor Soong could be provided with certain weapon components without significantly compromising the tactical systems." Tilting his head and allowing his antenna to twist and bend until it was pointed at Tucker, the general added, "Commander?"

Knowing he had been backed into a corner, the engineer nodded, though Hoshi saw the reluctance in his eyes. "I suppose we could pull the aft torpedo launcher, and maybe one phaser bank, but that'd be pushing it."

Mayweather was not pleased. "Even losing those components would leave the ship vulnerable. It could be all the advantage the rebels need if they decide to attack."

Shran shook his head. "It cannot be helped, Captain. We cannot let our future depend on a single ship, no matter how powerful. Its technology *must* be duplicated and spread throughout the Empire in order to secure Imperial supremacy."

Turning to regard her husband, Hoshi could not help but be impressed by Shran's impromptu speech. He seemed almost human in his passion and determination, taking to heart his pledge to serve her as well as protect his home world.

Perhaps the future she had conjured for the Empire—and herself—might have a chance of being realized after all.

Having found refuge near the master systems display located in the service alcove at the forward section of the *Defiant*'s engineering spaces, Arik Soong managed to avoid further discussions with Empress Sato during the remainder of her inspection. Here, tucked away from the main engineering floor, the professor sat quietly and enjoyed the brief private interlude. He closed his eyes and listened to the hum of the ship's enormous impulse power plant, naturally more pronounced here in the heart of the vessel.

Finally, he watched as the Empress departed, followed by Captain Mayweather and Doctor Phlox. Soong released a sigh of relief, realizing too late that his exhalation was audible and looking around to see if he had been overheard. The last thing he needed was for some sycophant to inform the Empress of his lapse in "loyalty."

Swiveling his chair around until he once more faced the console, Soong wiped his hand along its polished black surface, his eyes taking in its rows of raised, multicolored buttons and banks of switches. The professor had come to appreciate the surprisingly simple yet elegant arrangement of the control interface. Several hours spent perusing the *Defiant*'s library of technical documentation had given him a wealth of insight into this vessel's many marvels. His mind all but reeled at the ship's military superiority as well as the unmatched array of science laboratories, featuring equipment surpassing anything that might be found even within the Empire's most advanced research and development facilities.

Despite the excitement he felt welling up within him, Soong still was troubled, certain that he was living on borrowed time. If the professor had learned anything during his brief tenure as her science adviser, it was that Sato I was a consummate liar.

"Professor."

Soong flinched at the sound of the single word, even spoken as it was in a low, conversational tone by someone standing just behind his chair. Drawing a sharp intake of breath, he swung the chair around until he found himself looking up into the blue, scarred face of General Shran. How had he crossed the engineering deck, heavy polished boots and all, without making the slightest sound to announce his presence? Soong felt a knot of unease forming in his gut as his gaze locked on the Andorian's dead left eye, which still seemed to be studying him with disturbing intensity.

As he rose from the chair, Soong's hands absently moved to smooth any wrinkles—real or imagined—from his leather jacket. "General," he said, pausing to clear his throat. "My apologies. I must admit to being rather . . . distracted." He smiled and reached out to caress the control console again.

"I admire those who are not afraid to profess a love for their work," Shran said after a moment, keeping his voice low as though avoiding potential eavesdropping. "It is precisely the level of dedication I require for a special assignment. Few people are suited to such a task, and fewer still rise to the level of trustworthiness I demand."

Soong could not help the frown tugging at the corners of his mouth, his brow furrowing as he regarded the general. As always, Shran's manner was as polished as his boots. He spoke with a deliberate cadence that to the professor seemed almost practiced in its delivery. Instinct told Soong that the Andorian had been waiting for precisely this opportunity, when the two of them could speak alone and unobserved.

"You've certainly aroused my curiosity," Soong said after a moment.

Glancing over his shoulder as a crewman walked past the entrance to the service alcove, Shran leaned closer before continuing in an even lower voice. "I understand that you are an accomplished computer specialist. What do you make of the *Defiant*'s systems?"

Soong shrugged. "There are numerous fundamental similarities, of course, but the main computer's central processing components resemble nothing we have today." The ship's technical schematics referred to "duotronic circuits," which processed and transferred data at speeds Soong would not have believed possible. Software was another matter entirely. He estimated it would be months before he fully understood the basic framework of the computer's operating system.

Clasping his hands behind his back, Shran said, "I am most interested in the historical database."

"I assume you mean 'what remains of it.' The files have been deleted—by an expert." Then, probing tentatively, "I've heard that your wife—Her Imperial Highness—has the only existing copy."

"She guards it jealously," Shran said with the slightest hint of frustration.

Ah—the Empress won't even permit her husband to access the historical files, Soong thought. *Theirs must be a very happy marriage.*

The professor adjusted his glasses. "You know, I wouldn't mind seeing it myself. Might be able to make some real money at the track."

Shran didn't so much as crack a smile. "Knowledge of the future can be dangerous . . . particularly if one cannot examine the details for one's self."

What was Shran trying to tell him? And why was he being so cryptic? *Perhaps we are being observed,* Soong thought. He considered his next words carefully.

"Yes, I can see why *one* might find that frustrating."

"Professor," Shran asked, "may I confide in you?"

Finally. "Of course."

Shran circled the small control room, pretending to examine the data displays. "Given the magnitude of what I am asked to accomplish, I'm not prepared to accept any information at face value, even if my beloved wife is the source."

Surprised by the stark admission, Soong lowered his head until he could study the battle-scarred Andorian over the rims of his mirrored glasses. "You don't trust our Empress? That is treasonous talk, General."

"Indeed it is," Shran said, his lone antenna curling over until it nearly rested atop his close-cropped white hair. "Rest assured that you and I will stand together before the firing squad if the Empress learns of this conversation. It is therefore in our mutual best interest to keep that from happening."

Soong could not argue with that. Given his uncertain standing with Sato, he already had cultivated a habit of discretion. He remained alive only because the Empress believed he was one of the few people capable of reverse engineering the *Defiant*'s tactical systems. Once that task was complete, he was certain an unpleasant death awaited him.

Shran appeared to be offering him a different path.

Clearing his throat, Soong asked, "What do you want me to do?"

4

The slight breeze wafting through the open window of her bedchamber cooled the light sheen of perspiration on Hoshi's bare skin as she lay on her side, looking over at the reposing form of her husband. She ran her hand lightly over Shran's chest, her fingers tracing the scar that ran from his right pectoral muscle to his hip. The scar was thick and dark, standing out against his otherwise-pale indigo skin.

"How did you get this?" she asked, shifting her weight so that her right leg rested over his.

Without opening his eyes, Shran replied, "Fending off the amorous advances of a lover to whom I had been inattentive."

Laughing at that, Hoshi leaned over and pressed her lips against the scar's upper edge. "Hmm. Interesting," she said. "Judging from what I've seen so far, it seems you haven't learned much from those past mistakes."

She meant the comment in jest, of course, knowing full well that Shran had been occupied with Imperial business. Following their return from the *Defiant* inspection tour, Shran had met with his command staff in the war room he had established on the palace's lower level. Such were the responsibilities of her highest-ranking military adviser, and the general's unwavering dedication to his duty was but one of the reasons she had chosen him to oversee the planning of what she hoped would be the final, decisive battle against the rebellion.

Opening his eyes, Shran placed his left forearm beneath his head as he turned to regard her. "My aides showed me some startling new information, Your Majesty," he said, his tone soft and yet missing any trace of the passion and warmth he had exhibited mere moments before. Gone was her consort, Hoshi realized; she was now sharing her bed with the taciturn military strategist. "New intelligence from our operatives working inside the rebels' command structure. It seems they may have overcome their fears about the *Defiant,* and are planning a renewed offensive."

Hoshi sat up in the bed at that, frowning as she felt new irritation welling up within her. "And you didn't think this important enough to tell me before you came to my bed?"

For the first time since arriving in her bedchamber, Shran smiled. "It is not as though the rebels are attacking at this moment, Your Majesty," he said, a hint of amusement in his voice. His one antenna bent and curled as though angling to gaze upon her. "Besides, you *were* rather insistent upon my arrival." Glancing down at himself, he added, "I fear you may actually have inflicted permanent injury."

"A battle-hardened veteran like you?" Hoshi asked as she rose from the bed and retrieved the cream silk kimono draped over the chair next to her bedside table. "Something tells me you'll survive." She picked up a carafe on the table and poured water into a squat, thick-based glass. "Now that you've carried out your marital duties, tell me about the rebels."

Pulling himself out of the bed, Shran crossed the thickly carpeted floor to where his uniform lay scattered. "They are gathering their ships for a direct assault on the Proxima shipyards," he said as he donned his tunic. "Doing so is proving difficult. Despite the damage they inflicted on your fleet at Tau Ceti, the battle was even more costly for them." He reached for his polished boots before turning to regard Hoshi with a grim expression. "They are determined, but they are also vulnerable. We can repel this attack before it has a chance to begin."

Hoshi took note of her husband's current state of undress. "You mean, catch them with their pants down." Shran gave her a look of complete bewilderment, the metaphor lost on him. Then, more plainly: "You're suggesting a preemptive strike."

The Andorian nodded. "According to my informants, the rebels are assembling the remnants of their fleet—within a debris field located in the Devolin system."

"I've never heard of it," Hoshi said before sipping from her water glass.

Shran shook his head as he stepped into his black leather trousers. "I am not surprised, as it is well outside Empire territory. It's a trinary system, no planets, just the debris field, which according to my informants is being used as a staging area."

Hoshi remained skeptical. "It sounds like it would be pretty heavily defended."

He had moved to the large mirror mounted on the wall opposite the bed, standing before it as he smoothed wrinkles from his uniform and reached up to straighten his rank insignia. "Their defenses will be no match for the *Defiant*."

So that's where this is all leading.

"You have all of Starfleet at your disposal," Hoshi reminded him, setting down her water glass and pulling her kimono belt tighter around her slim waist. "Why don't you send the Sixth Fleet after them?"

They both were aware that the Sixth Fleet was comprised primarily of *Andorian* warships—until recently, those ships had been under the command of the Andorian Imperial Guard, but were now sworn to defend the *Terran* Empire. Would Shran order his own men to attack rebels with whom they were recently allied?

Shran moved away from the mirror, spreading his hands apart, as if suggesting the matter were beyond his control. "The Sixth Fleet is deployed along our border with the Klingons," he reminded her gently, a fact she already knew. "It would do us little good to destroy the rebels only to face an invasion from those foul-smelling barbarians."

Hoshi gave him a stern look, unconvinced by his arguments. Shran pressed on.

"They may be subversives, but the rebels are not fools. They're hiding in that system because they know our battleships won't be able to maneuver in a debris field that dense—but *Defiant* can. With our flagship leading the attack, we'll be able to finish them and end this war."

"And if you're wrong?" Hoshi countered.

The general shrugged. "Then we will still destroy what is there and deal the rebels a crippling blow. Their death will only be slower, if not more painful."

Instinct told the Empress that Shran's plan seemed rather straightforward, perhaps too much so. Then again, based on what little understanding she possessed regarding military strategy, history had shown that the intricate schemes more often than not were the ones that ended badly. The more complex the plan, the greater the opportunity for failure.

Additionally, Hoshi could not deny the lure of perhaps being able to put down the rebellion with a single strike. This was precisely the scenario Jonathan Archer had envisioned when he learned of the existence of *Defiant*. It was Archer's drive and determination that had seen to the recovery of the mighty starship. If the Empire was to endure, it would do so because of bold, resolute action as Archer had championed. It was time to take the fight to the rebels and end the conflict once and for all.

Fine, then.

"How soon can you be ready?" she asked, still not convinced, but willing to hear the rest of her husband's plan.

Stepping toward the open window that provided a breathtaking view surrounding the villa, Shran replied, "Final preparations are already under way." As though sensing Hoshi's disapproval, the general added, "It was not my intention to overstep my bounds, Your Majesty. The ships I require were already being readied for final inspections. I simply reprioritized their maintenance schedules in the event this plan should meet with your approval."

Smooth as always, the Empress reminded herself, though something about Shran's report still bothered her. "You're planning to lead this attack yourself?"

"Of course, Your Majesty," Shran replied, his expression one of confusion, though whether it was genuine or manufactured was something Hoshi could not determine. "My place is at the head of the armada, leading our loyal warriors into battle."

"That might have been acceptable in the Andorian Guard," Hoshi countered, "but you are the supreme commander of my military. You cannot consume yourself with a single battle, no matter how important. Oversee the attack from Starfleet Headquarters. Appoint whomever you want to head up the task force, but Captain Mayweather will retain command of *Defiant*."

Shran said nothing for several seconds, his eyes narrowing as he studied her. Then, a small smile tugged at his lips, and his antenna moved to stand up almost ramrod straight. Clasping his hands behind his back, he said, "Your Majesty, am I to understand that even though you have welcomed me into your inner circle, your life, and your bed, you still do not trust me?"

Matching his smile, the Empress replied, "Of course I trust you, my dear husband, but only to a point." She certainly had no intention of allowing Shran to assume command of *Defiant*. With the starship under his control, there would be precious little to prevent his unseating her from the throne. Hoshi held no illusions that the general had not considered that possibility, among others.

Shran had the good sense to appear slighted by her unspoken suspicions. "Surely the *Defiant*'s historical database does not include any information about my betraying my wife?"

"Let's just say I'd rather not tempt fate," Hoshi said before turning on her heel and walking toward her private bath, certain she felt Shran's steely eyes boring into her back. Whatever agenda he was pursuing, she was certain she had just confounded it, at least for a time.

Tempting fate, indeed.

5

Wie have taken a great risk to meet with you, Vulcan," the paunchy Tellarite said in a huff to T'Pau. "What purpose does it serve to bring all of us here? Aside from giving the Empress a chance to cripple our rebellion with one decisive blow!"

T'Pol, sitting to the right of the former minister, studied the Tellarite from her seat across the polished black table. They were in the wardroom of the *Suurok*-class combat cruiser *Ni'Var*, the vessel that had been T'Pol's home these past months. It was difficult for her to take any Tellarite seriously—they argued with extreme passion over whatever topic was presently on the table, whether it was military strategy or the temperature of the room. This Tellarite was introduced to her as General Gral, retired, but she knew him by the sobriquet given to him by Imperial propagandists—the "Butcher of Berengaria."

It was a title Gral wore with pride. T'Pol may not have appreciated his flair for verbal sparring, but she did recognize his proficiency in military matters. The general was widely acknowledged as the finest strategic thinker on Tellar Prime—he was the mastermind behind the brazen hit-and-run attacks on the Empire's starbase network, which had cost the Terrans dearly in manpower and ships. For a time, Imperial Intelligence considered his capture their number one priority—perhaps only T'Pol now rated higher on their list. The Tellarite had proven adept at eluding capture, primarily by avoiding face-to-face meetings like the one he was presently attending.

T'Pol noticed the distracted look on the face of the taller, pudgier Tellarite seated next to the general. This one had been introduced to her as Rog, the commander of the *Moedigesnuit,* the frigate currently holding station off the bow of the *Ni'Var.* At the moment, his attention was focused on the two Orion sisters seated to T'Pol's left, as if locked in a hypnotic trance with one of them.

The olive-skinned females were clad in wisps of ragged, strategically placed pieces of fabric—oddly, their attire actually revealed more flesh than it covered. One of the women returned Rog's gaze, tracing a finger along a corner of her sly smile. The Orion's sister, Commander Navaar, ignored the stare of the corpulent alien.

"What '*rebellion*' do you speak of, General?" Navaar asked him sharply. "Your ships haven't engaged the Terran fleet for months."

Commander Navaar had accelerated her own raids since the rebels' victory at Tau Ceti, claiming responsibility for numerous attacks along the Empire's periphery. During her time on *Enterprise,* T'Pol had personally witnessed Navaar's handiwork. Captain Forrest had responded to a distress call from a Terran outpost that had been decimated by the Orions. The casualties were more than Phlox's sickbay could handle—broken bodies overflowed into the corridor. Navaar was ruthless but efficient—she delegated many responsibilities to members of her extended family, including the sister at her side, who at the moment was taking delight in the exquisite torment she was inflicting on Rog.

Gral was about to reply to Navaar's challenge when he noticed his colleague's distraction, and nudged him hard with his elbow. Rog snapped out of his reverie, somewhat annoyed. "I told you to take the pheromone suppressant," the general growled at Rog under his breath.

"It must have slipped my mind." Rog's tone suggested to T'Pol that his omission was no accident. She knew it was dangerous for males to remain in close proximity to Orion women—as pleasurable as Rog may have found the experience, the airborne biochemicals the females were secreting made him susceptible to even the slightest suggestion. No doubt Rog would walk into an airlock and begin the depressurization sequence if one of the Orion women commanded it.

Gral turned back to Navaar, his ire rising. "If I reveal the location of my forces, the Empress's new battleship will blast us out of the sky."

"Your forces aren't in hiding," Navaar shot back, "they're making preparations to *flee* the quadrant. You've already abandoned our cause."

The Orion woman struck a nerve with Gral. "I wouldn't expect a former *slave* to understand the meaning of the term, 'strategic redeployment.' "

"In my language: *kohl'ash,*" Navaar replied with an edge.

Gral was incensed. "*Retreat?* The Andorians are on *my* border, not yours, and now the Empire has allied themselves with those blue-skinned demons. My men can't wage a war on two fronts!"

"Then I suggest a new strategy, General—*surrender*. Your men would do more damage to the Empire by crowding their prisons and consuming their food."

The Tellarite started to rise. "You promiscuous little . . ."

"*Kroyka!*"

T'Pau had gotten to her feet at the head of the table—T'Pol noticed that even at her full height, the minister was barely taller than those seated around her. Behind T'Pau, an Orion corsair and a Tellarite warship could be glimpsed through the window, the view of the ships partially obstructed by tendrils of gas and dust from the nebula the ships were using to conceal themselves.

"We have allowed ourselves to be intimidated by the Empire and their new vessel," T'Pau said, lowering her voice. "The time has come for unified action."

Gral shook his head. "That flagship of theirs is more powerful than anything in the quadrant! Starfleet's begun refitting their entire fleet with its weapons."

"Then logic dictates we strike now before the upgrades can be completed. For that, we will need *all* of our forces."

The general scoffed at T'Pau. "It's common knowledge that the *Vulcans* have been planning an exodus out of the quadrant for months. Your people gave up on this rebellion long before anyone else."

T'Pau didn't flinch at the accusation. "That is a factual statement. However, our plans have changed. We are not leaving."

"Then you're a *fool,* T'Pau. This war is lost."

"Come with me."

In the center of the *Ni'Var*'s launch bay, the Federation shuttlecraft *McCool* sat in stark contrast to the utilitarian Vulcan craft surrounding it. Gral and Navaar entered with the two Vulcans, and moved cautiously toward the vessel as if it were an object of reverence. The Terran media had broadcast holographic images of the *Defiant* in action—this auxiliary craft obviously shared the same slate-gray hull and clean lines of its mothership.

"Is this thing real?" Gral asked, almost afraid to believe it.

Minister T'Pau nodded.

Navaar ran her fingers along one of the nacelle support struts, as if needing physical confirmation of what her eyes told her. "How did you get your hands on this?"

"It is a long story," T'Pol said simply as the Tellarite began to trace a path around the shuttlecraft. Access panels on the aft section of the *McCool* had been opened; several engine components had been removed for examination by Vulcan engineers. On a workbench nearby, one of the shuttlecraft's computer modules was being disassembled by technicians. The computer interface was blinking and flashing, obviously still active—a network of cables snaked their way from the computer to the *McCool*'s cabin, providing power to the component.

"Is this warp capable?" Gral asked, as Rog peered into access ports and ran his short, fat fingers along the cool surface, marveling at its features.

The minister nodded. "Yes. Its speed is comparable to your merchant vessels."

T'Pol had allowed herself a small measure of satisfaction for her decision to present the *McCool* to the minister as a gesture of trust and goodwill. It had taken somewhat longer for T'Pau to extend that appreciation to the former Starfleet officer, but in the months since joining the resistance cell, T'Pol had become intimately involved in the group's strategic planning, leveraging her in-depth knowledge of Imperial protocols and military capabilities. T'Pol was careful to share her expertise on a "need to know" basis, making her all the more valuable to the minister.

"Wait," Gral said, examining the unfamiliar Starfleet pennant on the side of the craft. "Where is the Imperial emblem?" He stepped closer, reading the name emblazoned on the hull: "This should read *I.S.S. Defiant*—not *U.S.S.*" Gral looked to the Vulcans, expecting some sort of acknowledgment that their ruse had been uncovered. "It's a fake!"

"You're mistaken, General," T'Pol told him calmly. "This vessel is not from our future. It comes from a reality where the Empire does not exist—where it *never* existed."

As the general absorbed this new revelation, Navaar shook her head, unable to resist a clever smile. "Sato lies better than any privateer I've ever known."

Gral had apparently accepted the Vulcan's explanation. "Well, then, what about weapons?"

"It is unarmed," T'Pau replied, "but my engineers are gaining valuable insight into the *Defiant*'s technology."

Gral had heard enough. "This is all very impressive, but we're going to need much more than 'Vulcan insight' to destroy Sato's flagship."

T'Pol stepped toward the workbench. "We have an additional resource." She removed the data card Tucker had generously given her and inserted it into the slot under the monitor. The screen flared to life, displaying a rapidly scrolling series of technical images and diagrams.

"Detailed schematics of the *Defiant*," she said.

Gral tried to take in the moving images all at once. "Slow it down, I can't read it!"

"There will be ample time to examine the data," T'Pau said. "Before I give it to you, I require a commitment—from both of you."

Now it was Navaar's turn to look skeptical. "What sort of commitment?"

6

Travis Mayweather caught sight of his bodyguard in the corridor outside his quarters—lying dead in an expanding pool of his own blood. The image registered in his mind a heartbeat before light glinted off the polished steel of the stained blade that had taken his loyal servant's life.

It came from his right and just behind him, the attacker having pressed himself against the bulkhead near Mayweather's door. Training and instinct took over, and the captain ducked, pivoting until he was inside the arc of his assailant's swing. He threw up his right arm and blocked the strike, connecting with the other man's wrist and eliciting a grunt of surprise. Not bothering to wrest the knife from his opponent's grasp, Mayweather instead drove his elbow toward his assailant's face. He felt the satisfying crack of cartilage as the man's nose broke from the impact—Mayweather received a cry of pain as reward for his effort.

Pulling away and giving himself some maneuvering room, Mayweather got his first good look at his enemy: human male, bald but sporting a thin black mustache that drooped over his mouth and a well-groomed goatee. He was wearing a dark blue Starfleet uniform with insignia identifying him as an enlisted member of the ship's security force. That made him one of Malcolm Reed's men, but whether that indicted the good major himself was a matter for another time, once Mayweather had dispensed with the short-sighted fool now standing before him.

To his credit, the man said nothing as he faced off against Mayweather, moving to his left and studying the captain as he searched for a new opening. His movements indicated that he was well trained, and the fact that he hadn't used the phase pistol holstered at his waist signaled his apparent awareness of the defensive measures currently active aboard *Defiant,* particularly in the vicinity of Mayweather's quarters. Were the man to use the weapon, the starship's computer would immediately detect the energy release and seal the entire deck.

Such measures, however, did not rule out the possibility that the man might do something rash or simply stupid. Mayweather saw no reason to give him that opportunity.

The assailant lunged forward in a renewed attack. Mayweather was ready for him and lashed out with a savage kick that caught the man in the throat, knowing as his boot made contact that the blow was a lethal strike. His opponent staggered backward, eyes wide with panic and agony as he reached both hands to his crushed windpipe and fought for breath. Tortured wheezing echoed in the confines of the corridor as the man sank to his knees, suffocating with every passing second.

Mayweather considered taking pity on the man and ending his suffering by way of his phaser, but the errant thought evaporated as the captain noted the arrival of other crew members, watching from a discreet distance at opposite ends of the passageway. His gaze fixed on his opponent as he slumped to the deck, the crewman's body racked by a last string of violent spasms. *No,* he decided. His attacker's slow and excruciating death would serve as a warning to anyone who might be contemplating similiar action.

Looking up from the still-dying man, the captain caught sight of Sergeant Hayes and Corporal Madden, two members of his own trusted security contingent—both human males with weapons drawn—approaching at a rapid clip up the passageway. Madden stopped to inspect the body of Sergeant McCain, who had fallen near the door to Mayweather's quarters. Hayes stood before the captain, snapping to attention and offering the traditional imperial salute. "Are you all right, sir?" he asked. "We came as soon as we were alerted to the emergency."

"I'm fine," Mayweather replied. With a small smile, he added, "I figured it was about time somebody tried to take me out." He indicated the dead assailant. "I don't recognize him. Who was he?"

"Sergeant Haffley, sir," the MACO replied. "He was only with the crew a week or so. Major Reed approved his transfer from the *Invincible.*" Looking around as though to ensure they were not being overheard, he added, "Rumors are he's one of a small group the major's putting together—loyal officers he's served with."

Obviously not loyal to me. Mayweather considered what that might mean for him. Was Reed already positioning key personnel among *Defiant*'s crew? Even if that were the case, the major was no fool; he would not strike here and now, with *Defiant* so far from home and without the protection of the many friends Reed had made at Starfleet Command—few of whom were truly loyal to the Empress.

No, Mayweather decided. Instinct told him this attack was the result of one man's enthusiasm getting the best of him, but the captain had no intention of again being the victim of such zeal. He was not about to write off the possibility that Reed—or someone else with a similar agenda—might take advantage of any random opportunity that presented itself.

He indicated his slain bodyguard with a nod of his chin. "McCain was a fine soldier, but he was careless. Tell your people to remain alert. I want security doubled in the armory, engineering, and auxiliary control. No one steps onto the bridge without my authorization." Indeed, Mayweather was more than irritated with himself for not taking such precautions sooner.

I'd better get the hang of this job, he said to himself, *and pretty damned fast.* His path to command was atypical, to say the least. Only eight months ago, Mayweather was a lowly sergeant attached to the MACO detail aboard the ill-fated *Enterprise.* His startling advancement was a result of his decision to betray Captain Archer and ally himself with the woman who would soon become the first-ever Empress of the Terran Empire. Had Mayweather remained loyal to his former commander, at this moment he would probably be serving as Emperor Jonathan's personal guard—an assignment he hardly coveted, but one he would not be at liberty to turn down. Those men unfortunate enough to be selected for that "honored" position had a notoriously short life expectancy.

Mayweather had agreed to help Sato ascend to the throne. In return, all he had asked for was "a tall ship," as one lesser poet had once put it. The new Empress had been true to her word—Mayweather was now a man to be feared, the commander of the most lethal weapon in the known galaxy, as well as the youngest captain in the history of the Terran Starfleet.

And don't forget, the dumbest one, too, he often reminded himself.

Since being appointed captain, Mayweather had enrolled in an unofficial crash course in starship command, reading everything he could about naval history, battle theory, and the essentials of combat tactics. Every spare moment was devoted to earning the job he had already been given. Mayweather was determined to become not merely a competent officer—but the best captain in the fleet. Otherwise the Empress would be forced to replace him. After all, her promise said nothing about how long he would remain *Defiant*'s commander.

In his position, a sudden and violent death could come at any moment, from anywhere. The average captain only had to keep a watchful eye on his own crew—but Mayweather had to pay attention to the officers *above* him as well. The recently demoted fleet captain made no secret of the fact that he desired this command for himself. Rumors had even reached Mayweather's ears, alleging that Robinson had openly boasted of the "personal assurance" he had received from the Empress that *Defiant* would eventually be his.

The captain wasn't concerned—Robinson was probably lying. If he wasn't? Mayweather would see to it that his current mission was such a success that Sato *couldn't* replace him.

A troubling thought then occurred to him. Robinson was

Invincible's executive officer eight years ago—perhaps this assailant *wasn't* working on his own, as Mayweather's instincts told him. The two men may have known each other. If the theory was correct, the fleet captain may have decided to make a preemptive move against Mayweather—Robinson must be aware that if *Defiant*'s current mission is a success, it will be much more difficult to eliminate its captain.

Mayweather smiled inwardly at the paranoid conspiracy he had plotted in a matter of seconds. *You're not paranoid if they really are out to get you,* he thought.

Mayweather heard a new chorus of running footfalls echoing in the corridor behind him, and turned to see Major Reed sprinting toward him, phase pistol at the ready, leading a contingent of three security guards. Though the security chief's expression was one of concern, Mayweather thought he detected a hint of displeasure in Reed's good eye as the chief of security analyzed the scene before them.

"Captain," the major said as he approached, lowering his phase pistol. "What happened here?" Did Mayweather detect *disappointment* in Reed's voice?

Mayweather almost laughed at the near-sincerity lacing the major's words. Indicating the dead man with a nod, he said, "Someone looking for a promotion. One of yours, I understand."

"Yes, we served together previously." Reed's lips pressed tightly together as he holstered his sidearm. "Captain, I assure you, I had no inkling that he was planning something like this."

For once, Mayweather thought, *I believe you.*

Practically everyone on the ship believed he had made a catastrophic mistake by asking his former superior to become *Defiant*'s security chief. Reed's ambitions were evident—he practically wore them on his sleeve, next to the skull and crossbones MACO patch. Mayweather had to admit Reed was an excellent tactician and a superb officer, even if he wasn't particularly popular among the crew. If he *were* to make an attempt on his life, Mayweather hoped it would be more competently executed—or else he really *had* made a mistake. The ship's security could not be entrusted to an officer so inept.

His father often quoted dialogue from an old 2-D film that they watched together many times on their long cargo runs, "Keep your friends close, but your enemies closer." Mayweather wasn't sure he particularly agreed with that advice, and it certainly wasn't his rationale for keeping Reed on board. The major was here so that Mayweather could put an end to their rivalry once and for all. Now that *Defiant* was finally being sent on assignments that would take them out of Earth orbit, there would be many opportunities to send Reed on off-ship missions, some of which would be more dangerous than the major anticipated. Once Mayweather found a suitable replacement, he would dispatch Reed without hesitation.

"Sergeant McCain upheld the finest traditions of the Empire," the captain said. "I want a proper ceremony with full military honors. There will be a memorial service at nineteen-hundred this evening. I expect the ship's entire security contingent to be on hand."

Offering a succinct nod, Reed replied, "Aye, Captain." He nodded toward the lifeless body of Sergeant Haffley. "And him?"

"Put him out the airlock."

"Drop out of warp. Go to impulse power."

Seated at the center of *Defiant*'s bridge, Mayweather felt a momentary adjustment in the inertial dampers as the warp engines disengaged and the vessel transitioned into normal space. On the main viewscreen, elongated streaks of light receded to distant points in space, partially obscured by the dense field of asteroids and debris drifting ahead of the ship. *Defiant* had arrived in the Devolin system.

On the viewscreen, Mayweather could make out two flickering points of cool blue light—a pair of main sequence stars at the center of this somewhat inaccurately named trinary system. The third member of the trinary was no longer luminous in wave-lengths that humans could see—a half million years ago, it collapsed and formed what was now a class-four black hole. At close range, radiation from the singularity would overwhelm even *Defiant*'s deflector screens and kill Mayweather's entire crew. They were safe so long as they maintained a minimum distance of ninety million kilometers.

"We're at the outer boundary of the system," reported Ensign Zona, the Orion woman seated at the station in front of the captain. "Thirty million kilometers to the perimeter of the debris field." The words themselves were soft and sultry—much like the ensign herself, as Mayweather recalled from a previous evening rendezvous.

Rank hath its privileges.

Standing at the science station on the upper deck to Mayweather's right, Major Reed bent over the hooded viewer, analyzing the telemetry being fed to him from *Defiant*'s array of sensors. "The assault fleet has dropped out of warp behind us, Captain," he reported.

Six ships, Mayweather thought. *Not a very intimidating assault fleet.* These six vessels were all the Empress would spare—the rest of the fleet was spread thin across Alpha and Beta quadrants, tasked with protecting the Sol system and the major Terran colonies. At the tactical briefing, Mayweather had been told he could expect to find the bulk of the rebels' *Suurok-* and *Kumari-*class ships drifting among these asteroids—most of those ships were believed to be undergoing repairs and were not battleworthy. If Shran's informants were wrong, and the rebels are at combat stations, waiting for them . . .

We may find out if this crate is as "indestructible" as Imperial propaganda claims.

"Go to yellow alert," Mayweather ordered. "Shields up and weapons on hot standby. Helm, set a course for the coordinates Shran gave us." It was time to verify the reliability of the general's informants.

Zona's attention was divided between her console and the viewscreen, which now filled with thousands of tumbling, mountain-sized rocks. "It's going to get a little dicey in there, sir."

Mayweather looked to Reed. "Anything on sensors?"

Without turning away from his console, the major shook his head. "Many of the asteroids on the periphery are composed of phyllisite ore—it's scattering our sensors."

"Options?"

"The debris thins out closer to the stars. I should be able to scan the entire system if we move in, say, another twelve million kilometers."

"I wouldn't recommend that, Captain." Zona said, looking toward Reed. "At that range, solar radiation will significantly compromise our shields."

"A little bit of sunburn never killed anyone," Reed playfully shot back at her.

Mayweather thumbed the intraship comm button on his armrest. "Radiation exposure protocols, all decks." Weakened shields also meant *Defiant* would be vulnerable if the rebels were waiting for them in there.

"Slow to one-quarter, Ensign."

The minutes passed uneasily as the ship moved deeper into the field. As Mayweather watched his crew go about their assigned tasks, he found himself momentarily forgetting about the deadly radiation, and rebel ships hiding behind asteroids. For a few precious moments, the captain was distracted by the pleasant, almost mesmerizing sounds of his bridge—the beeping and whirring of relays, capacitors, and automatic scanners. It was an electronic symphony that the captain tended to think of as his personal background arrangement.

"Debris field is clearing," Zona said, snapping Mayweather out of his reverie.

"Long-range sensors are online." The major peered into his viewer, making adjustments to the selection lever.

"Major," Mayweather said, growing impatient.

Reed finally looked up from his scanners, the color having drained from the part of his face Mayweather could see.

"There's nothing here, Captain. Nothing at all."

Son of a bitch. "You're certain?"

"No ships—no bases—no artificial constructs of any kind."

How could we have trusted him?

"Could Shran's informants have been wrong?" Zona asked.

Mayweather's abdomen went cold. "We've been betrayed."

"Captain . . . ?"

Mayweather practically leaped from his chair, fighting the urge to take control of the helm. "Set a course for Earth, maximum warp!"

"Our fleet won't be able to keep up with us—" Zona protested.

"To hell with them. Warp factor eight, *now!*"

Zona relayed the captain's orders to her controls and *Defiant* lurched hard, accelerating at full impulse along the Z-axis relative to the ecliptic. A moment later, the ship cleared the debris field and plunged into subspace.

Mayweather cursed himself for not comprehending it sooner. Shran had given them exactly what they wanted—the rebel fleet, gathered in a single location, defenseless. On a platter. The moment they had been waiting for.

They had believed it because they *wanted* it to be true.

"How long to Sector 001?" Mayweather asked tightly.

Zona checked the astrogator display. "If we can maintain this speed . . ." she hesitated. "Eighteen hours."

Might as well be a million years.

Earth, the planet of his birth, the heart of the Terran Empire, waited . . . undefended and alone.

7

G et down!"
Her ears still ringing from the explosion tearing through
the hull of the shuttle she had just vacated, Hoshi heard the
warning the instant before a large hand gripped her shoulder and
forced her to the ground. She felt the sensation of displaced air as
something flew past her head and landed somewhere on the side-
walk behind her. It was answered by the deafening whine of a
phase pistol, and the Empress caught sight of the orange energy
beam overhead.

I brought this on myself!

The thought taunted her as she crouched on the ground, the
palms of her hands digging into the loose rock and other debris
littering the otherwise-smooth cobblestones on the outer wall of
Kyoto Palace.

"This way, Your Majesty," Solomon Carpenter said, the bodyguard pulling her to her feet while at the same time aiming his
phase pistol at the unruly mob of perhaps twenty people who
were approaching along the graded path that served as an entrance to the palace grounds. Her trusted guardian guided her
across the stone path, passing a spot where a section of the
palace's perimeter wall had collapsed. Other members of her security detail—one human and two Andorians—stood watch near
the breach, each of them carrying pulse rifles and occasionally firing the weapons through the ragged hole into the city street that
lay beyond.

Using his body to shield the Empress, Carpenter's attention was focused on the gap in the wall as they moved past, his phase pistol ready to answer any threat. He saw the next attack even before the guards at the wall did; another protestor attempting to leap through the jagged opening, his face a mask of hatred as he wielded a large machete. Carpenter did not hesitate, firing his weapon at the attacker and dropping him to the stone floor of the palace courtyard.

Beyond the wall, Hoshi heard the cries and shouts of her enraged and terrified subjects. Through the breach she could make out the wasteland of rubble and smoking craters that had been the city's business district. To her left was the smoking pile of debris that was all that remained of the *Shishinden*—the ceremonial hall in which she had held her coronation. One of her favorite places on the palace grounds, it now lay in ruin, like much of her capital.

A large piece of rock or brick sailed through the opening in the wall and struck one of the Andorian guards in the head. He fell backward, stumbling over loose debris scattered behind him and crashing in a heap to the ground. Cobalt blood ran from his temple, and Hoshi saw that his right antenna was now broken. None of that mattered, the Empress realized, as she saw the guard's open, fixed eyes.

In response, the two remaining guards opened fire, their weapons screaming as they poured a hailstorm of energy into the crowd. A half dozen were struck down, but there were ten times as many to take their places.

"Set to stun!" Hoshi ordered.

"We can't hold them back!" shouted the remaining Andorian.

These people have lost everything, she thought. *And it's my fault.*

She knew that the scene here was no different than the ones she had witnessed—either in person or via satellite communications feeds—at numerous locations around the world. The attacks had been devastating, coming without forewarning and far too fast for any appreciable defenses to be brought to bear. *Defiant,* still racing back from the Devolin system, had transmitted desperate alerts to Earth that came too late. Rebel ships, nearly two dozen of them, had emerged from warp space dangerously close to the planet, unleashing a series of fierce coordinated strikes. Eventually, the Terran defenses responded and destroyed all but one of the invading vessels. By then the damage was done—cities had fallen, millions of her subjects were dead.

And I let it happen.

Kyoto was hit hard, but had been spared a direct bombardment. Other cities had been less fortunate. Overriding the protests from her security detail, Hoshi had emerged from her underground bunker and traveled by shuttle to the scenes of the worst of the devastation. She had hoped her presence would be a source of comfort, but in every devastated city she visited—Chicago, Mumbai, Paris, Beijing, Rio de Janeiro—the shock and grief of the survivors quickly turned to outrage when she appeared. It had taken several days, but even the citizens of her birth city were now turning against her.

Hoshi heard the engines of an approaching ship. She turned as a second transport descended toward them—a replacement for her personal shuttle, now a heap of smoking, twisted metal. The craft passed low over the perimeter wall on the western edge of the palace grounds, drawing small arms fire from the angry crowd. This craft was better armored—it absorbed the damage, pivoting on its axis as it settled roughly on the landing pad.

"We have to go, Your Majesty!" Carpenter said, gripping her again by her upper arm and pulling her to her feet. Using his own body as a shield, he led the Empress across the courtyard. A trio of Andorians emerged from the transport, taking up defensive positions near the nose of the craft. To her right Hoshi saw the figures of at least a dozen rioters scaling the high perimeter wall, and the Andorians wasted no time opening fire.

Something tore into the cobblestones at Hoshi's feet, slowing her and Carpenter's progress. The bodyguard whirled to his right in time to see a lone figure brandishing an antique firearm. He dropped to one knee and aimed his phase pistol at the attacker, felling him with a single shot.

"Get aboard!" Hoshi heeded Carpenter's instructions and closed the remaining distance to the transport's entry ramp. An instant later he boarded the craft, followed almost as quickly by the trio of Andorian security officers. Carpenter reached with his free hand to slap a control set into the bulkhead near the entrance, cycling the hatch shut.

"Get us out of here!" he shouted.

Collapsing into a jumpseat in the craft's passenger compartment, Hoshi gulped air, gripping the armrests of her seat and feeling the deck shift beneath her feet as they rose from the landing pad. She lifted her head, locking eyes with Carpenter.

"You saved my life," she said between breaths. "A couple of times."

The bodyguard nodded as he holstered his phase pistol. "It is my honor to serve, Your Majesty." She caught the hint of a smile at the edges of his mouth.

He loves me, that's why he saved me. Hoshi had avoided any further intimate encounters with Carpenter since her marriage, but the separation had not been easy for her. She had genuinely cared for few men—there was Maximilian, certainly—but no one else recently. There was much she needed to tell Carpenter, but this was not the time or the place.

Her attention was caught by movement coming from the transport's cabin. She was startled to see Shran walking toward her.

"Your Majesty, I'm relieved beyond words." As the general moved to embrace her, Hoshi jumped out of her seat and slapped him hard across the face.

"Where the hell have you been?"

"It's good to see you as well," he replied dryly. Shran removed a leather glove and wiped the warm cerulean blood from the corner of his mouth. "I've been attending to our defenses. I'm pleased to report the rebels have been repelled."

Hoshi indicated a small viewport—dark columns of smoke hung in the air over the capital. "Look out that window and tell me how '*pleased*' you are."

"I think it would be premature to assign blame until a full inquiry is complete."

For the Empress, there was no need for an inquiry. "This is *your* doing! Millions of Terrans are dead because of the strategy *you* proposed."

"With all due respect, my beloved, let's not forget that *you* left Earth defenseless by ordering *Defiant* to proceed to the Devolin system."

So that's how we're going to play it, Hoshi thought. She felt for her hip instinctively, reaching for her ceremonial dagger. That's when she realized she must have lost it when she fled the palace. If that blade was in her hand right now, she would plunge it into Shran's chest.

"We must not second-guess ourselves," he pressed on. "What's done is done. All that matters now is your safety."

"My safety is the least of our problems."

"The citizens of Earth are calling for blood. They're demanding that someone take responsibility for this disaster."

Hoshi put aside her anger for a moment, long enough to realize he was right. "I'll address the people tonight," she said. "The command council will step down immediately. If they won't go voluntarily, they'll be shot."

"I think not."

Her forehead burned hot with rage. *"What did you say?"*

"How can I put down the rebellion if I'm deprived of my most trusted and loyal officers?" Hoshi had allowed Shran to appoint Andorian Guardsmen to some of the highest positions in Starfleet. She had hoped this would demonstrate to the Andorian people that they were now the equal of Terrans. It was clear she had made a terrible miscalculation.

"The rebels will be punished—we should not take out our frustrations on our own people. Soon, we will give the public a victory to celebrate, and their anger will pass. In the meantime, it would be best if we . . . *reduced* your profile."

She could feel everything slipping away from her now. Aside

from Carpenter, no human guards were aboard the transport. "I'm *not* going into hiding," she said defiantly.

"I'm merely proposing a short-term remedy—it's too danger-ous for you to remain on Earth."

That's his plan—exile.

"You *knew* this attack was coming. You told the rebels *Defiant* had left orbit."

That insufferable smile of his again. Shran raised his palms, as if making a peace offering. "You're angry—I understand." His tone turned threatening. "I urge you, *my beloved*, don't do some-thing that both of us will regret."

"Mister Carpenter." Her bodyguard stepped forward. "My husband is under arrest. Lock him in the aft compartment."

Before Carpenter could even acknowledge her command, a bright blue bolt of energy slammed into his chest, punching a hole straight through his torso. The scent of burned muscle and bone stung Hoshi's eyes. Her bodyguard was dead before he col-lapsed on the deck.

Enraged, she threw herself at Shran, lashing out toward his face, but he caught her in mid-strike. The three Andorians took flanking positions around their commander. He held Hoshi's wrists, im-moblizing her. Unable to lay a finger on him, she spat in his eye.

Two of the guards pulled the Empress off Shran, holding her. He wiped the spittle from his face. Then, he reached out and grabbed her by the throat. She gasped as her windpipe con-stricted, painfully.

"You're dead," she hissed at him.

His eyebrow arching in almost Vulcan fashion, he shook his head. "Your reign is over, Your Majesty."

He tightened his grip, nearly lifting Hoshi off her feet. She grasped at his gloved hand, choking. After an agonizing moment, Shran finally shoved her into one of the jumpseats.

Coughing, Hoshi rubbed her neck, obstinate as ever, gasping for air. "Do you expect . . . my people . . . to accept an *alien* . . . as their Emperor?"

"No, but they will accept me as *Lord Protector.*"

Lord Protector of the Realm—a title given to those who exercised the Emperor's powers in the event that the *true* heir to the empire—say, a child—was too young to assume those duties.

"You fool—we don't have a child!"

"Not yet."

For Hoshi, the temperature in the compartment seemed to abruptly plummet as she realized his strategy. Terran law and tradition forbade an alien—even her husband—from ascending to the throne. However, there was nothing in the law to keep Shran from acting as a *caretaker* to their child—even if it were nothing more than a clump of cells in a gestation chamber.

If the union of Earth and Andoria had proved fruitful, Hoshi had planned to order the creation of a *binary clone*—a human-Andorian hybrid made from their DNA. A son to continue the Sato Dynasty, as "foretold" by the *Defiant* historical database, or so she had informed Shran. She had intended the child to be born a few years from now, after the rebels were defeated and Shran and his people had demonstrated their fidelity to her and the Empire.

She realized that Shran was not content to wait. He intended to bring this child into existence *now,* and rule in its name.

Shran nodded to one of his guards, who approached her menacingly. He turned her head to the side and plunged a cold syringe into her carotid artery. She cried out in anguish—more mental than physical—as he drew blood.

"Doctor Soong will require more genetic material from you before he can sequence a viable embryo," Shran informed her calmly, "but he requested a sample of your blood to begin."

When the guard was finished, Hoshi tried to get to her feet, but found her shoulders pinned down by a pair of powerful blue hands. She struggled against them as her husband approached her.

Hoshi had a trump card. At least, she hoped she did. She played it.

"You're forgetting something, my dear *husband,*" she said.

Shran finished her thought. "The *Defiant* database. How could I possibly do harm to you if it wasn't predicted by your history book from the future?" He leaned in close, his voice almost a whisper, his remaining antenna circling to point at her like an accusing finger.

"I know it was all a lie."

Hoshi couldn't contain the shock that she felt. Shran read the truth on her face. This pleased him. "Your mistake, if I may be so bold, was assuming I would accept your word at face value. I had Doctor Soong reconstruct the *Defiant*'s data core—while he wasn't able to recover the entire database, what he found was more than sufficient." He laughed. "The *Defiant* is not from our future, but that of another universe? How *very* fascinating."

Hoshi's confidence was waning with each second. "You gave your word to me—to the Empire," she said to him.

"Let's keep in mind, my beloved," he said, moving close enough to kiss her, "that *you lied to me first.*"

The craft trembled—Hoshi could see the blue glow of atmosphere slipping by the viewport. They had been ascending all this time and were now in Earth orbit.

"What are you going to do with me?" she asked.

He wouldn't give her the satisfaction of an answer. Taking the vial of bright red blood from the guard, he slipped it into his belt. Shran disappeared into the cockpit, leaving Hoshi to be tortured by her thoughts.

8

E nergize."

Mayweather watched as Admiral Talas and her personal guard shimmered into existence on *Defiant*'s transporter pad. She bounded down the steps to Mayweather with purpose. *Still can't get used to the sight of an Andorian in a Starfleet admiral's uniform,* Mayweather thought as he saluted his superior.

"Permission to come aboard," Talas asked.

"Granted, Admiral. May I ask to what we owe the pleasure?"

"Congratulations are in order. Your ship has been selected to lead the new task force." Talas moved for the door, which sighed open. Mayweather and the Andorian guard followed her into the corridor. The captain had to practically jog to keep up with her long strides.

"What task force would this be?"

"General Shran has ordered us to find the rebels who planned the attack on Earth and wipe them out."

"We're leaving orbit?" he said, not quite believing it.

Talas cocked her head at Mayweather. "Very astute, Captain. I can see why the Empress promoted you so quickly."

Mayweather resisted the impulse to knock the admiral on her ass. "The last time *Defiant* left the system, the rebels took advantage of our absense. Millions of the Empire's citizens died." *None of them were Andorians,* he wanted to add.

"I'm well aware of what transpired," Talas replied evenly. "That's why the rebels must be made to understand they haven't weakened our resolve."

"And if they attack Earth again? Who's going to stop them if we're off on another wild-goose chase?"

Talas didn't entirely grasp the metaphor, but she understood his point. "The rebels aren't capable of launching a follow-up strike so quickly."

Mayweather could barely hide his contempt. "You know this—how?"

Talas didn't see the need to respond, but the captain pressed his point. "Admiral, our so-called intelligence told us we'd find the entire rebel fleet sitting defenseless in the Devolin system. We found *nothing.*"

"I'm certain you'll h`ave better hunting this time." She pressed on, not waiting for Mayweather to object again. "Inform your transporter chief that additional personnel will be beamed over from the *Warship Kumari* within the hour."

Mayweather recognized the name—the *Kumari* was Shran's former command. *More Andorian spies aboard* my *ship. "Defiant* already has a full crew complement, Admiral."

"Several of your officers will be transferred planetside."

"May I ask *which* members of my crew you're planning to get rid of?" Mayweather asked tightly.

The admiral handed him a blue data card. "Everything you need to know is on here." Talas stopped outside a door leading to crew quarters, eyeing the signage on the bulkhead.

"This room is unoccupied, is that correct?"

"That's right."

"Please tell the quartermaster that these are now my quarters. Inform your senior officers that we're warping out of orbit at nineteen hundred hours." Then she stepped through the door and was gone. The guard that had accompanied her spun on his heel, rifle in hand, taking his post, ready for anything.

For a moment, Mayweather found himself longing for the uncomplicated duties of a MACO sergeant.

★ ★ ★

Charles Tucker's face itched, but his hands were too busy to do anything about it. He was pulling himself upward, rung over rung, climbing through an access tube toward the heart of his ship. As much as he wanted to stop his ascent and dig through his radiation-poisoned skin, the gesture would have been futile. He knew the prickling sensation wasn't really physical in nature; it was triggered by the anxiety he was feeling—anxiety at having two of his most competent engineers replaced by blue-skinned flunkies. Anxiety at having his ship ordered away from his home planet, still smoldering after an attack that was less than a week old. Anxiety at not knowing why he had been ordered to meet with the captain deep inside the bowels of the ship.

Tucker climbed into a horizontal tube that was tall enough for him to walk in and pressed deeper into the engineering hull. The bulkheads surrounding him were lined with vibrant red and yellow conduits and cabling. He found it strange that the inside of a ship as powerful and as lethal as *Defiant* was painted in a variety of bright, cheerful colors—not just the conduits, but the doors, the corridors, even the ship's command deck. *Maybe it's designed to keep us in good spirits, so we don't kill each other,* he mused. The color scheme had proved of no benefit to *Defiant*'s original crew, who *had* in fact killed each other, for reasons still unknown.

At least the outside of the ship is a more appropriate tritanium gray, he thought to himself.

As he probed farther, Tucker could feel the heat of the warp plasma passing through large conduits over his head. He was approaching the main plasma junction, where the superheated gases were channeled upward into the diagonal pylons, en route to the warp nacelles suspended far above. The noise and the EM interference generated by this network of conduits frustrated all known types of recording and surveillance devices—making this part of the ship an ideal place for a clandestine meeting.

He entered the junction and found Mayweather leaning against a support strut, arms tightly folded. The captain must have been here for a few minutes—the heat was getting to him and sweat beaded on his forehead. *Or maybe it's not the heat, the kid is finally cracking under the pressure,* Tucker thought.

"Funny meeting you here, *Cap'm.*" He swallowed his pride a little every time he said Mayweather's rank aloud. The notion that a twenty-nine-year-old *grunt* was in charge of this magnificent ship . . .

"Seemed a little more discreet than the briefing room," Mayweather said. After a moment, he asked, "This may sound a little odd, but . . . have you received any communiqués from the Empress in the last week?"

"Hoshi?" Tucker almost laughed. "Why would Her Imperial Highness send a message to a lowly engineer like me?"

"I know the two of you have a history—I thought she might've contacted you."

He sneered at Mayweather's suggestion. "I'm sure Hoshi crossed me out of her little black book a long time ago." With a little bitterness, he added, "The minute she got what she wanted."

As much as Tucker resented his new captain, he realized the two of them probably had more in common than either cared to admit. They both had been used by the Empress during her climb to the top—yet they had also profited handsomely from their association with her. Maybe she only saw them as the most competent officers for their respective positions—or maybe all of her old conquests received some kind of "consolation prize." All things considered, Tucker still resented being used.

"I hope she's all right," Mayweather said. "Otherwise, humanity is in a heap of trouble."

"That's certainly the case if those blue bastards have anything to say about it."

Neither of them had heard Malcolm Reed climbing up the Jefferies tube. Both whipped out their sidearms as the major entered the junction. Reed indicated the pulsing conduits overhead. "Gentlemen, I don't think you want to be discharging particle weapons in here."

Tucker holstered his phase pistol, somewhat reluctantly. In

truth, he'd like nothing more than to blast a fist-sized opening in Reed's chest. Eight months had passed, and yet Tucker still had vivid memories of his time in "the booth," a heinous contraption designed to inflict the maximum amount of pain a human nervous system could comprehend. The device—an invention of Reed and Doctor Phlox—was destroyed when the *I.S.S. Enterprise* was crushed in the Tholian's energy web.

Too bad he wasn't atomized along with his damn booth, Tucker thought. The major had operated the device that day with his usual level of ruthless efficiency—but more than that, he had *enjoyed* torturing the engineer. In the white haze of searing pain, Tucker had promised he would kill the major when he was finally released. Tucker still had not disavowed that promise.

Reed eyed Tucker warily, then turned to the captain. "I didn't realize you'd invited anyone else, sir."

"Stand down, both of you," Mayweather chided, noting the disdain in their eyes. Reed and Tucker moved a little away from each other. "We need to pool our knowledge and figure out what the hell is going on." He turned to Reed. "Has there been any response from the personal transceiver?"

"I've been hailing it every thirty minutes, piggybacking on our transponder signal. No response so far."

"What personal transceiver?" Tucker asked.

"It's Hoshi's," Mayweather replied, dropping the title. "She told me to contact her in the event of . . . trouble."

Reed snorted. "I suppose a *coup d'état* could be classified as 'trouble.' "

"Wait a sec," Tucker said. "Who said anything about a *coup*?"

"Open your *eye,* will you, Commander?" Reed said scornfully. "Shran's installed his own people in key positions on this ship. They're just waiting for his order. Half of Earth is in ruins after the worst attack in a century, and the Empress hasn't been seen in public for nearly a week."

"Can you blame her? You should've seen the reception they gave her in Stalingrad . . ."

"Hoshi told me if there was any trouble on *Defiant,* I could reach her day or night on that transmitter," Mayweather said. "There's been no response for three days."

They shared disturbed looks as the warp conduits thrummed over their heads. Reed finally broke the silence. "We have to assume the Empress is dead and that General Shran is now in control of the Empire."

"Listen to yourself!" Tucker retorted. "It's called the *Terran* Empire for a reason—the council would never let an alien claim the throne."

"Shran may not be Emperor in name, but it's clear he's the one calling the shots."

Tucker knew it wouldn't have been the first time a world leader had been usurped by a spouse. In the early twentieth century, a North American dictator by the name of Wilson was poisoned by his wife, who proceeded to rule in her husband's stead for half a decade. It was years before anyone figured out what really happened. Or so Tucker had been told in high school.

"Shran doesn't need to claim the throne," Mayweather offered. "All he has to do is undermine and weaken the Empire from the *inside*—long enough for the rebels to win a decisive victory."

Reed picked up on the captain's chain of thought. "Next thing you know, Andoria secedes from the Empire—with Shran leading the charge."

On the whole, Tucker thought the notion of a quadrant-spanning human empire was probably a bad idea. Still, he didn't want to live in a universe where the Empire had collapsed and humans were no longer feared. Every species that had ever been victimized by Earth would declare open season on Terrans. Tucker would do anything in his power to prevent that from coming to pass.

"All right," Tucker said. "What the hell do we do?"

Mayweather considered. "First order of business, we bury the hatchet."

"Cap'n?"

"The three of us have had our differences," Mayweather continued. "From this point forward and until further notice, we have to put the welfare of this ship, her crew, and the Empire ahead of our personal concerns or vendettas. We work *together*. Do I make myself clear, gentlemen?"

Tucker couldn't help but smile a little at the captain's proposal. He even felt a slight jolt of electricity travel up his spine. *Maybe I'm more of a patriot than I thought.*

Reed looked to Tucker. *Until further notice,* they seemed to say to each other silently. A truce—both knew it was the right course of action for now.

He could see Reed's thin lips twitch upward in an imitation of a smile. The major was obviously itching to rid this ship of every single blue blood. Tucker recalled seeing this exact expression on Reed's face once before—on *Defiant*'s bridge, when he watched their old ship get blown to smithereens on the viewscreen.

"I'm with you to the bitter end, Captain," Reed finally said.

The hell with it, Tucker thought as he unashamedly scratched at the itch that had nagged him since he climbed into the Jefferies tube. "Where do we start?"

9

Hoshi screamed.

Her universe was white, cold, foreboding. An antiseptic odor permeated everything, and an intense white light flared from somewhere over her head. She tried to move, but there was something smooth and unyielding pinning her down. Was she lying atop a bed, or a table? She could not turn her head to see.

A shadow fell across her vision, and the silhouette of a figure blocked out part of the blinding light. Hoshi caught sight of her own face reflected and distorted in a pair of blue lenses—eye-glasses on the person's face. She knew that face! It was a man, looking down upon her with an almost-paternal smile.

Throughout it all, she heard a baby crying. Why? Where was it? She looked around but could not see it. There was only its plaintive wailing, growing ever louder. Then the cries stopped, and everything faded, seemingly pulling away from her as she fell.

That sensation was shattered as Hoshi was jerked from sleep by the sound and sensation of something colliding with the ship, her body momentarily suspended in midair as her yacht's artificial gravity fluctuated. Her bed disappeared from beneath her and she sensed her body floating out and away from it. Then the gravity returned and she dropped hard to the deck of her private bedchamber in a disjointed heap.

What the hell?

"Guard!" she yelled from the floor, her mind still fighting off the last vestiges of sleep. Shaking her head, she forced away the haunting memories that had infected and perverted her dreams in the days since her forced departure from Earth. A last fading image of Arik Soong loomed in her vision, and she buried it as she had every time she had awakened from sleep for . . . how long? Four days? Five? Hoshi could not remember, and gave up trying as she rolled to her feet, pushing hair away from her face as she padded barefoot across the room toward the door.

"*Guard!*" she yelled again, this time punctuating the call by slapping the locked smooth metal door with the heel of her hand. "What the hell's going on?"

Hoshi really did not expect an answer, as none of the Andorians had said so much as a single word to her since her banishment from Earth on her husband's orders. Nor did she expect the door to open. Except for times when a guard delivered her meals, the door had remained locked. Her personal yacht, one of her favored refuges from ceremony and duty as leader of the Terran Empire, had become her prison. She had no idea how long the vessel had been under way or what course it currently was pursuing. Most of the past few days were enveloped in a sedative-induced fog, which was only now beginning to fade. Her memories were returning, and Hoshi felt herself gripped by renewed anger as she recalled what Shran had done to her.

Shran, you bastard, she seethed. *You'll regret you didn't kill me.*

Another blast rocked the ship, and this time the lights flickered as Hoshi gripped the doorjamb for balance. The yacht was under attack, but by whom? Surely not imperial forces. Shran would not have gone to all this trouble if his intention was simply to kill her. Unless this attack was part of a cover story. Shran may have arranged to destroy her yacht, so he could blame her death on the insurgents.

Whoever it was, Hoshi had no intention of remaining trapped in her cabin waiting for the bulkheads to explode around her.

Blinking away the mental fog, the Empress looked around the lavishly furnished room, considering her options. An inspection conducted during one of her more lucid moments—yesterday, or perhaps the day before—had confirmed the removal of anything that could be used as a weapon. Although it was still possible that her captors had overlooked something.

The deck shifted and her stomach lurched as the yacht suffered another impact. This time Hoshi heard the near-omnipresent hum of the ship's warp drive begin to fade, followed by a shudder as the vessel dropped out of subspace. Reduced to impulse power, the yacht wouldn't last long.

Another frantic search of her desk and dresser turned up nothing. Hoshi had already checked the closet, but her attention now returned to it. The clothing included five sets of ceremonial robes. She felt a tinge of hope as she searched through the extravagant garments. How thorough would Shran's guards have been? Would they have been familiar with some of the ritualistic fashions she had adopted? Stepping closer to the wardrobe, Hoshi slipped one hand into the inner pocket of one robe, smiling as her fingers wrapped around the metal *kanzashi*.

She extracted her prize—a pair of long, ornate hair pins that were a gift from the citizens of Denobula, if she remembered correctly. Clutching them close to her chest, Hoshi reached into the closet for one of the robes before rushing back to the still-locked door. She eyed the control panel set into the bulkhead before wedging the tip of one *kanzashi* into the panel's seam. Straining, and with the smooth pin sliding in her grasp, she forced the point deeper into the seam until she felt a satisfying snap and the faceplate popped free, revealing the panel's internal circuitry. Pausing to draw a deep breath, Hoshi wrapped the robe around her hand and renewed her grip on the *kanzashi* before jamming them into the panel's main processor.

She pulled her hand and the pins free as sparks and smoke belched from the small compartment, followed an instant later by the satisfying sight of the door opening. It was still sliding aside as she plunged through the widening gap, her eyes locking on the Andorian guard standing with his back to her. He was still reacting to the sound of the door when Hoshi slammed into him, sending them both careening into the opposite bulkhead.

The Empress screamed in pent-up rage, lashing out at the guard and catching his face with the points of the *kanzashi*. Hoshi heard the Andorian grunt in pain as twin cuts appeared below his right eye. He tried to reach for his weapon, but Hoshi struck at him again, driving her knee into his groin before taking one of the long pins in each hand and plunging their length into either side of his neck. She felt blood on her face and heard a gurgled wheezing as the guard struggled for breath. Hoshi maintained her grip on the *kanzashi,* shouting through gritted teeth as she forced the Andorian against the bulkhead and held on until she finally felt his body go limp.

Only when the guard had dropped in a lifeless heap to the deck did Hoshi release her hold on him, leaving the pins still in his neck. She reached for his Imperial-issue phase pistol, and considered her options. Should she try to make her way to the bridge? There would probably be no point. The yacht had been out of warp space for several minutes now. If they had been attacked by pirates, then boarding parties were probably on the way if they had not already arrived.

Let them come, Hoshi decided. Better to die fighting, here and now, than to accept the exile that awaited her on some miserable planet.

As Hoshi pushed down the corridor, she heard weapons' fire from somewhere below and behind her, probably a lower deck near the yacht's stern. Had their assailants boarded the ship through the aft airlock? It was possible the Andorians on the bridge may have left their posts to intercept the intruders. If so, then perhaps the bridge was unmanned. If she could reach it, Hoshi would need only a few moments—just long enough to dissolve the magnetic barrier between the matter and antimatter in the vessel's reactor core. She was determined to deprive the attackers of whatever spoils they were seeking. That she would also kill the entire boarding party with the ship's destruction was merely an unexpected bonus.

Approaching the end of the corridor, she saw the entrance to the maintenance shaft that ran vertically through the yacht's four decks. Its length was spanned by a narrow metal-rung ladder that Hoshi knew would allow her access to the bridge. She was reaching for the ladder when she heard the telltale beeping of a scanner, growing louder with each passing moment and accompanied by the unmistakable sounds of someone—several someones—descending the ladder.

They're searching. For me?

She quelled her rising panic, backing away from the ladder and turning to head back up the corridor when she stopped short. Ahead of her, blocking her path, were four Vulcans: three large males—all armed with what Hoshi recognized as Starfleet-issue pulse rifles—and one lithe female whom the Empress immediately recognized.

T'Pol.

Dressed in a simple, earth-toned woven shirt and matching pants, T'Pol regarded her with what Hoshi was certain was restrained amusement. Her right eyebrow arching, she nodded in mock greeting.

"It is agreeable to see you again, Your Majesty."

Hoshi felt renewed rage as she beheld her former crewmate, this traitor to the Empire. Jonathan Archer believed T'Pol was working with the rebels all along, and it now appeared his suspicions were correct. The Empress seethed, furious with herself for not killing the Vulcan when she had the chance.

I'm not making the same mistake again. Hoshi felt her jaw clench in determination as she raised her phase pistol.

T'Pol's companions moved to react, but Hoshi's finger never found the weapon's firing stud. Instead she felt pressure at the junction of her neck and shoulder before everything gave way to blackness.

Standing with his hands clasped behind his back, one hand holding a data padd containing the latest in an unending series of status reports, General Shran looked out from the window of what had once been Empress Sato's office in the Kyoto palace. His eyes fell on the almost-repaired perimeter wall on the far side of the *oikeniwa*. The gardens had been restored in a matter of weeks. Shran could understand why Hoshi was enamored with this place. For a brief moment, he could almost forget the near-total destruction of the structures that stood just beyond the palace walls.

From the corner of his good eye, Shran noticed one of his personal guards standing at the entrance to the office. "What is it?"

"The Imperial Adviser on Technology has answered your summons, General."

"Show him in," Shran said, smirking a bit at hearing the officious title Doctor Soong had insisted upon. The gray-haired, bespectacled human shuffled into the office, cradling a pair of data padds to his chest.

"Your Excellency." Soong bowed his head.

Shran tossed his padd on a desk covered with flimsies, battle maps, and more padds. "I trust you bring good news, Doctor."

Soong's excitement was such that he could hardly contain himself. "General, General. The components I removed from that ship—I could spend the rest of my life examining them!"

"Your prediction will come true sooner than you think if you don't deliver results."

Soong used his hands as he spoke, as if disassembling an imaginary component in midair. "I've taken apart one of the food synthesizer units—its power is completely self-contained. You could feed half a *continent* with one of these devices. I turned a pile of organic goo into a prime rib steak better than anything your personal chef has ever . . ."

Shran moved to him, threatening. "I'm interested in *weapons,* Doctor. Technology with tactical applications. Have you managed to reproduce any of the Federation weapons?"

The doctor hesitated. Although he had some good news to report, there was precious little of it and he was uncertain how Shran would react. "The development of the ship-mounted phasers is showing a lot of promise," Soong offered hopefully.

"The biggest obstacle right now is reproducing the trifaceted crystal in the discharge emitter—without it, the beam would be scattered, unfocused. Useless. But I'm confident we're very close to duplicating this crystal."

"*How* close?"

"Another week at most."

Shran nodded, neither pleased nor displeased. "The torpedoes?"

Soong smiled nervously. "They've proven to be a little more of a challenge."

"Why should that be? The Klingons already have similar weapons."

The doctor winced. "Ah . . . they're not so much alike, it turns out. *Defiant*'s photon torpedoes aren't giant "capsules" like our standard warheads. They're really nothing more than a magnetic bottle containing slugs of antideuterium—it's like a miniature warp reactor *without* the reactor casing. Now imagine that field of energy hurtling through space at relativistic velocities and you'll have an idea of the technology I'm trying to duplicate!"

"You have a reputation as the most brilliant human alive," Shran said. "If the task I've given you is too difficult, perhaps I should turn it over to an *Andorian.*"

Soong swallowed hard. "I have no doubt your scientists are the best in their respective fields—but if they have to start over you'll lose months, General, and that's something you can't afford."

"Why would they have to start over? They'll simply use the data you've gathered."

"All of my data and research is encrypted with a zeta-level algorithm—for security purposes, of course," Soong said pointedly. "Wouldn't want the rebels to get their hands on it, would we, Your Excellency?"

He eyed the doctor, impressed. If Shran decided to eliminate his chief technology adviser, all of the work Soong had done would be lost. *A wise insurance policy,* Shran thought.

"All right, Doctor. What do you need from me? Personnel? Resources?"

"I need *time*."

Shran grabbed one of the data padds from his desk and hurled it into the window, which cracked from the impact. Soong held his tongue, wondering if the next thing he would hear would be the sound of the general removing his phase pistol from its holster.

"How long until our shipyards can build another *Defiant*? I want a realistic estimate."

Soong considered his response carefully. His next words could be his last. But at least they would be honest words. "Twenty-five years," he finally said. "If I was permitted to tear *Defiant* apart, I could probably cut that estimate in half." The look on Shran's face caused Soong to hastily add, "Keep in mind that everything we're learning will enable us to build *new* vessels with vastly improved tactical capabilities. They just won't be in the same class as *Defiant*."

Shran weighed what he heard as he contemplated the spider-web pattern he had made in Hoshi's window. She would no doubt be very upset that he had spoiled the view.

I need those ships now, not a year from now, not twenty-five years in the future.

"General, I must confess I'm puzzled," the doctor said. "From what I hear on the official broadcasts, the war's going well. Three rebel outposts destroyed, their leaders captured—"

"Lies and propaganda, all of it."

"So . . . we *haven't* destroyed any outposts?"

"Actually we did," Shran said evenly. "P'Jem, Weytahn, Tantalus V—every structure on those planets reduced to dust." He turned to look directly at Soong, his tone almost confessional. "There's only one minor complication—as it turns out, none of those colonies actually harbored any rebels."

This surprised even Soong. "P'Jem is a monastery, I believe."

"It was. One of the most revered among all Vulcans."

Soong read the general's tone and body language carefully— this was no lapse in intelligence gathering. Starfleet had targeted these worlds fully aware there were no rebel elements present.

Shran picked up a decanter of blue liquid and started to pour a glass for himself, asking him casually, "Could I interest you in a glass of ale, Doctor?"

Soong nodded. The Andorian poured. "Humans are an unforgiving species," Shran finally said. "The citizens demanded vengeance. I gave them what they asked for."

The public had responded to the attacks just as Shran had anticipated—instead of filling the streets in protest, they came out to praise their Empress for her resolve. Shran's actions had ironically renewed the people's faith in Hoshi. *It's a shame that my dear wife is not present to appreciate the effectiveness of her leadership.*

He handed Soong the glass of liquid. "Hearts and minds, Doctor. That's what it's all about. The public's appetite for blood is sated. I've bought the Empire a little bit of time. A real victory still eludes us—fortunately, it eludes the rebels as well."

Soong quickly downed the drink, stifling a gasp at the nearly two hundred proof fermented beverage. After a moment he managed to squeak out his next words. "I have every confidence you'll end this war, General."

"One way or the other," Shran said with resignation. He put down his drink, rubbed his eyes with the palms of his hand. "What of our *other* project, Doctor?"

Soong perked up at the change of subject. "I was hoping you'd ask. Genetic engineering has been something of a pet project of mine for years." He entered a sequence of commands on one of his data padds. "There were a few minor difficulties, but Mister Paxton's research proved most helpful during the post-fertilization resequencing." He handed the device to Shran. "In about thirty weeks, the Empire will have an heir to the throne."

Shran took the proffered data padd. On the miniaturized display appeared an image of a gray, metallic cylinder with four translucent panels. Inside, a viscous green fluid circulated. Shran pressed a key to enhance the image, and saw suspended within the fluid the unmistakable silhouette of a humanoid fetus.

A child of my own once again.

Long-suppressed feelings of paternal pride and excitement welled within him, sensations he had buried long ago after the death of his daughter, Talla, killed in a tragic accident before she had even been able to walk.

It had been a distasteful proposition, obtaining a selection of eggs from the Empress. The proceedure itself was something Shran had been anticipating ever since Sato had told him of the historical record of the child they would bear together. Even after her lie was revealed, Shran was surprised to realize that he still wanted this child. Its joint human-Andorian heritage would make it ideally suited as an acceptable future leader of the Terran Empire. Assuming he would allow the child to reach adulthood.

"General Shran?"

His personal guard had entered the office again. Rather than waiting at the entrance as he had before, the subordinate crossed the tiled floor and held out his hand. He carried a memory card, which he offered to Shran. "Imperial Intelligence has just delivered this, General. It's coded urgent."

Shran accepted the card and inserted it into the data padd. The image of the gestating fetus was replaced by a jumble of random, scrolling symbols, indicating an encryption scheme at work. With a sudden knot of unease, the general entered his personal access code, and the display coalesced into a short message rendered in Andorian alpha numerics.

"My wife never arrived at Deneva," he said, the words barely a whisper.

Soong leaned forward in his chair. "What's happened?" Soong asked with concern.

Shran read the message to himself again. "All contact with the yacht has been lost." He set the data padd on his desk. Feeling a chill on his skin, he looked to his personal guard.

"Get me Admiral Talas."

10

Despite her best efforts, it was impossible for Hoshi to keep track of the twists and turns as she was hustled through the narrow, dimly lit subterranean passageway. Shadowy rock walls and ceiling were almost a blur in her vision, with the two muscled Vulcan males charged with transporting her to their as yet unknown destination barely letting her feet touch the ground. Hoshi knew that resistance was useless; even if she somehow were able to escape her escorts and free herself of the manacles around her wrists and ankles, she would doubtless become lost in the maze of tunnels and chambers that seemed to be the primary feature of whatever planet, moon, or asteroid her captors had chosen for this, their current hiding place.

The corridor's illumination increased as they rounded yet another curve, the tunnel itself widening into a sizable cavern that Hoshi guessed was what passed for the command post for T'Pol and her cadre of rebels. Cargo containers were stacked nearly to the chamber's jagged, uneven ceiling. Power and data transfer cabling crisscrossed the stone floor, or was strung in haphazard fashion from bolts driven into the rock walls. Portable computer and communications equipment was positioned atop simple, utilitarian worktables and cargo crates from which they had been extracted. She heard the muffled hum of a power generator from farther back in the cavern.

This was the first time she had seen such an arrangement in the weeks that had passed since she had fallen into captivity, but it was obvious to her that her hosts preferred practicality to aesthetics in the finest Vulcan fashion, the entire scene suggesting that the rebels were ready to pack up everything and evacuate at the first sign of trouble.

"Move," a stern voice said from behind her before a firm hand between her shoulder blades propelled Hoshi farther into the room, her feet shuffling as they fought the short length of chain connecting the manacles around her ankles. The chamber's cool, damp air chilled her exposed skin and she even felt it already beginning to seep through the material of the gray, oversized one-piece garment she had been given to wear upon her arrival.

Situated near the far wall of the room was a long, narrow table, which to Hoshi looked to have been fashioned from the bulkhead of a large cargo container. T'Pau sat behind the table, a Tellarite male occupying the chair to her right while a male Andorian and an Orion female sat to her left. While none of the quartet appeared genial or welcoming, there was no mistaking the angry, determined set to T'Pau's jaw.

"Greetings, *Your Majesty,*" the Vulcan said, making no attempt to disguise the derision lacing her words. "I realize that the accommodations we've been able to provide while you've been our guest are somewhat less extravagant than the imperial palace on Earth, but I trust you are reasonably comfortable."

"I'm adapting," Hoshi replied, drawing herself to her full height and doing her best to put out of her mind her disheveled, servile appearance. Casting a glance at the Andorian seated at the table, she said, "How's your friend?"

Bristling at the question and all it suggested, the Andorian replied, "He is recovering in our infirmary. The damage to his pride was worse than the injury you inflicted to his body, but it is safe to say that he will not attempt to . . . ingratiate himself to you with such fervor in the future."

"I would have thought you appreciative of such overtures," the Orion woman said, leering at Hoshi, "given your choice . . ."

"That is enough, Navaar," T'Pau snapped, and this time there was no mistaking the annoyance in her tone.

No, the Empress decided, *there's something else going on here.*

It was clear that the rebel leader was angry and was doing her level best to keep that rising ire under some semblance of control. What possible reason could the learned Vulcan have for struggling for command of her own emotions?

"Why am I here?" Hoshi asked. "If you were going to kill me, you'd have done it by now."

T'Pau replied, "Rest assured that your death is inevitable. It is only a question of how that event best serves our ends." Rising from her seat, she made her way around the makeshift table. "Your husband has been quite busy these past weeks," she said as she moved to stand before Hoshi. "Claiming to the public that he is acting on your orders, he's dispatched your Starfleet to devastating effect, meting out revenge for our attack on Earth. Several of our bases have been destroyed, and rebellion sympathizers throughout the quadrant have suffered, as well."

"You'll forgive me if I don't shed any tears," Hoshi said, her eyes locking with the Vulcan's. She wondered if the doubt she heard in her own words was as noticeable to T'Pau, for the Empress found herself unable to understand Shran's motives in the face of what she now was hearing.

"Among his targets of choice was the monastery on P'Jem," the Andorian said from where he sat at the table. "It was obliterated. Hundreds of Vulcans were killed, absolutely none of whom had ever so much as raised a finger in support of the rebellion."

Despite her bluster, Hoshi blinked in disbelief at this new revelation. "That's impossible." From what she had read of Vulcan history, the monastery had stood unmolested for thousands of years. Even during the war between Andoria and Vulcan, both sides had agreed that religious sites such as P'Jem or the Andorian worship temples on Syrinx were to be declared off-limits. To the best of her knowledge, it was an agreement that had been respected for generations. Even the Empire had agreed to leave such sanctuaries undisturbed, though they of course had been subjected to scrutiny and inspection since.

"According to Shran," T'Pau said, "you put forth the accusation that the caretakers on P'Jem were harboring rebel leaders. Even if that were true, which it was not, there has been much public outcry over the massacre, both within and beyond the Empire's borders."

Still struggling to absorb what she had been told as well as trying to comprehend the long-term consequences of the unprecedented actions Shran was carrying out in her name, Hoshi felt her anger and renewed sense of betrayal threatening to boil over once again. Forcing her ire back down, she frowned as she regarded T'Pau. "Why are you telling me this?"

"She's a fool," said the Tellarite from where he still sat behind T'Pau, "just like the rest of the humans. She has no idea how deep Shran's treachery runs."

Breaking her gaze from T'Pau, Hoshi regarded the burly rebel. "I know enough," she snapped. "He's been working with you from the beginning. He directed *Defiant* to the Devolin system, and he informed you that Earth was vulnerable so you could attack." Despite the horrific wounds inflicted upon her planet, the Empress could not resist adding, "It is a testament to the inadequacy of your rebellion, that it can succeed only through such underhanded methods."

"Under other circumstances," T'Pau said, her right eyebrow rising as she leveled a knowing, accusatory stare, "the irony of your lecturing us on this particular topic would be amusing." Folding her arms across her chest, she began to pace in a circle around Hoshi. "Regardless, Gral is correct. Shran's duplicity extends far beyond what he has done to you. He's taken it upon himself to further betray those who helped him rise to power. He is continuing the objective you set out for the Empire and working to stamp out the rebellion, but not for anything as noble as freeing the downtrodden from the grip of oppression."

Hoshi released an audible sigh. Was it genetically impossible for Vulcans to get to whatever point they labored to make under the weight of such vocabulary?

"Shran never had any intention of helping us," T'Pau continued. "It was always his goal to seize the throne for himself and to use your Starfleet to do what Andoria could not accomplish on its own: conquer Vulcan and its allies. Thanks to your negligence, he apparently was able to succeed with a minimum of effort."

"If what you're telling me is true," Hoshi said, doing her best to contain her mounting anger, "then it looks like I'm in good company." Despite her acerbic comment, she could not help but agree with T'Pau's assessment. That Shran had gone so far as to use her own deceptions against her only added to her festering rage. Even as she stood before these rebels in a cave buried beneath the surface of some unknown world, the seeds of her husband's latest campaign were being sown. The fetus that had been conceived from her egg—taken from her via a surgical procedure performed by Arik Soong—had been fertilized with Shran's eager assistance. The result would be a child born of two races, a representation of Earth and Andoria's binding union and their joint destiny to rule the galaxy.

Traitorous bastard, she fumed, as outraged with herself as she was with the general. The violation she had suffered in order to set that aspect of Shran's scheme into motion was but one more item on the list of crimes for which she hoped he would answer. If the fates were kind, one day she would see the expression on his face and hear him utter his final words as her own dagger pierced his heart.

At the moment, however, that did not appear likely.

T'Pau's pacing brought her around to face Hoshi once more. "Shran's audacity will be his undoing, Your Majesty," she said, though this time there was no hint of her earlier disrespect. "Never before has any Terran Emperor ordered the slaughter of innocents on such a scale, even with provocation. While humans are renowned for their brutality toward those they conquer, an apparent unwillingness to murder indiscriminately is one of the few commendable traits your species still possesses."

"Shran has crossed a line from which there may be no retreat," the Andorian added. "History—ours and yours—has shown that whenever a ruling power commits such heinous acts, they are but the first of many steps along the path leading to their eventual downfall."

"Trev speaks wisely," T'Pau said, "and we have an opportunity here. People throughout the Empire have begun to question their new ruler. How fortunate for us that we have you in custody, where you can now stand trial for the Empire's crimes against those it has terrorized for generations."

Hoshi's eyes widened in disbelief. "You can't be serious."

"Vulcans are always serious," T'Pau replied, now standing close enough that Hoshi briefly considered an attempt to use the chain binding her wrists to choke the rebel leader. She dismissed the thought just as quickly. Even if T'Pau were unable to counter her attack, the two Vulcan guards who still flanked Hoshi would overpower her with even less effort than it had taken to bring her here.

"A tribunal representing the worlds crushed beneath the Empire's heel will hear your case and pass judgment upon you," Navaar said, rising from her chair. "It should prove most entertaining."

Leaning closer, T'Pau's eyes narrowed as she regarded Hoshi. "It is our hope that your trial and subsequent execution, broadcast throughout the Empire, will provide a much-needed boost to the rebellion's flagging morale. To use one of your human idioms, we will cut off the snake's head, leaving the body to wither and die."

She nodded to the guards, who ushered Hoshi without ceremony from the command post. Powerless to do anything except stumble and stagger in the custody of her escorts, the deposed Empress once again felt the stifling press of the narrow, dark passages leading deeper into the earth and to her detention cell, though this time the sensation echoed the oppressive grip of defeat that seemed now to be closing around her.

★ ★ ★

"Your accommodations appear adequate, if somewhat lacking."

Hoshi opened her eyes at the sound of the familiar voice and stared for a moment at the stone wall forming the rear of her holding cell. An abrasive woolen blanket provided the only barrier between her and the wall-mounted metal platform serving as her bed, and she felt the twinge of muscle ache as she rolled over to face the bars separating her from her visitor.

"*Vulcan* adequacy never did much for me," she said, swinging her legs off the so-called bed and planting her feet on the cell's cold, dusty floor.

Expressionless, T'Pol turned her gaze to the cell's far wall, now stained with a fresh spatter that dripped in thick brown streaks to a puddle on the floor next to a battered metal bowl. "However, your apparent actions will not help meet your nutritional needs."

"Spare me your *spa'ash plomeek* broth," Hoshi snapped, hoping her choice of a Vulcan slur might needle her former shipmate even if only the slightest bit. "Or whatever else you put in that bowl."

"Drugging or poisoning someone already in secure custody is not lo—"

Hoshi rolled her eyes in disgust and held her palm out toward the Vulcan. "Spare me *that,* too," she said. Releasing a tired sigh, she shook her head. "You're wasting your time, you know. All of you."

T'Pol replied, "It is you who requested my presence. If anyone is wasting time, it is you."

"I'd almost forgotten what an insufferable pain in the ass you can be," Hoshi said, rising from the cot as she glared at the other woman. It was her first time seeing the Vulcan since their unexpected meeting aboard her yacht. Prior to that, the Empress's last memory of T'Pol was of her being thrown into *Defiant's* brig, months earlier. She had escaped, doubtless with assistance, though the traitors responsible for that action were never found.

"You betrayed me," Hoshi said.

T'Pol shook her head. "Incorrect, given that I never pledged loyalty to you."

"Damn your semantics," the Empress countered, glaring at her rival. "You betrayed the Empire."

Pausing, T'Pol nodded after a moment. "Possibly."

Hoshi offered a wan smile. "What's more, you betrayed your own people, though you didn't know it at the time. You're only aiding in the slaughter now. It's a pity you can't see that. As I said, you're wasting your time. The longer you cower in the shadows, the more time you're giving Shran to push his strategy. You've already seen what he's done. Imagine what he'll be able to do in six months once he's had the chance to replicate *Defiant*'s technology."

"Such attacks are to be expected," T'Pol countered. "We will be prepared for them. I will remind you that the *Defiant* is only a single vessel, and its weaknesses are not unknown."

"That's right," Hoshi said, gritting her teeth in realization as she reached forward to grip one of the bars of her cell door in each hand. "More of your treachery at work." The Empress herself had caught T'Pol downloading *Defiant*'s schematics, the very treason for which she had been imprisoned. Had he not met an untimely end in his own right, Jonathan Archer might well have executed her for her crimes. "I'm guessing you managed to obtain another copy of the schematics before you escaped?" When T'Pol did not answer, Hoshi affected what she hoped appeared as a disinterested shrug. "Not that it matters. As we speak, Shran is replicating *Defiant*'s technology. Soon, he'll have a fleet of warships, all with weapons far more powerful than anything Starfleet or the rebels have."

T'Pol said nothing in immediate reply, her expression telling Hoshi that the Vulcan was mulling over what she had heard. "You will understand if I do not find you the most credible source of information in this regard."

"You don't have to believe me," Hoshi said, clutching the bars even tighter now. "What does your logic tell you about how this will play out? What are the rebellion's real chances against the Empire?"

Offering a conciliatory nod, T'Pol replied, "There is a greater probability of the Empire's eventual success in this conflict."

"And what do you think Shran will do the minute he knows he's won?" Hoshi asked. "With every political and military resource he'll control, what do you think he'll do first? He'll make sure that no one can rise up to challenge the Empire ever again. He'll grind Vulcan under his boot with such force that your past conflicts will look like a playground shoving match."

T'Pol remained silent.

"Let me guess," Hoshi said after a moment. "Vulcans don't *have* playgrounds."

Exhaling audibly at the remark, T'Pol clasped her hands behind her back. "Am I to assume that, given your certainty of the war's outcome, you summoned me merely to gloat?"

Hoshi grunted in mounting irritation. "I called you here to offer an alternative," she said. "An opportunity."

That finally got a reaction out of the heretofore stoic Vulcan. Her right eyebrow arched, a sure indicator of her piqued interest. "Elaborate."

"There's been too much death and destruction because of the rebellion," Hoshi said, "but the Empire itself is as much to blame for that. I want it to end. As for Vulcan, your people have enjoyed a measure of autonomy that others have not. That . . . latitude . . . could be expanded. I've come to understand that if the Empire is to survive, it will need powerful allies. Vulcan could be one such ally."

"Why should I believe your offer is genuine?" T'Pol asked. "You have lied and schemed to attain the throne, and you are about to stand trial for your crimes against entire worlds. It is logical to presume that you would say or offer anything which might facilitate your freedom."

Shaking the bars in frustration, Hoshi stepped away from the door. "You've seen the *Defiant*'s historical database, the real one. You know that in the other universe, Earth and Vulcan formed an alliance that lasted decades and was the basis for an interstellar coalition consisting of numerous worlds. They found a way to work together, T'Pol, despite their obvious differences. We can do that here." Captain Forrest had, years ago during one of their frequent trysts, mentioned that he often had wondered how the Empire might have expanded its sphere of influence if it had chosen to ally with the Vulcans rather than conquer them.

"I see the doubt in your eyes, T'Pol, even through that mask you wear to hide your emotions. I can accept that." Turning from the door, Hoshi moved to her bunk. "Humans have an old saying that it's better to deal with the devil you know than the devil you don't." Taking a seat atop the bed's dirty blanket, she said. "Consider the alternatives: unending servitude or perhaps genocide at the hands of Shran and Andoria, or a future under my benevolent rule."

For a brief moment, the Empress saw T'Pol's features soften as she considered what she was hearing. Were her words making an impression?

"You can play a role, T'Pol," she pressed, realizing as she spoke that her voice had lowered and that her body language had taken on a more seductive posture as though of its own volition. "Imagine guiding the future of your people, sitting at my right hand as we chart our course . . . together."

If she was enamored with the proposal, T'Pol maintained her composure so as not to show it. "Why have you not shared this proposal of yours with T'Pau?"

"She's been fighting the war too long," Hoshi replied. "She'd never trust me, and even if she did, I wouldn't trust her. You and I don't have to like each other in order to lead our people, but at least you're the devil *I* know."

Hoshi watched as T'Pol stood silent, her gaze fixed and her features betraying nothing. What was she thinking?

"You don't believe me, do you?" Hoshi asked after a moment.

Rather than reply, T'Pol stepped away from the bars, her eyes narrowing as she moved to leave.

Hoshi pushed herself from the bunk until she once again was gripping the cell bars. "I'm the only hope your people have!"

Pausing at the entrance to the passageway leading from the holding cell, the Vulcan turned to look over her shoulder. "I find that . . . unlikely, Your Majesty." She held her gaze a moment, as though hesitating over her decision, before disappearing into the subterranean corridor.

"T'Pol!" Hoshi shouted once more. What had she seen in the Vulcan's eyes? Uncertainty? It was fleeting, but the Empress was sure it had been there.

Think about that for a while, she mused, with only a small amount of bitterness. *I'm not going anywhere.*

11

If nothing else, Hoshi decided, the rebels certainly possessed a flair for the dramatic.

The interior of the spacious, drafty subterranean cavern had been reconfigured since her last visit. Gone were most of the cargo containers she remembered being stacked around the chamber. Most of them, along with the makeshift workstations and their pilfered computer and communications equipment, had been moved to the cave's far wall. There was no sign of the table at which T'Pau and her peers had sat in judgment of her.

Wooden torches were placed around the cavern, the flickering light from their flames reflected by the mineral deposits embedded within the rock walls and ceiling. To her right was a table with four wooden high-backed chairs, and arranged along the wall before the Empress were three rows of tiered bench seating, which appeared to have been constructed from metal plating scrounged from cargo crates or whatever other raw building materials the rebels might have brought with them to this world.

She counted perhaps three dozen individuals—Vulcans, Andorians, Orions, Tellarites, and even a few humans—occupying the stands. Some of the onlookers were talking in low voices among themselves, but most simply sat in silence, regarding her with expressions ranging from irritating indifference to barely disguised disdain to open, unfettered loathing. A railing had been erected in front of the stands, from which hung colorful banners representing Vulcan, Andoria, Tellar, and the Orion colonies. Hoshi noted that the flags bore symbols used by the individual worlds before they had become subjects of the Empire.

Vive la résistance, the Empress mused. Everything in the room, including her, was deliberately staged for visual effect. Hoshi stood atop a metal pallet at the center of the cavern, stationed before the assembled audience. Her improvised dais was ringed by a railing similar to that bordering the viewing stands. While the manacles had been removed from her ankles, those binding her wrists had been further secured to the rail in front of her. She had been allowed to bathe and was once again clothed in the silken robes she had been wearing at the time of her kidnapping. The garments had even been cleaned prior to her receiving them, all so that she might put forth the best possible appearance for the events that would unfold—and be broadcast via subspace throughout the Empire. To her left, a Vulcan female and a Tellarite male had attached a portable subspace transceiver interface to a tripod, aiming it so that its audiovisual receiver pointed toward Hoshi and the table on her right.

"All rise!"

The bellowing command echoed through the cavern, issued by a nondescript Andorian standing at the entrance to the cave and dressed in what the Empress recognized as the black, form-fitting uniform of the Andorian Guard. All the conversations taking place in the viewing stands faded into silence as the audience rose to their feet.

The show is about to begin. It was a bitter, sardonic thought that crossed Hoshi's mind as she turned her head in the direction of the speaker and saw T'Pau, dressed in a traditional light-colored Vulcan meditation robe, enter the chamber. She was followed by the same three rebels who had been with her the last time Hoshi had been brought to this place. Gral, the Tellarite, sported a cleaner version of the dark blue jumpsuit she had seen him wearing earlier, whereas the Orion woman, Navaar, was wrapped in a black gown that hugged every curve of her lean, sultry body. The Andorian, Trev, wore an unembellished sand-colored shift that reminded Hoshi of a poncho one might wear during inclement weather. None of the quartet resembled guerrilla warriors so much as diplomats, though the Empress was well aware of the role they actually would be playing here today.

"Be seated," T'Pau directed the audience as she and her companions moved behind the wooden table. She remained standing, turning her attention to the subspace transceiver interface. "We offer greetings to the people of the Terran Empire, particularly those of you who are presently involuntary subjects of that corrupt entity. For generations, the Empire has continued to push beyond the confines of its home planet, not for noble purposes such as expanding their knowledge or seeking out other worlds and civilizations which they might befriend.

"Instead, the people of Earth have embarked on a campaign of oppression, enslaving other worlds and subverting populations, resources, and technology for their own ends. This reign of tyranny has gone unchecked for far too long. Today, we will force the Empire to answer for its numerous crimes against sentient life."

T'Pau stepped around the table, moving to stand next to Hoshi before returning her focus to the subspace transceiver. "I present Empress Sato, your self-appointed ruler. In reality, she is nothing more than a scheming opportunist who rose to power through treachery, greed, and murder, and who now holds on to that authority only through fear and deceit."

Knowing the camera was on her as well as T'Pau, Hoshi stood straight and still, putting forth every appearance of the calm and control her position demanded while at the same time using all of her willpower to remain silent. How dare they sit in judgment of her? Did they actually think that doing so would bring sympathy to their cause? Even the most obtuse individual would have to see that this trial was to be little more than a circus, a staged entertainment designed to rouse those who already were sympathetic to the rebellion's cause.

"People of the Empire," T'Pau continued, "the proceedings

will unfold here, with you as witnesses. You will hear the charges leveled against the accused. You will listen to the testimony of learned colleagues who have thrown off the shackles of subjugation and instead pursued a long, arduous path toward regaining their freedom. The accused will be given the opportunity to defend herself and the actions of the Empire she rules. Nothing will be edited, nothing undertaken behind closed doors. Once that has concluded, and if the Empress is found guilty, then you will bear witness as justice is served."

"Charge number seven: That the Empire deliberately engaged nonmilitary targets on the planet P'Jem, an action resulting in the deaths of four hundred seventy-two civilians."

Sitting behind the ornate mahogany desk in what until recently had been Empress Sato's spacious office occupying the topmost floor of the Kyoto palace, General Shran watched the events unfolding on the viewscreen before him with increasing agitation.

"Fools." The single word was enveloped in bile. He slammed the desk with the palm of his hand, upsetting the crystal sculpture perched near one corner, and he heard it break as it tumbled to the office's carpeted floor.

Profound apologies, my beloved wife, he mused, frowning at the errant, sarcastic thought.

"Why could they not have simply killed her?" he asked, folding his arms across his chest as he began to pace the width of the lavish office.

From where he stood near the oval-shaped picture window that overlooked the western perimeter of the *oikeniwa* encircling the palace, Professor Arik Soong cleared his throat before replying, "I assume that was a rhetorical question, General?"

His eyes narrowing as he turned to regard the professor, Shran said, "Yes, much as if I had asked why you were still alive." Emitting a disgusted grunt, the general continued his pacing.

"The broadcast is being transmitted throughout the Empire,"

Soong said after a moment, his tone more reserved this time. "They're limiting their transmissions to ten minutes, and resuming them at irregular intervals, as well as scrambling the signal and embedding it within other subspace comm traffic. It's proving most difficult to trace the broadcast to its source."

Shran nodded. The so-called trial had paused and resumed in this manner without warning for nearly a day, owing to the frequent interruptions.

Looking down at the data padd he carried in his right hand, the professor continued, "Preliminary reports are already starting to come in from across the planet. There is much unrest among the people, General." Aiming the forward edge of the data padd toward the viewscreen, the professor pressed a control and the image shifted to show a series of scenes, all of them depicting crowds of shouting people standing outside the gates or steps of what Shran recognized as imperial military installations here on Earth. Though no violence appeared to be taking place, there was no mistaking the citizens' growing disapproval.

"Apparently," Soong continued, "they take issue with their leader being portrayed as a common criminal, particularly when the majority of crimes she's being charged with were committed in the name of the Empire." Peering over the rims of his glasses, he added, "The people have embraced the Empress. Unusual thinking, to say the least, considering the anger shown toward her after the rebels' attacks here."

Shaking his head, Shran released a tired sigh. The professor was correct in that Hoshi Sato's brief reign as ruler of the Terran Empire had been relatively bloodless, the murders of her immediate predecessors notwithstanding, of course. She had also eliminated a host of enemies immediately after seizing power, taking such action as a defensive precaution. Otherwise, Sato I had appeared well on her way toward being a truly benevolent ruler once the rebellion was quashed.

It had been a calculated risk on Shran's part, making it appear as though Hoshi had ordered the shocking attacks—particularly the strike on P'Jem—as retaliation for the assaults on Earth. Though there was a great deal of outrage voiced by the peoples of Earth and Vulcan, much of that indignation was tempered by the "evidence" Shran had presented to support claims that P'Jem was in fact a covert military installation loyal to the resistance. The general knew that such fabrications would never withstand intense scrutiny, but that did not matter. By the time the truth behind the violent actions was revealed, it would be far too late for anyone to do anything about it.

Of course, none of that addressed the more immediate problem.

"I feared something like this might happen," Shran said as he moved to stand before the office's picture window. He stared out at the quiet gardens, but the soothing environs did nothing to ease his worries. "From a tactical perspective, it makes perfect sense for the rebels to put her on trial as a shining example of their continued fight against the Empire. It might even suggest that the resistance is gaining ground in the war." This trial could very well be the impetus needed to bring the rebels out of hiding, their confidence renewed as they set out to achieve more than a simple symbolic victory.

To that end, the general quietly had dispatched the *Defiant* to search for Sato and the rebels who had taken her. The starship's advanced sensors were capable of detecting warp emissions and distinguishing between them with greater accuracy than the scanners aboard other Imperial vessels. Admiral Talas had reported a disturbing lack of progress on that front, however, with the *Defiant* encountering signs of multiple, overlapping warp emissions at the last known location of Sato's shuttle. Shran agreed with Talas's theory that the trails had been deliberately left as a means of thwarting the efforts of any pursuing vessels. That presupposed a more thorough knowledge of the starship's superior technology than would be gained simply through the news reports offered by the Empire.

T'Pol.

It was logical, Shran decided, loath as he was to consider that term. The meddlesome Vulcan had escaped the *Defiant* months ago, taking with her one of the ship's shuttlecraft—itself more advanced than anything possessed by the rebels or even the Empire—before disappearing somewhere into deep space. There was no reason to believe that T'Pol had not succeeded in linking up with a resistance cell and offering her knowledge of *Defiant* as proof of her allegiance to the insurgents' cause.

One more reason for me to destroy Vulcan at my first opportunity.

"The people are looking to you for answers, General," Soong said, interrupting Shran's reverie. Turning away from the window, Shran saw that the professor had changed the image on the viewscreen so that it once again displayed Empress Sato, standing regal and silent as the next in a seemingly unending list of charges continued to be read aloud. A moment later the transmission faded into static, the rebels once again terminating their broadcast.

Stepping forward, the professor removed his glasses and leveled a withering glare at Shran as he pointed toward the screen. "General, with time, the *Defiant*'s sensors can track that transmission to its source, even with the countermeasures the rebels are employing. The admirals at Starfleet Command are ready to act on your order. Why are we waiting? This trial is an obscenity against the Empire itself. Insolence on any scale cannot be tolerated, but this must be answered with crushing, decisive force."

"Why, Professor," the general said, smiling gently as he regarded Soong, "I had no idea you were a man of such patriotism."

Soong waved a hand before him as though pushing the notion aside. "This has nothing to do with patriotism and everything to do with survival." Pointing to the screen again, he added, "You heard T'Pau. Sato's just the first of what they hope will be a long list of trials and public executions. I for one have no desire to stand before a firing squad."

The smile faded from Shran's lips. "I could simply kill you now and save you the worry, Professor."

Before Soong could react to the blunt statement, the general stepped away from the window and moved back behind his desk. "We must act, if only to satisfy the people and prevent full-scale revolution from erupting across the planet." Thanks to the rebels, he simply had no choice now. Any perceived failure to answer this assault on the Empire or to rescue Sato would turn the upper echelon at Starfleet Command against him. Better to direct their attention, to say nothing of their considerable skill, resources, and mounting lust for vengeance, toward another enemy.

12

The aroma of *lap-wadi* incense teased her nostrils, and the flickering of sparse candlelight registered through her eyelids as she sat cross-legged on the floor of her quarters aboard the *Ni'Var.* T'Pol focused on none of that, instead using the sensory stimulation simply to enhance her mental focus as it allowed her mind to rest, freeing it if only momentarily from the burdens of the past hours. Matters of defensive resources and battle strategy that had consumed her for most of the day were set aside, finally allowing her to relax and benefit from therapeutic meditation.

Despite her best efforts, the same questions and concerns continued to plague her, relentless in their bid for her attention and energy. Even in her subconscious the variables of the strategy she labored to create danced before her mind's eye, moving and shifting much like the components of a *kal-toh* match. As she had for the past several days, she struggled to see the order and symmetry of the game pieces, in this case the ships comprising the small rebel fleet tasked with countering any forthcoming Starfleet offensive.

T'Pol had felt the same stresses pressing upon her since learning that T'Pau had chosen her to command the *Ni'Var* and assigned to her the task of devising a battle plan for defending the resistance cell's base on Aldus Prime. Now that the insurgents were broadcasting the encrypted and scattered transmission of Empress Sato's trial, the rebel leader was predicting Starfleet's eventual discovery of their temporary sanctuary, and wanted a contingency should that event come to pass. Though briefly taken aback at being asked to shoulder the dual responsibilities, T'Pol had accepted both without hesitation. The assignments were an indication of T'Pau's confidence in her ability, as well as a tremendous gesture of trust on the part of the former minister.

Of course, T'Pol mused, *it might all be a ruse on T'Pau's part—a test of my loyalty.*

She knew that T'Pau was aware of her conversation with Hoshi Sato. What the rebel leader did not know was that T'Pol had been forced to admit to herself that there had been some merit in what the exiled Empress had said. Based on the latest reports supplied by rebel operatives within the Empire, General Shran was maneuvering Starfleet and his own forces in a manner consistent with what Sato had described. Was his end game as she had foretold?

Sinking deeper into her meditative trance, T'Pol almost did not hear the pneumatic hiss of her quarters' door sliding open before her. Irritated at the unexpected interruption, she pulled herself back to full consciousness and opened her eyes to see who had called on her.

"You have arrived ahead of schedule, Staal."

Was it her imagination, or did her friend actually appear uneasy? Perhaps it was some odd manifestation of his human appearance, which he was forced to keep until such time as he could reach a qualified surgeon who could restore his Vulcan features.

"It was not my intention to disrupt your private meditation," he said. "I can return at a more appropriate time."

T'Pol rose to her feet. "Now is acceptable. We still have much work to do with regard to finalizing the battle plan, and your assistance would be most appreciated." At T'Pau's request, she had included Staal in the development of the defensive strategy. His contributions had been most helpful, not only with the plan itself but also in how she related to the other members of the resistance cell, particularly the commanders of the other vessels in their small fleet. Working with Staal had helped her build credibility within the cell leadership, and she even allowed herself a minor sense of satisfaction at the progress made to this point.

"Your unique perspective on Starfleet," Staal said, "as well as the *Defiant*'s capabilities will almost certainly yield a sound and comprehensive counteroffensive strategy. I am confident that your strategy will serve us adequately."

It was true that her knowledge of the *Defiant*'s specifications was unmatched within the resistance—at least, so far as she knew. Thanks to her zealous protection of the technical information she had stolen from the starship, there was no one else better qualified to carry out the task T'Pau had in mind.

"My early arrival is due to T'Pau's wish to review the plan ahead of our prescribed schedule. Have you completed it?"

"Yes," T'Pol said, crossing her quarters to the desk set against the far wall. Reaching for the card reader slot of the desktop computer station on her desk, she extracted a data card. "This is a copy of the . . ."

She sensed rather than heard the movement behind her, Staal doing his best to affect a stealthy approach. An instant later she felt his fingers on either side of her neck. Even as she jerked to one side, using practiced moves to break Staal's hold on her before he could tighten his grip, she immediately recognized the tactic he had attempted to employ.

Tal-shaya. There could be no mistaking Staal's intent, for the ancient martial art served but a single purpose: Her friend had come here to kill her.

Saying nothing, Staal renewed his attack, lashing out at her with his open right hand. T'Pol parried the attack, blocking his arm before thrusting her knee upward into his groin. Not giving him a chance to recover, she struck him across the face with the edge of her left hand. She stepped back in search of maneuvering room, driving her foot into his knee and sending him falling to the deck. A satisfying grunt of pain exploded from his lips as he rolled to one side in an effort to regain his footing.

"Staal, explain yourself," T'Pol said, maintaining a defensive stance as she watched him roll to a kneeling position. A trickle of green blood from his nose belied his human appearance. No sooner did Staal pull himself to his feet than T'Pol chose to go on the offensive. She lunged for him, closing the distance between them even as he readied for an attack of his own. Striking out at him once more, she thrust the heel of her hand up into his chin, driving it upward with more force than even she had anticipated. Reeling from the blow, Staal could only stand defenseless as T'Pol kicked him in the midsection, pushing him off his feet and sending him crashing into her array of meditation candles. He lay motionless, and only when T'Pol moved to stand over him did she notice the pool of green blood expanding out from beneath his head.

Reaching down, she rolled Staal onto his side, catching her first look at the centimeters-long shard of amber-tinted glass buried into the side of his neck. The amount of blood hemorrhaging from the wound could only have been caused by the severing of a major artery, an injury that likely would prove fatal if he did not receive prompt medical attention.

He must not die! Her mind screamed the declaration. She had to know why he had come to betray and murder her, but his condition prevented any immediate interrogation.

A single option remained to her, she knew, but it was a distasteful one. She knew from a lifetime of training—almost all of which had been held in secret in order to protect the knowledge of such ability—that forcing a meld upon an unwilling participant was one of the most heinous, vulgar acts one Vulcan could commit upon another, second only to murder. Despite that, T'Pol could not see that she had a choice, not if she was to learn the truth behind the attempt on her life.

Extending her right hand until her fingers rested on the *katra* points of Staal's face, T'Pol ignored his faint, labored breathing as she felt the initial quiver that always accompanied this most sacred and closely guarded of Vulcan mental disciplines.

"My mind to your mind," she whispered, as much to herself as to Staal. "My thoughts to your thoughts."

Shadows encroached upon her consciousness, pushing inward from the outer boundaries of awareness and reaching out to capture her mind within its grasp. T'Pol sensed another presence— weak, fading, but there nonetheless.

"Why did you try to kill me?"

T'Pau.

Even the simple response appeared to tax the mortally wounded Vulcan, and with that effort came T'Pol's need to avoid becoming too closely linked with his dying mind. Still, she pressed on, continuing to refine and focus the joint thoughts until an indistinct image of T'Pau appeared in her consciousness. T'Pol explored further, realizing she now saw herself standing next to the rebel leader, acting in Staal's stead as she forced him to relive this memory.

I no longer have confidence in our ally T'Pol, said the indistinct, wavering image of T'Pau.

"If true, that is regrettable," T'Pol replied aloud, sensing her near immersion into the mind-meld experience.

I do not believe her intentions are what they appear to be. Her loyalty to Empress Sato is something I have suspected from the beginning.

"I have not yet witnessed this firsthand."

You have found her presence welcome to you?

"She has served adequately in many ways, but has not ingratiated herself to me."

Then this task I present to you will not be problematic?

"No more so than when you asked me to kill T'Les."

In the face of this startling new revelation, T'Pol had to struggle to maintain the already tenuous, fading link. T'Pau, responsible for the death of her mother. Even with the life draining from Staal's body with every passing moment, T'Pol pressed onward, deeper into the recesses of her friend's mind.

"Why?" she asked, her own question shadowed by the same word released only with supreme effort from the mouth of the dying Staal. "Why did you have her killed?"

*She became an unknown quantity. There was no choice but to elimi-
nate her. She jeopardized what we have worked to create, apart from the
Empire. Now her daughter seeks to do the same thing. She must be
elimin . . .*

The word *and*, indeed, everything that remained of the consciousness dwelling within Staal's wounded form, faded from existence. T'Pol sensed it happening in time, withdrawing from the
meld and returning to the sanctuary of her own body as the final
flicker of light faded forever from Staal's mind.

Her hair matted with sweat, she pulled her hand away from
Staal's corpse. The full treachery of T'Pau had been laid open
for her mind's eye, and the knowledge filled her heart with a
nearly unchecked rage. The revered Vulcan leader—the would-be
savior of her race from the savage Terran Empire, the woman
who called T'Pol a trusted adviser and confidante—also was the
cold-blooded murderer of her beloved mother. The more she
processed this knowledge, the more intense her passionate hatred
became.

Vengeance is emotion run wild. Vengeance is not logical. T'Pol's mind
rang with the words that her boiling blood would not heed.

So furious was her mounting anger that she realized she had
not heard the chime of the intraship communications channel
until it sounded for the third time. Her fist clenched so tightly
that she thought she might draw blood, T'Pol slammed her hand
down atop the comm panel set into her desk. "What is it?"

"Your presence is requested on the bridge," replied a taciturn male
voice. *"Sensor probes have detected the presence of six Starfleet vessels entering this sector."*

Had Shran found them? Even if that was so, T'Pol found that
she simply did not care.

"Set a course back to Aldus Prime," she said.

13

At long last, Malcolm Reed smiled in satisfaction as an emerald-colored indicator light on his science station console began to blink.

"It's about bloody time," he said under his breath before turning his chair to face Captain Mayweather. "We've confirmed the source of the transmissions."

Mayweather rose from the command chair and moved to the bridge's upper deck to stand next to the major. "You're sure it's not another relay beacon?"

"I'd stake my life on it," Reed replied, turning back to the console and entering a new string of commands.

"That's about what it'll probably cost if you're wrong," Mayweather said.

In response to Reed's instructions, the image on the main viewer shifted to a tactical display of nearby planetary systems in the starship's vicinity. "The signal is coming from Aldus Prime," he said. "Practically under our noses."

Tracking the source of the signal had not at all been an easy task. Reed had spent nearly all of the past two days sifting through volumes of data collected by *Defiant*'s sensors, cursing in mounting frustration as—time and again—what at first had appeared as legitimate communications streams turned into phantoms and decoys, a product of the rebels' impressive encryption and scattering equipment. Only after the vessel maneuvered close enough to scan the Aldus system with short-range sensors was Reed able to make a positive determination.

Turning from his console, the major noticed Mayweather looking away from the main viewer and followed the captain's gaze to a workstation on the bridge's port side. An Andorian officer was hunched over his own console and speaking discreetly into an inset communications speaker.

"Ch'Berro's informing Talas," Reed said, although he was sure Mayweather needed no explanation. At every turn, the Andorians aboard *Defiant* had been working to undermine Mayweather's command in favor of the admiral. Talas was the physical manifestation of a greater, more insidious political climate: the covert transference of the Terran Empire into the hands of these blue-skinned, bug-headed bastards.

And Reed, for one, was itching to do something about it.

However, Mayweather himself had cautioned Reed as well as a growing cadre of imperial loyalists aboard *Defiant* that any action to seize the futuristic starship for themselves needed proper timing and coordination in order to succeed. Too many key personnel aboard ship had been replaced by Andorians, and well-trained replacements—preferably humans—needed to be ready at a moment's notice to fill those roles. Despite ongoing, covert efforts, Mayweather still believed they were not quite ready.

"Helm, increase to warp five and order the fleet to match our speed," the captain ordered.

Nodding, Ensign Zona replied, "ETA is five minutes, twelve seconds."

No sooner had the words left her mouth than the turbolift doors at the back of the bridge opened and Admiral Talas stepped onto the bridge.

"Status report," she said as she stepped into the command well and sat in the empty captain's chair. Reed turned to Mayweather, who was offering the admiral a cold stare.

"The situation's under control, Admiral," Mayweather said. "We've located the source of the transmissions, and I've just ordered a course change. I didn't see a need to inform you."

Talas knit her brow. "Why, Captain," she said in a condescending tone that made Reed bristle, "at what point did you assume leadership of my task force?"

"I merely anticipated what seemed to be the obvious next step, Admiral," Mayweather replied with an obvious effort to maintain a civil tone. "We've located the Empress, and our orders are to affect a rescue."

Pointing a long finger at Mayweather, Talas countered, "Your *orders* are to observe the chain of command, Captain. Any new instructions will come from me, and you do not take action with this ship so long as I am the ranking officer aboard. Am I clear?"

"Yes, Admiral," Mayweather said, biting down on every word. Reed sensed the anger raging beneath the captain's calm exterior. "With your permission, I'd like to finalize our assault plan."

Talas shook her head. "That won't be necessary, Captain. Such planning has already been completed." To Zona, she said, "Set a course for the planet, and notify weapons crews to stand by for orbital bombardment. Notify the ship captains to implement the deployment strategy."

"What?" Mayweather said, making no attempt to hide his surprise. "Admiral, what about . . . ?" He stopped in mid-sentence, casting a look over his shoulder at Reed. He said nothing more, but the look in his eyes told Reed that the captain had reached the same abrupt conclusion.

"We're not going to help her, are we?" Reed asked.

Turning in her chair to face him, Talas replied, "Remember your place, Mister Reed," she said, each word laced with venom.

Unfazed by the threat, Reed pressed forward. "Shran. He told you to only put forth the appearance of trying to rescue the Empress, but only so the people on Earth won't hunt him down and burn him at the stake. Your real orders are to destroy the planet and her with it."

"You're relieved, Major," Talas hissed. Gesturing to ch'Berro, she said, "Place him under arrest and throw him in the brig."

The young Andorian had no time even to rise from his station before red-alert klaxons began wailing across the confines of the bridge.

"What is that?" Talas shouted above the din.

Turning back to the science station, Reed bent over the hooded viewer and activated it, setting its selection controls to offer him incoming data from *Defiant*'s tactical systems. "Sensors are picking up seventeen ships approaching at high warp. Orion interceptors, Vulcan *Suurok*-class vessels, Tellarite cruisers, all on an intercept course. They were hiding on the far side of the Aldus star. They'll be on us in less than two minutes!"

"Ambush," Mayweather said.

Just kill me and get this over with.

The thought repeated in Hoshi Sato's mind as she once more was led down the narrow subterranean passageway back to her holding cell, where she would—again—wait until the unscheduled resumption of her "trial."

For more than two days, Hoshi had witnessed a seemingly unending stream of testimony from representatives of half a dozen races throughout the Empire, who all had taken their turn before the ersatz tribunal to relay their accounts of life under imperial rule: savaged cities, slaughtered innocents, and devastated global cultures as a result of oppressive actions and heinous crimes perpetrated in the name of the Terran Empire. That Hoshi herself actually was free of blame for many of these heinous acts was, of course, a fact of little importance to her prosecutors.

As had become habit, her two Vulcan escorts guided her from the rebels' command post to her cell. While she might be fed during this intermission, what Hoshi really wanted was sleep. With the measures in place to keep the rebels' transmission from being detected, the frequent interruptions and calls to the chamber where the trial was being broadcast came at all hours of the day or night. Sometimes she was left alone for several hours, other times she was hurried back and forth. Hoshi wondered whether the chaotic schedule might also be a ploy by T'Pau to erode her physical and mental resolve.

I wouldn't put it past her.

They rounded yet another bend in the corridor, and Hoshi's toe caught on a loose stone. She stumbled forward, but her fall was arrested by one of her guards, who easily pulled her back to her feet.

"Thank you," Hoshi said, surprised that the guard had not simply allowed her to drop to the tunnel floor. "I didn't . . ."

The rest of her words were drowned out by the high-pitched whine of a phaser. Harsh blue energy erupted from the darkness of the corridor ahead of her, striking the guard on her left in the chest. The Vulcan had no time even to cry out in shock as his body dissolved into nothingness. Hoshi pulled away from the other guard as he drew his own phase pistol, but the weapon never cleared its holster as another beam lanced from the shadows and touched him, wiping him from existence.

Rescued? Hoshi's mind screamed the single word. *Can it be?*

Now standing alone in the tunnel, she watched as a lone figure emerged from the darkened passageway ahead of her. Her savior wore a simple, dark cloak with a hood that concealed her face. Hoshi recognized a twenty-third-century phaser in her benefactor's right hand.

"Who . . . ?" she began, but the words died in her throat as the new arrival pushed back the cloak's hood, and she found herself staring at T'Pol.

"It is agreeable to see you again, Your Majesty," the Vulcan said, mimicking the greeting she had offered during their encounter aboard Hoshi's yacht.

"I don't suppose you're here to kill me?" the Empress asked. Though still shaken by what had just transpired, she made no effort to hide her sarcasm.

T'Pol shook her head. "The thought did occur to me, but other matters must now take precedence." Pausing to look ahead and behind her, she added, "You cannot remain here." Reaching into the folds of her robe, the Vulcan extracted what Hoshi recognized as another piece of futuristic technology from *Defiant*: a communicator. Flipping open the unit's antenna grid, T'Pol pressed one of the two small buttons set into the device's faceplate, and Hoshi saw the center red indicator light begin to blink.

"I have activated its homing beacon," T'Pol said before closing the communicator and handing it to her. "Once the *Defiant* is in range, you will be transported aboard." She reached once more into her robe, this time extracting a data padd. "Give this to Commander Tucker, and have him program the communicator with the information he'll find encoded here. He will understand and explain everything to you."

Frowning, Hoshi asked, "Why are you doing this?"

"I am a loyal subject of the Empire," T'Pol replied, her expression—as always—revealing nothing.

"You've said that same thing the whole time I've been your prisoner," Hoshi countered. "What's changed?"

"Perspective," T'Pol answered before turning to leave. "Live long and prosper, Your Majesty, and pledge to do what you told me you would do if given the opportunity." Without waiting for a response, the Vulcan moved off down the corridor at a fast clip, disappearing around a bend.

Then the sound of increasing energy echoed in the tunnel, and Hoshi felt the familiar tingle of a transporter beam playing across her body . . .

. . . and she materialized in *Defiant*'s transporter room.

"Welcome aboard, Your Majesty," said Commander Tucker from where he stood behind the transporter console, the small grin teasing the corners of his mouth making him appear as though he was insufferably pleased with himself. Behind him, MACO Sergeant Hayes and Corporal Madden stood at attention, each offering her a traditional salute.

Then everything lurched to her right as something slammed into the *Defiant*. Hoshi staggered to maintain her balance, reaching out to put her hand on the wall of the transporter chamber.

"What's going on?" Hoshi asked as she stepped down from the transporter platform. "Where are we?"

"The Aldus system," Tucker replied, moving around the console. "We're under attack by rebel forces. You can thank your husband for that, by the way. From the looks of things, he let the rebels set a trap for us when we came looking for you."

"Get me Mayweather," Hoshi said as she crossed to the transporter console and reached for its inset comm panel.

"That might be a problem, Your Majesty," Tucker replied. "Admiral Talas is in command of the *Defiant* and our task force. Shran's orders. He's pretty much replaced anyone in a key position with an Andorian."

Hoshi shook her head. She did not recognize the admiral's name, but quickly dismissed the officer as one of Shran's followers.

"I'm taking command immediately, Mister Tucker," she said, feeling some of her weariness squelched as adrenaline kicked in, fueled by her renewed drive to seek vengeance on her husband. When another blast struck the *Defiant,* she gripped the console for support as she looked to Tucker. "What about our task force?"

"We have five other ships," Tucker explained, "including the *Imperator.*"

Nodding at the report, Hoshi ran a hand through her hair. "I need to contact Fleet Admiral Robinson." Even as she spoke the words, she knew that would be a tall order. Communications outside the ship were routed through the main station on the bridge.

However, Tucker cocked his head toward the console. "I think we can manage that," he said. When Hoshi offered him a questioning look, he added, "I've been a little busy while you were away, Your Majesty. Making a few adjustments here and there in the event we needed something like this." He reached for the comm panel and activated it. "Computer, this is Commander Tucker. Initiate secondary communications system control at this station location, secured under my voiceprint lockout. Authorization Tucker-Two-One-One-Two, enable."

"*Working,*" answered the *Defiant* computer's synthesized voice. "*Reroute complete.*"

Offering a wan smile, Tucker regarded the Empress. "It's all yours, Your Majesty."

Damage reports from nearly every deck flooded the comm channels, adding to the already tense atmosphere on the bridge. Listening to the reports detailing damage to *Defiant*'s defensive systems, Reed gripped the edge of his station as the ship lurched under yet another salvo that hammered its stressed deflector shields.

"Forward shields are back up!" reported Mayweather from where he now manned the helm. The captain's face was a mask of concern even as he continued his task of maneuvering the starship farther into the rapidly escalating battle. "I don't understand what the hell just happened."

Leaning forward in the command chair, Admiral Talas turned to Reed. "Notify engineering that defensive systems are first priority. Route power from life support if you have to, but keep those shields up!"

Reed nodded. The assault by the rebel ships had so far been fast and brutal, with the *Defiant*'s task force outnumbered nearly three to one as the enemy ships dropped from warp and immediately maneuvered into multiship assault configurations. Though she actually had signaled a retreat at the outset of the skirmish, Talas had just as quickly relented, ordering full power to weapons and shields and giving the order to take the battle to the rebels. Her wavering commitment to a decisive course of action had not gone unnoticed, with Reed and Mayweather exchanging matching looks of concern. Still, there was nothing to be done about that now, as *Defiant* and her escort ships waded into the fray.

To his right, Reed saw the ensign at the communications console turn in his chair, his right hand reaching up to grasp the Feinberg receiver he wore in his ear. "Admiral, *Dauntless* reports the *Bismarck* has been destroyed."

Despite the flurry of noise washing across the bridge, Reed sensed the silence gripping his fellow crew members at the tragic news. As soon as the report was heard, however, he and everyone else knew that they had no time now for mourning; that could come only later, once this current crisis had passed.

"Tellarite cruiser off the port bow," he called out as an alert indicator cried for his attention and he bent over the science station's hooded viewer. "Range forty thousand kilometers and closing. Its shields are failing." *Brave, yet stupid,* Reed mused.

Gripping the arms of her chair, Talas called out, "Target and fire at will."

Looking toward the main viewer, Reed saw the image on the screen shift from that of Aldus Prime, the planet rolling and pitching around the edges of the screen as a consequence of the evasive maneuvers conducted by Mayweather. In its place appeared the incoming enemy ship, a squat, bulky construct that did not at all look as though it represented a threat. The overhead lighting flickered as the phaser batteries engaged yet again, and he saw twin beams of blue energy lance across space to strike the unshielded vessel, carving parallel trenches into its hull as it moved past. An instant later Reed watched as the ship erupted into a ball of energy and flames before dissolving into an expanding cloud of debris. It was followed immediately by a chorus of cheers from around the bridge.

Be seeing you, the major mused as he returned to his sensor display.

"Admiral," the communications officer shouted above the noise. "Receiving an incoming distress call from *Akagi!*" Without waiting for an order, the ensign moved his hands across his console, silencing the flow of status reports coming from the rest of the ship and directing the new signal to the bridge's intercom system.

"*. . . bandoning ship! Warp reactor breach is . . .*"

The signal exploded into a burst of static that made Reed wince, even as the communications officer fumbled to reduce the volume. That accomplished, he turned back to face Talas. "That's all there was, Admiral."

Keeping his attention focused on his station, Reed gritted his teeth in mounting frustration. Two *NX*-class ships destroyed in as many minutes? A third of the task force gone within moments of their arrival at Aldus Prime?

"Continue evasive maneuvers," Talas ordered, though Reed was sure he heard uncertainty in her voice as she issued the instructions. Her confidence had been shaken by the early losses, he realized, and the admiral now was battling to maintain her bearing amid the rapidly deteriorating situation. How long would it be before her increasing doubt affected her ability to issue commands and see them through the battle?

As he gripped the sides of his sensor viewer and watched the fight continuing to unfold in the cold, sterile graphics rendered by the *Defiant*'s tactical sensors, Reed heard the same answer beginning to repeat in his mind.

Not long at all, I'd imagine.

14

Alarms echoed throughout the underground complex. The lighting in this section of the outpost had been reduced, casting the tunnel network farther into shadow. Phaser in hand, T'Pol rounded a bend in the passageway and caught sight of figures running from the cavern ahead of her. A full-scale evacuation was under way, and she knew that—assuming everything went according to the plan she had put into motion—only minutes remained until the planet fell victim to orbital bombardment by the *Defiant* and her task force.

The rebels had good reason to flee. Alone, the starship was more than capable of laying waste to the entire planet. Her Starfleet escort of five ships would no doubt have received upgrades to their tactical systems thanks to efforts to reverse engineer the *Defiant*'s advanced technology. As a result, they would be more than prepared to engage the rebel ships currently maneuvering to intercept them.

Pausing perhaps twenty meters from the entrance leading to what she knew to be the resistance cell's command center as well as the stage from which Empress Sato's trial was broadcast, T'Pol used the shadows for cover. She watched as rebels scurried from the chamber, some of them carrying crates or other equipment, taking along anything portable. From the tunnel to her left, she heard the hum of a transporter in operation as personnel and equipment were evacuated to rebel ships waiting in orbit.

T'Pol cared about none of that. At this moment, she was concerned only with a single objective: T'Pau.

★ ★ ★

Mayweather gripped the edge of the helm station's polished console as *Defiant* shuddered beneath the brunt of another salvo. All around the bridge, display screens and consoles flickered as power distribution nodes strained under the onslaught of the continued attack. The overhead lighting had already dimmed to a low crimson as emergency power systems came online, and it too blinked in protest of the new assault.

"Our shields are holding at seventy-three percent," Reed called out from where he stood at the science station, both hands gripping the console's hooded sensor viewer. "Some minor buckling in the port nacelle strut."

"Bridge to engineering," Admiral Talas shouted above the klaxons from where she sat at the center of the bridge, her hands gripping the armrests of the command chair in an effort to keep from being thrown to the deck. "Route emergency power to the structural integrity field. Helm, evasive maneuvers. Fire at will!"

Bristling at the orders that he should be issuing, Mayweather forced himself to focus on his console, his fingers moving across the rows of multicolored buttons before him. He peered into the targeting scanner near his left hand, waiting with mounting impatience as the ship's weapons struggled to lock onto a target. It seemed to take an eternity before the fire control system finally offered him the telltale tone. A Tellarite ship was in his sights.

Without hesitation the captain stabbed the firing control and the overhead lighting dimmed again as power was drawn by the vessel's forward phaser banks. On the main viewscreen, twin blue-white phaser beams lanced across open space and impacted the enemy vessel's shields, an orange firestorm erupting as conflicting energies collided.

"Their shields are down," Reed reported from the science station. "Picking up a hull breach!"

Not waiting for the order to fire, Mayweather reset the targeting scanner and once more took aim on the now-damaged Tellarite vessel. He tapped the firing control again and when the phaser beams found their mark this time *Defiant*'s bridge crew was rewarded with the sight of the enemy ship breaking apart, consumed by an explosion that just as quickly was snuffed out by the vacuum of space.

"Nice shooting, Captain," Talas offered from behind him. Turning to Reed, she asked, "What about the other ships?"

Still bent over the sensor viewer, the major did not look up as he replied, "*Imperator* has engaged an Orion marauder and a Tellarite cruiser. She's holding her own. *Dauntless* and *Interceptor* are circling back over the planet's north pole, trying to draw fire." A moment later, he added, "Admiral, two more Orion cruisers are moving in behind us."

"Stand by photon torpedoes," the admiral ordered. "Continue evasive, Mayweather. Get us some breathing room."

Even with his attention all but consumed with the task of maneuvering the mighty starship, Mayweather still was able to keep tabs on the sensor telemetry being fed to his station by Reed. Though the ambush had cost them in the opening moments of the battle, the task force had wasted no time regrouping from the loss of *Bismarck* and *Akagi*. While the Earth vessels were outnumbered and the Vulcan ships possessed better shielding than their Starfleet counterparts, the *Imperator* and the remaining two NX-class ships still possessed more powerful weapons thanks to Professor Soong's upgrade efforts. Even with the Tellarite and Orion cruisers aiding in the battle, no side seemed to be enjoying a decisive advantage.

Damn Shran, Mayweather thought, feeling his ire rise at the mere thought of the traitorous Andorian. One way or another, the general was to blame for the fleet's current predicament. The captain did not know the exact nature of Shran's involvement with the rebels, and he no longer cared. Shran would die; Mayweather would see to that.

Assuming he and *Defiant* survived the next few minutes, of course.

"*Imperator* is maneuvering into position to commence orbital bombardment, Admiral," reported the ensign at communications.

Talas nodded. "Excellent," she said, though her next words were interrupted by the shrill tone of the ship's intercom system blaring to life.

"This is Commander Tucker. By order of Empress Sato, all Andorians are to be taken into custody. Intruder alert protocols are now in effect."

"What the hell?" Talas said, the shock evident in her voice. Mayweather saw her rise out of her seat from the corner of his eye and he tensed in anticipation. To his right, he saw the Andorian navigator turn from his console, no doubt seeking guidance from the admiral. Mayweather caught sight of the Andorian's hand moving for the phase pistol on his belt.

Pushing himself from his own chair, Mayweather slammed into the navigator, wrapping his arms around the Andorian and driving him from his chair to the deck. He heard the piercing whine of a phase pistol firing in the confined space of the bridge and orange energy rippled in his vision. A console to his left exploded, and Mayweather sensed movement along the upper bridge deck. Then a shadow fell over him and he rolled aside in time to see Reed hurdle over the railing that encircled the command well, launching himself at Talas as the admiral attempted to adjust her aim for a second shot.

Mayweather kicked away from the navigator, rolling to his feet in an attempt to help Reed. Movement to his right caught his attention, and he looked up to see the Andorian lieutenant at the engineering station rising from her chair and aiming her phase pistol at him. An instant later orange light flooded his vision and a sledgehammer drove into his chest before everything went dark.

T'Pol heard the whistling sound as she stepped into the rebel command center. She turned toward the noise, aiming her phaser ahead of her but realizing too late that she had walked into a trap.

The heavy, woven strap sliced through the air, wrapping around her weapon arm. Instinct made T'Pol yank away from the attack, but her assailant was faster. The *ahn-woon* tightened around her wrist, and T'Pol felt herself pulled off her feet. She crashed to the cave's unyielding stone floor, her phaser dropping from her hand as she grunted from the force of the impact. Ignoring the pain, T'Pol reached for the *ahn-woon* with her free hand, grabbing the slackened strap and preventing her attacker from pulling it away to use again. She rolled to her feet, detecting movement in the corner of her eye, and saw T'Pau glowering at her as she gripped the other end of the *ahn-woon*.

T'Pau the liar. T'Pau the murderer.

"You should have fled when you had the chance," T'Pau said, the strap of the ancient Vulcan weapon wrapped around her right wrist. She reached with her free hand for the disruptor pistol tucked into her wide leather belt.

Pushing to her left, T'Pol tightened her own grip on the *ahn-woon* as she struggled to pull her opponent off balance. T'Pau reacted to the maneuver by attempting to set her feet and pulling back the other way.

"You killed my mother," T'Pol hissed through gritted teeth, her muscles straining as she held her ground. Dropping to one knee, she grabbed the dagger on her hip and slashed across her body, the gleaming blade slicing through the strap's heavy material. Momentum sent T'Pau stumbling backward and she fought for balance on the cave's rocky, uneven floor, which was all the time T'Pol needed to regain her feet and lunge forward, dagger at the ready.

T'Pau was prepared. Shaking the now-useless *ahn-woon* free of her wrist, the minister stepped into the knife attack, left arm raised to block T'Pol's right and arresting its downward swing. The blade of the dagger was halted mere centimeters from T'Pau's left eye as she shifted her weight and attacked with her free hand. The heel of her hand slammed into T'Pol's chest, and she groaned in new pain from the brute force of the impact. She lashed out with the edge of her left hand, but T'Pau was faster, blocking the strike and stepping forward to reach for the junction of T'Pol's neck and shoulder. T'Pol pivoted away, spoiling her opponent's aim long enough to slash once more with her dagger. This time the blade found a mark, ripping through the sleeve of T'Pau's heavy woven shirt. The minister hissed, yanking her arm back, and T'Pol saw that her knife had drawn blood.

Not giving her opponent any opportunity to recover, T'Pol lunged again but was forced to alter her attack when T'Pau pulled the disruptor from her belt and fired. The shot was wild but close enough that T'Pol scrambled away, diving between two nearby stacks of cargo containers. Another disruptor bolt pierced the air and she felt the reverberation as the energy pulse chewed into the side of one cargo crate. Using the disorganized stacks of supplies and equipment as cover, T'Pol pushed deeper into the cavern, chased by a steady stream of disruptor fire.

Then the ground trembled beneath her feet and the piles of supplies shook. A deep rumble echoed through the cave, and dirt showered down from the ceiling.

The bombardment had begun.

Emerging from the turbolift with phaser drawn and aimed ahead of her, Hoshi leveled the weapon at Talas as the admiral swiveled around in the command chair. The Andorian's expression was one of shock as she beheld the bridge's newest arrival.

"Your Majesty," Talas said, moving to rise from the chair.

"Don't," Hoshi cautioned as Sergeant Hayes and Corporal Madden emerged from the lift behind her, both MACOs moving to disarm the other three Andorians manning bridge stations. "Stand down, Admiral. It's over."

Her eyebrows furrowing and her antenna moving to face the Empress, Talas remained seated, ramrod straight in the center seat. "I answer only to General Shran."

"Shran's not here," Hoshi countered. "Surrender now and you might just survive the day."

The order came an instant before Hoshi felt the entire bridge shake around her as *Defiant* suffered yet another direct hit on its deflector shields. She reached out with her free hand to steady herself against the bulkhead of the turbolift alcove. All around the bridge workstations and overhead lighting wavered in the face of the latest assault.

"Empress," Talas said, "as you can see, we still face considerable opposition. Now is not the . . ." As she spoke, Hoshi saw her right hand move ever so slightly toward the holster on her hip.

Hoshi fired.

The phaser whined and its energy beam reached out for Talas, enveloping her in a cocoon of blue-white energy that pulsed for an instant before it and the admiral faded from existence.

"She's even worse than Shran," Hoshi said, shaking her head. Moving toward the command well, she looked to where Madden was kneeling beside the still forms of Captain Mayweather and Major Reed. "Are they all right?"

The corporal nodded. "Yes, Your Majesty. They've only been stunned."

Though she schooled her features to betray no reaction, Hoshi nevertheless was relieved at the report. Mayweather was a loyal officer, and while Reed was a career-minded opportunist on the best of days, the truth was that he had become the closest thing to an expert with *Defiant*'s tactical systems. Assuming he could be controlled, he would make a valuable resource—in the short term, at least. "I need them conscious."

Another blast rocked the ship, and Hoshi fell against the railing near the command chair. The effects were more pronounced this time, she sensed. "Route power from all nonessential systems to shields and weapons!"

She looked to the four aliens—three Andorians and an Orion woman—who manned other stations around the bridge, her expression cold and unwavering. "I have no more time for this foolishness. Swear loyalty to me now and live, or remain silent and die. Choose now." When she received a chorus of four pledges, Hoshi nodded in satisfaction, though she still turned to Sergeant Hayes. "Kill them all the instant any of them tries anything."

The ensign working at the science console turned to Hoshi. "Your Majesty, several rebel ships are altering course to converge on us. Others are setting off in pursuit of *Imperator.*"

Moving to sit in the captain's chair, the Empress nodded at the report as she turned to Ensign Zona, seated at the helm. "Continue the bombardment. I want every trace of rebel scum erased from that planet."

15

Somewhere above T'Pol another muffled explosion reverberated through the cavern. She pushed herself away from a stack of cargo crates as the topmost container teetered above her before falling from its perch and crashing to the cave floor.

Crouching near the cave wall, T'Pol knew that the attacks would only become more ferocious. If whatever remained of the *Defiant*'s strike force truly was back under Sato's command, the bombardments would continue until no trace of the rebel headquarters remained.

It does not matter.

The thought screamed in her mind, forcing away all other considerations. Unmoving and holding her breath, she strained to listen over the sounds of the ongoing attack as well as the sirens and the shouts of alarm. She ignored everything, searching instead for some clue as to . . .

There.

Faint footfalls to her right, the sounds of leather against rock. T'Pol waited no longer, pushing off from the wall and gripping the edge of a nearby cargo container to pull herself around until she saw T'Pau, facing away with her disruptor aimed ahead of her. Obviously hearing her approach, the minister turned with only enough time to set herself, answering T'Pol's unspoken challenge.

They smashed into one another, the impact jarring T'Pau's disruptor from her hand. The next seconds were but a blur in T'Pol's vision as bone slammed against bone or cartilage, muscle strained against muscle. Dust rose from the cave floor, stirred by the skirmish. Every fiber of T'Pol's being protested at the abuse being inflicted upon it, but she ignored it all. Anger seethed with each passing heartbeat, her blood flowing with rage as she unleashed a lifetime of willfully suppressed emotions on the enemy before her.

With a fierce howl she lashed out a final time, the flat of her hand connecting with T'Pau's jaw and sending the other Vulcan staggering backward to collapse to the ground. Her lungs screaming for oxygen in the dirt-choked air of the cavern, T'Pol pushed herself away, lurching along the uneven floor until the toe of her boot caught on the edge of a flat rock and she stumbled before falling in an exhausted heap against the nearby wall. Gasping for breath, she tried to push herself to a sitting position but failed, the sour taste of blood filling her mouth.

Another strike, this time a series of blasts, echoed through the cavern, and T'Pol heard the sounds of rock cracking overhead. Chunks of the ceiling fell between her and T'Pau, pushing new clouds of dust into the cave's already choked air.

"You will . . . die here," she heard T'Pau say. "The entrance . . . collapsed." T'Pol looked up to see the minister glaring at her through pain-racked eyes, her expression hard as she too struggled and failed to regain her feet. As with T'Pol herself, green blood oozed from cuts and scrapes on her face and hands.

T'Pol winced as pain lanced through her midsection, perhaps the result of a fractured rib. She felt the fine shower of dust on her exposed skin, mixing with perspiration and sticking to her body. "I will not be alone," she replied, the words almost a growl in her throat. While she was prepared for death, it could come only after she had achieved her goal. She glimpsed T'Pau's dropped disruptor a few meters to her left, and surmised that even if she could pull herself up, the rebel leader was in a better position to retrieve the weapon.

"Why?" was all she could muster as she locked eyes with her adversary.

Her eyes closed as she fought back her own pain, T'Pau replied, "Though she joined the resistance, your mother clung to the pacifist ways that have doomed us to subjugation by the humans for generations."

T'Pol regarded the minister with a skeptical look. "I do not understand."

"Had T'Les been successful, she would have betrayed us all," T'Pau said, "notifying Starfleet of our base locations and our supply routes. She claimed she was working toward a resolution that would end the war without further bloodshed, but she underestimated the previous Emperor. He would have used that information to slaughter us all, as well as anyone who aided us. I had no choice."

A wave of relief swept over T'Pol, easing her mounting pain and fatigue. Her mother—as she had done all her life—had honored the teachings of Surak to the best of her abilities and to her dying breath, working for peace for all of Vulcan even in the face of bitter Imperial oppression.

I should never have doubted you, Mother.

The revelation about T'Les's actions also gave T'Pol hope, reinforcing her belief that the action she had taken—freeing Sato and affording her the chance to regain the throne of the Terran Empire—was correct. If everything went according to plan, the rebellion could end today and with minimal further bloodshed.

Her mother might well have approved.

Another quake shook the cavern, the tremors longer and more intense this time, and T'Pol pulled herself along the craggy floor toward the wall, seeking any sort of protection from the new avalanche of rock falling from the ceiling. She heard a scream of agony and turned to see that a sizable piece of stone had landed on T'Pau's legs, crushing them and pinning her to the ground. Green blood streamed from the corner of her mouth, and her features were contorted in renewed suffering. Still more fragments of the cavern were falling, and T'Pol pressed herself against the wall, covering her head with her hands. She was helpless to do anything but watch as two larger hunks of rock dropped from the roof and T'Pau disappeared from view forever.

Then T'Pol felt the familiar tingle of a transporter beam, and the sounds of the cavern's collapse faded as her vision filled with a shower of golden energy.

"Transporter room to Bridge. T'Pol is aboard, Your Majesty."

"Shields up," Hoshi ordered. "Helm, bring us about."

At the science station, Major Reed looked over his shoulder. "*Imperator* is showing damage to its hull plating. Four cruisers are converging on its position. *Dauntless* has lost warp power. *Interceptor* is engaging two Orion marauders."

His report came just as *Defiant* was rocked by yet another attack. Hoshi felt her stomach lurch, and she gripped the arms of the command chair as the deck shifted beneath her feet. All around the bridge, crew members struggled to remain at their posts as workstations and the overhead lighting flickered yet again in response to the starship's overburdened power systems.

"Route emergency power to tactical and navigation," Mayweather shouted over the new alarms. Hoshi watched as the captain, his shoulders hunched with effort, fought the helm for control of the vessel. "Controls are sluggish," he said, casting a glance over his shoulder. "I'm losing maneuverability."

Sato gritted her teeth as she took in the steadily worsening reports. On the main viewscreen, a trio of Vulcan ships loomed before them, each a deadly wedge seemingly suspended within an immense outer ring that pulsated with power.

"Two more Vulcan ships are approaching aft," Reed reported. "It's a standard enveloping maneuver."

Though the major did not say anything else, Hoshi comprehended the unspoken addendum. *Defiant* would be caught in a crossfire designed to overload its already stressed deflector shields. Despite the starship's superior weaponry as well as the modifications her escort ships had received, the task force was outnumbered and outgunned. Further, the rebels had finally decided to concentrate their attacks on the two ships posing the greatest threat, *Defiant* and *Imperator,* and the lopsided battle was finally beginning to take its toll.

"Empress," said the young male human manning the communications station, "we're being hailed by one of the Vulcan ships."

"Really," Hoshi said, her eyebrows rising in mild surprise.

Turning from the helm, Mayweather said, "It makes sense. They'd probably rather capture *Defiant* than destroy it. Think of the advantage it gives the rebellion."

"We'll destroy it first," Hoshi countered, her voice hard. "Open the channel."

On the viewscreen, the image of the three rebel ships was replaced with that of a lean, older Vulcan male, seated in a high-backed chair. Dressed in a stark gray uniform with no visible insignia, he possessed a full head of graying hair, and a long, thin mustache drooped to either side of his mouth.

"I am Vanik, captain of the Ti'Mur *and leader of this assault force. Deactivate your weapons and lower your shields. Surrender your vessel and prepare to be boarded."*

"Any attempt to board this vessel will result in its destruction," Hoshi countered, rising from her seat. She reached into the folds of her gown, extracted the communicator T'Pol had given her, and flipped open the unit's cover. Placing her other hand on her hip, she affected what she hoped was an appearance of confidence in her mastery of the current situation. "Stand down, Captain, or be destroyed."

Vanik was unconvinced. *"Perhaps your sensors are malfunctioning, Empress, but you are surrounded. My fleet is merely waiting for my order to finish you."*

"They'll be waiting quite a while," Hoshi countered before pressing the control blinking on the face of the communicator.

The effect of her action was immediate. On the viewscreen, she saw the lights on the bridge of the *Ti'Mur* flicker before dying out altogether, and she caught a fleeting look of shock on Vanik's face before the communication frequency itself was severed.

"What the hell just happened?" Mayweather asked, turning from the helm with an expression of utter confusion.

"They've lost primary power," Reed replied, once more bent over the science station's sensor viewer. "All of the rebel ships are powering down. Weapons, shields, even life support." He looked up from his console. "They're completely immobilized. I don't understand."

Hoshi held up the communicator. "T'Pol. She provided me with the override codes for every ship in the fleet." Following the Vulcan's instructions, she had delivered the communicator and the codes to Commander Tucker, who had programmed the device to transmit the override information to every rebel ship within range. T'Pol had used her temporary position as captain of the *Ni'Var* to avail herself of the tightly guarded information, obviously planning for the betrayal she suspected would be visited upon her by resistance leaders.

Loyal, after all, Hoshi mused.

"Your Majesty," said the communications officer a moment later, "I'm picking up weak distress calls transmitting from several of the rebel ships. They're probably being sent on battery backup systems."

"They are completely at our mercy," Reed added. "Shall we destroy them?"

Hearing the anticipation in the major's voice, Hoshi was tempted to allow him to follow through and finish the battle in a decisive fashion. It would take only moments for *Defiant* to obliterate the now-helpless rebel fleet, and would almost certainly signal to any remaining resistance cells once and for all the folly of defying the Empire.

Or, it might only serve to strengthen their resolve, thereby dragging the rebellion on for months, even years, until both sides suffered irreplaceable losses and uncounted innocents died as the two warring parties carved destruction wherever their conflicts took them. While Hoshi aspired to rule over an Empire, she preferred a vibrant, thriving civilization to the shattered remnants that surely awaited her if the war was allowed to continue.

"Empress," she heard a voice say, and looked up to see Captain Mayweather regarding her from the helm, his features a mask of uncertainty.

No, she decided.

There was another option.

16

G eneral," the guard said from where he stood at the threshold to Shran's office, "the *Defiant* task force has dropped out of warp and is entering Earth orbit."

From where he stood next to the general's desk, Doctor Soong released a relieved sigh. "That is wonderful news."

Rising from his desk, Shran nodded in acknowledgment, though even that simple gesture was laced with irritation. "Notify Captain Mayweather to report to me immediately."

In the two days that had passed since the battle at Aldus Prime, the reports he had been given by Captain Mayweather remained unsatisfying. The general naturally was suspicious upon hearing of the death of Admiral Talas, an apparent casualty of the conflict. Mayweather's report of the incident was thorough, but it somehow rang hollow, and Shran vowed he would learn the full truth behind what happened, even if he had to rip it from the young captain's body with his own bare hands.

Still, Shran was pleased to learn about the destruction of the planet that had served as the base for a key resistance cell. Though there naturally would be a large degree of outcry when the public learned that their Empress was included among those lost, at least now the general could show proof that he had done everything in his power to rescue her, including sacrificing two starships in a pitched battle against enemy forces. It would do much to ease the expected formidable anxiety when he named the heir to Sato's crown, the as yet unnamed child still immersed in the gestation chamber in Doctor Soong's lab. Such worry no doubt would be heightened when the people of Earth learned that Shran himself would act in the new Emperor's stead until such time as he was of age to assume his responsibilities, and that his staff would "assist" those personnel in key imperial positions to ensure a smooth transition and period of rebuilding in the aftermath of the prolonged rebellion.

A faint whine echoed across the office, and Shran felt a slight tingle on his exposed skin as he turned to see five columns of energy coalesce into existence, rapidly expanding into the shapes of humanoid figures. The transporter beams solidified, and the general recognized the face of Major Malcolm Reed, along with two MACOs, a Vulcan woman he thought looked familiar, and Hoshi Sato.

The transporter beams faded, and Shran saw that all five of the new arrivals were armed, and aiming their weapons at him.

"Hello, my dear husband," Sato said, her expression one of complete confidence.

"Your Majesty," Shran replied, feeling his throat constrict as he uttered the words. Holding his hands out, he stepped toward her. "You have no idea how pleased I am to—"

He stopped as Sato raised her phaser to point directly at his head. Looking to where Shran knew Soong still stood next to the desk, she asked. "Professor, how is my child?"

Shran turned to see the professor nod rapidly, his eyes wide with mounting fear. "Wonderful, Your Majesty. Everything is proceeding without any complications or concerns. My staff oversees him every hour of every day. He will be a healthy, beautiful child."

"Thank you, Professor. You've done well," Sato replied, before moving her arm until the phaser aimed at Soong and without another word fired the weapon. Shran flinched at the burst of howling energy as the phaser struck Soong and he was enveloped in a burst of blue energy. Despite himself, Shran's eyes widened in fear as he watched the professor's body dissolved by the phaser's restrained fury. His pulse pounded in his ears, and it required physical effort to keep his breathing under control as Sato moved the phaser back to point once more at him.

Muffled footsteps sounded in the corridor outside his office, but Reed and his MACOs were ready when the door opened and a pair of Andorian security guards burst into the room, weapons at the ready. Both MACOs fired their pulse rifles, each catching one of the guards with the force of their energy bursts and dropping them to the office's tiled floor.

As the echo from the fleeting skirmish faded, Sato said, "I have returned from my 'temporary exile,' General." One thin eyebrow arched as she regarded him. "Isn't that how you described it? If I remember correctly, this is the part where you rededicate your life to my service."

The tone of her voice, the way she held her stance as she scrutinized him down the length of the phaser in her hand, told Shran that no matter what he said, he would die here, today. She would not kill him outright, of course; the Empress had far too many reasons to prolong his execution and to ensure that any time spent leading up to that event would be anything but pleasant for him. Drawing a deep breath, he pulled himself to his full height, adopting a confident posture of his own in an attempt to match Sato's. He looked to the Vulcan woman, who until this point had remained silent, standing slightly behind Sato's right shoulder and brandishing a phaser of her own. "Am I to understand that you've forged some sort of alliance with this Vulcan? Your people are supposed to be smarter than this." Frowning, he realized that he in fact did know the woman accompanying the Empress. "You're the traitor, from Captain Forrest's ship, the one who sabotaged his vessel as well as the *Defiant*."

The Vulcan nodded. "T'Pol."

"If you are responsible for seeing to Empress Sato's safety," he said, the plea spilling from his mouth even as the thoughts took form in his mind, "then your previous crimes might well be forgiven, and you will be amply rewarded for your efforts."

Her face betraying no hint of emotion, T'Pol replied, "I have been informed that the rewards will be even greater for capturing enemies of the Empire."

"One could argue that I have acted in the best interests of the Empire," Shran said. "Earth cannot conquer an entire galaxy on its own. It needs allies, those with far greater influence than humans have been able to muster." He looked to Sato. "You're infants compared to races who have been traveling space for centuries while your ancestors beat each other with the bones of animals they killed for food. Imagine what you'll discover the farther you push beyond the confines of this insignificant planet. Think of the enemies you'll face."

Sato shrugged. "I've no intention of facing them alone, Shran." Nodding to T'Pol, she added, "The rebellion is all but over. I have already been in contact with Vulcan, and they have accepted my offer: I have released them from their servitude and granted all Vulcans the status of citizens of the Empire, effective immediately. Never again will they live in slavery, and they will live as equals to humans. Together, we will chart a new destiny for both our peoples, and it's already started, Shran. A fleet of Vulcan warships waits in orbit above us, pledged to me."

Unable to stifle the sudden, humorless laugh exploding from his lips, Shran stared with openmouthed shock at the Empress. "Pledged to you? Vulcans living as equals to humans, and simply because you order it to be so? Your species does not possess that level of cooperative spirit, *Empress*. Even if the Vulcans believe they have been granted their freedom after a century of enslavement, what's to stop the rebels from continuing to fight you?" Looking to Sato, he added, "To say nothing of how my own people will react when they learn that you're abandoning them for this alliance of convenience. Andoria will not rest until the Empire is crushed, along with anyone foolish enough to ally with them."

Instead of Sato, it was T'Pol who replied, "The proposal of a human-Vulcan alliance to secure the future of the Empire is logical. Once Vulcan resistance cells stand down, others will soon see the futility of their actions. The rebellion will end quietly, with little more loss of life. Perhaps in time, other peoples will understand that aligning with the Empire is more beneficial than taking up arms against it."

"Or, they can continue to resist," Sato added, "and be destroyed."

Shaking his head at the incredible depths of naïveté he was hearing from this representative of a race long known for its logic and ability to reason, Shran looked upon T'Pol with disgust. "Your shortsightedness will be your downfall."

"Perhaps," the Vulcan replied after a moment, "but there are always possibilities."

Sato nodded to Reed, and the major directed his two MACOs toward Shran. The soldiers wasted no time flanking the general and each taking an arm in hand. He felt their muscled grip on him, lifting him nearly off the floor as they proceeded without further direction toward the door, escorting him to his still-unknown fate.

Struggling in their grasp, Shran jerked his head to look over his shoulder. "She'll betray you, T'Pol!" he shouted, his words echoing off the walls of the office. "The Empire will die on the sword of its own treachery!"

Sato signaled for the guards to halt their departure, indicating for them to pull Shran around so that he faced her one final time. Handing her phaser to T'Pol, an overt gesture of trust to her new-found ally, she stepped forward until her body nearly pressed up against his. She reached up to stroke his chin, her hand moving upward to caress the side of his face in the way he remembered from the last time they had shared her bed. Her expression never wavered, remaining fixed and determined as she stared into his eyes.

"Regardless of what happens," she said, her voice low and soft, "I'm sorry to say that you likely won't be around to see it." Then she cocked her head, the corners of her mouth tugging upward. "Though I'll certainly do my best to see that you're kept alive that long."

The obvious threat was like an icy hand reaching out to grip Shran's heart.

Epilogue

Fading rays of sunlight filtered through the trees lining the Kyoto palace's western wall. As night descended upon the *oikeniwa,* Hoshi stood on the balcony outside her office and took in the peaceful surroundings for the final time that day, bookending the ritual she observed each morning from her bedchamber on the opposite side of the palace. No trace remained of the damage inflicted upon the far edge of the grounds weeks ago during the rebel attack, a testament to the small army of landscapers and other staff charged with maintaining the palace's picturesque appearance.

Not for the first time since her return to Earth, Hoshi considered the symbolic nature the gardens now seemed to hold. Once more marking the heart of the Terran Empire as far as its subjects were concerned, the *oikeniwa* now also embodied the new peace that had come with the ending of the rebellion. As the Empress had hoped, the remaining resistance cells had surrendered in the wake of the Vulcan contingent's recusal, taking with them the need for prolonging hostilities. Her promise to elevate all of Vulcan to equal status with Earth in the Empire had achieved its intended effect, and the two planets now found themselves in unfamiliar territory as they charted a new, joint destiny for their respective peoples.

Stepping away from the balcony rail, Hoshi turned and reentered her office. Her new bodyguard, Brooks, stood vigil near the door, the man having been promoted to her personal security detail following the death of her steadfast guardian, Carpenter.

Seeing her, the muscled bodyguard snapped to attention and rendered the traditional salute. She acknowledged him with a nod as she crossed to the office's other occupant, who currently sat at the oval conference table situated before a large rectangular monitor mounted on the wall opposite Hoshi's desk.

"I have completed my analysis of the star charts," said T'Pol, Supreme Regent of Vulcan. Dressed in a simple yet stately ensemble of earth-toned robes that were highlighted by a heavy necklace featuring an arrangement of shaped and polished stones from her homeworld, the regent showed no outward sign of the injuries sustained during her fight with T'Pau on Aldus Prime, all of which Phlox had mended upon her return to *Defiant*. "I believe you will find this most interesting."

Reaching for the portable computer positioned near her right hand, T'Pol tapped a sequence of commands and the wall-mounted monitor activated, its screen coalescing into a two-dimensional, computer-generated representation of an area of space. The black background was overlaid with a light blue grid, and cutting a curving, diagonal swath down the center of the image was a thick gray line emblazoned with the words "Neutral Zone." To the left of the line—which to Hoshi was obviously a territorial boundary—was a series of seven numbered black triangles, highlighted with the caption "Earth Outpost Sector Z-6." On the right of the Neutral Zone were two large red circles, each denoting a planet.

"The Romulan Star Empire," T'Pol said, reading the caption aloud. "In the other universe, these two planets, Romulus and Remus, are at the center of what according to the *Defiant*'s database is a militaristic, totalitarian regime. Earth fought and won a massive war against them." Looking away from the monitor, the regent regarded Hoshi. "A war that is supposed to start within the next few years, in fact. After its ending, Earth, Vulcan, Andoria, and Tellar will be among the signatories for the creation of their so-called Federation of Planets."

"What do we know about that area of space in our universe?" Hoshi asked, her attention still focused on the star chart.

T'Pol shook her head. "Almost nothing. It has never been explored. All we have are unsubstantiated rumors about whoever or whatever is there."

"So," Hoshi said, folding her arms across her chest as she began to pace the width of her office, "even if these Romulans do exist there, they might be nothing like those found in the other universe. They may be much weaker than us."

"Or far more powerful," T'Pol countered. "Likewise, they may be open to an alliance, rather than seeking conflict."

Frowning, Hoshi considered the notion. Though it had become apparent within hours of discovering *Defiant* that the universe from which it had originated possessed many differences from her own, it also was apparent to the Empress that there were a great deal of similarities, as well. Indeed, in many cases perceived disparities were not black and white but merely shades of gray. With that in mind, she wondered: How did the Romulans of this universe—assuming there were any—compare or contrast to their counterparts in the other universe?

There was only one way to find out.

"We need to see for ourselves," Hoshi finally said. "I'll send *Defiant*. It will lead an armada to that area of space, and we'll learn what awaits us there." While the technological upgrades to the remaining Starfleet vessels were continuing at a pace slower than she would have preferred, the Empress was confident that *Defiant* still was the premier warship in the known galaxy. It would certainly be a match for whatever the Empire might find at the mysterious location designated on the star chart she now studied.

"If our intention is to seek a new ally," T'Pol said, "this mission will require someone skilled in diplomacy, particularly with regard to first contact situations. You should also be prepared in the event these Romulans reject the offer of cooperation and instead desire conquest. With all due respect to Captain Mayweather, he does not yet possess the necessary experience."

Hoshi nodded in agreement, reassured once again that her decision to appoint T'Pol to the highest position of leadership on

Vulcan had been the correct choice. In only a short time, the Empress had come to value T'Pol's counsel, which she considered correct in this matter. Though Travis Mayweather was a capable and loyal officer, *Defiant*'s current master still lacked the proper seasoning—something he would acquire, certainly, but not fast enough for what Hoshi now needed.

Fortunately, the Empress had anticipated such eventualities.

The special research laboratory Hoshi had ordered constructed on the palace's lowest underground level was abuzz with power and activity. In stark contrast to the damp stone walls lining the passageways leading down from the ground floor, the lab was the very picture of cleanliness and sterility.

As she entered the lab with T'Pol following a step behind, Hoshi regarded the lab's stark white walls and dull metal floor plates and was momentarily reminded of the infirmary aboard the late *Enterprise*. Work tables and storage lockers lined the walls, and the Empress recognized a variety of equipment and components taken from several of *Defiant*'s fourteen science labs as well as its own sickbay. The lab's most notable feature was the hyperbaric chamber. Essentially a large, squat rectangle, it was composed of thick plates of gray duranium, much like the outer hull of *Defiant* itself, from which the chamber had been removed.

For the moment, Hoshi found herself drawn to a smaller construct situated to her left as she entered the laboratory. Essentially a cylinder on its own freestanding frame, it possessed a quartet of frosted-glass viewing ports through which the Empress could see only the shadowy outline of a small, fragile figure floating within a green, gelatinous fluid. Limbs were visible, as was its elongated head, which she knew would soon be in proportion to the rest of the body as the baby continued to mature. A single tube ran from the creature's abdomen to a device mounted inside the chamber, delivering needed nourishment and vitamins to the gestating fetus.

Her son. Hers and Shran's.

Upon returning to her rightful place on the imperial throne and seeing for the first time the results of Shran's insidious scheme, Hoshi had been tempted to terminate the unborn child's life, destroying with it any remaining vestige of her former husband's grand plot to unite the people of Earth and Andoria before carrying out his final goal of ultimate conquest of the Empire. When faced with the decision, however—seeing the fetus confined to this laboratory and being harvested as though it were nothing more than the genetic samples used to create it in the first place—she found she did not possess the will to carry out the abortion, unwilling to punish the child for the actions of his father.

Perhaps he represented the Empire's future? Did he hold its life in the palm of his still-maturing hand? Of course, Hoshi did not know. There was no historical database to consult. She had only her instincts to guide her, and for now they were enough.

"Your Majesty?"

Hoshi turned at the sound of the voice and saw Doctor Phlox. Dressed as always in his dark leather uniform over which he wore a blue physician's lab coat, he regarded her with a smile. "He is doing quite well. All life signs appear normal." Shrugging, he added, "Well, so far as I can tell with respect to a human-Andorian hybrid. However, I am confident."

Nodding, Hoshi replied, "Thank you, Doctor." Putting aside her personal feelings for the moment, she indicated the larger chamber. "What about . . . ?"

Moving to stand before the unit's massive circular door, the Denobulan peered into the chamber through the door's porthole while reviewing the contents of a data padd he held, the fingers of his right hand tapping across its surface as he entered whatever information he considered important at that moment. "You are just in time. I've begun synaptic stimulation, and the patient is already responding most favorably. From what I can tell it's a rather painful process, but certainly better than the alternative."

The report was heartening news for Hoshi. Though she had at first resisted this course of action, logic eventually had prevailed. In her haste to ascend to the throne, she had neglected to consider all of the long-term consequences for removing all of her potential enemies. Even her most devout adversaries might still harbor some potential value, T'Pol had advised, and such possibilities should be explored at length before any rash action was taken.

Thankfully, on this occasion, when a decision needed to be reconsidered or even recanted, technology from the future had once again come to her aid.

"It's taken me several weeks to perfect the process," Phlox said, "but between the information in the *Defiant*'s medical banks as well as a few things I learned from some friends of mine on Antos IV, I am confident we will be successful this time."

"So you're saying . . . ?" The words trailed off, squelched by disbelief. Was it truly possible?

Nodding at the rest of the unspoken question, Phlox replied, "Yes, Your Majesty. He lives." He stepped back, indicating the viewing port to her.

"I do not understand," T'Pol said, her brow creasing in confusion. "What have you done, Empress?"

Rather than reply, Hoshi gestured for the Vulcan to join her at the viewing port, and both women stared in awe at the scene before them.

Suspended in the null gravity environment created by Phlox inside the chamber was a human male. Nude but for the spider-web of wires and tubing running to and from his body to a host of instruments lining the chamber's interior walls, the patient twitched and jerked as his body was repaired, erasing the neglect and decay of the past months. He soon would be whole again, but only time would tell if he would be her enemy or her ally.

Hoshi flinched as the patient's body spasmed again, and this time his eyes opened. With a start, the Empress felt triumph, uncertainty, and even fear grip her heart as she stared into the face of Jonathan Archer.

The Sorrows
of Empire

David Mack

For what could have been,
if only we'd had more courage.

Historian's Note

The Sorrows of Empire begins in mid-2267 (A.C.E.), shortly after the four crew members of the *U.S.S. Enterprise* crossed over to an alternate universe ("Mirror, Mirror"), and concludes in 2295, two years after the Khitomer Accords were signed by the United Federation of Planets and the Klingon Empire (*Star Trek VI: The Undiscovered Country*). All events occur in the mirror universe.

In every revolution, there is one man with a vision.

—Captain James T. Kirk

Part I

Sic Semper Tyrannis

2267

1

The Marriage of True Minds

Crushing Captain Kirk's windpipe was proving far easier than Spock had ever dared to imagine.

The captain of the *I.S.S. Enterprise* struggled futilely in the merciless grip of his half-Vulcan first officer. Kirk's fists struck at Spock's torso, ribs, groin. His fingers pried at Spock's grip, clawed at the backs of the hands that were strangling him. Spock's hands only closed tighter, condemning Kirk to a swift death by suffocation.

Killing such an accomplished officer as Kirk seemed a waste to Spock. And waste, as Kirk's alternate-universe counterpart had reminded Spock only a few days earlier, was illogical. Unfortunately, as Spock now realized, it was sometimes necessary.

Kirk's strength was fading, but his eyes were still bright with cunning. He twisted, reached forward to pluck Spock's agonizer from his belt—only to find the device absent. Removing it had been a grave breach of protocol, but Spock had decided that willfully surrendering to another the means to let himself be tortured was also fundamentally illogical. He would no longer accede to the Terrans' obsessive culture of self-inflicted suffering. It was time for a change.

Marlena Moreau stood in the entryway of Kirk's sleep alcove, sharp and silent while she watched Spock throttle Kirk to death in the middle of the captain's quarters. There was no bloodlust in her gaze, a crude affectation that Spock had witnessed in many humans. Instead, she wore a dark expression, one of determination tinged with regret. Her sleepwear was delicate and diaphanous, but her countenance was hard and unyielding; she was like a steely blade in a silken sheath.

Still Kirk struggled. Again it struck Spock how great a waste this was, and the words of the other universe's Captain Kirk returned to his thoughts, the argument that had forced Spock to confront the futility of the imperial mission to which his civilization had been enthralled. The other Kirk had summed up the intrinsic flaw of the Empire with brevity and clarity.

The illogic of waste, Mister Spock, he had said. *Of lives, potential, resources . . .* time. *I submit to you that your empire is illogical, because it cannot endure. I submit that* you *are illogical, for being a willing part of it.*

And he had been unequivocally right.

Red stains swam languidly across the eyes of this universe's Captain Kirk. Capillaries in the whites of his eyes had ruptured, hemorrhaging blood inside the eye sockets. Seconds more, and it would be over.

There had been no choice. No hope of altering this Kirk's philosophy of command or of politics. His doppelganger had urged Spock to seize command of the *I.S.S. Enterprise,* find a logical reason to spare the resistant Halkans, and convince the Empire itself that it was the correct course.

Spock had hoped he could achieve such an aim without resorting to mutiny; he had never desired command, nor had he been interested in politics. Science, reason, research . . . these had always been Spock's core interests. They remained so now, but the circumstances had changed. Despite all of Spock's best-formulated arguments, Kirk had refused to consider mercy for the Halkans. Even when Spock had proved through logical argument that laying waste to the Halkans' cities would, in fact, only impede the Empire's efforts to mine the planet's dilithium, Kirk had not been dissuaded. And so had come Kirk's order to obliterate the planet's surface, to exterminate the Halkans and erase their civilization from the universe.

To speak out then would have been suicide, so Spock had stood mutely by while Kirk grinned and chuckled with malicious self-satisfaction, and watched a planet die.

Now it was Spock's turn to watch Kirk expire in the grip of his fingers, but Spock took no pleasure in it. He felt no sense of satisfaction, nor did he permit himself the luxuries of guilt or regret. This was simply what needed to be done.

Kirk's pulse slowed and weakened. A dull film glazed the captain's eyes, which rolled slowly back into his skull. He went limp in Spock's grasp and his clutching, clawing hands fell to his sides. Dead weight now, he sagged halfway to his knees. Not wanting to fall victim to a ruse, Spock took the precaution of inflicting a final twist on Kirk's neck, snapping it with a quick turn. Then he let the body fall heavily to the deck, where it landed with a dull thud.

Marlena inched cautiously forward, taking Spock's measure. "We should get rid of his body," she said. Stepping gingerly in bare feet, she walked over Kirk's corpse. "And his loyalists—"

"Have been dealt with," Spock interjected. "Show me the device." He did not need to elaborate; she had been beside him in the transporter room when the other universe's Kirk had divulged to him the existence of a unique weapon, one that Kirk had promised could make him "invincible." The device, which Marlena called the Tantalus field, had, apparently, been the key to the swift rise of this universe's Kirk through the ranks of the Imperial Starfleet. Marlena led Spock to a nearby wall, on which was mounted a trapezoidal panel. She touched it softly at its lower right corner, then its upper right corner, and it slid soundlessly upward, revealing a small display screen flanked by a handful of buttons and dials.

"This is how you turn it on." With a single, delicate touch, Marlena activated the device. "These are the controls."

"Demonstrate it," Spock said. "On the captain's body."

He observed her actions carefully, memorizing patterns and deducing functions. With a few pushed buttons, she conjured an image of the room in which they stood. Some minor adjustments on the dials narrowed the image's focus to the body on the floor. Then she pressed a single button that was segregated from the others inside a teardrop-shaped mounting, and a blink of light filled the room behind them.

Marlena lifted her arm to shield her eyes, but Spock let his inner eyelids spare him from the flash. It was over in a fraction of a second, leaving him with a palpable tingle of electric potential and the lingering scent of ozone mingling with Marlena's delicately floral Deltan perfume. On the floor there was no trace of Kirk—no hair, no scorch marks, no blood . . . not a single bit of evidence that a murder had occurred. Satisfied, he nodded to Marlena, who shut down the device. "Most impressive," he remarked.

"Yes," she replied. "He let me use it a few times. I only know how to target one person at a time, but he told me once that it could do much more, in the right hands."

"Indubitably," Spock said. The communicator on his belt beeped twice. He lifted it from its half-pocket and flipped it open. "Spock here."

"This is Lieutenant D'Amato. The ship is secured, sir."

One detail loomed paramount in Spock's thoughts. "Have you dealt with Mister Sulu?"

"Aye, sir," D'Amato replied. *"He's been neutralized."*

"Well done, Mister D'Amato. Spock out."

Spock closed his communicator and put it back on his belt. He crossed the room to a wall-mounted comm panel, and opened an intraship PA channel. "Attention, all decks. This is Captain Spock. As of fourteen twenty-six hours, I have relieved Captain Kirk and assumed command of this vessel. Continue on course for Gamma Hydra IV. That is all. Spock out." He thumbed the channel closed and turned to face Marlena. "It would seem, for now, that circumstances favor us."

"Not entirely," she said. "Last night, Kirk filed a report with Starfleet Command about the alternate universe. He called its people anarchistic and dangerous . . . and he told Starfleet that he suspected you of helping breach the barrier between the universes."

Her news was not entirely unexpected, but it was still unfortunate. "Did the captain speculate why I might have done such a thing?"

"No," Marlena said. "But he made a point of mentioning your attempts to convince him to spare the Halkans."

He nodded once. "It would have been preferable for there to be no official record of the other universe's existence," he said. "But what has been done cannot be undone. We must proceed without concern for details beyond our control." Looking into her eyes, he knew that, for now, she was the only person on the ship—perhaps even in the universe—whom he could really trust, but even her motives were not entirely beyond suspicion . . . at least, not yet. But if the Terran Empire and its galactic neighbors were to be spared the ravages of a brutal social implosion followed by a devastating dark age unlike any in recorded history, he would have to learn to trust someone beyond himself—and teach others to do the same.

Picturing the shifting possibilities of the future, he knew that he had already committed himself, that there was no turning back from the epic task he had just set for himself.

The great work begins.

"Congratulations, Captain," said a passing junior officer as he saluted Spock, who dutifully returned the gesture while continuing down the corridor to his new cabin.

Pomp and fanfare had never appealed to Spock. Pageantry had its uses in the affairs of the Empire, but aboard a starship it was a needless frivolity, a distraction ill afforded. He preferred to focus on tasks at hand, on the business of running the ship. The crew, sensing his mood, had obliged him. But the human compulsion to laud success was irrepressible, and he accepted it with stoic grace.

His ascendance to command, however, was only the second most compelling item of news aboard the *Enterprise*—the crew was buzzing with hearsay of the alternate universe. Chief Engineer Scott, Doctor McCoy, and Lieutenant Uhura, despite having been ordered to secrecy during their debriefings, apparently felt liberated to speak freely of it now that Kirk had been assassinated. Spock had made no effort to curtail the rumors or to interdict the crew's personal communications. The truth was out; attempting to rein it in would be futile. It had a life of its own now, and he decided to let it be.

He arrived at the captain's cabin, which he had claimed as his own. The door opened with a soft hiss. On the other side of the threshold he was met by the dry heat and dim reddish-amber glow that he preferred for his private quarters, a crude approximation of the light and climate of his homeworld of Vulcan. He was pleased to see that the last of Captain Kirk's belongings had been removed from the compartment, and that his own possessions had been moved in. On the far side of the room, Marlena was gently hanging his Vulcan lute on the wall.

Spock stepped farther into the room, clear of the door's sensor. The portal slid shut behind him. Marlena turned and folded her hands in front of her waist. "I assumed this was where you would want it displayed," she said.

"It is," Spock said. He had not expected her to still be there. She had been Kirk's woman for some time, and though she had sympathized with Spock's cause, he had anticipated little more from her than silent acquiescence. Apparently, she had taken it upon herself to supervise the transfer of his personal effects and to complete the preparation of his new quarters.

"You've received several personal transmissions in the past few hours," she said, moving to the cabinet where beverages were stored. "Some from other starship captains, some from the Admiralty . . . even one from Grand Admiral Garth himself."

"Yes," Spock replied. "I have already read them."

She opened the cabinet and took out a bottle of Vulcan port and two short, squarish glasses. "Missives of congratulation, no doubt." She glanced up at Spock, who nodded in confirmation, then she half-filled both glasses with the bright green liquor.

He accepted the glass that she offered to him. By reflex, he sniffed it once, to try to discern any telltale fragrance of toxins lurking in its tart, fruity bouquet.

Keen to his suspicion, Marlena smirked. "It's not poisoned. But if it will make you more comfortable, we can swap glasses."

"Unnecessary," Spock said, and he took a drink.

At that, she genuinely smiled. "Trust?"

His tone was calm and even. "A calculated risk."

Carefully, with slow and languid grace, she reached up and stroked her fingertips across his bearded chin. "I've been a captain's woman, Spock. . . . Am I still?"

A stirring in the dark corners of his soul, the animal cry of his human half. It felt something for this woman—a hunger, a need. Dominated by his Vulcan discipline and his credo of unemotional logic, his human passions were deeply buried, strange and unfamiliar to him. But they paled in comparison to the savage desires of his ancient Vulcan heritage, whose lethal furies were the reason his people relied on the dictums of logic for their continued survival as a culture.

As if with a will of its own, his left hand rose and cupped Marlena's cheek, then traveled through her warm, dark hair. It was soft and fell over his fingers like a lover's breath. Her skin was warm. His fingertips rested on the side of her scalp, while she traced a line with her nails down his throat.

"You are still the captain's woman," he said.

Her hand moved along his clavicle, to his shoulder, down the length of his arm, until it came to rest atop his own hand, on the side of her face. "When I was a girl, I heard stories about Vulcans who could touch minds," she said. "Is it true?"

"Yes," he said, revealing his people's most closely guarded secret, one for which entire species—such as the Betazoids and the Ullians—had been all but exterminated. "We hide our powers from outsiders, and such a bond is never performed lightly. The melding of two minds is a *profound* experience."

She took a half step closer to him, all the while holding eye contact with him and keeping her hand pressed against his. "Do both people know it's happening?"

"They become as one," Spock said. "No secrets remain."

Resting her free hand against his chest, she whispered, "I wouldn't resist if . . . if you wanted to . . ."

It was subtle, nimble, and quick. His fingers changed position on the side of her face, spreading apart like the legs of an arachnid, seeking out the loci of neural pathways.

Marlena tensed and inhaled a short, sharp breath. Though she had said she wouldn't resist, she couldn't have known what the touch of a Vulcan mind-meld would really feel like. Nothing could have prepared her for the total loss of privacy, the ultimate exposure of her inner self to another consciousness. Even the most willing participants resisted their first time.

"My mind to your mind," Spock intoned, his rich baritone both soothing and authoritative. "Our thoughts are merging. I know what you know. Our minds become one. We become one."

The dark flower of her mind bloomed open in his thoughts, and the coldly rational structures of his logic gave form to her chaos of passions and appetites. Fears fell silent, motives were laid bare, and the union of their psyches was complete.

Years, days, and moments wove together into a shared tapestry of their past. The cold disapproval of Spock's father, Sarek, stood in sharp contrast to the volcanic fury of Marlena's father, François: an icy stare tore open a silent gulf between a father and son; a broad palm slapped a young girl's face again and again, leaving the hot sting of betrayal in its wake.

I have made my decision, Father.

I'm sorry, Daddy! Please stop! Don't!

Defenses took root, grew coarse, became permanent barriers.

Marlena's weapon of choice was seduction; Spock's preferred implement was logic. He planned ahead, a master chess player thinking two dozen moves beyond his current position; she lived in the moment, moved with the shifting currents of power and popular opinion, never planning for tomorrow—because who knew what the universe would be like by then?

Yin and yang, they stood enmeshed in one another's thoughts. She, quick to anger, rash to act, desperately seeking one moment of tenderness, one solitary moment of affection, in a life that promised nothing but strife and loneliness. He, aloof and alone, desiring only knowledge and order, but watching the Empire begin an inexorable slide toward collapse and chaos.

All they had in common was the shared experience of meeting the humans from the other universe, the glimpse of a reality so much like theirs yet so different. He admired their discipline, their restraint, their stability. Marlena yearned to live among people of such nobility and compassion. Blending her memories with his own, Spock knew that the qualities he had so respected in the visitors, and the ones that Marlena envied, were inseparable. The others' self-control and focus in collective effort were made possible by the peaceful ethos they embraced.

Spock also had not forgotten that the visitors' merciful ways had saved his own life, when the alternate Doctor McCoy had risked being left behind in this cosmos in order to save Spock from what would have been a fatal subcranial hemorrhage. Marlena had witnessed that moment as well, with Kirk's alien assassination device. What she hadn't seen was that, after Spock had risen from the table, he had mind-melded with McCoy to force the truth from his weak human brain—and beheld a vision of the universe the visitors called home.

It was not without its conflicts, but the civilization to which the humans belonged was no empire; it was a federation, a democratic society, committed to peaceful exploration and coexistence, eschewing violence except in its own defense or that of others who ask for their aid.

That would be a society worth fighting for. Worth saving.

In every revolution . . . there is one man with a vision.

Marlena reached up and gently pressed her fingertips against the side of Spock's face. "I share your vision."

There were no lies in a mind-meld. Spock knew that she spoke the truth; she knew his thoughts, understood what he meant to do, though she likely did not realize all the consequences of what would follow. But her sincerity was unimpeachable, and for the first time in his life, he knew what it was to be simpatico with another being. They were each the first person whom the other had ever truly trusted. Though they knew the galaxy would likely align itself against them and their goals, they were not afraid, because at that moment, in that place, they had one another, they were one another . . . they were one.

He pulled back from her mind. Loath to be left alone once more, she resisted his departure, clung to his thoughts, pleaded without words for a few more moments of silent intimacy. It was a labor to leave her mind, and for a moment he hesitated. Then discipline reasserted itself, and he gently removed her fingers from his face as he severed their psychic link. Tears welled in her eyes as she looked up at him. His mien, masklike and vaguely sinister, did not betray the swell of newfound feelings he had for her . . . but then, despite his best intentions, a savage chord in his nature asserted its primal desires. He pulled her close and kissed her with a passion that no Vulcan would admit to outside the sacred rites of *Pon farr.*

She kissed him back, not with hunger or aims of seduction, but with devotion, with affection . . . with love.

Though he would never have imagined himself destined for such a fate, he realized that he might almost be able to let himself reciprocate her feelings. *How ironic,* he mused, *that after all the times I have chided Sarek for choosing a human mate, I should now find myself emulating his behavior.*

Embracing Marlena, he knew that he would never give her up and that she would never betray him. Whether that would be a strong enough foundation upon which to erect a new future for the people of the Empire, he didn't know, but it was an ember of hope, one with which he planned to spark a blaze that would burn away a failed civilization already in its decline, and make way for a new galactic order that would rise from its ashes.

For the love of a woman, Spock would destroy the Empire.

He would ignite a revolution.

2

The Inevitability of Change

*M*ain shuttlebay doors secure," intoned a masculine voice over the *Enterprise*'s intraship address system. *"Repressurizing shuttlebay. Stand by."*

Captain Spock, Doctor McCoy, and the *Enterprise*'s newly promoted first officer, Commander Montgomery Scott, walked together down the corridor to the ship's main shuttlebay. The three men were attired in their dress uniforms, as were the members of the security detachment that was gathered at the shuttlebay door. As soon as the guards saw Spock, they snapped to attention, fists to their chests; then they extended their arms, palms forward, in unison. Spock returned the salute.

"Shuttlebay repressurized," the voice announced.

With a nod, Spock said, "Positions, gentlemen."

The guards entered the shuttlebay single file, forming an unbroken line from the door of the shuttlebay to the hatch of the just-returned *Shuttlecraft Galileo*. Phasers drawn and clutched reverently to their chests, they stood at attention, eyes front. A group of Vulcan delegates debarked from the shuttlecraft, boarding the *Enterprise* for transport to the imperial conference on the planet code-named Babel.

At the front of the procession, moving with confidence and

radiating personal power, was the head of the Vulcan delegation: Ambassador Sarek of Vulcan, Spock's father. Trailing behind him was Amanda, his human wife, followed by the junior members of his diplomatic entourage. They all carried with them the spicy scents of the Vulcan homeworld. It had been four years since Spock had last been there, and eighteen years since he had last exchanged words with his father. It was likely, Spock knew, that Sarek would resist any overture of reconciliation he might offer, but he would not be able to avoid interacting with Spock now that he was the captain of the *Enterprise*. Under different circumstances, Spock might have found the necessity of contact to be distasteful, but as matters now stood it was a fortunate arrangement, and one he intended to exploit.

Sarek halted in front of Spock, eyed the gold tunic that Spock wore, and made a silent note of the rank insignia. He looked Spock in the eye and said in a level voice, "Permission to come aboard, Captain."

Spock lifted his right hand in the Vulcan salute and waited until Sarek reciprocated the gesture before he replied, "Permission granted, Ambassador Sarek." He nodded at his two fellow officers. "Our chief medical officer, Doctor McCoy, and our first officer, Commander Scott." Scott and McCoy nodded curtly to Sarek, who returned the gesture.

Speaking more to them than to Spock, Sarek motioned to the retinue that followed him. "My aides and attachés, and she who is my wife." He held up one hand and extended his index and middle fingers together. Amanda joined him directly and pressed her own fingertips to his. They both were stoic in their quiet companionship. It was a quality of their relationship that Spock had always found admirable.

"Commander Scott will escort you and your wife to your quarters, Mister Ambassador," Spock said. "Once you are settled, I look forward to offering you a tour of the ship."

"Captain, I'm certain you must have more pressing matters to attend to," Sarek said, as verbally agile as ever. "Perhaps one of your junior officers could guide us." He clearly did not want to interact with Spock any more than was necessary to complete his assignment for the Vulcan government, but the protocols of military and diplomatic courtesy prevented him from saying so.

Spock intended to turn that limitation to his advantage. "It would be my privilege, Mister Ambassador," he said. "I insist."

Of course, Sarek could simply decline the invitation entirely, but Spock knew that Sarek's devotion to the minutiae of decorum would prevent that. A subtle exhalation of breath signaled Sarek's grim acceptance of the inevitable. "Very well," he said. "My wife and I shall look forward to receiving you at your earliest convenience."

"Ambassador," Spock said with a half-nod, bringing the discussion to a close. Sarek looked to Commander Scott, who led the middle-aged Vulcan and his wife away, toward a turbolift that would take them to their quarters. The rest of the diplomatic team was escorted from the shuttlebay by the security team, as much for their own protection as that of the other Babel Conference delegates currently aboard the *Enterprise*.

McCoy turned and smirked at Spock. "Your father didn't look too happy to see you, Captain."

"My father is a Vulcan, Doctor. He feels neither happy nor unhappy."

The doctor snorted derisively. "You can tell yourself that if you want, *sir*, but that man is *not* looking forward to seeing you later." He frowned. "Pure logic, my ass. I know a grudge when I see one."

"Perhaps," Spock said. "But be that as it may, I will not tolerate being interrogated on the subject by a subordinate—particularly not by one who tortured his own father to death."

McCoy bristled at the mention of his father. "Dammit, I was under orders! You know that. I was *under orders*."

"Indeed, Doctor. As are we all."

The tour of the ship passed quickly. Spock escorted his parents from their quarters first to the bridge, then through the various scientific and medical laboratories in the primary hull. Sarek made a point of limiting his remarks to no more than a few words—"I see," or, "Sensible," or, "Most logical"—never asking follow-up questions, and suppressing any attempt Amanda made to engage Spock in more than the most perfunctory manner.

After a brief visit to the astrophysics labs and sickbay, they had arrived in main engineering, which had been busy with activity, most of it directed from the bridge by Commander Scott, who still groused to anyone who would listen that he had been forced to leave his beloved engines in less capable hands.

Less than an hour later, the tour was finished, and Spock escorted his parents to his own quarters. He walked a step ahead of them, moving in long strides that he knew his father would easily match. Stopping in front of his door, Spock turned and said curtly, "Mother, I wish to meet privately with Sarek. Please excuse us."

"Of course, Spock," she said, and started to step away.

Sarek caught her arm and stopped her, all the while keeping his hard, dark eyes fixed on Spock. "No, my wife. Stay with me."

Undeterred, Spock steeled his tone. "I must insist, Mister Ambassador. It is a matter of great urgency."

"I have nothing to say to you, Spock," Sarek declared. "You made your decision, and you must live with the consequences."

Amanda looked torn between them. "Sarek, please, listen . . ."

"Be silent, Amanda," Sarek said, his voice quiet but forceful. Returning his attention to Spock, he continued. "You could have been a leader on Vulcan, Spock. A man of power and influence. You rejected that for this? Most illogical."

Spock hardened his resolve. "I disagree."

"Naturally," Sarek said. He tried to walk away. "Let us pass. It has been a long day for my wife. We should retire."

"Ambassador," Spock said sharply, "I will speak my mind to you, and you will listen. As the captain of this ship, I have the power to compel your audience—and much more, if I so desire. I respectfully suggest that the wiser course of action would be not to force me to resort to such barbaric tactics."

For several seconds Sarek regarded Spock and took his measure. Spock waited while his father pondered his options. At last, Sarek folded his hands together and sighed. "As you wish, Captain. I am most interested to hear what you consider to be of such grave importance." He turned to Amanda. "I will rejoin you when my conversation with Spock is finished." She nodded her understanding and walked away.

Spock unlocked the door. It swished open, and he stepped aside to let Sarek pass. "After you, Mister Ambassador."

Inside Spock's cabin, the thermostat had been adjusted to a much warmer level than normal, and almost all traces of humidity had been extracted from its air—both changes being for Sarek's benefit. Seated across a small table from Spock, Sarek's face was steeped in long vertical shadows from the dim, crimson-hued overhead illumination. He shook his head.

"Your proposal is not logical, Spock," he said. "It is grounded in sentimental illusions."

"I assure you," Spock replied, "it is not." He picked up the ceramic urn of hot tea that rested on the table between them and refilled both their cups as he continued. "You yourself have admitted that conquering Coridan for its dilithium resources will inevitably consume more time, personnel, and resources than it can repay. Advocating a policy of waste is illogical." He set down the tea urn and looked Sarek in the eye. "However, enticing Coridan to join the Empire of its own volition, particularly if it can be accomplished without resorting to threats or force, would represent a significant and immediate gain for the Empire, at a relatively moderate long-term cost."

Sarek sipped his tea slowly, then set down his cup. "Even if I acknowledge the logic of your analysis, Spock, you must concede that negotiating such an agreement with a planet we could just as quickly invade would make the Empire appear weak. If our enemies come to believe that we would rather talk than act, they will not hesitate to strike. Introducing supplication into our foreign policy will only invite attack."

"Your analysis is flawed, Sarek."

The accusation almost provoked a glare of anger from the elder Vulcan. He reined in his temper, then said, "Explain."

"I agree that opening talks with Coridan will cause the Klingons and the Romulans to question our motives," Spock said. "But their scanners will still show our border defenses to be intact, and our fleet vigilant. They will not attack."

Pensive now, Sarek folded his hands in front of his chest. "The other delegates will not be receptive to this idea."

"Then you must persuade them," Spock said. "It will cost the Empire less than conquest, and reap it greater benefit."

Spock almost thought he noticed a frown on Sarek's face as the older man rose from the table and paced across the cabin. Watching his father stroll the perimeter of the room as though it were an activity of great interest reminded Spock of his youth, growing up in Sarek's home on Vulcan. Whenever Sarek had become displeased with him, he'd paced like this. "As it ever was, so it remains," Sarek said, half under his breath. "You have served the ambitions of humans all your life—no doubt thanks to the influence of your mother and your own human DNA. Assuming command of a starship has only made your devotion to the Terrans' cause more strident."

"Why do you assume it is their interests that I serve?"

Spreading his arms to gesture at the space around them, Sarek said, "You command one of their starships. You ask me to help increase their power and wealth by proposing that we invite Coridan into the Empire. What other conclusion should I draw?"

"You have heard only the first step in my proposal," Spock pointed out. "I think you will find its later stages *intriguing*, for their anticipated effect upon the status quo."

"I am well acquainted with how the Terrans adjust the status quo," Sarek replied. Many times had Spock listened patiently while Sarek recounted, with thinly veiled bitterness, the manner in which humans, immediately following their first contact with the crew of a Vulcan scout ship, had captured the scouts and tortured them into divulging the secrets of interstellar navigation. In short order, the Terrans had turned the Vulcans' knowledge to their own aims, laying the foundation for their nascent star empire.

"You assume facts not in evidence, Sarek." He waited until he once again commanded Sarek's full attention, then continued. "Strengthening the Empire is not my objective. In fact, I aim to do quite the opposite."

A twinge of emotion fluttered across Sarek's countenance. Fear, perhaps? He moved slowly, positioning the table between himself and his son. In a milder tone than he had used before, he said, "Speak plainly, Spock."

"Fact: The Empire's policies of preemptive warfare and civil oppression are not sustainable, and will soon collapse."

Cautiously, Sarek nodded. "Stipulated."

Emboldened, Spock pressed on. "Fact: Within approximately two hundred forty-three Earth years, uprisings will compromise the security of the Terran Empire from within, even as it wages a war against multiple external threats. The ensuing collapse will most probably destroy millennia of accumulated knowledge, triggering an interstellar dark age without precedent in the history of local space."

Sarek nodded gravely. "Vulcan's Council has reached the same conclusion. The Empire's collapse is inevitable."

"Agreed," Spock said. "The Empire cannot be saved. But the civilization that it supports can be—with a different, more benign form of government."

The upward pitch of Sarek's tone would barely have been noted by a non-Vulcan, but to Spock it registered as indignation. "You speak of treason, Spock."

"I speak of the inevitability of change, Sarek." He picked up

Sarek's half-full cup of tea from the table and held it before himself. "The Empire will fall. And when it does—" He let the cup fall to the deck. It broke into dozens of small jagged fragments, spilling tea in an irregular puddle across the carpet. "All within it will be lost. Unless—" He picked up his own cup from the table, opened the lid on the ceramic pot in the middle of the table, and poured his leftover tea back inside. Then he casually hurled the cup against the wall, where it shattered into countless tiny earthen shards.

Several seconds passed while Sarek considered Spock's point. The metaphor had been obvious enough that Spock had not felt the need to elaborate after throwing the empty cup. He was certain that Sarek understood that he meant to transition the imperial civilization to a new form of government before making a sacrifice of the Empire itself, casting it aside after it had been gutted and reduced to a hollow shell of its former self.

"My son," Sarek began, sounding as though he were selecting each word with great care. "I ask this with genuine concern: Do you suffer from a mental infirmity?"

The question was not unexpected. Spock shook his head once. "I am in full possession of my faculties, Father." He took one step toward Sarek. "It will take time for my plan to come to fruition. I must cultivate allies and fortify a power base. But it *can* be done—and if we wish to prevent the sum of all Vulcan thought and achievement from being erased less than three centuries from now, it *must* be done."

Sarek emerged from behind the table. He stepped slowly between the shards of the broken cups. "For the sake of our discussion, let us assume that you can seize power over the Empire, and maintain your hold long enough to push it toward its own demise. What do you propose should replace it?"

"A constitutionally ordered, representative republic," Spock said. As he'd expected, Sarek recoiled from the notion.

"Most illogical," Sarek replied. "The Empire is too large to be governed in such a manner. It would fall into civil war."

Nodding, Spock said, "As an Empire, yes. But as a coalition of sovereign worlds, united for their mutual benefit, much of its administration could be localized. Each planet would be responsible for its own governance and would contribute to the interstellar defenses of the republic."

"Madness," Sarek retorted. "You would never be able to maintain control."

"Irrelevant," Spock said. "When it is in each world's best interest to remain united with the others, it will no longer be necessary to compel their loyalty. Self-interest will dictate that the good of the many also benefits the few—or the one."

The elder Vulcan stopped in front of the food slot and pushed a sequence of buttons to procure more tea. High-pitched warbles of sound emanated from behind the device's closed panel. "The populace is not ready for self-rule, Spock. After centuries of dictatorship, the responsibilities of civic duty will be alien to them. They will reject it." The food-slot panel lifted, revealing a new ceramic pot and two empty cups on a tray. Sarek picked up the tray and moved it to the table. "And our enemies will capitalize on the chaos that follows from your reforms."

"I am not suggesting we dismantle Starfleet," Spock said. He moved to the table and stood opposite his father. "If reform is to have a chance to succeed, foreign interference must be prevented." He gestured for Sarek to be seated. As his father sat, so did Spock. He reached forward, lifted the teapot, and filled his father's cup with a slow, careful pour. "I do not propose to effect my changes all at once," Spock said. "Progress must come by degrees." Spock set down the teapot. "By the time our rivals are aware of the true scope of my intentions, they will be ill-prepared to act."

Leaning forward, Sarek said, "But when they do act, Spock, their reprisal will be catastrophic." He picked up the teapot and, with the slow measured motions of an old man in no hurry to reach the end of his life, poured tea into Spock's cup. "It is logical to conclude that the Empire cannot endure, but to contend that the solution to that problem is to prematurely destroy the Empire is . . . *counterintuitive,* at best."

"Indeed," Spock replied as he watched Sarek set down the teapot. Spock picked up his cup and savored the gentle aroma of the herbal elixir. "But to do nothing is more illogical still."

"True," Sarek replied, then he breathed deep the perfume of his own tea. They sipped their drinks together for several minutes, each contemplating what the other had said. It was Sarek who finally broke the silence. "I find much of what you propose troubling, Spock. However, given the inevitable decline and fall of the Empire, yours seems the most logical course."

"Most generous," Spock said.

"I offer you this caveat, however," Sarek added. "Even the most thoroughly logical agenda can be confounded by the actions of an irrational political actor—and humans are nothing if not irrational. They can be passionate, vindictive, sometimes even loyal . . . but more than any other species I have ever met, they are willing to kill and die for ideology. Most any species will fight for territory, resources, or survival. But Terrans, far beyond all the others, will readily slaughter billions and lay waste to entire worlds for the sake of an idea. Choosing the nobler of two paths will not come naturally to them. . . . They will have to be fooled into acting in their own best interest."

There was wisdom in Sarek's words, Spock knew. "Your point is well taken," he said. "Perhaps it is my own human ancestry that has spurred me on this admittedly ideological course of action. That, most of all, is why I humbly seek to enlist you as my chief political counsel."

"I would be honored."

Rising from his seat, Spock said, "There also is one other matter of importance." Gesturing toward the sleep nook in the back of the cabin, he called out, "Marlena. Join us."

Sarek also stood up as Marlena appeared from the shadows. She was attired in her nightclothes, and her long, dark hair was thickly tousled. She strode to Spock's side and clutched delicately at his arm. "You shouldn't have woken me," she said with a glare. "I was having a good dream for a change."

Spock ignored her complaint. "This is Lieutenant Marlena Moreau—my fiancée." Turning to her, he continued. "Marlena, this is Ambassador Sarek of Vulcan . . . my father."

She looked quickly from Spock to Sarek, then blushed with shame. "Forgive me, Ambassador. I didn't mean to . . . I mean, I wanted to make a better first impression than this. I . . ." She stammered for a few seconds more without forming any actual words. Spock and Sarek waited, each with one eyebrow raised.

"Emotional, isn't she?" Sarek noted.

"Indeed," Spock admitted.

"Why do you wish to marry her?"

With a tilt of his head, Spock gave the only honest answer. "It seems the logical thing to do."

Sarek nodded. "I understand." He took two short steps toward the door. "Rest tonight, Spock. We will speak again before the conference." He glanced once at Marlena, then, almost imperceptibly, signaled his approval to Spock with the barest hint of a nod. "The future awaits us; we have much to do."

2268

3

The Quality of Mercy

Elaan, the Dohlman of Elas, paced like a caged tiger. Spock watched the swarthy, lavishly bejeweled beauty prowl back and forth. She threw angry glances in his direction. They were alone together in Lieutenant Uhura's quarters, which Spock had designated as Elaan's cabin for the duration of this mission.

Grabbing a small statuette off a nearby shelf, she shouted, "You have no right to keep me here!" She hurled the figurine at Spock, who remained still and let it fly past, confident from the moment she'd thrown it that her hysteria had compromised her aim. "I am a dohlman! On my world, you would be—"

"We are not on your world," Spock corrected her. "We are aboard the *Enterprise*. And as a passenger on this ship, you are required to recognize my authority."

A fiery fit of temper propelled her across the cabin to confront him. Her eyes glistened with tears, and she looked on the verge of weeping. "Have you no mercy? No compassion? I am a dohlman, born to rule . . . to conquer." A single tear rolled down her left cheek to her jaw, then it crept forward toward her chin. Spock noted the subtle manner in which she lifted her chin, an invitation for him to wipe away her concocted grief.

He turned his back on her. "I am well acquainted with the

reputed properties of Elasian tears, Dohlman." Spock stepped over to the small table that stood against one wall and set the toppled teacups upright once more. "Let us continue reviewing the protocol for your introduction to the Troyian Caliph."

Her footfalls were soft, the gentle pattering of bare feet on the carpeted deck. She approached from behind him, and his keen Vulcan hearing was alert for any warning of an attack. Elaan had already stabbed and wounded Petri, the Troyian ambassador who had originally been given the task of educating her in Troyian protocol. Because of Petri's subpar combat reflexes and ensuing convalescence in sickbay, the only person from whom Elaan would consent to receive further instruction in etiquette was the highest-ranking individual on the ship: its captain.

She slipped past Spock, eyeing him first with suspicion, then with perverse amusement. "The Empire's never taken an interest in our conflict before," she said, dropping her voice into a slightly lower register, giving her words a smoky, seductive quality. "Some of the Empress's envoys have even encouraged us." Moving behind her seat at the table, she continued. "But now you arrive and convince Caliph Hakil to accept a marriage as grounds for a truce and a treaty. Why?"

"A nonviolent resolution to the situation is the most desirable outcome for all parties," Spock said.

"Not for me," Elaan shot back. "I'd much rather kill the Troyians, down to their last infant. I've dreamed of cleansing their world in fire and salting its ashes. How is this a desirable outcome for me?"

Spock pulled his communicator from his belt and flipped it open. A triple chirp signaled that his standby channel was open. "Bring him in," he said into the device, then he closed it and placed it back on his belt.

Moments later, the door to the corridor opened, and two security guards dragged in Elaan's bodyguard, Kryton. The young man's clothes were torn, and his face was bruised and bloody. He was barely conscious. "We caught him sending transmissions to a nearby Klingon cruiser," Spock said. "He has been conspiring with them to sabotage this mission, because he desires you for himself."

"Absurd!" Elaan cried. "I am a dohlman!" She stared in horror at Kryton, who hung limply in the hands of the two Starfleet guards. Disgust filled her voice with venom. "You're but a lowly soldier—you could never be my mate!"

Calmly, Spock explained, "Not as long as you remained Dohlman of Elas. However, once he had helped the Klingons conquer the Tellun system, you would be equals—as slaves of the Klingon Empire. A minor step down the social ladder for Kryton . . . but a significant demotion for you."

As she looked back at Kryton, her pity turned to fury. "You will pay dearly for this betrayal, Kryton."

The bodyguard's eyes were dull and half-glazed with pain. He lifted his head at the sound of her anger. "I did what my heart bade me, Dohlman," he croaked through bloody, swollen lips. "I love you. . . ."

"You are not permitted to love one such as me!" She whirled toward Spock. "Captain, please tell your men to remove this presumptuous worm from my chambers!"

The captain nodded to the guards, who pulled Kryton out of the cabin and took him back to the brig for his imminent execution, which Spock had postponed only until after this planned exhibition. For a change, Elaan was silent. Spock concluded that she most likely was brooding over the sudden revelation that her staunchest defender had been about to sell her into slavery.

Finally, she broke her reverie. "Captain," she asked, "is that Klingon ship still nearby? Do they still plan to attack, to prevent my wedding to Hakil?"

"No," Spock said. "I have dealt with the Klingons."

Elaan looked quizzically at him. "I heard no alerts, no sounds of combat. Did they flee? Or did you strike your own bargain with them?"

"They are no longer part of the equation, Dohlman," he said. "I suggest you leave it at that."

The less said, Spock reasoned, the better. The Tantalus field device had enabled him to uncover Kryton's treachery; once the Klingon ship's precise coordinates had been locked in, Spock had found it remarkably easy with the Tantalus field to eliminate the Klingon crew en masse while leaving their vessel intact. He had already ordered Mister Scott to capture the Klingon cruiser and tow it back to Starbase 12 for a complete analysis, from its disruptors to its spaceframe. It was a fortuitous addendum to his growing list of accomplishments, but his principal objective for this mission remained incomplete.

"I have spared you from becoming a slave of the Klingons," Spock said. "And I would also spare you the indignity of being enslaved by the Empire. Marry the Caliph of Troyius and end the war between your worlds. United for your mutual defense, you will be able to negotiate from a position of strength for your worlds' immensely valuable commodity."

Perplexed, she tilted her head and squinted suspiciously. "What commodity, Captain?"

"This one," Spock said, reaching forward. He touched the long crystalline jewels that formed her ornate neckpiece, arcing down in a semicircle atop her chest. "Dilithium crystals, more abundant on your planet than on Halkan or even on Coridan. Elas and Troyius are in possession of the largest natural deposits of high-quality dilithium in all of known space."

"But the Imperial engineers surveyed our planets decades ago," Elaan said, unable to hide her surprise. "They said they found nothing of value!"

"They lied," Spock said. "Because your two worlds are so well armed and well fortified, it would have been exceptionally costly for the Empire to conquer you in open combat. It was easier to provoke you into a prolonged war of attrition, so that when your worlds became so weakened that they could no longer oppose an invasion, the Empire would eradicate you all."

The more he told her, the sharper her focus became. "Why are you telling me this now?"

"Because the Klingons apparently are ready to conquer your worlds by force—an outcome that Starfleet cannot permit. My orders were to halt your conflict by force of arms, and to subdue your worlds in preparation for an occupying force."

"Then the marriage . . . ?"

Spock nodded his affirmation. "A plan of my own making. If the Klingons do plan to annex your worlds, you will be better able to repel their attacks if your defenses are intact and united. This will also reduce the number of Starfleet vessels and personnel that must be committed to defending you, freeing our resources for other objectives—and preserving your autonomy from direct imperial oversight."

"Slaughter would have been quicker," Elaan said.

"But less effective," Spock replied. "And more costly. Better for all if peace can be achieved without impairing the value of either world to the Empire."

For the first time since he had met Elaan, she smiled. "You speak almost like a statesman, Captain Spock. And I say 'almost' only because I've never heard one sound quite so reasonable."

"Then you accept my proposal? You will wed Caliph Hakil?"

She gave an enthusiastic nod. "I will," she said with conviction. "And I shall do more besides. Once our worlds are united, I will see to it that the exclusive mining rights for our dilithium are not given to the Empire." Before Spock could counsel her that defying the Empire might undo all the benefits of uniting with Troyius, she added, "I will, instead, grant them directly to you, Spock." She strode to the bed and sprawled herself across it. "As a sign of my enduring gratitude."

"Most kind," he said, fully aware of the understatement. With control over such an enormous wealth of dilithium crystals, Spock's path to the Admiralty was all but assured. It was more than he had hoped for; he had intended only to cultivate a future ally in the person of Elaan. Instead, he had acquired himself a patroness—and a very generous one, at that.

Perhaps, he mused, *I have underestimated the persuasive value of fairness and mercy. If it can spur such generosity in one, how will it affect the many?*

He resolved to find out.

"First the Halkans, then that business with Coridan," whispered Montgomery Scott. "Now a peace treaty? It's damned peculiar, that's what it is."

Huddled with him were Doctor McCoy and the communications officer, Lieutenant Uhura. Their clandestine meeting was safe from eavesdropping here, in a dimly lit maintenance bay on one of the lowest decks in the secondary hull of the *Enterprise*. Scott himself had personally rid the compartment of listening devices and set up surveillance countermeasures in the bulkhead around it. There was no place on the ship more private than this.

"I agree," McCoy said, leaning forward on the scuffed work bench. "Spock's behaved oddly ever since the Halkan mission, when he asked Captain Kirk not to destroy the planet."

Uhura got a ferocious look in her eyes. "Our duplicates," she said. "From the other universe. You think they got to him."

"I don't know, lass," Scott said. "I can't prove it."

McCoy's tone was sharp. "You don't have to prove it. Starfleet ordered Spock to subdue Elas and Troyius, but he went and made them stronger than ever—then secured their dilithium rights for himself. He disobeyed fleet orders, Scotty—you can assassinate him for that."

"Not without orders from Starfleet Command," Scott said. "I keep filing reports, but nothing happens."

Pushing away from the work bench, Uhura sighed with anger and frustration. "It's as if he's protected by the gods," she said. "He disobeys Captain Kirk, and nothing. Seizes the ship, and nothing. Defies Starfleet Command, and nothing. It's like they're afraid of him!"

"Maybe they are," McCoy said. "After that business with the Klingon cruiser, I'm starting to fear him a little myself."

Scott nodded. "Aye. You didn't see it, lass. The whole ship was deserted, like the whole crew just up and vanished." His stare became distant and creased with horror, and his voice, already quiet, hushed even lower. "Mess hall tables covered with plates of food half eaten, the gravy still fresh on the knives. A half-buffed pair of boots next to a bunk, the rag and the polish just lying on the deck. You could tell what every man on that ship was doing right before he vanished." He looked Uhura in the eye. "And not one bloodstain. Not a single phaser burn, no carbon scoring, no sign of a struggle at all. Just the pieces of the lives they left behind. I've never seen a weapon that could do that, lass."

She looked skeptical. "Then what did it, Mister Scott? Magic? Fairies and elves? A genie from a bottle?"

McCoy folded his arms and shrugged his shoulders. "Maybe the legends are true," he said. "Even in medical school I heard about Vulcan psionics. Some people think they're telepaths. Others say they can be clairvoyant or precognitive. Hell, I heard that in ancient times Vulcans could kill with a thought."

Uhura rolled her eyes. "And you really believe that?"

"I don't know what I believe," McCoy said. "But what I *know* is that three days ago that Klingon ship was stalking us in the Tellun system. Then, less than an hour after Spock found it, it went adrift, and we boarded it to find every last member of its crew gone without a trace."

Scott looked from McCoy to Uhura and lifted his brow imploringly. "You have to admit, Uhura, it seems a bit too convenient to be mere coincidence."

"But we have no proof," she said. "We can't send a message to Starfleet Command that says we think Spock is using ancient telepathic powers to crush his enemies."

"You're telling me," McCoy grumbled. "They'd probably give him a medal and call him a hero of the Empire."

They stood apart from one another in the shadows and remained silent for a long moment. "So," Uhura finally said. "What are we going to do?"

Scott shook his head. "There's nothing we can do. We don't

have any proof that Spock's been compromised, and Starfleet hasn't ordered us to take action."

"Maybe I could declare him mentally unfit," McCoy said. "I could say his brokering a peace treaty was irrational, and—"

"And he'd give you a half-dozen reasons why it's completely logical," Scott cut in. "You should know better by now than to argue logic with Spock. It's a losing proposition."

Uhura's temper flared higher by the moment. "Listen to the two of you!" she hissed. Backpedaling away from them, she continued. " 'Nothing we can do. Losing proposition.' You're not men. Men would stand and fight! Men would eliminate Spock now, before his brand of appeasement spreads. But since neither of you seems willing to act like a man"—she drew her dagger from her boot—"I guess I'll have to do it for you."

Scott tried to interpose himself between Uhura and the door, but he wasn't quick enough. She cut him off and was backing out of the room. "Where do you think you're going, lass? What do you think you're going to do?"

"What you should have done, Mister Scott," she replied. "I'm going to kill Captain Spock before he—"

An incandescent flash of light and a lilting, almost musical ringing sound filled the air around Uhura—and when it faded she was gone. No bloodstain. No phaser burns. No sign that she'd ever been there at all.

All that Scott could do was stare at the abruptly empty space in the room where she had stood. He tried to control his terror as he realized with a shudder that the same fate might be about to befall him, as well.

A glance to his right confirmed that Doctor McCoy was harboring the same brand of paranoid musings.

Their shared horror was interrupted by the shrill whistling note of the intraship comm, followed by Captain Spock's baritone voice. *"Spock to Mister Scott."*

Trading fearful looks with Doctor McCoy, Scott moved to a nearby panel and thumbed open a secure, encrypted channel that would mask his location if anyone happened to be monitoring for that information. "Scott here."

"Mister Scott," Spock said over the comm. *"Please meet me on the bridge at once. We need to discuss an adjustment to the bridge duty roster."*

A sick feeling churned in Scott's gut. He knew what was coming, but the protocol of the situation demanded that he play along as if he didn't. "The duty roster, sir?"

Spock's voice was ominous. *"Indeed, Mister Scott. . . . We appear to have an opening for a senior communications officer."*

Rumors spread quickly on any starship, but some traveled faster than others. "I heard it directly from Doctor M'Benga," Lieutenant Robert D'Amato said in a nervous whisper across the mess hall table. "And he heard it from Doctor McCoy himself."

"It's just not possible," Lieutenant Winston Kyle said, hunched over his soup. "People don't just wink out of existence."

"Mister Scott saw it, too," D'Amato said. "Just zap—and she was gone. No blood, no ashes, nothing."

"Big deal," Kyle said. "A phaser on full power can do the same thing. Seen it a hundred times."

"But there weren't any phasers in the room," D'Amato said. "It's been torn apart three times, nothing."

Kyle swallowed a spoonful of his soup and shook his head. "You ask me, I think Scott and McCoy killed her, then they made up this stupid story to cover their tracks."

Lieutenant Michael DeSalle, who had recently taken over for Mister Scott as chief engineer, put down his tray next to Kyle's and joined the conversation. "Be careful what you say," he said, keeping his own voice low. "Captain Spock hears everything."

Rolling his eyes, Kyle asked, "Now you're paranoid, too?"

DeSalle shrugged. "Caution pays dividends on this ship. Always has. You know that." He sliced through a rubbery-looking breast of chicken. "I heard Palmer got Uhura's job. She's keeping her distance from Mister Scott, though."

D'Amato shook his head. "I don't know. Way I heard it, Scotty's being set up."

"Forget 'set up,' he did it," Kyle said. "Don't you guys remember that flap on Argelius II? Three women dead, all evidence pointing at Scotty, then all the charges got dropped?"

"Thanks to Kirk," D'Amato said. "Like any of *us* would've gotten that kind of favor."

"That's what I'm saying," Kyle continued. "He has a history of it. And you know McCoy must have helped bury those forensic reports. So it's a lot easier to believe that Scott sliced up Uhura and disintegrated the evidence than to pin it on some kind of crazy Vulcan psychic mumbo-jumbo."

DeSalle took a sip of his drink, then smirked at Kyle. "Don't be so quick to write off the Vulcans' psionic powers. If they can do half the things I've heard, we're lucky we outnumber them seven to one in the Empire."

"You ought to hear what Doctor M'Benga says about the Vulcans," D'Amato said. "He interned on Vulcan. Saw things you wouldn't believe. He says they can read minds, plant delayed suggestions, even control weak minds from a distance. And in one of their oldest legends, the most powerful Vulcans used something called the Stone of Gol to kill people with just their thoughts—destroy people's minds, even erase them from reality."

"Sounds like someone's been hitting the Romulan ale again," Kyle quipped to DeSalle.

D'Amato's temper rose to the surface. "You don't believe me? Go ask M'Benga, he'll tell you."

"Proving what?" Kyle said. "That he's crazy, too?"

"I think you're forgetting something," DeSalle said.

Turning slowly to face DeSalle, Kyle asked, "What's that?"

A wan smirk crept across DeSalle's face. "The Klingon cruiser," he said. "Its entire crew missing, like they'd been beamed out of their seats into space."

"Oh, you've got to be kidding me," Kyle said. "Can you really not think of a single way that could've been done without some kind of magical trick? Occam's razor, guys. What makes more sense—that cloaked Romulan ships used transporters to kidnap and dematerialize the Klingon crew, or that Captain Spock thought about it *really hard* and made all the Klingons go *poof*?"

"There's no evidence that the Romulans were anywhere near here," D'Amato said.

DeSalle added, "Or that they can even use transporters while cloaked."

Kyle nodded. "Exactly. And there's no evidence that Vulcans have amazing psionic powers that can vaporize people. But which explanation sounds like it has a better chance of being true?" When neither DeSalle nor D'Amato replied after several seconds, Kyle shook his head in disgust, stood, and picked up his tray. "And you call yourselves men of science," he grumbled, then stalked away to turn in his half-eaten lunch.

D'Amato and the chief engineer watched Kyle leave the mess hall, then they continued eating their own lunches. "Kyle's story does actually make more sense," D'Amato admitted.

"I know," DeSalle replied. He washed down another mouthful of chicken before he added, "But I still think M'Benga's right."

Checking to make sure no one was eavesdropping, D'Amato whispered back, "So do I."

It didn't take long for the stories to spread beyond the confines of the *Enterprise*. Missives sent via subspace radio carried word of Captain Spock's eldritch powers throughout the Empire. Tales traded from crewman to crewman, and officer to officer, during shore leaves and transfers, inflated the story with each retelling. Within a few months, Spock's powers were said to be on a par with those of ancient Vulcan myths. His name became synonymous with power, and the terror that preceded him made his growing reputation for mercy, compromise, and restraint all the more beguiling. *Why,* many wondered, *would a man who could destroy any foe choose to promote peace?*

That question now preoccupied Empress Hoshi Sato III. At

the head of an oblong table, she presided over the meeting of her senior advisers in the situation room of the imperial palace on Earth. Sheltered deep below the planet's surface, the vast, oval underground chamber was illuminated solely by the glow of its massive display screens, which ringed the walls.

"Grand Admiral Garth," she said, eyeing the notorious flag officer from Izar. "Where is Captain Spock now?"

Side conversations around the table fell away to silence as Grand Admiral Garth straightened his posture and replied to the young monarch. "Your Majesty, Captain Spock and the *Enterprise* have just returned from their successful mission to the Romulan Neutral Zone. They are en route to Starbase 10 with a captured Romulan bird-of-prey in tow."

"And the disposition of the Romulan crew?" Sato asked.

Garth shifted slightly before he answered. "Eliminated, Your Majesty. The ship is empty."

A nervous murmur worked its way around the table. Empress Sato did not like the fearful tune that this report was striking up among her cabinet. In a pointed manner she inquired, "By what means were they dispatched, Admiral?"

Garth cocked his head nervously. "The boarding party was not able to determine that, Your Majesty."

"But the ship had been manned when the *Enterprise* made contact with it, yes?"

The admiral nodded. "Yes, Your Majesty."

Sato nodded slowly. Pressing the question further would serve no purpose but to embarrass Admiral Garth and make herself seem insecure or fearful. She had ascended to the throne less than sixteen months ago and was determined not to be perceived as weak. *What would my first royal namesake have done?* She adjusted her tactics to turn this scenario to her advantage—or, at the very least, to postpone the crisis until she had amassed sufficient political capital to entertain greater risks.

"If memory serves, Admiral, similar circumstances attended

Captain Spock's capture of a Klingon cruiser just a few months earlier, correct?"

"Yes, Your Majesty," Garth said.

"And his family and heirs have secured the dilithium mining rights in the Tellun system?"

Again, Garth dipped his chin and confirmed, "Yes, Majesty."

"Then it seems to me that Captain Spock is an officer of greater resources than we thought," Sato proclaimed more loudly, projecting her voice to the far end of the table. "Admiral Garth, move Captain Spock to the top of the list for new Admiralty appointments."

"As you wish, Majesty," Garth replied, "but granting him that kind of power could be dangerous."

Sato frowned. "Clearly, Spock is already dangerous," she said. "Prudence would suggest we try to make an ally of him."

Apparently, Garth was unconvinced. "And if elevating his rank only fuels his ambition . . . ?"

"In that case," she said, her melodic voice laced with menace, "we shall make an example of him, instead."

2277

4

Fortunes of the Bold

Commander Will Decker, first officer of the *I.S.S. Enterprise,* greeted Admiral Spock as the Vulcan C.O. entered transporter room one. "Your landing party is ready, Admiral."

Spock nodded his acknowledgment as he strode past Decker and stepped onto the platform. Awaiting the admiral there were four young Vulcan officers, three male and one female, all personally selected by Spock to accompany him to the Starfleet Admiralty's strategic conference on Deneva. Lieutenant Xon, the *Enterprise*'s new science officer, was a boyish-looking young man with long unruly hair. Ensign Saavik, the woman, had come to the ship directly from the Academy, and now served as its alpha-shift flight controller. The other two, Solok and Stang, were lieutenants in the security division.

Like the admiral, the other Vulcans all wore full dress uniforms—which, thanks to their dark gray, minimalist styling, looked almost identical to regular duty uniforms, right down to their ceremonial daggers and mandatory sidearms.

Lieutenant Commander Winston Kyle stood at the transporter control station. "Coordinates locked in, Admiral," he said.

"Stand by, Mister Kyle," Spock said. In a sepulchral tone of voice, he added, "Mister Decker, please join the landing party."

The request caught Decker by surprise. He concealed his alarm. "Me, sir? But I'm not dressed for a formal conference."

"A technicality," Spock said. "Overriding protocol is one of the privileges of rank."

Decker realized that he had become the center of attention in the transporter room. Debating a direct order from Admiral Spock aboard his flagship would only exacerbate the situation. Refusing it was not an option. Decker wondered if Spock knew what had been arranged on the planet's surface—or what Decker's role in it had been. "Aye, sir," he said, stepping up to join the landing party. Moving past the Vulcans, Decker found an available transporter pad at the rear of the platform.

In the six years since Will Decker had been appointed by his father, Grand Admiral Matthew Decker, as Spock's executive officer aboard the *Enterprise,* the notorious Vulcan flag officer had made a point of keeping him at a distance. Except for the most perfunctory communications, Spock rarely conversed with Decker and generally declined to include him in tactical planning or diplomatic efforts. It was easy for Decker to guess why. Because Spock had never shown any particular affinity for his previous first officer, Montgomery Scott, Decker had ruled out resentment as a factor. In fact, any emotional basis for Spock's decision to ostracize Decker was denied by the simple fact of the admiral's Vulcan heritage. The more Decker thought about it, the more convinced he became that Spock simply did not trust him.

And why should he? I wouldn't, if I was him. I'd assume that my first loyalty would be to my father. It's a wonder he hasn't "disappeared" me like so many others. He still might.

Decker's musings were disrupted by Spock's level baritone. "Mister Kyle . . . energize."

Wrapped in the transporter beam, Decker saw the room swirl with light and color. He unfastened the loop on his phaser before the annular confinement beam ensnared him and restrained his movements. The same irrational fear always raced through his thoughts as the dematerialization sequence began: *What if being disassembled is actually fatal? What if the person who comes out on the other side is just a copy of me, perfect in every detail, but completely un-aware that I'm dead and he's a copy?* A wash of whiteness brought him up short, then the swirl of light and euphonic noise ushered him back to himself, now in a corridor of the imperial adminis-tration building in Deneva's capital city. Though he knew he could never prove his idea or disprove it, he still wondered, *What if I'm a copy now? What if the person who stepped onto the transporter pad on the* Enterprise *is dead?*

The landing party was in a dim hallway with bare, dark gray walls of a smooth, prefabricated material. Open panels on the wall revealed complex networks of wires and optronic cables. A musty odor permeated the cool air, suggesting to Decker that they were underground, in some kind of subbasement.

Recalling the pre-mission briefing, he realized that some-thing was wrong. "This isn't where we were supposed to beam in," he said.

"Quite correct, Commander," Spock said. "Follow me." With-out hesitation, Spock led the group at a quick step down the cor-ridor, then right at a T-shaped intersection. Within a few minutes, he had reached a locked portal marked "Auxiliary Security Con-trol." Next to the door was an alphanumeric keypad. Spock stood aside while the four Vulcans gathered at the door and stared at it, as if concentrating on something beyond it. They and Spock all were perfectly still and quiet, and Decker followed their example.

Then Saavik blinked, stepped forward, and tapped in a long string of characters and digits on the security keypad. The door swished open, and the four young Vulcan officers rushed in, swift and silent. Sharp cracking noises were followed by heavy thuds. Spock walked inside the security control center, and Decker fol-lowed him.

Four human Starfleet officers lay unconscious on the floor, and Spock's team now occupied the fallen officers' posts. Banks of video screens lined three walls, packed with images from the building's internal security network. Spock and Decker watched as the four Vulcans worked. Finally, Stang turned his chair to face Spock. "There are no other members of the Admiralty in the conference hall, Admiral."

"As I suspected," Spock said. He looked at the science officer. "Lieutenant Xon, scan the conference hall for any life signs." To Saavik he said, "Scan the corridor outside the conference hall for evidence of concealed explosives or other antipersonnel devices." Both officers nodded in acknowledgment and set to work.

Decker stood and watched, dumbfounded. It was all falling apart. Spock noted Decker's dismayed expression. "You appear troubled, Commander."

Still trying to make sense of what was happening, Decker said, "You came down here *expecting* a trap?"

"Naturally," Spock said.

"But why?"

Folding his hands behind his back, Spock replied, "Mister Decker, in the ten years that I have commanded the *Enterprise,* I have been forced to suppress six mutinies, two of them instigated by senior officers."

"None on my watch, Admiral," Decker said proudly.

"True," Spock said. "Discipline has improved markedly under your supervision. Regardless, I have been forced on many occasions to defend my command from persons and factions who oppose my methods. Precaution becomes a necessity." Decker couldn't fault Spock's reasoning. From the alleged "malfunction" of the experimental M-5 computer, which had caused the *Starship Excalibur* to attack the *Enterprise,* to Grand Admiral Garth's failed ambush of the *Enterprise* at Elba II, the Empire had given Admiral Spock more than sufficient cause to treat any invitation it proffered as being instantly suspect.

Ensign Saavik turned from her screen to report. "Explosives have been installed at one-meter intervals beneath the floor in the main corridor outside the conference hall."

"Fascinating," Spock said. He looked at Xon.

Xon, sensing the admiral's attention, turned to face him. "Two life signs inside the conference hall, Admiral. Close together, in a concealed position opposite the main entrance. Both armed with phased plasma rifles."

"Snipers," Spock said. "Lieutenant, can you deactivate the building's transport scrambler from here?"

"Negative, sir," Xon replied. "Doing so would alert the personnel in the primary security control center."

Spock raised his voice. "Solok, Stang, use the emergency exit stairway to reach the conference hall undetected. Eliminate the two snipers. Saavik, Xon, initiate a command override and then execute an intruder protocol inside the primary security control room. Trigger their anesthezine gas module. As soon as they are incapacitated, we will return to the *Enterprise.*"

"Aye, sir," Xon and Saavik answered in near unison, while Stang and Solok swiftly exited the auxiliary security control center on their way up to the conference hall.

Standing near the door, Decker listened to their retreating footfalls. Inside the room, Spock conferred with Xon and Saavik at the main console. All three had their backs to him.

Slowly, carefully, as quietly as he was able, Decker drew his phaser from his belt, extended his arm, and leveled his aim. *Three against one, but I have the element of surprise,* he assured himself. *This is the best chance I'll get.*

He squeezed the trigger.

Nothing happened. He released the trigger and looked at his weapon, as if it were a friend who had betrayed him.

Spock, still facing away from Decker, said, "It would seem, Commander, that you are the only member of the landing party who is not aware of the phaser-dampening field inside this room." The admiral turned to face him. Saavik and Xon swiveled their chairs to do likewise.

The door swished closed behind Decker. *Oh, no.* Panic swelled in his gut as he lowered his sidearm.

"Thank you, Mister Decker, for all your assistance," Spock continued. "Without your unwitting complicity, I would have been hard-pressed to ascertain the specific time and place of this assassination attempt, arranged by your father."

Decker smiled sadly. "You know I had no choice, right?"

"One always has a choice," said Spock. "Even refusing to decide is still a choice. And choices have consequences."

Saavik stood and walked slowly toward Decker. Xon followed a step behind her. Both unsheathed their daggers.

Not content to let himself be murdered without a fight, Decker drew his own dagger and squared himself for combat.

They were so fast, and he felt so slow.

He met a lunge with a block, dodged a thrust, slashed at an opponent who had already slipped away—

—then cruel agony, sharp and cold. Steel plunged into his body below his ribs. Gouging upward, ripping him apart from the inside out. Then the serrated Vulcan blades tore free. He dropped to his knees and clutched his gut. Blood, warm and coppery-smelling, coated his fingers.

Xon and Saavik stood above him, the blood-slicked blades still in their hands. Spock remained at the far console. All the Vulcans wore the same dispassionate expression as they watched Decker die. For people from a scorching-hot planet, they were the most cold-blooded killers that he had ever seen.

Decker tried to swallow, but his mouth was dust-dry and his throat constricted. "My father will kill you all," he rasped.

"It is very likely that he will try," Spock said, then he nodded once to Saavik.

Another flash of steel landed a stinging cut across Decker's throat. He felt himself slipping away and going dark, and his last thought was that it felt not all that different from vanishing into a transporter beam.

"That rotten, scheming, Vulcan sonofabitch!" Grand Admiral Matthew Decker hurled an expensive bottle of Romulan ale against the wall of his quarters, showering his first officer, Commander Hiromi Takeshewada, with broken glass and pale blue liquor.

A few seconds later, she felt reasonably certain that none of the glass had penetrated her eye. A light sweep of her hand wiped the splatter of liquid from her sleeve. The grand admiral, meanwhile, was almost literally tearing at his gray hair while thumping his forehead heavily against the bulkhead.

For all the times that being the right-hand officer to the Grand Admiral of Starfleet had been a boon to Takeshewada, it was moments such as these that made the job a horror. Being the one to inform him that his son, Will, had been slain—cut down by Admiral Spock's loyal Vulcan operatives—marked a low point in her Imperial military career. Now she had the unpleasant task of delivering a second piece of news to the grand admiral.

"There's one more thing, sir."

His face was scrunched almost into a knot from his efforts to muzzle his grief and fury. Through clenched teeth he replied, "What is it?"

She cast her eyes downward. "The Empress commands you to make contact with her at once."

An angry, bitter chuckle rumbled inside Decker's throat. "Of course she does."

Takeshewada pointed toward the door. "Should I . . . ?"

"No," Decker said. "Stay. I want you to hear this. So you can be glad you'll never have to deal with it."

Long hours of training for months at a time enabled Takeshewada to suppress any reaction to Decker's almost-reflexive insults. At first, his mocking reminders that her career would never advance beyond its current position had grated sorely on her nerves. It was well known that the empresses of the Sato Dynasty had refused for more than a century to grant female officers the rank of admiral. A lucky few made captain, but such an honor was rare and usually restricted to noncombat vessels—in other words, to ships of little value to the Empire. Takeshewada's own ambitions had never been a secret, and as a result she had endured continual mockery by her peers and shipmates for more than two decades.

A few years ago, with the help of a sympathetic Vulcan officer, she had started teaching herself how to suppress her emotional reactions to Decker's taunts. No longer did a snarl twist her lip or a grimace crease the corner of her mouth. Her eyes didn't narrow, nor did her face flush with anger when he hurled another of his unthinking japes in her direction.

He powered up the private viewscreen on his desk. "Computer," he said. "Establish a secure, real-time communication channel to Empress Sato on Earth."

"Working," said the computer's masculine, synthetic voice.

Decker took a few deep breaths while he waited for the channel to open on his screen. He had just composed himself into a semblance of his normally grim, imposing visage when the face of Empress Hoshi Sato III appeared on the viewscreen.

"Grand Admiral Decker." She sounded almost amused. *"It's my understanding that the trap you set on Deneva was unsuccessful."*

He bowed his head like a common supplicant to the throne. "Yes, Your Majesty. Admiral Spock anticipated the ambush."

"I warned you not to underestimate him," Sato said. *"His promotion of compromise and nonviolence might seem irrational, but I am beginning to comprehend a method to his madness."*

Vengeful wrath usurped Decker's demeanor. "He's just a man, Your Majesty. And I'm going to kill him."

Her voice was hard and unyielding. *"You will kill him, Admiral, but you will do so because I order it, not for your personal satisfaction."* She waited until he bowed his head before she continued. *"And he's more than just a man. For dissidents and malcontents throughout the Empire, he has become a symbol. The longer he remains free to promote his agenda, the more allies he attracts. He enjoys an unprecedented level of popularity among civilians, and my sources warn me that more than half of Starfleet is prepared to follow his banner."*

"Any who follow him are traitors," Decker declared. "Any crew that mutinies will be put to death."

"Really?" The empress tilted her head, again with an intimation of mockery. *"You were incapable of killing one man, but you're prepared to declare war on half your own fleet?"*

"Ambushing Spock is extremely difficult, Your Majesty," Decker said. "After today, he'll be even more cautious. It'll take time to prepare another trap."

Her tone became one of dark menace. *"We're long past the time for clever ploys, Admiral. Spock is poised to launch a coup for control of Starfleet. He must be put down immediately. Assemble a fleet and destroy the* Enterprise. *Act with extreme prejudice; kill Admiral Spock. Is that understood?"*

"Explicitly," Decker said.

As she closed the channel, she said simply, *"Good hunting."*

Decker deactivated the viewscreen and turned his chair to face Takeshewada. He was so alive with purpose that he looked reborn. "Commander, send on a secure channel to all confirmed-loyal ships, 'Rendezvous at Terra Nova, await further orders.' And start running battle drills." He stood and straightened his posture into one of defiant pride. "When we catch up to the *Enterprise,* I want to be ready to blast her to kingdom come."

A soft hum coursed through the deck of the *Enterprise*'s bridge. The ship was cruising at warp six toward Xyrillia, having made an unharried departure from Deneva. By now, word had certainly reached Starfleet Command regarding the outcome of Grand Admiral Decker's trap and the fate of his son. Though it was possible that Matt Decker and the Empress might choose to regroup following such a setback, Spock doubted that they would afford him or his crew such a reprieve.

Spock leaned forward in the center seat while reviewing a short list of candidates to succeed the late Will Decker as first officer. He had narrowed the roster to three names since his last sip of bitter tea, and much careful consideration now reduced it to two: either Lieutenant Commander Winston Kyle or Lieutenant Commander Kevin Riley.

He looked up from the display tablet in his hand and made an effort to shift his focus to points at different distances around the bridge, as a relaxing exercise for his fatigued ocular muscles. The bridge of the *Enterprise* seemed darker to him since its 2271 refit—its curves more pronounced, its shadows deeper. Overall, the more somber ambience suited Spock, who had always found its two previous incarnations garishly bright. Another definite improvement of the refit was that the chairs had been securely fastened to the deck and equipped with optional safety braces. Though little more than a half-measure in a pitched battle, they nonetheless represented progress.

As his gaze passed the communications station, Lieutenant Elizabeth Palmer turned toward him. "Admiral," she said. "I'm picking up encrypted signal traffic on multiple Starfleet channels. None of the regular decryption protocols are working." She thought for half a second, then added, "It appears that the message is intended for all Starfleet ships *except us,* sir."

Turning toward the opposite side of the bridge, Spock looked to his science officer. "Lieutenant Xon," he said. "Tie in to Lieutenant Palmer's station and help her decrypt the signal from Starfleet."

"Aye, sir," Xon replied, then he went to work on the task.

Tense minutes passed while Xon and Palmer worked to decipher the fleet's urgent communiqués. Finally, Xon moved away from his station and stepped down from the upper level to stand beside Spock's chair. He spoke softly. "Admiral, we have decrypted the signals. The message is audio only, and is available for your review at my station."

In a normal speaking voice, Spock said, "Put it on the speaker, Lieutenant."

Xon remained calm and replied simply, "Aye, sir," then he returned to his post. From there, he relayed the message to the bridge's main overhead speaker. A recorded male voice spoke calmly and plainly. *"Attention all Starfleet ships, this is a direct order from Grand Admiral Matt Decker, commanding the fleet from aboard the* Starship Constellation. *All vessels in sectors one through seven are to rendezvous at once in the Terra Nova system. Under no circumstances is any vessel to exchange communications with the* Starship Enterprise.

This is an imperial directive issued by Empress Sato III. Further orders will be forthcoming at the rendezvous. Constellation *out.*"

Spock arched one eyebrow with curiosity at this turn of events. Glancing to his right, he saw his expression mirrored on Xon's young, clean-shaven face. Nervous looks were volleyed between the non-Vulcans on the bridge. Before idle speculation could take root, Spock seized the initiative. "Helm. Increase speed to warp nine, and set course for Terra Nova."

Ensign Saavik began punching in the coordinates for the course change, then she paused and turned her chair to face Spock. "Admiral, please confirm: You wish to rendezvous with Grand Admiral Decker's attack fleet?"

"Affirmative, Ensign," Spock said.

Even Xon seemed perplexed by Spock's order. "Sir, the fact that Grand Admiral Decker excluded us from the initial transmission, and barred the rest of the fleet from communicating with us, would seem to suggest—"

"I am well aware of what it *suggests,* Lieutenant. Grand Admiral Decker has been ordered to destroy this ship. First, however, he hopes to intimidate us into retreat, so that he may frame the conflict as one of loyal soldiers versus deserters." Steepling his fingers against his chest, Spock finished, "I will force him to accept a different narrative—one of my choosing."

Saavik continued to press the debate. "Admiral, would it not be prudent to seek reinforcements before confronting an entire fleet of hostile ships? As the ancient Terrans might have said, 'Discretion is the better part of valor.' "

"True enough, Ensign. But the ancient Terrans were also fond of a different maxim: 'Fortune favors the bold.' . . . Set course for Terra Nova and increase speed to warp factor nine."

The *Enterprise* was still more than a light-year from the outer boundary of the Terra Nova system when Grand Admiral Decker's attack fleet intercepted it. Less than ten minutes after Spock's ship had registered on the *Constellation*'s sensors, it had been met and surrounded, all without a shot being fired. *Enterprise* hadn't attempted a single evasive maneuver, nor had it fired a shot. Every scan that Decker's crew performed showed that the *Enterprise*'s shields were down, and its weapons were not charged. The only thing that had postponed Decker's order for its immediate destruction had been the signal of surrender transmitted by Admiral Spock himself, along with a formal request for parley.

Decker didn't like this at all. It smelled like a trap.

Lieutenant Ponor, the communications officer, looked up to report, "I have Admiral Spock on channel one, sir."

"On-screen," Decker snapped. The main viewer wavered and rippled for a moment, then the visage of Admiral Spock appeared, larger than life. Decker scowled at the Vulcan. "Admiral Spock, by the authority of Empress Sato III, I order you to surrender your command and relinquish control of your vessel."

"I have already surrendered," Spock replied. *"Forcing you to destroy the* Enterprise *would serve no purpose when it can still be of service to the Empire."*

If Spock had a strategy here, Decker wasn't seeing it.

"Very well," Decker said. "Prepare to be boarded."

"Hardly necessary," Spock said. *"I am prepared to allow myself to be transported to your ship."*

It took a moment for Decker to formulate his response. "Who said any of this was up to you? You're in no position to—"

"I merely suggest," Spock interrupted, *"the most logical and least time-consuming alternative."*

Decker was literally now on the edge of his chair, tensed to spring to his feet at the slightest provocation. "You're not dictating the terms here, you Vulcan sonofabitch."

"My apologies, Grand Admiral," Spock said, lowering his head slightly. *"Do you wish to accept my surrender in person?"*

"What?" He didn't know why Spock even had to ask. The protocol for a formal surrender demanded that Decker receive it face-to-face. "Yes, of course."

"Shall I then arrange to have myself transported into custody aboard your vessel?"

Only belatedly did Decker realize what Spock was doing. Though Spock had framed his statements as interrogatives he still was directing the process of the surrender, usurping Decker's own authority. "A security detail from my ship will beam aboard your vessel immediately," he said, then continued quickly to keep Spock quiet. "If they meet with any resistance, Admiral Spock— *any* resistance whatsoever—I will not hesitate to destroy your ship and its crew." Before Spock could even acknowledge Decker's statement, the grand admiral forged on. "My guards will escort you back here, to my bridge, where I will accept your surrender and pass sentence for your treason against the Empress Sato III. Decker out." He made a slashing motion in Ponor's direction, and the communications officer closed the channel before Spock could sneak in another word.

Commander Takeshewada stepped down from one of the aft consoles and stood beside Decker's chair. "The boarding party has just beamed over, sir," she said. "They'll notify us the moment they have Admiral Spock in custody."

"Good," Decker said. "Have extra security guards meet them in the transporter room when they get back. I don't want to take any chances with Spock." He heaved a tired sigh. "The sooner we get this over with, the better."

As Spock had pledged, no member of his crew interfered with the *Constellation*'s boarding party, and he himself gave no resistance when the six-man team placed him under arrest and ushered him at phaser-point off the bridge of the *Enterprise*.

Now they were aboard the *I.S.S. Constellation,* Grand Admiral Decker's flagship, crowded together in the turbolift. Deck after deck blurred past as they ascended toward the bridge.

The doors opened with a gasp and swish, and the soft chirps and hums of the bridge, all but identical to those aboard the *Enterprise,* met Spock as he was prodded forward out of the turbolift. The *Constellation* was a refit *Constitution*-class vessel, just like the *Enterprise,* and only a handful of tiny differences in console layout distinguished the two ships' command centers.

On the main viewer was the image of Empress Sato III. A string of symbols beneath the bottom edge of the screen alerted Spock to the fact that this was a two-way transmission being broadcast in real time on an open subspace frequency.

Decker stood beside his chair, facing the turbolift, as Spock and the security detail filed out. The bridge officers also stood, each next to his or her station, observing Spock as he was led in and guided to within a meter of Grand Admiral Decker. When the procession came to a stop, boot heels clapped together as the guards snapped to attention and thrust out their arms in salute to Decker. Spock saluted the grand admiral, more out of respect for the rank than for the man. While keeping eye contact with Spock, Decker returned the salute to one and all.

Hands pressed down roughly on Spock's shoulders. "Kneel," said one of his guards. He was forced to his knees in front of Decker, who glared fiercely down at him.

"You killed my son," Decker said.

Raising one eyebrow, Spock replied, "No, sir. My operatives slew your son. I merely sanctioned it."

"Spare me your Vulcan semantics," Decker said. "You ordered it. You're responsible. Hand me your agonizer, Admiral."

Spock calmly answered, "I no longer carry it. Nor does any member of my crew."

"That's a court-martial offense," Decker said.

Unfazed, Spock said, "If you wish to convene a court-martial, I am more than willing to defend my decision."

Decker practically quaked with rage. "I've heard enough," he said, his disgust evident. "Admiral Spock, I order you, as a Starfleet officer and subject of the Terran Empire, to profess your loyalty to Empress Sato III before you are put to death, so that you may die with some measure of honor."

Emboldening his voice for the benefit of those watching via the subspace channel, Spock answered, "I pledge my loyalty and my life to the Empire." He noticed, at the edge of his vision, the Empress on the viewscreen, casting a poisonous glare at Decker. He waited for Decker's reaction. It took only a moment.

"I ordered you to pledge your loyalty to the Empress Sato III," Decker said, trembling with fury.

"The Empress and the Empire are one," Spock said. "Fealty to one is fealty to both. It is a founding principle of the Empire."

Decker smirked arrogantly. "Do you really think this grand-standing will delay your execution, Spock?"

"I think," Spock said, "that this will all be over in a few moments."

A screech of phasers, flashes of light, and agonized cries filled the bridge of the *I.S.S. Constellation*. The security detail surrounding Spock dropped to the deck, shot dead. Spock, already aware of what was happening, stayed where he was. Decker cringed, looked around in a sudden panic—and watched his bridge officers act in concert to ambush the security team.

It was a mutiny.

Decker began to back away from Spock. The voice of his first officer stopped him. "That's far enough, Decker." Spock watched Decker turn and face Commander Takeshewada, whom Spock had long ago cultivated as an ally. Her resentment at the suppression of her potential had made her a prime candidate for a revolt against the status quo, and her access to information as Decker's first officer had provided Spock's people with critical intelligence—such as the means to break the *Constellation*'s latest encryption codes.

Trapped between Takeshewada and Spock, Decker started to lose his stature. He was cowering. "What are you doing, Hiromi?"

"Something that should've been done a long time ago," she said.

The grand admiral turned away from his first officer to find Spock, now standing tall again, surrounded by the charred corpses of the fallen, gazing down upon him. Mustering all the sound of authority in his rich baritone, Spock declared simply, "You are relieved, sir."

All at once Decker understood what was transpiring, and he straightened himself back to a pose of dignity and defiance. Looking Spock in the eye, he answered, "The hell I—"

Takeshewada fired and burned a hole halfway through Decker's back. He convulsed, then twitched grotesquely as he fell facedown at Spock's feet.

On the main viewer, Empress Sato III watched with wide-eyed attention but said nothing. The bridge crew of the *Constellation* all looked to Spock for direction. "Stations," he ordered, and everyone leaped into motion. "Commander Takeshewada, secure from general quarters. Lieutenant Ponor, request status updates from the ships of the fleet."

While the officers around him scrambled to collect data and remove the dead bodies from the bridge, Spock settled easily into the center seat and waited, patient and stoic, for word of whether his plan—triggered prematurely by Decker and the Empress's blatant move against him—was unfolding as intended. He passed the minutes looking at the Empress on the screen. For her part, she seemed equally willing to reciprocate his stare.

Finally, Takeshewada concluded her conference with Ponor and stepped down into the middle of the bridge, next to Spock. "We have reports from all sectors, sir," she said. "Officers loyal to you have successfully taken control of sixty-one-point-three percent of the ships in Starfleet. The remaining vessels are under the control of officers who have expressed a desire to remain neutral."

"What is the disposition of the other ships in Admiral Decker's attack fleet?"

She handed him a condensed report on a data slate. "All are with you except for the *Yorktown* and the *Repulse,* but their captains have ordered their crews to stand down."

"Very well," Spock said. He stood and took two steps toward the main viewer. He put his closed fist to his chest, then extended his arm in salute to the Empress. "Your Majesty," he said, lowering his arm. "In accordance with the imperial rules of war, and Starfleet regulations regarding the criteria for advancement, I hereby assume the rank of grand admiral of Starfleet, and designate the *Enterprise* as my flagship."

It was done. He had thrown the gauntlet and appointed himself the supreme military commander of the Terran Empire. Now all he could do was await the Empress's response. She could refuse to grant him the title, but to challenge him would spark a civil war—and with the majority of Starfleet supporting his bid for control, and the bulk of the remainder choosing to sit out the confrontation rather than risk becoming caught in a cross fire, the odds favored Spock's triumph. Alternatively, she could implicitly endorse his coup, thereby cementing his hold on power and legitimizing his control of the Empire's vast military arsenal. If she was as shrewd and logical as his observations had led him to suspect she was, she would not elect to plunge her Empire into a disastrous, internecine conflict.

The monarch's neutral expression never changed as she spoke. *"Grand Admiral Spock, redeploy your fleet to fortify our defenses on the Klingon border near Ajilon,"* she said.

"As you command, Your Majesty," Spock replied.

"Then," Empress Sato III added, *"set your flagship's course for Earth. It's customary for a promotion of this magnitude to be honored with a formal imperial reception. I look forward to welcoming you to my palace on Earth in seven days' time."*

Spock bowed his head slightly, then returned to attention. "Understood, Your Majesty. My crew and I are honored by your invitation."

Without any kind of valediction, the Empress cut the channel, terminating the discussion. The collective anxiety on the bridge diminished palpably the moment the viewscreen reverted to the placid vista of a motionless starscape. Spock turned away from the screen. "Captain Takeshewada," he said, granting an instant promotion to his chief ally aboard the *Constellation*. "Take this attack fleet and proceed at best speed to the Ajilon system. From there, redeploy to secure the border. The Klingons will see this change in our military leadership as an invitation to test our discipline and organization. Encourage them not to try more than once."

"Aye, sir," Takeshewada said.

"I return now to the *Enterprise,*" Spock said. He raised his right hand and spread the fingers in the Vulcan salute. "Live long, and prosper, Captain Takeshewada."

"And the same to you, Grand Admiral Spock," she said, then she took her place in the center seat and beamed with pride.

He took his communicator from his belt and flipped it open. "Spock to *Enterprise.*"

It was Lieutenant Xon who answered. *"Go ahead, sir."*

"One to beam over, Lieutenant," Spock said. "Energize."

5

The End and Object of Conquest

*E*nter," said Grand Admiral Spock from the other side of the door to his quarters. It opened and Saavik stepped inside.

As soon as she crossed the threshold she felt more comfortable. Inside, the light was dimmer and tinted red; the heat was dry and comforting; even the gravity was slightly greater. It was as accurate a facsimile of Vulcan's climate as the ship's environmental controls could create. She stepped farther inside, and the door shut behind her.

Saavik turned and saw Spock. His back was to her. He was wearing his full dress uniform, complete with regalia and medals, and standing in front of a mantel on which stood a smoking cone of incense. Without turning to look in her direction, he said, "Join me, Ensign."

Hands folded together behind her back, she walked slowly to his side. Several seconds passed while she stood beside him. "We have received your transport coordinates from the imperial palace," she said, breaking the silence. "They are standing by for your arrival."

"I am well aware of our itinerary, Ensign," Spock said.

Duly chastised, Saavik lowered her chin. "Aye, sir."

This time she respected the silence until he spoke.

His eyes remained fixed on the twists of pale smoke rising from the ashen cone of mildly jasmine-scented incense. "Do you know why I asked you here?"

She followed his example and stared at the serpentine coils of dense smoke. "No, sir."

"Do you know why the Empress ordered us here to Earth?"

Electing to eliminate obvious answers, Saavik replied, "To honor your promotion to grand admiral of Starfleet."

A soft, low *harrumph* was Spock's first reaction. "That was her stated purpose for the invitation."

Saavik cast a furtive, sidelong glance at her Academy sponsor and mentor. Phrasing her supposition as a statement rather than as a question, she said, "You believe the Empress's invitation is a prelude to an assassination attempt."

He gave a brief nod. "I do."

"If you are correct," Saavik said, "do you concede that her decision is logical? You have, after all, orchestrated a coup over Starfleet and usurped a rank that traditionally is appointed by the throne."

Turning to face her, he replied, "I concede that her decision to eliminate me is consistent with her objectives. But as I consider her long-term goal to be untenable, I am forced to conclude that the entirety of her agenda and the actions that she takes to support it are illogical."

"Then the rumors are true," Saavik said. "You intend to challenge her for control of the Empire."

His expression betrayed nothing as he stepped away from her to a nearby table, on which sat a tray that held a ceramic teapot and two low, broad cups of a matching style. He poured a cup of tea, then lifted it and held it out toward Saavik. She walked over and accepted the tea, then returned the gesture by filling the other cup, then offering it to him. He took it from her with a solemn bow of his head. They sipped the bitter libation together. Finally, he said, "Share your thoughts."

Challenging him felt improper; she was a lowly ensign, and he was the supreme military commander of the Empire—at least, he was for the next hour, until his audience with the Empress. His invitation had sounded genuine, however, so she collected her thoughts, then began cautiously. "I am familiar with the predicted future collapse of the Empire," she said. "And I agree that it is not logical to continue expending time, resources, and lives on an entity that we know to be doomed." Growing bolder, she continued. "But I have grave misgivings about your proposed solution, Admiral. Many of your ideas seem laudable for their nobility, but I think they will ultimately prove impractical."

"Should we instead do nothing?" Spock asked.

She put down her tea. "Perhaps your domestic adjustments could be accommodated, with a more graduated timeframe. But your platform of diplomacy and exclusively defensive power as the basis for a new foreign policy strikes me as politically naïve at best, and possibly suicidal at worst."

"And yet, by employing those very tactics within Starfleet, I have amassed more direct support than any officer ever to precede me in this role."

"Enacting reforms within Starfleet is hardly analogous to effecting a total reversal of the Empire's foreign policy."

Setting aside his own tea, he asked, "On what do you base your assumption that our adversaries will reject diplomacy? Or that renouncing wars of choice would provoke them?"

"I have based my arguments on my observations and studies of the Klingons, the Cardassians, and the Romulans as large-scale political actors," Saavik said. "Each is ambitious and highly aggressive. Historically, none of them have been receptive to diplomatic efforts. As for your civil reforms, the regional governors would certainly revolt, and you might lose much of your current support within Starfleet."

He paced slowly away from her and stopped next to a wall in the middle of the cabin. "Put aside what you know, Saavik," he said. "And consider this hypothetical question: If there existed a means by which my power could be assured, and my enemies kept at bay, would you support a more logical approach to the governance of the Empire?"

"Hypothetically?" Arching one eyebrow, she replied, "Yes."

"And if I were to place the fate of the Empire into your hands," he said, "which path would you choose?"

"The one that was the most logical," Saavik said, almost as if by instinct.

With one hand, he beckoned her to him. As she stepped over to join him, he reached up toward an empty trapezoidal frame on his wall. He touched its lower right corner, then its upper right corner. At that, the main panel of the frame slid upward, revealing a small device: just a screen, a few knobs, a keypad, and a single button set apart in a pale, sea-green teardrop of crystal. "This," he said, "is the control apparatus for an alien weapon known as the Tantalus field. With it, the user can track the movements of any person, even from orbit." He activated the device and called up an image of Empress Sato III, in her throne room on Earth. "It can strike even within such protected domains as the imperial palace." He pointed at the various controls. "These are used to switch targets, these are for tracking. And this one"—he pointed at the button inside the teardrop crystal—"fires the weapon. It can eliminate a single target as small as an insect . . . or everyone in a desired zone of effect. To the best of my knowledge, there is no defense."

Saavik stared at the device, transfixed by the macabre genius of it. Undoubtedly, this had been the secret of Spock's swift ascent to power, and the source of the legends about his terrifying psionic gifts. Then she realized that knowing about the Tantalus field might make her a liability to him. "Admiral," she asked carefully, "why are you showing me this?"

"Because, Saavik, when I meet with the Empress, you will have three choices." He stepped close to her, invading her personal space and towering over her. "One: Serve your own agenda—let the imperial guards kill me, then take the Tantalus field device for yourself. Two: Assassinate me yourself, and try to curry favor with the Empress. Or three: Defend me from the Empress, and help me initiate the logical reformation of the Empire. . . . The choice is yours."

It took several seconds before Saavik understood the exact nature of the responsibility Spock had just entrusted to her. He was one of the most powerful men in the Empire, and he was about to make himself infinitely vulnerable to her whim. It was one of the most illogical decisions she had ever seen a Vulcan make. "I do not understand, Admiral," she said. "You would actually *trust me* to remain here, alone with this unspeakably powerful weapon? You would entrust your life . . . to my goodwill?"

"No, Saavik," he replied. "I am entrusting my life to your good judgment. Logic alone should dictate your correct course." He frowned, then continued. "We live in a universe that tends to reward cruelty and self-interest. But I have seen irrefutable evidence that a better way exists—and if our civilization is to endure beyond the next two centuries, we must learn to change."

His assertion fueled her swelling curiosity. "You say you have seen 'irrefutable proof.' What was that proof, Admiral?"

"A mind-meld," he said. "With a human from an alternate universe, one much like our own." He lifted his hand and gently pressed his fingertips against her temple and cheek. "Open your mind to me, and I will share what I have seen."

He had already volunteered so many secrets that Saavik saw no reason for him to lie now about his intentions. She lowered her psionic defenses one layer at a time and gradually permitted his mind to fuse with her own.

And then she saw it.

Flashes of memory, a third mind, fleetingly touched but now forever imprinted in Spock's psyche. Another Doctor McCoy. A man of compassion and mercy. From a Starfleet whose officers don't kill for advancement, but are willing to die to protect each other.

A Federation founded on justice, equality, and peace, and, like the Terran Empire, beset by powerful, dangerous rivals. But unlike the Empire, this Federation amasses its strength by means of consensus and alliances of mutual benefit, and it assuages its wants and its injuries through mutual sacrifice.

Stable. Prosperous. Strong. Free.

Spock withdrew the touch of his mind and his hand, leaving Saavik with the lingering images of the alternate universe. It was no psionic illusion; it was genuine. Just as Spock had said, it was irrefutable. And yet . . . it was not this universe. Its lessons, its ideals—they weren't of this reality. To think that two such divergent universes could belatedly be steered onto the same course struck Saavik as dangerously wishful thinking.

She was still considering her reaction when Spock stepped back from her and said, "The choice is yours." Then he walked away, out the door, to keep his appointment with the Empress.

With a few simple turns and taps of the device's controls, Saavik conjured an image of Spock on its viewer. She watched him stride through the corridors of the *Enterprise,* on his way to the transporter room and not at all resembling a man willingly walking into a trap. *I could eliminate him right now,* she realized, her fingers lightly brushing the outline of the teardrop crystal. *No one would ever know.*

Ultimate power lay in Saavik's hands—and she had less than five minutes to decide what to do with it.

Flanked by a trio of his most trusted Vulcan bodyguards, Spock rematerialized from the transporter beam. He and his men were on the edge of a vast plaza, at the gargantuan arched entryway on the southern side of the imperial palace. The polished titanium of the massive, domed structure reflected the lush green vista of the Okinawa countryside—and the legion of black-and-red-uniformed soldiers standing at attention in formation on the plaza, to Spock's left. He turned and faced the ranks of imperial shock troops. As one, thousands of men brought their fists to their chests, then extended their arms in formal salute. He returned the salute, then turned about-face and entered the palace proper, his guards close behind.

Like so many edifices dedicated to human vanity, the palace was a conspicuous waste of space and resources. Thoroughfares that receded to distant points were bordered by walls that ascended to dizzying heights. From the floors to the lofty arches of the ceiling, the interior of the palace appeared to have been crafted entirely of ornately gilded marble. In contrast to the muggy, hazy summer air outside, the atmosphere inside the palace was crisp and cold and odorless. Heavy doors of carved mahogany lined the cathedral-like passageway, and on either side of every door stood two guards, more imperial shock troops.

A steady flood-crush of pedestrians hurried in crisscrossed paths, all racing from one bastion of bureaucracy to another, bearing urgent missives, relaying orders, coming and going from meetings and appointments. Then a booming voice announced over a central public address system: *"Attention."* The madding throng came to a halt. *"Clear the main passage for Grand Admiral Spock."* As if cleaved by an invisible blade, the crowd parted to form a broad channel through the center of the passageway, and an antigrav skiff glided quickly toward Spock. The pilot was another member of the Imperial Guard. He guided the skiff to a gliding stop in front of Spock, finishing with a slow turn so that the open passenger-side seat faced the grand admiral. "Good morning, sir," he said. "I'm here to escort you to Her Majesty, Empress Sato III." Spock nodded his assent, climbed aboard the skiff, and sat down. His guards occupied the rear bench seat. The vehicle accelerated smoothly, finished its turn, and returned the way it had come. The corridor and the faces that filled it blurred past.

Less than a minute later, the skiff arrived at the towering, duranium doors to the imperial throne room. Waiting there for Spock was his entourage, whose members the Empress had summoned specifically in the more formal invitation she had extended after their last subspace conversation: Lieutenant Commander Kevin Riley, the newly promoted first officer of the *I.S.S. Enterprise;* Lieutenant Xon; Doctor Jabilo M'Benga, who had taken over as the *Enterprise*'s chief medical officer after McCoy's untimely demise due to xenopolycythemia; and chief engineer Commander Montgomery Scott, whose loyalty to the ship, even after being ousted as first officer by former Grand Admiral Decker, had surprised Spock as much as anyone.

Spock and his bodyguards debarked from the skiff. After a curt greeting, he directed his men simply, "Places." He took his own place at the head of their procession, with his bodyguards in tight formation behind him. Riley and Scott formed the next rank behind the guards, followed by Xon and M'Benga. Spock signaled the senior imperial guard that he was ready.

After relaying the message ahead into the throne room, the guard received his orders from his superior, and he turned to face his men. "Open the door and announce the grand admiral."

Resounding clangs, from the release of magnetic locks inside the enormous metal doors, vibrated the marble floor beneath Spock's feet. He lifted his chin proudly but kept his expression neutral. The doors parted and swung inward. Golden radiance from the other side spilled out in long, angled shafts. In a blink of his inner eyelid, his sight adjusted to the luminous appointments of the throne room.

A great fanfare sounded, and a herald stepped in front of the door and faced the throne. "Your Majesty: presenting His Martial Eminence, Grand Admiral Spock, supreme commander of your imperial armed forces." Another fanfare blared as Spock stepped through the doorway, trailed by his retinue.

The imperial court was resplendent with trappings of gold and crimson. Legions of imperial shock troops manned the upper balconies, from which were draped gigantic red-and-gold banners emblazoned with the imperial icon, the Earth impaled on a broadsword, stabbed through the heart by its own martial ambitions. The expansive lower concourse was crowded with courtiers, pages, personal bodyguards, foreign ambassadors, imperial advisers, and members of the cabinet. Several planetary governors also were present, among them Kodos of Tarsus IV, Oxmyx of Sigma

Iotia IV, and Plasus of Ardana. The majority of the guests hovered around the overfilled banquet tables like vultures feasting on a killing field.

Walls covered in damask were lined with portraits of members of the royal family, but none were so commanding in their presence as the ones that were holographically projected behind the throne at the far end of the great hall. Twenty meters high, the trio of high-definition likenesses formed the portrait of a dynasty in the making: Empress Hoshi Sato I, Empress Hoshi Sato II, and Empress Hoshi Sato III—the currently reigning Imperial monarch, who presided from her throne high atop a truncated half-pyramid of stairs, surrounded by another company of her elite guards.

Spock and his retinue marched in solemn strides toward the throne. Quickly, the chaotic crowd formed itself into orderly rows, aligned by rank. Thunderous applause swelled and became almost deafening as Spock continued forward. The Empress and her soldiers, however, remained still and silent.

The broad base of the stairs to the Empress's platform was surrounded by a ten-meter-wide border of obsidian floor panels. Polished to perfection, their glassy black surface reflected Spock's weathered visage with such clarity that he could see every graying whisker in his goatee. It was here that a quartet of imperial guards blocked him and his retinue. The captain of the guard said gruffly, "Grand Admiral Spock: By order of Her Imperial Majesty, from here you proceed alone." Then he motioned for Spock to follow him up the stairs, toward the throne.

Spock passed through the invisible energy barrier that protected the Empress's throne. A galvanic tingle coursed over his skin and bristled the hairs on the back of his hands. Once he was on the other side, he heard a subtle hum, gently rising in tone, as the force field returned to full strength behind him. As he had suspected, a small gap had been opened only long enough to grant him ingress to the Empress's inner circle. Now that he was separated from his bodyguards, they would be unable to intervene when the Empress gave the order for her troops to execute him. Directed-energy weapons, projectiles, and most other forms of ranged armaments could not penetrate the shield in either direction. And because imperial law forbade him from bearing arms into the presence of the Empress, he would have no means of defending himself.

He climbed the stairs without hesitation.

Ten steps from the top, Empress Sato's voice commanded him, "Halt." Spock genuflected before the Empress. "Welcome, Grand Admiral Spock," she continued. "This court is honored by your august presence."

Because she did not bid him rise, he remained on one knee. "It is I who am honored, Your Majesty—by your most gracious invitation, and by the opportunity to serve the Empire as its grand admiral."

Irritation colored her words. "My dear admiral, I believe you have misspoken. You serve me, not the Empire at large. I am your sovereign."

"I acknowledge that you are the sovereign ruler of the Empire," Spock replied. "But I have not misspoken."

Her mouth curled into a smirk, but anger flashed in her eyes. "Your reputation is well earned," she said, her demeanor hostile and mocking. "A 'rogue,' that's what Grand Admiral Decker called you. Before him, Grand Admiral Garth of Izar labeled you a 'radical,' a 'free thinker.' Now I hear rumors that you see yourself as a reformer."

"I have been, remain, and will continue to be all those things," Spock admitted.

She abandoned the artifice of sarcasm and spoke directly. "Your penchant for compromise troubles me, Spock. Negotiation and diplomacy are the tools of the weak."

"Quite the contrary," Spock said. "Only from a position of strength can one afford to offer—"

"Silence!" she snapped. "Having someone of your temperament as grand admiral is a threat to the security of the Empire. It will invite attack by our enemies, both internal and external. How can the Empire be assured of its safety when its supreme military commander is an avowed appeaser of its rivals?"

Looking directly and unabashedly at the Empress, he replied, "Every action I have taken has been grounded in logic. I have never acted to the benefit of our enemies, but only to serve the best interests of the Empire and its people."

Empress Sato III blinked in disbelief, as if he had just committed a grievous faux pas. "The *people*?" she said, with obvious contempt. She rose from her throne and descended the stairs toward him. Her guards advanced quickly behind her, weapons at the ready. "Since when do the *people* matter, Spock? The people are fodder, a source of revenue to be taxed, a pool of raw material to be kept ignorant and afraid until I need them to be angry and swell with pride." With a sneer she added, "The people are *pawns*. Their 'best interests' are irrelevant." She ascended back to the top of the stairs, then turned and glared down at him with all the haughty grandeur that she could muster. "As irrelevant as you, my dear half-breed." Raising her arm, she called out, "Guards!"

Weapons were brought to bear with a heavy clattering sound. Spock kept his attention on the Empress, ignoring the dozens of phaser rifles aimed at his person from every direction.

A flare of light and a crackle of blistering heat. Spock gazed into the blinding brilliance, stoic in the face of sudden annihilation. Then a sharp bite of ozone filled his nose, and a warm breath of air passed over him. He heard the gasps of the crowd beyond the force field. Empress Sato and her company of elite guards were gone. Not a trace of them remained—not scraps of clothing, not ashes, nothing at all. Spock stood, turned, and gazed intently at the legions of guards on the upper balconies. Another massive pulse of pure white incandescence erupted on every balcony, leaving only the silhouettes of skeletons to linger for a moment in the afterglow. Blinks of light stutter-stepped through the crowd in the hall, finding every imperial guard in the throne room. Within seconds, it was over.

For a moment, all anyone below could do was look around in horror, dumbstruck with fright at this invincible blitzkrieg. Then, inevitably, all eyes turned upward, toward Spock.

He turned away from the crowd.

Climbed the stairs.

Seated himself upon the throne.

And he waited.

Then, from far below, outside the protective energy barrier, sounded a man's solitary voice, one that Spock didn't recognize, repeating his lonely declaration in the echoing vastness of the great hall, until his voice was joined by another, then by several more, and finally by the booming roar of a crowd chanting fervently and in unison.

All hail Emperor Spock!

With two gentle touches of Saavik's hand, the panel slid closed over the Tantalus field device's control panel. Seemingly unperturbed by the momentous and pivotal role she had just played in the fate of the Empire, she walked calmly out of Spock's quarters. The door hissed closed and locked behind her.

Concealed behind a false panel in the bulkhead opposite the secret weapon, Marlena Moreau breathed a tired sigh. She was greatly relieved to know that Saavik was loyal to Spock. It would make it easier for her to trust the young Vulcan woman from now on. If the targeting cursor of the Tantalus field had fallen for even a moment upon Spock's image, Marlena had been ready to strike instantly, a phaser set on kill steady in her hand. Though she was now ashamed that she had doubted Spock's judgment about his protégée, she was still frightened by his willingness to trust other people too much. She loved and admired his idealism even as she cursed its inherent risks.

Marlena emerged from behind the panel. Over the years, she had gradually become accustomed to the higher temperatures and gravity inside the quarters that she shared with Spock. The aridity, however, continued to vex her, so she tried to limit the time she spent there, preferring to pass her free hours in the ship's library or its astrometrics laboratory.

She eyed her reflection in the wall mirror and was able to tell herself honestly that, so far, the years had been kind to her. Spock, on the other hand, was already showing signs of the extreme stress inflicted by his rapid campaign to seize control over Starfleet. Now, less than a week after that decades-long effort had come to fruition, he had succeeded in placing himself upon the imperial throne. He was the Emperor.

Everything was changed now. Marlena could only imagine the toll that reigning over an interstellar empire would take on her beloved husband, and she feared for his health . . . and for his life. There were bound to be operatives loyal to the Sato Dynasty who would seek retribution. Even with the Tantalus field, how could she and Spock hope to find and eliminate them all? It seemed impossible.

We will find a way, she promised herself. *We have to.*

A thought occurred to her. She pulled open her closet and surveyed its contents. Dismayed, she realized that Spock's great achievement had caught her totally unprepared. *Damn. Fifty outfits to choose from . . . and not one is even remotely good enough.* She shut the closet. *I'm not ready to be an empress yet.*

In two regal strides, she was at the wall panel. With a push of her thumb she opened a channel to the bridge. Moments later, she was answered by Lieutenant Finney, whose youthful voice shook with a new undercurrent of fear. *"Bridge here."*

"This is the Empress Consort," she said, liking the sound of it as soon as she'd said it. "Have the imperial tailors sent to my quarters immediately."

"Right away, Your Majesty," Finney said, sounding like a scolded child. *"Bridge out."*

Despite her best efforts at equanimity, a slightly insane smile and wide-eyed mask of glee took over Marlena's face. Even after catching sight of her Cheshire cat grin in the mirror, she couldn't suppress it.

Just as she'd always suspected, it was good to be queen.

6

The Designs of Liberty

It had been slightly more than two months since Spock claimed the throne, and the ensuing cavalcade of pomp and pageantry had only just subsided. First had come the official coronation, followed by more than a hundred hastily dispatched state visits by the Empire's various planetary governors, each of whom had come to deliver gifts and pledges of loyalty, all of which Spock had accepted with politely concealed indifference. His thoughts had been occupied almost constantly by the intricate and politically delicate task of transitioning the imperial government to a new administration, one populated from its highest echelons down with reformers whom Spock had painstakingly cultivated as allies over the past decade.

As Spock had suspected, his wife had adapted easily and enthusiastically to her new role as Empress Marlena. To her care he had entrusted the coordination of the cosmetic overhaul of the government. For the most part, that had entailed removing the outrageously oversized holographic portraits in the throne room and minimizing their physical counterparts on the walls. Other, more radical alterations he had discussed with her would have to wait until the Empire's political climate was ready.

One element of imperial life remained constant during the

abrupt transition to Spock's reign, and that was the apparent mood of constant, muffled terror that suffused the halls of the palace. Even without the benefit of his spies' reports, Spock could overhear the whispered rumors, the hushed exchanges of frightened eyewitness accounts describing the manner in which the Empress Hoshi Sato III and her Imperial Guard corps had been annihilated. A few people had guessed, correctly, that an unknown weapon had been involved, but by far the most persistent and popular explanation was that Spock had used an ancient, formerly secret Vulcan psionic attack to seize power.

Encouraging untruths ran counter to the principles of logic, but in this case Spock permitted the rumors to spread unchallenged as a means of securing his power base during this vulnerable period of transition.

For his own part, Spock found life in the imperial palace to be quiet, comfortable, and opulently boring. The oversized chambers and furniture all offended his simpler, more austere sensibilities. The illogic of waste had been a primary factor in his decision to seek dominion over the Empire, and now he lived in the midst of the most ostentatious expression of wastefulness imaginable. The irony of his circumstances was not lost on him.

Clad in luxurious robes of Tholian silk, he stood on the force field–protected balcony outside his personal suite and looked upon the verdant countryside of Okinawa. The dawn air was cool. Despite his half-human heritage, this land, this world, felt alien to him. He was, in essence, a stranger here.

Behind him, inside the bedroom, Marlena slept blissfully behind the gauzy screens of the antique French canopied bed. Earth was her home. She had been born here, the youngest child of a common merchant. But though her family's origins had been modest, her homecoming had been nothing less than glorious.

A deep chiming signal indicated that Spock's staff wished to announce a visitor. He turned and watched the double doors that led to the parlor. They opened several seconds later, and a herald entered. "Your Majesty," he said, then briefly bowed his head. "Ambassador Sarek of Vulcan is here at your invitation."

"Show him into the study," Spock said. "I will join him there momentarily."

"As you command, Your Majesty," the herald said and withdrew in reverse, closing the bedroom doors as he exited.

Spock closed his eyes and meditated in silence for a few minutes, clearing his thoughts and preparing himself for the meeting with his father. Each breath was a cleansing intake and release, and the tension that attended the rulership of the empire gradually ebbed from his muscles. At last centered in his own thoughts, he allowed himself a solitary, sentimental glance in Marlena's direction before he left the bedroom.

He crossed through the parlor and passed the library on the way to his study. The shelves of the library were currently bare; Spock had found the Satos' collection of references and literature to be woefully inadequate, not to mention pedestrian and out of date. Thousands of more recent, and more worthy, tomes had been ordered and were due to be delivered within the week. Marlena had callously suggested simply burning the Satos' books, but the idea was anathema to Spock. Destroying books was out of the question. Instead, he had arranged for the Satos' volumes to be relocated somewhere more appropriate. It was doubtful that anyone would randomly stumble across them buried in a crater on Luna, but Spock knew that it wasn't impossible.

The doors of the study were open. Sarek stood opposite the entrance, in front of the antique writing desk. He bowed his head as Spock entered. "Your Majesty," Sarek said with all sincerity. "I am honored to be received."

"Welcome, Ambassador," Spock said. "We are alone. We may dispense with formalities."

Sarek nodded. "As you wish." Gesturing to a pair of large chairs on either side of a low, broad table, he added, "Shall we sit down?"

Spock nodded his assent and sat down opposite his father, who took a small holographic projection cell from his robes and set it on the table. The device activated with a small buzzing sound, and a complex document, written in High Vulcan, scrolled in glowing letters on the air, several centimeters above the dark tabletop. "Before we begin," Sarek said, "I wish to ask: Are you still committed to your plan of reform?"

"Indeed," Spock said. "My objective remains the same."

Nodding, Sarek explained, "You would not be the first head of state to amend his agenda after taking office." He sighed. "No matter. If you are ready, we should proceed."

"Agreed," Spock said.

His father leaned forward and manipulated the elements in the holographic projection with his fingertips. "The key to a successful transition will be to effect your reforms by degrees," he said. "A shrewd first move would be to increase the autonomy and direct control of the regional governors."

Moving a few items along the timeline, Spock replied, "An excellent idea. The erosion of imperial executive power will be subtle, but the governors will not object because they benefit."

"Exactly," Sarek said. "And it will pave the way for your first major reform: the creation of a Common Forum, for popularly elected representatives from each world in the Empire. You should expect the governors to object vehemently to this."

"Of course," Spock said. "It will be a direct affront to their authority. I presume that I will pretend to appease them by suggesting they appoint their own representatives to the newly reconstituted Imperial Senate."

"It will mollify them briefly," Sarek acknowledged. "Granting authority for drafting legislation to both the Forum and the Senate will turn them into rivals for power."

"And they will vie for my approval by drafting competing bills," Spock predicted. "I will then censure both for wasting my time with duplicated efforts, and force them to work together by declaring that I will only review legislation that they have approved jointly."

After a moment's thought, Sarek replied, "A curious tactic." He adjusted more items in the complex predictive timeline. "You will give them incentive to align against you."

"Yes," Spock said. "Fortunately, the conflicts in their interests will make that difficult for them." He pointed out another item on the timeline. "I should retain plenary executive authority long enough to liberate the imperial judiciary into a separate but equal branch of government."

Sarek made a few final changes to the timeline, then looked up at Spock. "With your permission, I should like to turn now to matters of foreign policy." Spock nodded his consent. Sarek touched a control on the holographic emitter and changed the image above the table to another timeline, this one superimposed over a star chart of local space. "Your proposition of détente as an official platform for imperial policy still troubles me."

He had expected his father's reservations, and was prepared to address them. "Nonaggression does not equal surrender, Sarek. We will continue to defend our borders from external threats. Only our approach to the growth and maintenance of the Empire will change." Pointing to the map, he continued. "A diplomatic invitation convinced Coridan to join the Empire of its own accord. Renouncing conquest and annexation as our chief modes of expansion will earn us the trust of more worlds, and enable us to expand by enticement rather than by extortion."

Spock waited while Sarek mulled that argument. The older man got up from his chair and paced across the room, then behind the desk, where he stood looking out the window for a minute. When he finally turned back toward Spock, his expression was darkened with concern. He spoke with careful diction, as if vetting each word's nuance before it passed his lips. "Spock, I have supported your call for reforms, because I know that they are necessary. However, the subtext of your recent proposals compels me to inquire: Is there more to your long-term plan than you have told me?"

"Yes, Father," Spock said. "The true scope of my reforms is more drastic than I have said so far."

Raising one eyebrow to convey both his skepticism and his annoyance, Sarek prompted him, "Go on."

"Preemptive war will be renounced as an instrument of policy," Spock said.

Sarek nodded. "I had assumed as much."

"Before I begin my final reforms, I will issue an imperial edict delineating a broad spectrum of inalienable rights for all sentient beings in the Empire," Spock said. "These rights will be comprehensive and will serve to greatly empower the individual at the expense of the state." He pointed at a data slate on the desktop. "A draft of the edict is there."

His father picked up the data slate and perused the document. With each passing moment, his grimace tightened, and the creases of worry on his forehead deepened. "Freedom of expression," he mumbled, reading from the device in his hand. "Rights of privacy . . . security from warrantless search or seizure." He set down the electronic tablet on the desk. "The governors will not stand for this."

"Irrelevant," Spock said, "as I intend to abolish their offices and replace them with elected presidents, their powers curtailed by law. Then, I will abolish the Empire itself. The Forum and the Senate will be given the right to elect one of their own as Consul, and the power to remove such an individual with a simple no-confidence vote when necessary. And at that time, I shall step down as Emperor, and cede my power to a lawfully constituted republic."

"Madness," Sarek said, his cherished mask of stoicism faltering. Spock realized that his father's anger and fear must be overwhelming for them to be so apparent. Stepping from behind the desk, Sarek crossed the room in quick strides to confront Spock. "My son, do you not see this is a recipe for disaster?" Disregarding all dictums of imperial protocol, he grasped Spock by his arms. "A republic without strong leadership from the top will be too slow to survive in this astropolitical arena. While the Forum argues, the Klingons will slaughter us. So will the Romulans, the Cardassians, the Tholians." His fingers clenched, talonlike, on Spock's biceps. "You will be writing the Empire's requiem with the blood of generations to come, Spock. What good will their freedoms be when they are dead?"

A single withering glare from Spock convinced Sarek to remove his hands from the arms of his son, the Emperor.

Spock answered calmly, with the conviction that came from knowing the endgame that so far had eluded even Sarek's keen foresight. "There is only one antidote to tyranny, Father, and that is freedom. Not the illusion of freedom, not the promise of freedom. Genuine freedom. When too much power concentrates in one person, civilization slips out of balance. Give the people real freedom, and the real power that comes with it, and no force of oppression will ever be equal to them again."

Sarek folded his hands together inside the deep, drooping sleeves of his robe. He paced away from Spock, his expression stern and telegraphing his pessimism. "It will take many decades to complete even your preliminary reforms," he said. "As for issuing your edict and erecting a republic on the ruins of the Empire . . . such fundamental changes in the status quo will take generations to enact."

"They cannot," Spock said gravely. "We do not have that much time."

Part II

Sic Transit Imperium

2284

7

Hearts and Minds

The echoes of Spock's voice faded away into the vastness of
the Common Forum, and for a moment stretched by anticipation, all was silent. He had delivered his proclamation of citizens' rights, uninterrupted, to a sea of stunned faces. It was done
now, and it could not be undone, and there was naught to do but
wait in the heavy swell of anxious quietude for the reaction.

A roar of applause surged up from the members of the Forum,
a wave of sound like floodwater breaking against a dam. Exultant
and energized, the thousands of gathered representatives from
worlds throughout the Empire stood and applauded and chanted
his name with almost-idolatrous fervor. Stomping feet rumbled
the hall, which once had been the imperial throne room. Its
lower level now was packed on three sides with tiers of seats for
the Forum members, and its spacious balconies had been con-
verted to a gallery for citizen observers, or for the Senate during
joint sessions of the Legislature such as this one.

In the balconies above, faces grim and forbidding communi-
cated the Senate's reaction. Like mannequins of stone, its members looked down with ashen-faced horror at the populist turn
their government had just taken. A few shook their heads in disbelief. Spock presumed that they were unable to comprehend

why he would have chosen to give more power to the citizenry than to himself. In all likelihood, he knew, they would never understand. Regardless, the one power that Spock still reserved for himself was that his word carried the absolute force of law.

He let the applause wash over him for a moment, not because he enjoyed it but because it would help cement this moment in the minds of those hundreds of billions of citizens throughout the Empire who would be watching it on the subspace feed. This was a threshold moment for their society, and he knew that it would be important for them to have the requisite time to absorb its full importance. Nearly two minutes elapsed as the cheering and applause continued unabated. Sensing that the moment had run its course, Spock bowed his head to the Legislature. As thousands of arms were extended in salutary reply, he withdrew from the podium in the center of the Forum and departed, surrounded by his elite Vulcan guard, through the rear exit.

Marlena was waiting for him in the turbolift, which carried them to their private residence on the uppermost level. She clutched his arm tenderly. "You were magnificent," she said softly. He glanced in her direction and saw her smile.

"Most kind," he said, his old habit of understated humility intact despite more than seven years of imperial privilege.

The turbolift doors opened, and they exited to their airy, sunlit residence. Sarek stood in the doorway to their parlor, flanked by two more of the elite Vulcan guards. "Your address went well," Sarek said as Spock and Marlena passed him.

"As well as could be expected," Spock replied over his shoulder to Sarek, who followed him into the parlor.

The guards closed the double doors behind Sarek, giving Spock at least a modicum of privacy with his wife and father. Marlena and Spock sat next to one another in matching, heavy wooden chairs. Sarek sat to Spock's right, at the corner of a long sofa. All three of them were aware of the servants hovering just out of sight at all times, and they kept their voices low. "You've won the hearts of the people," Sarek said. "But the elites are already conspiring against you."

"Enemies are a consequence of politics," Spock said.

Folding his hands in his lap, Sarek replied, "Your reign will not last forever, Spock. The most probable consequence of your latest action is that you will be assassinated by someone acting on behalf of your political opponents."

"I am aware of my rivals' ambitions," Spock said. He motioned a servant to come closer as he continued. "However, I do not consider them to be a risk." A female servant gracefully and unobtrusively took her place in front of the trio. To her, Spock said, "*Plasska* tea, service for three." With a genteel murmur of "Yes, Your Majesty," the servant slipped away.

Sarek waited until the woman was well out of earshot before he spoke. "Spock, the threat posed by your rivals is not a trivial one. If you are killed or deposed, your progressive regime will almost certainly be replaced by one of a decidedly reactionary temperament."

The cool demeanors of the two Vulcan men made Marlena's undercurrent of anger all the more palpable by comparison. "His assassins will not succeed," she said forcefully to Sarek. "I will see to that."

Expressing his incredulity with one raised eyebrow, Sarek asked, "And how will you do that, my dear? With what resources?"

"I am not without means, Sarek," she retorted hotly. "This would not be the first—" Spock silenced her outburst with a gentle press of his palm on the back of her hand. Marlena took his admonition to heart and pursed her lips while suppressing the rest of what she had intended to say.

It was Spock's opinion that Sarek need never be told of the Tantalus field device, or of the role it had played in Spock's assumption of power. It had been a terrible risk revealing its existence to Saavik, but his long-term plans for her had made it crucial to test her loyalty as early as possible.

Silence reigned over the parlor until the tea was delivered and poured. All three of them sipped from their cups, and nodded their approval to themselves. Then Sarek set down his cup and, once again with a conspirator's hushed voice, continued the conversation. "Let us assume," he said, "that your wife is correct, and that assassins pose no threat to you. Even if you succeed in your goal of abolishing the Empire, once you place its fate into the hands of a representative government, it will almost certainly be corrupted from within. The Senate will be first among those looking to consolidate their power; they will learn how to manipulate popular sentiment and fill the Common Forum with their own partisans. Gradually at first, then more boldly, they will steer the republic back toward totalitarianism. Ultimately, they will elect one of their own as dictator-for-life . . . and the Empire you are laboring to end will be reborn. The rights you granted to the people will be revoked; they will resist, and rebel, and be brutally suppressed. Civil war will rend the Empire, and its enemies will exploit that division to conquer us outright. All that you have done will have been for naught, my son."

Spock finished his own tea and set down the empty cup. "All that you predict, I have anticipated," he said. Leaning back in his chair, he continued. "That is why the republic must be destroyed by its enemies *before* it lapses back into empire."

The statement seemed to perplex Sarek. "What beneficial end would that accomplish?"

"Liberty crushed by one's own government carries the poison of betrayal," Spock said. "If so extinguished, it will be almost impossible to rekindle, and our cause shall be lost. But freedom lost to conquest focuses the people's anger outward, and unites them in common cause against a foreign oppressor."

"You intend to let the republic fall?" Sarek asked. Upon Spock's nod of confirmation, he continued. "A dangerous gamble. What if such a rebellion fails to materialize? Or simply fails? Staking the future of our civilization on the success of an insurgency seems a most foolish proposition."

As Spock rose from his chair, Sarek did likewise. Spock turned toward Marlena. "Will you excuse us a moment?" Marlena cast wary looks at both Spock and Sarek, then got up and walked with prideful calm from the parlor. Once she was in the next room, and the door closed behind her, Spock said loudly, for the servants lurking in the wings, "Leave us." Like spooked mice, the domestics scurried away. A clatter of closing doors marked their exits. Able to speak in full privacy at last, Spock still whispered. "Steps will be taken to ensure the success of the rebellion," he said. "The groundwork for an insurgency will be laid now, while we have time to prepare in safety. If my plan is successful, the Klingon-led occupation of the former Terran Empire will last fewer than one hundred fifteen Earth years."

With unconcealed suspicion, Sarek said, "And if it fails?"

"Then several millennia of Vulcan and human scientific achievement will be lost forever."

"And what are these steps you're going to take?"

"Not I," Spock said. "You."

8

Omega's Genesis

After living seven years as a virtual prisoner in the imperial residence, Emperor Spock appreciated the luxury of returning to a starship. Recent refits had made them faster, more comfortable, and more powerful than ever before.

At his behest, the *Enterprise,* now in its seventh year under the command of Captain Kevin Riley, had been standing by to beam up Spock from the palace after his meeting with Sarek. With the Empire devolving into chaos following his declaration of rights and freedoms for the people, it had seemed like an opportune time to slip away. During his absence, Marlena would reign as Empress, freeing him to make this journey incognito.

Liberating as his departure was, it carried an element of risk that he hadn't faced in close to seventeen years. For the first time since he had slain Captain Kirk, he was without the protection of the Tantalus field device, which remained safely concealed in his and Marlena's private quarters on Earth. Fortunately, the judicious use of the device over the years had cultivated such a profound culture of fear with respect to Spock's purported psionic powers that it was unlikely he would be challenged during this brief sojourn from the throne.

The bosun's whistle sounded over the ship's intercom.

"Attention, all hands. Stand by for secure transport. Captain Riley, please report to the bridge."

As the channel closed, the door signal buzzed. Turning to face the door, Spock said, "Enter."

The door slid open, and the ship's first officer, Commander Saavik, stepped inside. "Your Majesty," she said with a reverent bow of her head, then she looked up and delivered the formal salute. He noted that she avoided making eye contact with him, and her demeanor seemed stiff.

"At ease," he told his former protégée. "Is it time?"

"Yes, Majesty," she said. "The facility has been prepared, and a secure transport conduit is standing by."

"Then let us proceed," he said. Saavik nodded and led the way out the door into the corridor. Spock followed her. A pair of his elite Vulcan bodyguards fell into step a few paces behind him. Moving until he was almost parallel with Saavik, he said in a confidential tone, "You seem preoccupied."

"Not at all, Majesty," she said as she stepped into an open and waiting turbolift car. He and his guards followed her in.

The ride was brief. As soon as they stepped off, into another empty, sealed-off corridor, Spock subtly signaled his guards to fall back a few paces to give him privacy. "You are uncomfortable with the proclamation I made on Earth."

"I've said no such—"

"Prevarication does not suit you," he interrupted. "Speak plainly. I would know your thoughts."

Her apprehension was palpable. She eyed him with guarded suspicion. "Do I address the Emperor?"

"You address your mentor, and your Academy sponsor."

That seemed to reassure her. Glancing over her shoulder to make certain the bodyguards would not overhear her, she whispered to Spock, "Undermining your own power was an error."

Her assertion intrigued him. "How so?"

They turned a corner toward the transporter room. "The Empire and its ruler are one," she said. "By diminishing yourself, you diminish the Empire. You invite conquest."

"Which is stronger, Saavik? One man, or ten men?" He let the analogy sink in for a few seconds, then, before she could answer, he continued. "An empire that derives its strength and authority from one person alone is weak, because its foundation is too narrow. One whose power derives from the mutual consent of the many rests upon a broad and unshakable base."

"Which is stronger, Your Majesty? A sheet of metal foil twenty meters square, or the blade of the knife that slices through it?" She paused a few meters shy of the transporter room door, and Spock and his guards halted with her. "Diffusing the power of the Empire throughout its people robs it of focus," she added. "A quality that our enemies possess in abundance."

Spock considered her point for a few seconds. "When our enemies choose to conquer us," he said, "they will succeed. And it will be their undoing." At that, he stepped ahead of her and led the way into the transporter room. An engineer manned the transporter console, and another pair of Spock's elite guards stood at attention, awaiting his arrival. He stepped onto the platform, accompanied by the two guards who had followed him through the corridors.

Saavik stood between Spock and the transporter operator. Arching one eyebrow, she asked, "Majesty, do you really believe that conquering us would cause the fall of the Klingon Empire?"

With perfect surety, he replied, "It is inevitable."

Then, with a nod, the order was given, and Spock and his guards vanished into the white haze of the transporter beam.

Doctor Carol Marcus paced nervously inside the storage bay, awaiting the arrival of the most important VIP guest in the Empire. *Don't panic,* she kept telling herself. *It's a good proposal, he's a Vulcan, he'll see that what you're asking for is logical. . . . Don't panic.*

The transporter effect shimmered into existence just a few

meters away from her. She froze in place and watched three Vulcanoid shapes materialize, one in front and two behind. As the sparkling glow faded away, she found herself face-to-face with Emperor Spock, the supreme ruler of the Terran Empire.

Though she had been taught as a child how to curtsey, she had never had any need to do so until this moment—and suddenly she found herself awkwardly wobbling over her own crossed feet. "Your Majesty," she said while looking at the floor. "Welcome to Regula I."

Spock stepped toward her. "Thank you, Doctor Marcus." He looked around at their immediate surroundings. "Based on your preliminary report, I presume that *this* is not the second phase of your project."

"Certainly not," Marcus said, before adding belatedly, "Your Majesty." The Emperor's classically aloof Vulcan nature made it hard for her to tell if he was annoyed with her. She gestured toward the exit from this terminal chamber, which was located at the end of a long service corridor. "May I guide you through the rest of the facility?"

"By all means," he said.

They left the storage bay, their footsteps echoing crisply in the empty space. Indicating the drab, gray surfaces of the corridor, she noted, "It took the Imperial Corps of Engineers nine months to excavate the preliminary facility. Though it was a costly and time-consuming project, it was essential to—"

"I read your proposal for Project Genesis, Doctor," he said as they neared a T-shaped intersection. "It is not necessary for you to reiterate its contents."

Concealing her embarrassment, she replied, "Of course not, Your Majesty. My apologies. Obviously, you just want to know whether phase two was a success." At the intersection she turned to the right, then stopped and pivoted back to face Spock. "Well . . . you tell me."

The Emperor turned the corner and looked out upon Doctor Marcus's handiwork. True to his Vulcan heritage and his personal reputation, he showed no sign of surprise at the verdant splendor of the Genesis Cave. Kilometers across, the roughly ovoid excavation was teeming with vegetation. Ferns and fronds carpeted the lower half of the space, which was thick with stands of jungle trees whose branches were heavy with fruit. Flowers of variegated colors dotted the periphery of the enclosure at seemingly random intervals. Mist hung in gauzy layers, refracting light from the artificial solar generators in an adjacent cave, on the far side from where Marcus and Spock now stood. Off to the right, in the distance, an enormous waterfall cascaded in snowy plumes over jagged rocks, its wholly natural appearance a testament to its meticulous engineering.

"It's self-contained and self-sustaining," she said. "All except the solar generators, which will need to be refueled every sixty years." She waited for a reaction from Spock, but none came. "In transforming this limited volume of inanimate matter, the Genesis Wave was completely successful," she continued. "But to assess its full potential, we need to move on to phase three: a lifeless, geologically inactive planetoid. For that, we'll need an increase in our funding, and the services of an Imperial starship, to help us seek out an appro—"

"No," Spock said.

His answer caught her completely off guard. "Excuse me?"

"Your request for funding and operational support is denied."

She folded her arms and reminded herself not to raise her voice. Though Spock had seemed to be a benign and compassionate sovereign so far, she remained keenly aware that he was still the Emperor—and that he could make her disappear with a single word. "May I ask why, Your Majesty?"

"For the same reason that I terminated Operation Vanguard— what you propose is too dangerous. If I allow you to carry out your third-phase test, it will provoke an arms race and prematurely ignite our inevitable conflict with the Klingon Empire."

She knew he was right; the only reason she had dared to continue her work to this stage at all was because, unlike the opportunistic and belligerent Empress Sato III, Emperor Spock gave every indication of being a leader who would wield a power such as the Genesis Device wisely.

"But think of the potential, Your Majesty," she said, unable to give up on a project that had consumed the past fourteen years of her life. "We could transform dead worlds into new class-M planets. We wouldn't have to compete with the Klingons for habitable worlds anymore."

"I am aware of its potential, Doctor, but the risks it carries are too great." He turned his head and looked again at the cave. "How many people will this facility support?"

Still reeling from the rejection, it took Marcus a moment to answer. "Indefinitely? Perhaps a hundred. Why?"

"Because I want you to duplicate phase two of your project in a number of other sites throughout the Empire—sites whose locations will be known only to the two of us and to a handful of people who will be permanently attached to them."

She was confused now. "I thought you said you were terminating Project Genesis."

"I am," Spock said. "But your work will not go to waste. I need it—and you—for an infinitely more important project."

Alarmed but curious, she asked, "What kind of project?"

Spock met her questioning stare with his dark, hypnotic gaze. He replied somberly, "The future of our civilization."

2286

9

A World in Transition

Fingers brush across Lotok's graying temple. Thoughts, half formed, whisper from mind to mind, conveyed with equal parts urgency and discretion. Contact is fleeting and subtle, all but imperceptible, its gift unremarked, its purpose unquestioned. The mind-meld ends, and he looks at his grandson, Kerok; now they are co-conspirators, and there is much work to do.

Another dusky sunrise in ShiKahr, the cinnamon daybreak of dawn on Vulcan. Volkar rouses T'Len, his seven-year-old daughter, for school; their hands touch. He brushes a hair from her cheek. In a moment he shares the secret of a lifetime. Looking upon her sire with new eyes, T'Len understands.

Spock is summoning the future, and we must be ready for it.

A sullen storm front churns on the horizon, a dark stain on the crimson sky. Salok, a tenth-year *Kolinahr* adept, stands on a ledge near the peak of Mount Seleya. The crash of a far-off gong calls him to meditation. His walk across the bridge is long; his only companion is the wind, howling in minor chords, warm and rich with the clean smells of the deep desert.

In the Halls of Ancient Thought, he is handed his ceremonial sash. As the high priest lowers it into Salok's hands, they make contact. In between two more crashes of the gong, Salok sees the truth, shared by Emperor Spock with Sarek and passed on to a thousand more minds since: a vision of another universe, an incontrovertible mental image of a universe both like and unlike his own. The knowledge comes with a price: a call to arms.

Salok is ready.

Rebellion. It's an idea, a concept, a meme.

Viruslike, it travels and seeks receptive hosts, vessels who will carry it, nurture it, spread it.

Freedom. It is contagious in its simplicity, incendiary in its potential, complicated and inherently contradictory. Logic demands it; without the freedom to explore new thoughts and new ideas, knowledge cannot advance; without intellectual freedom, civilization stagnates. Progress halts. Hope dies.

It is only the germ of an idea. But it is spreading.

L'Haan is a defender of the peace, a law enforcement officer, and until three days ago she had held no other loyalty than to the Empire. Then the Emperor's vision of the future touched her mind. Today she realizes the Empire is doomed, and that Emperor Spock's dangerous vision is the way of tomorrow.

Her first duty now is to the people of Vulcan—and to the future. Time is short, and there are many minds to reach. Already she has encountered several who are already part of the movement. It is reassuring to know who her allies are, but theirs is an evangelical cause. Success will be measured not in the depth of their personal commitment but in their ability to recruit others. And so she continues to search, to seek out those individuals who seem most likely to sympathize with Spock's plan for the future.

She sees the man she has been looking for. His name is V'Nem. He is a professor at the Vulcan Science Academy, known for being slightly unorthodox. Statistically speaking, he is likely to be a receptive candidate for The Touch.

L'Haan concocts an excuse to detain him for just a moment. She demands to see what he has hidden in the folds of his loose desert robe. Predictably, he resists, citing the new imperial guarantees against warrantless search and seizure. It's a flimsy pretext for her to accuse him of resisting arrest, but it will do. She grabs his wrist for only a moment, long enough to reach out and try to make contact with his thoughts, to tell him to remain calm, that he is in no danger—

He is a Romulan. An infiltrator. A spy.

V'Nem reaches for a concealed weapon.

L'Haan attacks, a knifing blow of her stiffened hand against V'Nem's neck, which snaps instantly. His head lolls toward the ground, a limp and heavy mass with dull eyes. She releases his wrist and lets his body fall into the street.

A crowd gathers. There will be an inquiry, but even after Spock's legal reforms she still has the power of authority, the protection of being an officer of the law. In short order she will be vindicated, even applauded for exposing and disposing of a Romulan agent. The attention this will bring her will prevent her from spreading Spock's message for a few weeks, or longer.

This was a mistake of youthful inexperience, she knew. *In the future, I must be more circumspect in my actions.*

T'Meri slips out of her dormitory at the Vulcan Science Academy and steals away into the dark predawn hours. Halfway across the city, the young Vulcan woman finds her way to an unmarked door below street level. She does not knock; instead she scrapes her boot against the base of the door for a few seconds, then stands where she knows the security camera can see her clearly. The rust-mottled portal opens with fluid ease and surprisingly little noise. She slips inside, and the door is shut quickly after her.

T'Prynn is waiting for her. The older Vulcan woman is ex-Starfleet and, from what few fleeting personal glimpses T'Meri has had of T'Prynn's mind, privy to many terrible secrets. But the one that she has shared most vividly with T'Meri is the one she received, through a long chain of psychic transfer, of Emperor Spock's mind-meld with the man from the alternate universe. She has imparted the vision to T'Meri so that she can seek out others sympathetic to Spock's aims and pass it along to them, with the same directive. T'Meri has done exactly that.

She reaches up toward T'Prynn's face and gently rests her fingertips against the woman's smooth, pale skin. In turn, T'Prynn's fingers press delicately upon the side of T'Meri's bronze-hued face. Their minds touch, and T'Meri shows T'Prynn all the minds to whom she has conveyed Spock's message. T'Prynn is pleased—then she breaks the psychic link.

T'Meri opens her eyes and finds her face and T'Prynn's only a few centimeters apart. Their lips are parted and trembling with anticipation. The sensations are a mystery to T'Meri, whose next *Pon farr* is still four years away—until she realizes that T'Prynn is hiding the fires of her own desire, and that some of that ardor has been transferred in the mind-meld.

The urge to kiss the older woman is overpowering, and as T'Meri searches her thoughts, she realizes that, in fact, T'Prynn desires her. *Burns* for her.

She feels the heat of T'Prynn's breath inside her mouth, mingling with her own, but all she can think about is the fact that, despite Governor Sarek's attempts at liberal social reforms, Vulcan's laws—preserved for thousands of years by the Council of Elders at Mount Seleya—forbid her and T'Prynn from succumbing to their true natures.

T'Prynn's lips graze T'Meri's.

Surrendering to the swell of passion lingering from their mind-meld, T'Meri returns T'Prynn's kiss and gives herself over to a woman more than three times her age. T'Prynn is voracious in her desire, primal in her way of touching, almost savage in the way she removes T'Meri's garments.

We are already conspiring to help destroy the Empire, T'Meri rationalizes between desperate, fumbling gropes as T'Prynn pulls her toward a bed. *We are already criminals.*

2288

Men of Long Knives

Every warrior in the Great Hall could smell the scent of blood. The Terran Empire was starting to flounder, its Emperor Spock shedding power and control the way a gelded *targ* sheds fur. At long last, the greatest enemy of the Klingon Empire was faltering; it was time to strike.

All that remained now was to decide who would strike, with what forces, where, when, and how. This debate, unfortunately, was dragging on late into the night, and Councillor Gorkon was growing weary of the bickering. Regent Sturka—the latest warrior to hold the throne for Kahless, He Who Shall Return— looked haggard and sullen as Councillors Duras and Indizar argued while circling each other inside the small pool of harsh light in the middle of the Council chamber.

"You Imperial Intelligence types are all the same," Duras said with a sneer. "*Infiltrate* the Terrans, *sabotage* them, conquer them *by degrees.*" Lifting his voice to an aggrieved bellow, he added, "Where's the glory in that?"

Keeping one hand on her *d'k tahg,* Indizar replied with a voice like the low growl of a Kryonian tiger. "It's smarter than your way, Duras. You'd plunge us headlong into full-scale war with the largest fleet in known space. We might emerge victorious, but at what cost? Our fleet would be savaged, our borders weakened. The Romulans would overrun us the moment we finished off the Terrans. . . . Of course, maybe that's your *real* plan, isn't it, Duras?"

Duras's eyes were wide with fury. "You dare call me a traitor?" His hand went for his own *d'k tahg*—

Sharp, echoing cracks. One, two, three. Everyone looked at Sturka, who ceased smashing the steel-clad tip of his staff on the stone floor. "Both of you get out of the circle," he commanded Indizar and Duras. Then, to the others, he said, "I want to hear realistic strategies. Honest assessments." He looked at Gorkon, who had served for more than twenty years as Sturka's most trusted adviser, and who had thwarted an attempt by the late Councillor Kesh to seize the throne for himself. "Have Spock's reforms weakened the Terrans' defenses," Sturka asked, "or merely damaged his own political security?"

Stepping out of the crowd into the heat and glare of the circle, Gorkon gripped the edges of his black leather stole, which rested over a studded, red leather chimere; worn together, the two ceremonial vestments marked him unmistakably as the second-highest-ranking individual in the chamber. "The Terran Empire," he began in a stately tone, "is still far too strong for us to risk a direct military engagement." Before the rising murmur of grumbles got out of control, Gorkon reasserted his control over the discussion. "However, the reforms instituted by their current sovereign hold the promise of future opportunities." He began a slow walk along the edge of the circle of light, using his time to size up the commitment of both his rivals and his allies on the Council. "Emperor Spock has made significant reductions in military spending, with many deep cuts in the field of weapons research and development." He paused as he returned the steely glare of Duras, then moved on. "This will give us a chance to finally take the lead in our long arms race, after more than six decades of lagging behind the Terrans. This opportunity must not be squandered—it might never come again."

As Gorkon reached the edge of the circle that was farthest from the Regent's throne, Sturka asked, "What are you proposing, Councillor Gorkon?"

Gorkon grinned to Indizar, his long-time ally, then turned to answer Sturka. "A doubling of the budget for new starship construction and refits, and a separate allocation of equal size for new military research and development."

Sturka sounded skeptical. "And where will we find the money for this? Or the resources? Or the power?"

"Money is not a warrior's concern," Gorkon said, even though he knew it was undeniably a politician's concern. "If we need power, we all know that Praxis is not running at capacity—we can triple its output to power new shipyards. As for raw materials and personnel"—he paused and looked around the room, already plotting which of his rivals would end up bearing the brunt of his plans for the future—"sacrifices will have to be made. Hard choices. For the cost of a few worlds and a few billion people conscripted into service, we can transform the quadrant into an unassailable bastion of Klingon power."

"Whose worlds?" Councillor Argashek blurted out. Suspicious growls worked their way around the room. Many of the councillors no doubt were already aware of what Gorkon had in mind for them should he ever rise to the regency. Leaning over Argashek's shoulders, Grozik and Glazya, his two staunchest comrades, sniped verbally at Gorkon. *"PetaQ,"* spat Grozik, as Glazya hissed, "Filthy *yIntagh!*"

Councillors Narvak and Veselka conferred in hushed voices near the back of the room, while the Council's three newest—and youngest—members stepped to the edge of the circle from different directions, flanking Gorkon. Korax had come up through the ranks of the military, much as Gorkon had. Both his friends in this challenge were scions of noble houses: Berik, of the House of Beyhn, and Rhaza, of the House of Guul.

"Bold words, old man," Korax taunted. "But I bet it won't be your homeworld that gets ground up for the Empire."

Gorkon watched the three younger men moving in unison, circling him . . . and he smirked at them.

"Step into the circle, whelps," Gorkon challenged. "And I'll show you what being ground up really means."

Again came the thunderous rapping of Sturka's staff. "Enough. Korax, take your jesters and go back to the shadows. Gorkon, let them go."

With a respectful nod to Sturka, Gorkon said, "As you wish, my lord." Secretly, he wondered if Regent Sturka had lost his appetite for battle, his love of purifying combat. Twice today he had intervened when custom dictated the strong should reign. *Perhaps the Terrans' leader isn't the only one losing his edge,* Gorkon mused grimly.

Leaning forward from the edge of the throne, Sturka spoke slowly, his roar of a voice diminished with age to a low, ragged rumble. "Praxis is unstable. Doubling its output would be a mistake. And if a few of our worlds must be sacrificed to secure our victory over the Terrans, I will decide which worlds to cast into the fire, and when. But for now, this option is rejected."

Vengeful fury raged inside Gorkon, but his countenance was steady as granite, his gaze winter-cold. *Sturka has lost the will to fight,* he realized. *He doesn't have the stomach for casualties, for risk. His fire is gone; he's just a politician now.*

Looking at the Regent, bitter regret filled Gorkon's heart. Sturka had helped elevate Gorkon to the High Council more than twenty years ago. Since then the Regent had kept him close and taught him how to keep the other councillors fighting among themselves so that he and Sturka could be free to plot grander schemes for the glory of the Empire. Sturka had become like a second father to Gorkon, but now the old statesman was past his prime—enfeebled, vulnerable, and no longer able to lead.

Gorkon knew what had to be done for the good of the Empire. *It galls me that it must come to this,* he admitted to himself. *But better that it should be me than that* petaQ *Duras.*

Sturka was still talking. His eyes drifted from one side of the room to the other, gauging each councillor's reactions as he spoke. As soon as his gaze was turned away, Gorkon adjusted his wrist to let his concealed *d'k tahg* fall into his grip. His hand shot out and up and plunged the blade deep into Sturka's chest. A twist tore apart the Regent's heart. Lavender ichor spurted thick and warm from the ugly, sucking wound, coating Gorkon's hand. Sturka fell forward, into Gorkon's arms, hanging onto his protégé as his lifeblood escaped in generous spurts. As he looked up at Gorkon, the Regent's expression seemed almost . . . grateful. "I knew . . . it would . . . be you," he rasped through a mouthful of pinkish spittle, then his corpse fell off Gorkon's blade and landed in a blood-sodden heap on the floor.

Gorkon looked around the room to see if anyone wanted to challenge him. No one seemed eager to do so.

He sheathed his *d'k tahg* and kneeled beside Sturka's body. He pried the eyelids fully open and gazed into their lifeless depths. His warning cry for *Sto-Vo-Kor* built like a long-growing thunderhead, resonating inside his barrel chest. Within seconds, more gravelly hums were building in the bellies of all those around him. Then he threw back his head and let his bellicose roar burst forth, and the High Council roared with him, the sound of the *Heghtay* powerful enough to shake the dust from the rafters. The ranks of the dead could not say they hadn't been warned: A Klingon warrior was coming.

Pushing aside the empty husk of Sturka's body, Gorkon stepped up onto the raised dais and took his place upon the throne. Immediately, Indizar was at his right side, handing him the ceremonial staff. Alakon, a common-born soldier who had earned his place here through honorable battle, took his place at Gorkon's left and made the declaration, which was echoed back by the councillors without a challenge:

"All hail, Regent Gorkon!"

It was too early in Senator Pardek's political career for him to pick fights on the floor of the Romulan Senate. Fortunately for him,

Senator Narviat was stirring up enough ire in the Senate chamber for both of them.

Narviat shouted above the angry hubbub. "A wise general once said, 'When you see your enemy making a mistake, get out of his way.' Well, we're being given a rare treat: We get to watch *two* of our enemies making a mistake. So why aren't any of you smart enough to get out of their way?"

Pardek almost had to laugh; there were days when he was certain that Narviat simply enjoyed making the others crazy, especially Proconsul Dralath and Praetor Vrax.

Shouting back from his seat at the front of the chamber, Proconsul Dralath made his voice cut through the clamor. "We missed our chance to strike when the Klingons and Terrans clashed twenty years ago," he said. "Not again."

"Even at war with each other, they would still be a threat to us," Narviat retorted, ignoring the anonymously hurled epithets that filled the air: *Coward. Quisling. Pacifist.* "The best course," he added, "is to expand our covert intelligence opportunities inside—"

"The same old refrain," cut in Senator Crelok, her elegant features crimped with contempt. "Another testimonial for the Tal Shiar. The last time I checked, Senator Narviat, the Tal Shiar hadn't won any wars for the Empire."

Unfazed, Narviat shot back, "Without us, the military would never have won any wars at all."

Crelok, a former starship commander, bristled at Narviat's remark. She seemed poised at the edge of a reply when the Praetor rose from his chair, and the senators who were gathered in the chamber fell silent.

Praetor Vrax turned his head slowly and surveyed the room. Pardek had been a senator for nearly eleven years now, and this was only the fourth time he had seen the Praetor stand to address the Senate. Vrax was more than old; he bordered on ancient. Despite his advanced years, however, he remained a keen political thinker and military strategist.

"The Terran Empire," Vrax began, speaking slowly, "is on a

path to chaos." He lowered his head and cleared his throat. Looking up, he continued. "The Klingon Empire, now under Gorkon's control, is arming for war." He made a small nod toward Crelok. "Some of you say we should strike when the Klingons do." Vrax glanced at Narviat. "Others say we should use their war to infiltrate them both." Now Vrax's voice grew stronger, building as he spoke. "All the estimates I've seen tell me the Klingons will win this war, and the Terran Empire will fall. If so, we should let our fleet claim what it can. . . . But other reports, from within the Terran Empire—I must admit they worry me. It is impossible for me to believe that Emperor Spock is ignorant of the consequences his actions will carry. But he continues all the same, and his homeworld of Vulcan is awash in a tide of pacifism. Our spies on Vulcan—the few that haven't been exposed and executed—cannot explain the spread of that world's pacifist movement. It has no printed propaganda, no virtual forums for discussion, no broadcast messages, no public meetings." The Praetor allowed that to sink in for a moment, then he followed it with a succinct, pointed inquiry to the Senate: "Why?"

Speaking from the back of the chamber, Senator D'Tran, one of the elder statesmen of the Senate, trepidatiously asked the Praetor, "Why, what? Why are the Vulcans becoming pacifists? Or why is it happening outside the normal channels?"

"Start with the method," Vrax said.

Shrugs and eye rolls were passed from person to person as everyone sought to avoid answering the question. Pardek sighed with disappointment at his fellow senators' lack of courage. Lifting his voice, Pardek answered Praetor Vrax. "They are avoiding the normal channels in order to flush out spies."

The soft chatter of the room fell away and everyone looked at Pardek. Praetor Vrax cast an especially harsh glare at the young senator from the Krocton Segment. "Explain," he said.

"I have my own sources on Vulcan," Pardek confessed. "Based on the patterns of recruitment, people are seeking out their friends and family members and drawing them into the pacifist movement. It's not a government-directed initiative; it's a grass-roots campaign, with each person brought into the fold through a chain of accountable kith and kin."

Vrax nodded at first, then tilted his head as he asked, "But how would such a recruitment model help them expose our spies? Why have we not infiltrated this movement?"

It was a loaded question, one that Pardek dreaded answering. "I do have one hypothesis," he said carefully.

"Tell us," Vrax commanded.

Pardek steeled himself for the wave of ridicule he knew would follow. "I believe they are vetting new members by means of telepathy."

No one in the Senate Chamber mocked Pardek's theory. They were all too incapacitated to do so, because they were doubled over with paroxysms of cruel laughter. Much to Pardek's consternation, he noticed that the only two people in the room not guffawing were himself and Praetor Vrax.

It took several seconds for the contagion of hilarity to run its course and peter out. When a semblance of decorum at last returned to the Senate Chamber, Praetor Vrax coolly raised one eyebrow and said, in an archly skeptical tone, "Senator Pardek . . . shall I assume that you spoke in jest? Or are you seriously suggesting that the Vulcans are carrying out a vast planetwide conspiracy by means of a mythical psionic power?"

Before he answered, Pardek picked up his glass from the small desk in front of his seat and took a sip of water. He put down the glass and met Vrax's accusing stare. "My sources have told me that they believe the Vulcans' psionic gifts might be more than just the stuff of legend, Praetor."

Nobody laughed this time. Praetor Vrax ceased his pretense of civility and became openly sarcastic. "I suppose, Senator Pardek, that you'll next be telling me that Emperor Spock really does possess tremendous psionic abilities, and that it was the power of thought alone that enabled him to slaughter the Empress Hoshi Sato III and her entire Imperial Guard corps?"

Dead silence. A few stifled coughs echoed, then were lost amid the dry scrape of shuffling feet.

"No," Pardek said as diplomatically as he could. "I think that the Vulcans, who long resented sharing power with the Terrans who enslaved them, made a major leap forward in the arms race—and Spock chose that moment to show the Vulcans' hand."

Mumbles of agreement bubbled up in isolated patches around the Senate Chamber. Taking note of it, Vrax nodded. "Agreed. And until we know more about that weapon, I am inclined to support Senator Narviat's recommendation for discretion." He looked back at Pardek. "As to the spread of the pacifist movement on Vulcan . . . do you really have no better hypothesis, Senator Pardek?"

Abashed, Pardek answered, "Not at this time, Praetor."

Vrax shook his head. "Thank you, Senator Pardek. I would prefer an explanation that does not require me to believe in magic or mythology. You may sit down."

It hadn't been permission so much as a directive, and Pardek settled into his seat. The debate continued around him. He made no effort to conceal his disgruntled glowering.

So they don't believe my theory, he consoled himself. *Not surprising; I'm not sure I believe it, either. But there's one thing I am certain of: Spock is deliberately setting up his people to take a fall, and I have no idea why.*

Pardek considered a thousand reasons why Spock might sabotage his own empire; none of them made sense. As a junior senator, there was little he could do directly to guide the affairs of the Romulan Star Empire. Weighing his options, he decided he would back Senator Narviat's proposal of military disengagement when it came time to vote. Pardek doubted that the Tal Shiar would be able to infiltrate Vulcan any better than it had so far— which was to say, barely at all—but emphasizing covert intelligence rather than overt conquest would keep the Romulan Star Empire out of the Terran-Klingon cross fire. Pardek simply hoped it would buy his people enough time to determine what Emperor Spock was really up to.

★ ★ ★

"I must say, Admiral Cartwright," remarked Colonel Ivan West as he sat down at the dinner table, "this is by far the best-catered secret meeting I've ever been to."

Admiral Lance Cartwright chuckled as he settled in at the head of the table. Colonel West's observation had struck a chord because it was true. The table was dressed with crisp white linen and set with dishes of fine crystal and utensils of solid, polished silver. Cartwright's domestic servants had just cleared the appetizer course—a salad of baby greens tossed with warm slices of braised pear, walnuts, and a light vinaigrette—and brought out the next course, bowls of creamy pumpkin soup. Special dishes were served to the nonhuman guests.

Laughing with Cartwright were six visitors, high-ranking military officers who had been invited to his home this evening. They swapped small talk as a Bolian waiter refilled their glasses. Cartwright, West, and Admiral Thomas Morrow all were drinking cabernet. General Quiniven of Denobula was abstaining from liquor this evening and nursed a glass of Altair water instead. Admirals Robert Bennett and Salliserra zh'Ferro gladly accepted refills of their illegally imported Romulan ale. Commodore Vosrok, the Chelon director of Starfleet Intelligence, was half sitting, half kneeling on a piece of furniture designed for his nonhumanoid anatomy and drinking *n'v'aa,* a beverage from his homeworld that, up close, reeked of brackish vinegar. Cartwright made a mental note never to drink at Vosrok's home.

The banter remained light while the servants moved through the lavishly decorated dining room, serving soup, refilling water, replacing sullied utensils, and setting out freshly baked rolls and glass dishes of whipped butter.

"I'll give you credit," Morrow said to Cartwright. "You know how to live like a grand admiral."

Raising his glass in appreciation, Cartwright replied, "The amazing part is that I do it on a fleet admiral's salary." More polite laughter filled the moment. He watched the last of the servants exit, and the doors swung closed behind them, leaving him and his guests in privacy. "To business, then," he said, and his guests nodded in agreement. "I've sounded out each of you individually, so I imagine you're all aware why I've asked you here tonight." After a pause for effect, he stated plainly, "Emperor Spock is determined to destroy the Empire to which we have all devoted our lives. Before he's done, he'll kill us all. He must be stopped."

Cautious mumbles of assent traveled around the table, as each guest looked around to make certain they weren't alone in speaking treason against the Emperor. Their mutual affirmation seemed to encourage them. West, who sat to Cartwright's left near the head of the table, was the first to respond directly.

"I'm sure we all agree with you, Admiral," West said. "But opposing Spock won't be easy. I know of a few more admirals who are ready to turn against him, but most of the officer corps and almost all the enlisted men still support him."

Jumping in, Admiral Bennett said, "And don't forget how popular he is with the people. Assassinating him might just make him a martyr. A coup against Spock could start a rebellion."

Quiniven waved his hand dismissively. "No matter," he said with arrogant surety. "The people can be kept in line."

"Oh, really?" was Vosrok's sarcastic reply. "Have you forgotten that Spock granted the people such rights as—"

"Rights given with a word can be revoked just as easily," Quiniven said. "The citizens of the Empire have never had to shed blood to secure their rights. They wouldn't know how."

Cartwright sipped his dry red wine as the conversation took on a life of its own. Admiral zh'Ferro looked down from her end of the table and quietly remarked, "We will also have to kill Empress Marlena."

"Easily done," Colonel West replied.

Admiral Morrow, who had been enjoying his soup one carefully lifted spoonful at a time, set down his spoon and cleared his throat. "Neutralizing Spock and Marlena is only the first step," he said. "And I don't mean to say that doing so will be easy. But before we take that step, we should know what we intend to do next. Once they're gone, who should take their place?"

"Not another Vulcan," West said. "That's for damned sure."

Quiniven's upswept eyebrows and facial ridges gave a sinister cast to his broad grin. "And who would you rather see on the imperial throne, Colonel West?"

Defiantly lifting his chin to the Denobulan's challenge, West replied, "Someone who deserves it. . . . A human. Someone of noble lineage, verified ancestry."

"Please," implored Admiral zh'Ferro, "tell me you aren't suggesting who I think you are."

"Why not?" West retorted. "He was born to rule!"

Within seconds, it was apparent that everyone else in the room knew exactly of whom West spoke, and that no one agreed with his recommendation. All shook their heads in mute refusal. Despite trying to remain neutral, Cartwright himself joined the chorus of rejection. "I'm sorry, Ivan," Cartwright said. "They're right. We can't put Ranjit Singh on the throne. It'd be a disaster."

West pushed away his bowl of soup and fumed. "Ridiculous," he said. "He's a direct descendant of Khan Noonien Singh. No one has a better claim to the Terran throne than he does."

Quiniven tempered his usual haughtiness, no doubt in an effort to reach an accord. "With all respect, Colonel, bowing to the whims of megalomaniacs is what got us into this predicament. Installing another one as emperor is hardly the ideal solution."

"The general's right," Morrow said. "Besides, if I know our host, I think you'll like his plan for the future of the Empire even better than your own."

With new curiosity, Colonel West turned slowly and looked at Admiral Cartwright. "Do you have a plan, Admiral?"

Cartwright dabbed the corners of his mouth with his napkin. "It's more a vision than a plan," he said. "We need a military government at the imperial level. Martial law, no civilians. Kill Spock, the Senate, the Forum . . . all of them."

Shocked silence followed Cartwright's declaration. General

Quiniven was the first to recover his composure. "Assassinating Emperor Spock and his wife might be logistically feasible," the Denobulan noted. "But to wipe out the Forum and the Senate would require destroying the imperial palace, and that's far more difficult. Its shields can stand up to half the fleet—and Earth's orbital defense network would shred us before we could breach its defenses."

"All very true," Cartwright said. "Fortunately, we have an alternative." He looked down the table at the director of Starfleet Intelligence. "Commodore Vosrok, would you kindly tell the other guests what you told me last week, about S.I.'s latest innovation?"

Vosrok was a hard person to read by means of body language. His leathery face betrayed little or no emotion, and his thickly scaled body was stiff and slow-moving. Even as all the guests in the room fixed their shared attention upon him, he seemed like a dark, vaguely amphibian statue at the end of the table. Blinking his topaz-colored eyes, he said, "Starfleet Intelligence has discovered and refined a new explosive compound called ultritium. So far, it's undetectable by any of the security scanners inside the palace. It won't take much to incinerate everyone in the Forum Chamber—maybe a few kilograms. As I'm sure you're aware, the search protocols at the palace are quite stringent. To smuggle the explosive in, it will have to be disguised as something else, something that is above reproach, that will not be searched, and that can get close enough to Emperor Spock and Empress Marlena to ensure their annihilation."

At the first sign of Vosrok's pause, Admiral Bennett asked, "And that 'something' is what, exactly?"

The Chelon paused to sip his drink. Cartwright appreciated the sly sadism of Vosrok's dramatic timing. In molasses-slow motion, Vosrok put down his glass, swallowed, and took a breath. "The ultritium," he continued, "will be disguised as the armor of one of Spock's elite imperial guards. Our assassin will wear it into the Forum during a joint session of the Legislature, and, on a signal from myself, turn the entire government to dust in a single blast."

Vosrok's plan was met with the same incredulous stares that had stifled Colonel West's proposition. Quiniven shook his head and looked almost ready to laugh. "One of Spock's guards? Are you mad? He recruits only Vulcans and makes them spend years proving their loyalty before they can serve in the palace. You will never infiltrate his guard corps."

Vosrok looked to Cartwright, who broke the news to the table: "We already have."

2289

11

Missives and Messengers

K orvat was more than just a desirable place to start a colony, and it was more than the Klingon Empire's first solid foothold inside what had once been inviolable Terran space. Listening to General Kang address the assembly of Klingon and foreign dignitaries as the Klingons asserted their claim to sovereignty over the planet, Regent Gorkon knew that this annexation was nothing less than a test of the Terran Empire's collective will.

The Terrans' sole representative at the ceremony, a young male Trill diplomat named Curzon Dax, had arrived late and made no effort to be inconspicuous. Quite to the contrary, he had seemed intent on disrupting General Kang by walking brazenly up the center aisle, his footfalls snapping sharp echoes. Gorkon had watched from the balcony level as, down below, Dax forced himself into a front-row seat, jostling aside several high-ranking Klingons in the process. Kang, to his credit, had ignored the obnoxious Trill and continued his address, the force of his voice stealing back the attention of the audience and subduing its angry mutterings about the latecomer.

"This world," Kang bellowed, "has been the rightful territory of the Klingon Empire for more than a century. Too long has it been neglected, left under the careless dominion of the Terrans.

By right, we have reclaimed it in honorable combat. But the Terrans, unable to defend this world by force of arms, now wish to beg for its return with diplomacy!" The large number of Klingons seated in the auditorium roared with indignation, exactly as Kang had coaxed them to. "Once, the Terrans were warriors, and they understood that warriors do not talk, they act. They were an enemy we could respect." Grumbles of glum agreement rolled like an undercurrent through the crowd. "But now they are weak and fearful, plying us with concessions and bribes. They are not the warriors we used to know; they are nothing more than *jeghpu'wI,* waiting for us to put our boots on their necks!" Furious howls of approval and a thunder of stomping feet filled the hall.

Curzon Dax sat with his arms folded, looking quite bored. As the bellicose chanting of the crowd began to subside, the Trill stood and walked up the nearby stairs onto the stage with Kang. Quickly, the room fell silent as the two men faced each other. Kang returned Curzon's unblinking stare for several seconds, then Curzon spat at the ground in front of Kang's feet.

"Pathetic," Dax said with naked contempt. To the crowd, he added, "All of you." He prowled like a hunting beast across the front of the stage as he hurled his sarcastic verbal attacks. "Such mighty warriors! You conquered an unarmed farming colony less than a light-year from your border. *This* is the greatest victory you've scored against the Terran Empire in sixty years?" He shook his head and sneered. "What a miserable empire you have. Congratulating yourselves for the least audacious victory in our shared history. I'm ashamed to think I once respected you as soldiers." Now he turned and directed his comments at Kang. "I wasn't sent to beg for Korvat; I was sent to negotiate the safe return of its people. But I've changed my mind, General. I hereby request that you execute our colonists—because they would be shamed to death if they had to return home and admit they were conquered by *petaQpu* like you." Dax walked back to the stairs and looked out at the Klingons in the audience. "You want me to call you warriors? Bring your fleet to Ramatis. We'll send it back to your widows in a box." The Trill descended the stairs and strode back down the center aisle, ignoring the hostile jeers and overlapping threats. All the way to the exit, he never looked back. Then he was out the door, and the Terran-Klingon negotiations for Korvat were ended before they had begun.

Energized and enraged, the crowd surged with a magnetic fervor, but Regent Gorkon found himself more interested in General Kang's reaction. Kang had paced to the back of the stage, where he stood alone and silent, peering through the shadows into some dark corner of himself.

General Chang, Gorkon's senior military adviser, leaned over from the seat next to the Regent's and said in a low voice, "The Trill got under Kang's ridges." Gorkon grimaced at Chang, who sat to his left. The general always sat on Gorkon's left side, to make sure that his intact right eye—and not his triangular, leather eyepatch—faced the Regent.

"For a diplomat," Gorkon said, "Dax went out of his way to provoke us. Why would Spock send us such an envoy?"

Chang picked up a bottle of *warnog* and refilled his stein with the pungent elixir. "Perhaps Dax was chosen in haste," he said, offering to refill Gorkon's stein. The Regent declined. Resealing the bottle, Chang added, "It's possible that Spock did not realize how the man would comport himself."

"That doesn't sound like Spock," Gorkon said. "It also doesn't track with Curzon Dax's reputation."

"True," Chang said. In the decade since Spock had begun reforming the Terrans' political landscape, Dax had emerged as one of Spock's most skillful negotiators. For him to inflame the battle rage of the Klingon Empire by losing his temper over such a minor affront was horribly out of character.

An unlikely notion pushed its way to the forefront of Gorkon's thoughts. He guzzled the last dregs of *warnog* from his stein, then said, "Would Spock and Dax have deliberately set out to sabotage the Korvat talks?"

Chang squinted his right eye as he considered the question. "To what end, my lord?"

"To push us closer to war," Gorkon said.

This time the general chortled. "As if we needed the push." Becoming more serious, he added, "After all the efforts Spock's ambassadors have made to establish diplomatic relations, for him to suddenly reverse his foreign policy makes no sense."

"Then how should we interpret Ambassador Dax's actions?"

Leaning back in his chair, Chang said, "There is a third possibility, my lord, one that I have raised before. Maybe Spock's diplomatic efforts were strictly domestic. By using enticement and diplomacy to pacify his own people, he is free to deploy all his Starfleet assets against external threats."

It wasn't based on a social model that the Klingons would tolerate within their own empire, but Gorkon had to admit that Chang's theory made sense. For Spock, being able to direct all his empire's strength outward, instead of having to constantly redeploy forces to quell internal uprisings, would be an enormous tactical advantage. "If you're right," Gorkon said, "then all of Spock's progressive reforms have been a prelude to a war—one that he now feels confident goading us to begin."

"Vulcans aren't direct," Chang said, "but they are cunning. If he wants us to go to war now, he must believe he has the upper hand. But before we engage the Terrans, we should guarantee that we hold the advantage."

Gorkon understood exactly what Chang was referring to. For years the general had been overseeing a secret starship-design team, which was working on a bird-of-prey prototype that could fire torpedoes while cloaked. "How close is the prototype to being ready for assembly-line production?"

"Immediately," Chang said. "All we need to start building a new fleet is enough power to cloak the Praxis shipyard from the Terrans' spy arrays."

"I'll give the order to triple energy production at Praxis immediately," Gorkon said. "How long will it take to build a fleet capable of crushing the Terrans in a single offensive?"

Chang stroked thoughtfully at the two tufts of mustache above the corners of his mouth. After several seconds of consideration, he said, "Nine years."

"That's a long time to wait, General."

With a rueful grin, Chang replied, "The Terran Empire is vast, my lord. Subduing it all in one sneak attack will take a lot of ships. We could expand our starship production to other shipyards, but the more facilities that receive the prototype's design, the greater the risk of espionage."

"Very well, then," Gorkon said. "Keep the program secret at the Praxis facility. But work quickly, General. It's time for us to wipe the Terran Empire off the map, and I am eager to begin."

"As am I, my lord," Chang said. "As am I."

2293

12

The Architects of War

Marlena walked alone across the frozen gray expanse of the ocean. Thunderous rumbles trembled the ice under her bare feet. Great fissures cracked open the snow-dusted horizon, which churned with dark water, like blood erupting from a wound.

As she walked, the glaciated terrain was cleaved in twain beneath her, and jagged shards of ice sliced into her heels. She clutched the bundle in her arms, its cargo more precious than any she had ever held before. Warm against her bosom, safe in her embrace, the fruit of her womb was all that mattered to her now in this desolate, frigid wasteland.

Fire, on the horizon. The figure of a man robed in flames. Reddish-gold against the grayish-white emptiness that seemed to have no horizon, surrounded by widening gulfs of black seawater. A silhouette, a gaunt outline of a lanky form, burning bright in the falling gloom, ushering her onward against the bitter wind.

She trudged across the bobbing ice floes, her torn feet leaving bloody prints. The man in the flames was her father, François—it had to be. He was waiting for her, waiting to see her son, to reach out and give his blessing to her child. All she had to do was traverse a treacherous sea of broken ice.

A short leap, then a longer one. Deep cracking sounds, like the breaking of a giant's bones, filled the dreary dusk. The faster Marlena tried to reach her father, the more quickly the ice broke apart, the farther the pieces drifted.

I have to hurry, she knew. *Time is running out.*

From the back edge of a long strip of ice, she took a running start. Her final step, the push-off, dipped the leading edge of the floe under the inky surface of the sea.

Aloft, airborne, floating weightless upon a breeze, Marlena drifted through the air, the ghostly vapors of her breath ringed about her like a halo, a maternal blessing of mist. Below her, the bottomless ocean, darker than the deepest hours of the night, colder than an unforgiving heart.

Marlena landed like a feather at her father's feet. She looked up at the pillar of golden fire that surrounded him. Trapped inside his incandescent cocoon, her father resembled a dark statue, as unyielding and mysterious as he had always seemed to her during her childhood.

She extended her arms and held out her swaddled son. "Look, Daddy," she said. "My son. Your grandson."

Her sire of shadows looked down and spoke with disdain. "I see nothing but broken promises."

"No!" she protested. "He's your grandson! Look at him!" She pulled away the outer fold of the blanket, then the next, and the next. With every unfolded corner, she expected to reveal her glory, the heir of Spock, the offspring she had borne into the world . . . but then the blanket tumbled from her hands, completely undone, fluttering empty to the icy ground.

The wind howled in mourning. Bitter tears ran hotly across her frost-numbed cheeks. She collapsed onto her knees and pawed helplessly at the child's blanket, at its frayed edges. A low tender cry strained to break free of her chest. Looking up to her father for mercy, forgiveness, and comfort, instead she beheld Spock, frozen and one step removed from real, a sculpture chiseled roughly from soft ice. She reached out to touch it. It broke apart at the grazing brush of her fingertip, collecting itself into a mound of ash and snow.

Nighttime edged across the sky, swallowing the light, and Marlena was surrounded by the widening ocean, eternal and fathomless. She was alone in the world, with no one to hear her weeping. Hers was not the maudlin sobbing of a madwoman, but a funereal wail that was all the more terrible for its clarity.

Stinging cold water bit at her hands and knees as the ocean claimed the floe beneath her. There was nowhere to run to, no one to beg for rescue. Marlena fell forward and surrendered to the irresistible pull of the sea. Her arms and legs numbed on contact with the frigid water. As she slipped under the waves, she made no effort to hold her breath. She exhaled, felt heat and life escape in a flourish of bubbles. Pulling the sea into her lungs, tasting death in all its briny coldness, was easier than she had expected.

The scant light from above the water's surface was deep blue, then blue-black . . . but only as Marlena felt herself vanishing into the darkness did the last, desperate spark of terror ignite in her soul—lonely, afraid, not ready to let go, not ready to be extinguished . . . but darkness had no mercy, and its grip choked away her final cries for help. . . .

A gasp and a shudder, and Marlena was awake in her bed, her heart pounding, musky sweat coating her face and arms and chest. She stared at the ceiling of her bedroom in the imperial palace. Every undulating pattern of light and shadow on the walls and ceiling seemed infused with sinister intent. Her breathing was rapid and shallow. *You're hyperventilating,* she told herself. *Calm down. Force yourself to slow down. Breathe.*

Beside her in the bed, Spock lay on his right side, facing away from her. As she turned her head to make certain she hadn't disturbed him, he rolled slowly onto his back. He was awake. "Nightmares again?" he asked.

"The same one," she said, and he nodded. The journey across

the ice was a dream that had plagued her intermittently for more than a decade. She had discussed it with Spock after its third repetition, but he had offered no analysis. As much as she had hoped that merely sharing it would be enough to exorcise it from her thoughts, it remained with her, its rather naked symbolism growing more painful with each passing year.

Spock seemed to sense that tonight's recurrence of the dream had left her more agitated than it had before. "Perhaps you are concerned about the upcoming conference," he said.

"Of course I am," she shot back. She had told him openly that she feared someone would try to assassinate him at the interstellar summit two weeks from now. "But I know what this dream is telling me, Spock, and it's not about Khitomer."

With a stately economy of movement, Spock sat up in bed and folded his hands on his lap. "I know that this topic distresses you," he said. "For your own sake, I urge you not to pursue it."

"But you've never told me the truth, Spock. Not once. I've asked you a hundred times over the years, and you've given me a hundred different answers."

He raised his right eyebrow, which she knew was a prelude to his taking her exaggeration-for-effect and rebutting it with a precise fact that would utterly miss her intended point. "If memory serves," he said, "we have discussed this subject precisely forty-three times, including tonight. Our most recent previous conversation of this matter was—"

"Damn you, Spock," Marlena said, verging on tears. "Just tell me the truth—the real truth, not just your latest excuse. Why won't you have children with me?"

Her entreaty was met with aggrieved silence. Spock would not lie to her, she knew that just as certainly as she knew that he loved her—or, at least, that he *had* loved her once, long ago, before he became Emperor. But though he would never lie to her, he also was supremely talented at saying nothing at all.

Determined to force the truth from him, she pressed him harder. "Is it that you don't love me anymore? That you're sterile? Or do you simply have a concubine that you prefer instead of me? A Vulcan woman?"

"I assure you," Spock said, "that none of those are true."

Unable to hold back her tears, she took his arm in her gentle grasp and begged, "Then tell me. Please."

"The reason is simple," he said. "I do not want children."

"But I do," Marlena pleaded. "I know you don't need an heir to the throne, but why shouldn't we get to be parents like everyone else? Why can't we have a son or a daughter to call our own?" Spock got out of bed and walked toward the balcony. Marlena cast aside the covers and moved to the edge of the bed. She watched him stare out into the night for what seemed like forever. "It's been more than a year since you've touched me," she said in a timid voice. "I miss you, Spock."

He turned back to face her. As always, his expression was unreadable, but for once his voice was gentle. "The burdens of rulership weigh on us both," he said. "It was necessary for me to put matters of state ahead of your happiness." In slow, careful steps, he returned to her. He took her hands and helped her to her feet. "I apologize," he said, and embraced her. "Never doubt that I love you, Marlena," he whispered into her ear. "But for us to have children would be a mistake."

Struggling not to succumb to overpowering sorrow, Marlena clung to Spock's shoulder and whimpered, "Why?"

"You know why," he said. "Events are moving quickly. We are less than a year from ending the Empire and creating the Republic. But we must not delude ourselves, Marlena. The future of the Republic will be brutal and short-lived. And when it comes to its premature and violent end, it will claim us along with it. I will not sire children only to see them share our fate."

The truth was ugly and terrible and indisputable. But still, there had to be a solution, an escape. "What if I went into exile?" she said. "I could leave before anyone knows I'm pregnant, go into hiding—"

"Our enemies would seek you out," he said. "They will not rest until they have eliminated us. If a scan shows them you have borne children, they will seek out your offspring. They must be convinced that we represent the end of our dynasty, or they will lay waste to the worlds of the Republic searching for what has been hidden from them. And in so doing, they could potentially destroy all that I have labored to set in motion for the future." He tightened his embrace and ran his fingers through her hair. "I am sorry, Marlena. Duty demands a different path for us. This is how it must be."

She sobbed against his shoulder, dampening his nightclothes with her tears, mourning for their children who would never be. She knew that he was right, and that there would be no changing his mind. His decision was final; she would have to live with it. But it would torture her and haunt her until the end of her days, this hunger of her body to bear him children. It was an empty, tragic yearning that was matched only by her longing for his affection, which she knew would always be held at a remove, veiled behind logic and custom and protocol.

For her love of who Spock was, she had married him; for her love of what he stood for, she would die childless. All the lavish trappings of the imperium were cold comfort as she confronted the chilling finality of her situation: *When I'm gone, not one little bit of me will remain. I'll just be gone.*

Spock held her as she wept; he was stoic in his compassion.

When the well of her tears at last ran dry, she looked up through the kaleidoscope of her burning eyes into his serene face. "This is how it must be," he said.

"I know," Marlena said. She took his hands in hers. "I accept that I can't have your children, but promise me that when the end comes, you'll be with me, that I won't be alone."

"I promise that I will be with you," Spock said. "But in *the end* . . . everyone is alone."

The assassin's armor felt only slightly heavier than it had the day before. The field agent from Starfleet Intelligence had said as much when he'd delivered it, though his assurance had sounded too convenient to be true. Feeling the armor slide into place, however, there was no denying how remarkably lightweight and unobtrusive the ultritium lining was. Less than four kilograms was dispersed throughout the suit of polymer armor: some of it in the shin guards, some of it in the cuirass of the *lorica segmentata,* some of it in the red-plumed helmet. It felt perfectly balanced and was so evenly distributed that it was hardly noticeable. And when the time came, it would be enough to vaporize the entire Forum Hall and everyone in it.

But this was not that time.

A barked order from the captain of the guard—"Attention!"—and the members of Spock's elite guard snapped into formation inside the hangar bay, their plumes aligned, battle rifles shouldered, eyes front. One among many, anonymous in the ranks, the assassin stared ahead, careful not to betray the mission with a wayward glance or a moment of lost focus.

The door slid open, and a procession of diplomats and cabinet officials entered and marched quickly toward the open aft ramp of the personnel transport docked in the bay. Then Empress Marlena walked in. She was followed closely by Emperor Spock, who stopped, turned, and faced his troops. The captain of the guard, a middle-aged Vulcan named Torov, saluted the Emperor. As if acting with one mind, the rank and file of the elite guards saluted in unison a moment later.

Spock returned the gesture, then said to Torov, "Have you secured the landing site?"

"Yes, Your Majesty," Torov said. "And the transport has been inspected. We stand ready to depart on your word."

Spock dropped his voice to speak privately with Torov, but the assassin—and very likely every other Vulcan in the imperial guard detail—heard their conversation clearly. "Armed escorts," Spock said, "will not be allowed inside the conference center. Furthermore, my agreement with the Klingon Regent and the Romulan Praetor limits each of us to no more than one bodyguard inside the meeting chamber."

Above the bridge of Torov's nose, a V-shaped crease of concern betrayed his profound alarm. "Such measures will put you at risk, Majesty," he protested, careful to keep his tone steady. "Klingons are highly adept at disguising weapons as parts of their uniforms. If they should move against you—"

"Highly unlikely," Spock said. "With their homeworld in ruins after the explosion of Praxis, provoking us to war would not be in their best interest."

Torov seemed unwilling to concede. "Are the other delegates equally constrained, Your Majesty? What incentive do the Romulans or the Cardassians have to respect the armistice?"

"The Romulans are recluses," Spock said. "I suspect they accepted our invitation solely to gather intelligence. As for the Cardassians, they are a fledgling power. They are ill-equipped to challenge us directly." The Emperor's answers seemed to mollify Torov somewhat. "We need not commit to a decision now, Torov. Have your platoon accompany me aboard the transport. We shall make our final arrangements when we reach the surface of Khitomer."

"Yes, Your Majesty," Torov said, bowing his head. Spock walked away toward the Starfleet transport ship. With a crisp snap of one boot heel against the other, Torov straightened his back and shouted the platoon of elite imperial guards into motion. "Move out! Single file, double time, *hai!*"

Soldiers wove together into a long line, their feet moving quickly in lockstep, their boots ringing deep echoes from the metal deck plates, their armor clunking with the dull clatter of nonmetallic polymers. In less than a minute they were aboard the transport, clustered back into ranks inside its lower compartment, while the political VIPs traveled comfortably in the staterooms on the upper decks.

The rear ramp lifted shut and was secured with a rich hum of magnetic locks and the hiss of pressure-control vents. The ship's inertial dampers gave its liftoff a surreal quality for its passengers; there was no sensation of movement, even though the scene outside the porthole-style windows drifted past. It was more like watching a holographic video of a journey than taking one. Then the flatly lit, immaculate whiteness of the *Enterprise*'s hangar bay gave way to the endless darkness of space, dappled with the icy glow of distant stars.

Moments later, other ships came into view as the transport raced past them. Massive fleets maneuvered past one another—Starfleet cruisers and frigates, Klingon dreadnoughts, Romulan birds-of-prey, Cardassian battleships—all vibrant with the potential for catastrophic violence. An impulsive decision, a single error of translation, and Khitomer would be transformed into one of the largest, most politically incendiary battlegrounds in local galactic history.

Impulse engines thrummed with rising vigor as the Emperor's transport made its swift descent toward the lush, blue-green planet. The curve of Khitomer's northern hemisphere spread out and flattened as they penetrated its atmosphere. Spared an idle moment to think, the assassin harbored a seditious thought.

Four heads of state in one place, and me ready to strike. I could plunge four empires into civil war with a single decision. As quickly as the thought had emerged, it was suppressed. *No. That is not the mission. Galactic anarchy is not the objective. Stability and security for the Empire is the only priority.*

The transport pierced a thick layer of clouds and arrowed down toward the designated meeting site, dubbed Camp Khitomer. Sequestered in a bucolic nature preserve, the conference center itself was situated on a lake shore and surrounded by virgin forest. It was the sort of blue-skied, M-class world that humans and Klingons prized above all others.

A gentle shudder and a bump heralded the transport's landing on the surface. Almost on contact, Torov released the pressure seal on the rear ramp, which lowered with a hydraulic whine. "Twin columns! Face out! Double time, *hai!*"

The imperial guards deployed with precision and speed. Down the ramp, around the transport's fuselage to the VIPs' portal, which was perfectly aligned with an imperial-scarlet runner that extended from the transport's ramp to the conference center entrance. The guards arranged themselves in two rows, one on either side of the carpet, both facing away from the path to watch for any sign of danger.

Torov tapped the assassin on the shoulder. "Come with me."

The assassin followed Torov to the base of the VIPs' ramp.

Emperor Spock and Empress Marlena descended the ramp together, leading the Terran procession from the transport. At the end of the ramp, Spock acknowledged Torov with a curt nod.

Taking the Emperor's cue, Torov presented the assassin to him. "Your Majesty, duty precludes me from acting as your personal defender. Instead, I give you my best and brightest, the finest soldier under my command, to safeguard your life." Then the captain of the guard stepped aside and stood at attention while Spock studied the assassin.

"I have not seen you before," Spock said.

The assassin replied, "I was promoted to palace duty only last month, Your Majesty."

If the Emperor divined any fault, his dispassionate gaze betrayed nothing. "Very well," he said at last. Peering into the eyes of the assassin, Spock asked, "What is your name?"

"Valeris, Your Majesty."

Spock found it curious that the Klingons, despite their well-known martial austerity, were so enamored of pageantry and ritual. From the waving of smoking censers to prolonged chanting by an old Klingon monk from Boreth, Regent Gorkon's official introduction and entrance to the dimly lit private meeting chamber took nearly an hour, during which time Spock stood, hands folded inside the drooping sleeves of his imperial robe. Finally, a herald stepped through the portal reserved for the Klingons' use and announced, "His Imperial Majesty, He who holds the throne for Him Who Shall Return—Regent Gorkon."

The lanky Klingon head of state swept into the room with long strides, his bearing fierce and straightforward. His sole body-guard, a burly giant of a warrior, stepped just inside the doorway and stood near the wall, mirroring the pose of Spock's defender, Valeris, on the opposite side of the room.

Gorkon was taller than Spock, brawnier, heavier. His clothing was fashioned mostly of metal-studded leather dyed bloodred or oiled jet black, and loose plates of brightly polished lightweight armor. Glowering down at Spock, he flashed an aggressive grin of subtly pointed teeth. "Emperor Spock," he said. "I have antici-pated this meeting for some time."

"Greetings, Regent Gorkon," Spock replied. "Thank you for accepting our invitation."

A soft grunt prefaced Gorkon's reply. He smirked slightly. "We both know why I'm here," he said. "It's not because I was moved by your invitation."

Content to abandon small talk, Spock replied, "You are here because the explosion of Praxis has crippled Qo'noS."

The regent bristled at Spock's statement, then half smiled. "We are not crippled," he said. "Damaged, yes, but—"

"Your planet has begun a swift ecological decline," Spock said. "Toxic elements from the crust of Praxis are breaking down your atmosphere and tainting your fresh water. Within fifty Terran years, Qo'noS will no longer be able to support higher-order life-forms. In addition, nearly seventy percent of its population is dying of xenocerium poisoning as we speak."

Once again, Gorkon resorted to his emotionally neutral, insin-cere smile. "You make it sound as though the entire Klingon Em-pire were collapsing. Qo'noS is only one world."

"True," Spock said. "But its symbolic value as a homeworld is considerable. And you know as well as I that symbols can be just as vital to the stability of an empire as its arsenal."

The Regent's wan grin faltered. He stepped away from Spock toward a long window that wrapped in a shallow curve around one wall of the meeting chamber. The window looked down upon the main banquet hall, a dozen meters below. Spock followed Gorkon to the window, though he was careful to remain more than an arm's length away, to be respectful of the Klingon's personal space. Looking down, Spock observed that the delegations from the four major powers had, predictably, segregated themselves, despite a conscious effort by the Diplomatic Corps to mingle the preferred foods and beverages of the various species throughout the hall. Mutual understanding did not appear to be favored by the starting conditions of the summit.

Regent Gorkon lifted his eyes from the gathering below and turned toward Spock. "Let us not mince words, Your Majesty," he said. "We each walked into this room with our own agenda. What is yours?"

"A formal truce," Spock said. "A treaty declaring the permanent cessation of hostilities between our peoples."

This time, Gorkon's smile was honest but disparaging. "You really are out of your mind!" He laughed in great barking roars. "My empire is far from surrender."

"I did not ask for your surrender," Spock said. "I am offering what I want in exchange for what I know you need."

Pacing away from the window, Gorkon threw back his head and hollered, "Do tell me, Spock! What do I need?" His voice rebounded off the hard, close ceiling.

"Medicines that your scientists lack the skill to invent," Spock replied. "Technology and methods that can restore your planet's environment to balance."

"Both of which we could take by force," Gorkon said, turning like a caged animal at the end of its confines.

With perfect equanimity, Spock said, "You could try."

"Don't try to bluff me, Spock." Gorkon walked back toward him now, more slowly but still menacing. "You've been cutting your empire's defense spending for nearly a decade."

There was no reason to deny it. "Indeed," Spock said. "And the resources we have saved have spurred advances both scientific and social."

"Leaving your defenses soft!" Gorkon shouted. "Dozens of

your capital ships have dropped out of service, vanished into your spacedocks, scrapped for parts."

Spock's eyebrows lifted for emphasis: "Now it is you who underestimate your opponent, Gorkon." Before the Regent could retort and escalate the verbal confrontation, Spock changed its direction. "You now know my intention. What is your proposal?"

Gorkon hesitated, then his grin returned, this time conveying the dark glee of avarice mingled with bloodlust. "An alliance," he said. "Not just some pathetic cease-fire, a full merging of our power. Together, we can crush the Romulans, the Cardassians, the Tholians, and all the rest of the second-rate powers in the quadrant. United, we could reign supreme!"

It was a notion as crass as it was illogical.

"Only one entity can 'reign supreme,' Gorkon, as you are no doubt aware," Spock said, his tone deliberately rich with condescension. "Need I ask which of us would fulfill that role in our grand alliance?" Gorkon's ire rose quickly. Spock continued. "And when at last we lament that there are no more worlds left to conquer, should I not expect our Klingon allies to turn against us, after we have spent ourselves on war? . . . No, Gorkon, an alliance with your empire is not in the best interests of my people. We will come to your aid, but we will not enlist as your accomplices only to become your victims."

In just a few quick steps, Gorkon was all but nose-to-nose with Spock. The Regent's fanglike teeth were bared, his sour breath hot and rank in Spock's face, his eyes blazing with indignation. Their bodyguards tensed to intervene. In a whisper that sounded more like a growl, Gorkon said, "Make no mistake, Spock: You and your empire will bow to Klingon rule in my lifetime. I offered you the chance to correct your empire's failing course and claim your rightful power. Instead, you chose to grovel and bribe like a *petaQ*." He spat at Spock's feet. "Keep your precious medicines and your fancy devices. If Qo'noS fails, then it is weak and deserves death—*just like you and your empire*."

The Regent turned his back on Spock and marched from the

room, followed by his bodyguard. Their door closed behind them, and Spock turned his attention back out the window, to the banquet room below. A minute later, Gorkon emerged from a side corridor and bellowed at the assembled Klingons. All of them turned and glared at the Terran Empire's delegates, then upended their steins of *warnog* onto the floor. Hurling aside their fully loaded plates, they stormed together out of the conference hall, no doubt heading back to Gorkon's transport for a swift departure from Khitomer.

Spock had considered it unlikely that Gorkon would accept his offer of a truce, but after a sizable fraction of the Klingons' new fleet of ships had been lost in the blast at Praxis, it had seemed like a rare opportunity to attempt diplomacy. Had his bid for a permanent cease-fire been successful, Spock reasoned, he might have postponed the final, bitter end of his "great experiment" by a few decades. As it stood now, however, with the Klingons ostensibly committed to waging war with the resources they still had, the destruction of Praxis had only accelerated the coming conflagration. Gorkon, having already declared his intentions, would likely invade Terran space in less than two years.

There was still so much to do, and Spock's time had just become oppressively short. Many years earlier, his father had warned him that even the most logically constructed agenda could be derailed by the interference of a single "irrational political actor." In all Spock's years, he had never met another species that was even remotely so irrational as the Klingons.

Senator Pardek noted the departure of Regent Gorkon and his entourage from the conference center with muted interest. Exactly as Praetor Vrax had predicted upon receiving Spock's invitation, the Klingons had made a spectacle of themselves by arriving in force and leaving en masse after a theatrical display. Having observed their steady buildup of military resources in recent years, Pardek was not surprised. *They did not come here to negotiate,* he concluded. *They came to defend their pride by trying to intimidate the rest of us.*

He picked halfheartedly at his plateful of broiled *paszi*. It was undercooked and overspiced. *Until today,* he mused glumly, *I had thought there was no such thing as bad* paszi. *I was wrong.* Setting aside the plate on the end of a banquet table, Pardek slipped discreetly away from his fellow senators. To deflect attention and allay suspicion, he kept to the perimeter of the room and feigned interest in the various culinary delicacies on each table he passed. For appearance's sake, he even sampled a few of the Cardassian appetizers. Suppressing his gag reflex as he swallowed proved extraordinarily difficult.

Minutes later, he was on the far side of the room from the rest of the Romulan delegation, near the door reserved for the Praetor's use that led upstairs to the meeting chamber. Taking a risk, he strolled nonchalantly through the door, into the corridor on the other side.

A pair of Spock's elite imperial guards stopped Pardek the moment the door closed behind him. "Identify yourself," demanded the older of the two Vulcan soldiers.

"I am Senator Pardek, representing the Krocton Segment on Romulus. I seek an audience with Emperor Spock."

A look of suspicion passed between the guards. Again, the older one spoke for them both. "The Emperor's invitation was to Praetor Vrax."

Pardek flashed a grin to mask his impatience. "I did not say that I was invited. Only that I wish an audience with His Majesty, Emperor Spock."

To the younger guard, the older Vulcan said, "Watch him." Then he stepped away and spoke into a small communication device embedded in his wristband. His eyes took on a faraway stare as he listened to the response. When he looked back at Pardek, his expression was resigned but still distrustful. "Where is your escort?" he asked.

"I have none," Pardek said. "And I am not armed."

"You will be scanned and searched at the top of the stairs," the guard said as he stepped aside. He nodded to the younger Vulcan, who also stood clear of Pardek's path.

The senator offered polite nods to both men. "Thank you," he said, then walked up the stairs. As promised, another quartet of guards searched him there, both manually and with sensitive devices. At last satisfied that he posed no security threat, he was ushered through the door into the meeting chamber.

The large, oval room had a low ceiling that rose to a tentlike apex in its center. In the dimly lit chamber, Emperor Spock was a silhouette in front of the broad window to Pardek's left. As the senator entered the room, Spock turned away from his observation of the banquet hall to face him. His voice was deep and magnificent in the richly acoustic space. "Senator Pardek," Spock said. "Welcome."

"Thank you for seeing me, Your Majesty."

Spock gestured with an open hand toward a small table set with two chairs. "Please, join me." Pardek crossed the room in a cautious stride, wary of the sharp-eyed Vulcan woman who was standing in the shadows along the room's edge, watching him like a raptor eyeing her prey. He stopped at the table, on which rested a tray with a traditional Vulcan tea service. "Sit down," Spock said, easing himself into his own chair. Pardek sat down and struggled to remember the customs of Vulcan tea.

"Forgive my faulty protocol," Pardek said. "Is it customary for me to pour your tea?"

The Emperor lifted one eyebrow with apparent curiosity. "It is more a matter of familiarity than of protocol," he said. "The practice is usually reserved for friends and family members." Perhaps sensing Pardek's lingering confusion and hesitation, Spock added, "If you wish to pour my tea, I will take it as a gesture of goodwill."

Pardek nodded his understanding and picked up the teapot. Taking care not to spill any tea, he filled Spock's cup. When he set down the teapot, Spock picked it up and reciprocated the courtesy by filling Pardek's white ceramic cup. "You honor me, Your Majesty," Pardek said, half bowing his head. "I am humbled by your graciousness."

After savoring a slow sip of his tea, Spock set down his cup. "Why have you asked for this meeting, Senator?"

Gently setting down his own tea, Pardek replied, "This conversation is strictly unofficial." He took a moment to compose his thoughts. "I have paid close attention to your reforms, Majesty. In attempting to discern a pattern to your actions, all of my conclusions have seemed . . . implausible."

Mild intrigue animated Spock's expression. "How so?"

"Your promotion of civil liberties has come at the expense of your own executive power," Pardek said. "And in the face of growing belligerence from the Klingon Empire, you have been reducing Starfleet rather than expanding it. It seems almost as if you are acting with the intention of letting your empire fall." He picked up his tea to take another sip. "But of course, that's an outrageous conclusion."

"Indeed," Spock replied. He picked up his own tea.

"May I ask you a question, Your Majesty?"

Nodding from behind his tea, Spock said, "You may."

"Did you, just minutes ago, reject an offer of alliance from Regent Gorkon?"

"I did," Spock said.

At the risk of being hounded from the Romulan Senate for speaking out of turn, Pardek told Spock, "Praetor Vrax intends to make you a similar offer." He watched Spock's face for a reaction but could discern nothing behind that frown-cut visage and gray goatee. "You will reject the Praetor's offer as well?"

"I shall," Spock said.

None of it made any sense to Pardek, who set down his teacup a bit more roughly than he'd intended. "I'm sorry, Your Majesty," he said. "But I find your actions baffling. You are a wise and learned man—your public addresses and scientific policies have confirmed that. But in strategic and political matters, you seem committed to a suicidal agenda."

"I disagree," Spock said.

"Majesty, the Cardassians haven't come to Khitomer to broker a treaty with your empire; they're afraid of you, afraid that your democratic reforms will inspire a demand for the same in their own nation. And it's hardly a coincidence that the Tholians declined your invitation. Even after you disbanded Operation Vanguard, they've remained openly hostile toward your empire. I predict that within two decades they will ally with the Gorn to oust your colonies from the Taurus Reach."

"And with the Breen to seize all territory from Izar to Vega," Spock said. "We are well aware of the Tholians' plans."

Pardek sat stunned for a moment. "Then why do you not *act*?"

"Because I choose to *react*," Spock said. "I plan to renounce preemptive warfare as a tool of foreign policy. I will not incite conflicts based solely upon what *might* occur."

The Romulan senator didn't know whether to think Spock noble or naïve. "A risky policy given the current astropolitical climate," Pardek said.

"Perhaps," Spock replied. "But it is the most logical one. The resources of an empire are finite and in great demand. It is foolish and wasteful to expend them against *potentials* when they can be more effectively deployed against *actualities*."

Allowing himself a moment to absorb Spock's argument, Pardek leaned back in his chair and idly stroked his chin. "If I might be permitted to inquire, Your Majesty . . . what did you expect would be the outcome of this summit?"

"An alliance between the Klingons and the Cardassians," Spock said. "Now that Gorkon lacks sufficient fleet power to conquer my empire alone, he and Legate Renar of Cardassia will negotiate a pact predicated on the goal of destroying the Terran Empire. The Tholian Assembly and the Romulan Star Empire will declare themselves neutral even as they seize several remote systems. The Breen and the Gorn, being consummate opportunists, will work as mercenaries; they will aid the Cardassians and the Klingons in their conquest of Terran space. This will all transpire within approximately two years of this conference's end."

What horrified Pardek most about Spock's prediction wasn't

its specificity but rather that the Vulcan Emperor had delivered it with such tranquility. "If you know all this is coming to pass," Pardek replied, "why do you plan to refuse the Praetor's offer of alliance? Why let your empire be conquered when we could help you defend it?"

Spock replied with terrifying certainty. "Because the fall of my empire will mean the end of all of yours."

13

The Ashes of Empire

Nine years had passed since Doctor Carol Marcus had last met with Emperor Spock. It had been one of the most demanding and all-consuming periods of her life. There had been so few people whom she could trust, so few who were actually cleared to know the true scope of the project that Spock had code-named Memory Omega. Only her son, Doctor David Marcus, had she entrusted with the whole truth, shortly after he'd joined her on the project.

Memory Omega was the most ambitious project of its kind that she had ever seen. It was a repository of the collected knowledge of the Empire—all its peoples, all its worlds. Science, history, music, art, literature, medicine, philosophy—the preservation of all these endeavors and more was its mission. Multiple redundant sites were linked through a secret, real-time communications network unlike any other known in the galaxy: quantum transceivers, composed of subatomic particles vibrating in perfect sympathy even across interstellar distances, perhaps even across any distance. A frequency provoked in one linked particle vibrated its simpatico partner perfectly. Marcus had hypothesized that each pair of sympathetic particles was actually just one particle occupying two points in space-time simultaneously, but so far she had been unable to prove or disprove her supposition. What mattered was that the system worked, and its transmissions were undetectable and completely beyond interception. And what she found most amazing about it was that it had been invented by her own beloved son.

She wished that David could be at her side now. A trio of Vulcan imperial guards—one leading her, two following her—escorted her through the deserted, cordoned-off corridors of the *I.S.S. Enterprise,* which was now under the command of Captain Saavik. Acting on confidential orders from the Emperor, Marcus had booked passage on a civilian luxury liner to Garulon. Less than ten minutes ago, the *Enterprise* had intercepted the liner, though on what pretense Marcus had no idea. As soon as the luxury ship had dropped out of warp, a transporter beam had snared Marcus from her stateroom and rematerialized her aboard Spock's imperial flagship. This, she surmised, was to be a meeting with no official record and no unnecessary witnesses.

She was led to a door that glided open before her. The guard who had been walking in front of her stepped aside at the threshold and signaled with an outstretched arm that she should continue inside alone. Marcus walked through the open doorway and recognized the telltale signs of a Vulcan habitation: the artificial gravity was slightly stronger, the temperature a little higher, the humidity and the illumination significantly lower. The door closed behind her. Her eyes adjusted to the dimness, and she recognized Emperor Spock on the far side of the room. He nodded to her. "Come in, Doctor."

Marcus crossed the room, honored her host with a nimble curtsey, then replied, "Your Majesty."

Spock acknowledged her with a curt nod. "For a number of reasons," he said, "this meeting must be very brief. Recent developments have made it necessary for us to hasten the completion of the project."

Alarmed, she asked, "Developments, Your Majesty?"

"A Klingon-Cardassian alliance will soon move against us,"

Spock said. "In less than two years they will launch a massive, co-ordinated attack that will destroy Starfleet."

Shaking her head, she said, "I don't think that's enough time, Your Majesty. Too many sites are still off-line."

"The Imperial Corps of Engineers is at your disposal, Doctor," Spock said. "Memory Omega must be completed before the invasion begins."

Marcus replied, "I don't think we can finish the project in two years without compromising its secrecy."

Spock sat and steepled his fingers in front of him while he pondered the situation. "Can the last six sites be automated?"

She thought about that, then tilted her head and shrugged. "Yes, but they'd be little more than data-backup nodes."

"Precisely," Spock said. "We could halt the terraforming at those sites and relocate their teams to the existing ones."

Marcus shook her head. "That would overpopulate the current sites, Your Majesty. With fewer than one hundred fifty personnel, the sites can be sustained indefinitely. If we exceed that, then resource depletion becomes inevitable."

"Over what time period?" Spock asked.

It took her a few moments to do the math in her head—which was embarrassing, since she knew that Spock had probably already completed his own mental calculations with greater accuracy than she was capable of emulating. "Doubling the populations," she said, "reduces the sustainability period to just less than ninety-one years."

He considered that, then frowned. "Unfortunate, but it will have to suffice. I will make the necessary adjustments to the other aspects of the operation."

All the secrecy in which Spock had shrouded this grand project still worried Marcus. She, her son, and several dozen of the foremost scientific thinkers in the Empire—as well as forty-seven previously suppressed dissidents, artists, and progressive political philosophers—had been sequestered inside the Genesis Cave deep within the Regula I planetoid for close to nine years. From there, they had directed the creation of several more hidden redoubts just like it, in various remote sectors of the Empire, always in unpopulated star systems that were as devoid of exploitable resources as they were empty of life-forms. Though it had seemed at first like an intellectuals' paradise, it had soon come to seem increasingly like a prison.

"Your Majesty, I have a question about the project."

In a surprisingly candid tone, the Emperor said, "Ask."

Mustering her courage, she said, "Why are all the people who most strongly support you being hidden away? It's obvious that you're working to turn the Empire into a republic. We could help ease that transition. Why sequester us?"

"When the Klingon-Cardassian invasion comes," Spock said, "it will succeed, and we will be conquered. . . . But when the war is long over, Memory Omega will be the seed from which our republic will be reborn, rising from the ashes of empire." He got up, moved to a cabinet along one wall, and opened it. From inside he took a large black case with a handle. "Inside this case are data cards containing the final entries for the database." He handed it to her. "Guard them well."

The case was heavy enough that, as she took it from Spock, its weight wrenched her shoulder. Straightening her posture, she asked, "What's on them?"

"The truth," Spock said. After a pause, he added, "The transporter room is standing by to beam you back to your ship. You should return before your absence is noted."

"Of course, Your Majesty," she said.

He lifted his right hand and spread his fingers in the traditional Vulcan salute. "Live long and prosper, Doctor Marcus."

Remembering the proper response, she lifted her own right hand and copied the finger positions as best she could. "Peace and long life, Your Majesty." They lowered their hands, and Marcus walked toward the door. As the portal opened ahead of her, she stopped and looked back. "I just realized," she said, "I never thanked you for killing Jim Kirk. . . . I was always afraid of what he would've done if he'd known about David."

"You were wise to fear him," Spock said, sending a chill through her. "He would have killed you both."

The door buzzer sounded and Spock bid his visitor enter.

He turned at the sound of the opening door. Captain Saavik walked in and saluted him as the door closed behind her. "Doctor Marcus has been beamed back to her ship, Your Majesty."

"Well done, Captain." Now that he had a moment to actually look at her, he was pleased to see that commanding a starship flattered her. The hesitation of her youthful self was gone, the uncertainty of her Academy days supplanted by conviction and discipline. It would be a shame to make her give it up, but it was time for her to embrace a larger destiny. "Two days after we reach Earth," he said, "I will convene a special joint session of the Legislature, to make a statement about the results of the Khitomer Conference. But before I do so, you will resign from Starfleet and return to Vulcan."

Saavik's stoic countenance betrayed no reaction. "Permission to speak freely, Majesty?"

"Granted."

"Is there a connection between the timing of your address and your request for my resignation?"

Spock nodded. "There is. When my declaration is complete, nothing will be the same. It would be best if you were away by then, traveling under an alias."

For a few moments, she broke eye contact with him and processed what he had said. When her eyes turned back to him, they carried the gleam of cognition. "Then this is to be the moment you spoke of so long ago?"

"It is," he said.

His answer seemed to trouble her. "This is far more abrupt than I had imagined it would be, Majesty. Unrest, even rebellion might follow, and our enemies will—"

"I am aware of the risks," Spock said.

Small motions and expressions—a twitch near the creases of

her right eye, the subtle curling of her fingers into the first inkling of a fist—conveyed her profound anxiety. "This is not a time to deprive yourself of allies, Your Majesty."

"Nor am I doing any such thing," Spock countered. "I am, however, redeploying my allies to those locations where they can serve me best. And it is time for you to return to Vulcan."

The muscles of her face relaxed, and her fingers gave up their slow curl. Resignation brought her singularity of focus and tranquility of mind. "Then this is the end," she said.

"And the beginning," Spock confirmed.

Eyes downcast, Saavik said, "As you command, Majesty. I will resign." Then she met his gaze with her own steely look. "But before I do, I have one final duty to perform."

Orders filled the air, loud, crisp, and fierce. "Single file, left face! Atten—tion! *Hai!*" The emperor's elite guards snapped into formation, pivoted left on their heels, and stiffened to attention, eyes front.

In the middle of the line, Valeris kept her stare level and unblinking. The captain of the guard walked past her, reviewing the line before Emperor Spock and Empress Marlena exited the turbolift from the imperial residence. Moments from now, the guards would escort them on the short walk to the Forum Hall, where the Legislature awaited the Emperor's arrival. A live, real-time subspace transmission had already begun, to share with the entire population of the Empire what Spock's advisers had promised would be a "momentous announcement."

I must remain calm. Valeris focused on the well-rehearsed details of her mission. This was her appointed hour to strike. No strategy was required here, only commitment. Her armor, loaded with ultritium, was fully primed and ready to be detonated. *I will die, but this failed political experiment will end, and a stronger empire will be born.* She told herself that this was a logical exchange—her life for the continued safety of the Empire, under the more competent guidance of the military. Years of preparation had brought her to this threshold moment. One press of a button and her mission would be complete. The action would be simple; her readiness to act would be all.

One final check. She reached down to confirm that the detonator, disguised as a communicator, was secure on her hip.

It was missing.

The first flutter of alarm had barely registered in her mind when she felt a pair of blades stab up, under the layered plates of her *lorica segmentata,* and slice deep into her torso from both sides. Her cry of pain caught in her throat, which rapidly fountained with dark green blood.

To either side of her, none of the other guards moved to her aid. Not one of them even looked at Valeris as her knees buckled and delivered her rudely onto the floor. Torov, the captain of the guard, watched her crumple to the ground . . . then he turned his back on her.

Lying on the cold marble slabs, surrounded by her own lifeblood, Valeris watched as her killer stepped through the gap in the line where she herself had stood seconds earlier.

Captain Saavik towered above Valeris, the bloody daggers still in her hands. She squatted beside Valeris and spoke in a husky whisper, as though they were intimates exchanging secrets. "Your accomplice General Quiniven was exposed two months ago," Saavik said. Her dark eyes burned momentarily with venomous hatred. "Several weeks in a Klingon mind-sifter exposed the rest of your conspirators. So in case you think that Admirals Cartwright, Bennett, or Morrow will finish your grand plan for you, they will not. Nor will Colonel West, nor Commodore Vosrok, nor Admiral zh'Ferro."

Valeris's head lolled toward the floor. Saavik slipped the flat of one of her blades under Valeris's chin and gently turned the expiring woman's face so that they made eye contact again. Valeris saw Saavik's other dagger, held high, ready to deliver the coup de grâce. The turbolift doors opened at the end of the hallway, and Emperor Spock and Empress Marlena emerged.

"One man is about to summon the future," Saavik told Valeris. "But you will not live to see it." Saavik's dagger struck, sharp, cold, and deadly, but for Valeris the fatal blow was not nearly so terrible as the sting of her own failure.

Spock and Marlena paused together at the stairs to the podium. She took his hand. "Are you sure?" she asked.

"It is time," he said. "We cannot afford to wait."

Her trembling frown concealed her swell of emotions. "Then let it be done," she said, and she released his hand.

Alone, Spock climbed the stairs and moved to the lectern, awash in the percussive roar of applause, all of it from the floor of the Common Forum. The sound rebounded from the gilt dome of the ceiling, beneath which the ring of balconies were filled with scowling senators and governors of grim bearing. The Emperor rested his hands on the lectern's edges and waited. Moments later, the applause diminished, then dissipated like a summer rainstorm coming to a sudden end.

"Members of the Legislature," Spock began, enunciating with precision. "Distinguished Governors of the Empire. Honored guests. Please be seated." His standing audience sat down in a rustle of movement. When they had settled, he continued. "I have convened this joint session to issue an imperial proclamation with no precedent. In recent years, I have instituted reforms of a radical nature, altering the structure of our government and shifting the tenor of our domestic and foreign policies.

"Today shall mark another such change."

A worried murmur coursed through the thousands of people gathered in the Common Forum. Spock waited for the susurrus to abate before he pressed ahead. Just as he had done when making his declaration of citizens' freedoms nine years earlier, he had ordered this address to be transmitted on a live subspace channel to every world in the Empire and to its foreign neighbors. Hundreds of billions of people were about to witness the boldest, and last, reforms of Spock's imperial reign.

"Since the hour of its inception, our empire has been predicated on tyranny. Territory and resources have been seized by force of arms, dissent crushed and made criminal, loyalty secured through intimidation.

"The Terran Empire has expended as much blood and treasure on suppressing its own people as it has on defending itself from foreign powers. This ruthless policing of our own citizens is one factor in our cultural stagnation; another is that we can grow only as quickly as we can conquer.

"War is an inefficient means to an end. It leaves ruin in its wake, resources expended for naught, lives taken and given in vain. It is the most egregious form of waste known to sentient beings, and, like all waste, it is illogical. For more than a century, preemptive war has been the chief instrument of foreign and domestic policy for this empire.

"No longer. On behalf of the Empire, I renounce it."

The hubbub of alarm was stronger now, from the Forum members as well as the senators. Their reaction was just as Spock had expected; he had known from the outset that this moment would terrify them, but that could not be helped. And now that he had begun, there was no longer any choice but to push on to the inevitable end.

"A nation founded on waste and injustice cannot endure," he said with force, quieting the rumbles of the Legislature. "For several decades, the leaders of Vulcan have known that our empire is on a path to its own demise. Habitable worlds and energy reserves are both finite; we will exhaust our resources and collapse into civil war within two hundred fifteen years—unless we change the course of our civilization."

Spock hesitated before making his next statement. To make such a revelation as this to the galaxy at large was a gamble, one whose outcome had proved too complex to predict. He chose to let the truth speak for itself. "During my service in Starfleet, I met four people from another, parallel universe—one much like our own, and very different. Those four people were that universe's versions of my own captain and crewmates, transposed across the dimensional barrier by a transporter accident.

"In returning them to their own universe and recovering my crewmates, I was afforded a glimpse of their reality. They had come from a federation of planets, a coalition of worlds bound together by mutual consent. These worlds and peoples shared their resources and knowledge willingly, defended each other mutually, and valued life and freedom more than power. And they prospered for it. Harmony had brought them stability. Peace had made possible the eradication of hunger and poverty.

"Their way of life is peaceful. Sustainable. Logical."

Stunned, ostensibly horrified silence filled the Forum Hall. Determined to seize the moment, Spock continued. "The path that I have chosen for our future is modeled on that which I have seen succeed beyond even our most optimistic projections. Despotism is a path to self-destruction. Our best hope for survival and prosperity lies in reforming our civilization as a representative republic, with a system of checks and balances between strongly constrained and coequal branches of government, and a charter of inalienable rights and freedoms that guarantees the sovereignty of the citizen over the state.

"As of today, I issue my final decrees as Emperor: I revoke the authority of the planetary governors and command that they be replaced by elected presidents." He touched a single key on his lectern. "Second, I have just transmitted to every member of the Forum and Senate a proposed charter for this new political entity. It is now the duty of the Legislature to review this document, revise it, ratify it, and submit it to the head of state for enactment.

"My third and final decree: The Terran Empire is hereby dissolved, and the Terran Republic is established. I shall assume the role of Consul for a period of not more than four years, after which I shall be required to stand for reelection, like any member of the Legislature.

"Imperial fiat is hereby replaced by a charter of law, subject to legislative review and amendment.

"The Empire is over. Former governors, I thank you for your past service and discharge you. Distinguished members of the Forum and the Senate, when you are ready to discuss the charter proposal, I will be at your service. Until then, I pledge myself to defending the rights and freedoms of the citizens of the Terran Republic, whom I now serve. Thank you, and farewell."

Raging howls of protest wailed in the cavernous hall as Consul Spock walked away from the lectern, descended the stairs, and joined his wife for the rapid retreat back to the turbolift.

Even amid the din of shouting voices, Spock distinctly heard the epithets and slurs aimed in his direction. Change always frightened humans, he knew, and he had just upended their entire civilization. Even though he was no longer an emperor, his elite guards swiftly moved into a protective formation around him and Marlena and escorted them from the Forum at a brisk step. Without stopping to answer questions from the many furious Starfleet officers in the hallway, Spock and Marlena jogged into the turbolift. Marlena sighed with relief as the doors slid shut and they were once more cocooned in silence.

"It's really done," she said, sounding both amazed and terrified. "You did it. . . . The Empire's gone."

For once, Spock was at a loss for words. His emotional control almost faltered as he contemplated the enormity of what he had just done, and how irrevocable it was—or more precisely, how irrevocable it soon would be.

The doors of the turbolift opened, and he walked back into the formerly imperial, now consular residence. Marlena remained close behind him as he moved resolutely through the opulent foyer and parlor to the private antechamber where he kept the Tantalus field device. Incorrectly anticipating his intentions, she bounded ahead of him and keyed in the sequence to open its concealing panel, which lifted away to reveal the device's tarnished but still perfectly functional interface.

She spoke quickly, her voice pitched with excitement. "We'll have to move quickly, there won't be much time. I'd suggest getting rid of Senator ch'Neth before he—"

"Marlena," Spock interrupted, drawing a small hand phaser from beneath his robe. "Step away from the device."

Horror and panic made her look crazed, feral. She spread her arms, shielded the device with her body. "No," she protested. "Spock, you can't! We need it. Without it, we can't defend ourselves. All the work, everything we fought for—it won't mean anything without the power to enforce it. Think about what you're doing, for God's sake!"

"I have thought about nothing else for the past twenty-six years," Spock said. "Moments ago, I forced our government to renounce terror and preemptive violence as instruments of statecraft; I must now relinquish them as tools of politics." He stepped closer to her, keeping the phaser leveled at her trembling body. "This device must never fall into the hands of another tyrant, Marlena. It has served our purposes, but it is time to let it go. . . . Step out of the way."

Marlena's resolve weakened, then it collapsed. Her arms fell limp at her sides, and she stepped clear and moved behind Spock. He took careful aim and set his phaser to maximum power. A single, prolonged burst of phaser energy vaporized the interface of the Tantalus field device, melted its internal components, and finally reduced its mysterious, shielded core to a puddle of bubbling slag and acrid, blue-white smoke.

The deadliest implement of arbitrary power Spock had ever known was gone, destroyed with the secrets of its creation.

This, he knew, was the beginning of the end.

2295

14

In the Hour of Broken Dreams

Consul Spock and Marlena Moreau stood together on the floor of the Common Forum and awaited their executioners.

They faced each other, the tips of the first two fingers of their right hands pressed solemnly together, a sign of their bond of affection. Even from this slight union, Spock was able to touch Marlena's troubled thoughts; he counseled her to remain calm, to be at peace with the end that was coming for them both.

Deep rumbles shook the floor under their feet, and a sound like rolling thunder filled the palace-turned-people's-hall that surrounded them.

Energy weapons screeched somewhere outside.

He felt her love and quiet admiration for him as she looked up into his eyes. "It was nice while it lasted," she said.

Spock lifted his eyebrows, a sly admission of bemusement. "I presume you are referring to the Republic."

"All of it," she said. "The Republic, your reforms . . . us." She paused as the clacks of marching boots echoed louder outside the doors. "It was all worth it," she continued. "Even if it couldn't last, I'm glad I lived to see it."

"My only regret is that its tenure had to be so brief," he said. "I am curious to know how this great experiment might have fared on a longer time scale."

She smiled sadly. "Yes. That would have been interesting."

Interesting, but impossible, Spock reminded himself. Given the state of political relations between the Terran Empire and its neighbors in local space, Spock had known from the outset that a cautious, gradual transition of the Empire to a republic would never have succeeded. There had been too many variables to contend with. Just as important, Sarek had been right; at the first sign of weakness, the Klingons had redoubled their aggression against the Empire. Keeping them, the Romulans, and the Cardassians at bay had taxed the Imperial Starfleet almost to its breaking point.

Then, just more than one year ago, against the counsel of all his senior advisers, Spock had proposed the unthinkable: unilateral disarmament. Entire fleets of ships had been mothballed; hundreds of defensive installations were ordered to stand down; millions of troops found themselves discharged from active service. Then, before the furor over such a gross dereliction of executive duty could engulf the Legislature, the invasion had begun, and the time for debate was ended.

Today, Spock's civilization was reaping the bitter harvest of all his decisions. The invasion force of allied Klingon and Cardassian ships had overrun the defenses of the nascent Terran Republic. The Klingons had unleashed a fleet of birds-of-prey that could fire while cloaked, a tactical advantage that had proved all but invincible. Entire fleets of Terran ships had been annihilated, and one world after another had fallen with alarming speed.

Sixteen hours ago, Earth itself had been blockaded by an Alliance fleet. A hundred thousand Klingon and Cardassian shock troops were landing on the planet's surface every hour. Virtually unopposed, they had wiped out the planet's military and political targets and subdued its civilian population.

Thirty minutes ago, they had begun their siege of the Terran

Forum. Ten minutes ago, the Forum's external energy barrier had fallen, and its few remaining security personnel had mounted a doomed counterattack.

Two minutes ago the shooting had stopped.

One minute ago, Alliance troops had entered the building.

Booming impacts at the locked doors of the Forum Hall heralded the enemy's arrival.

Spock and Marlena waited in silence for the doors to break open. This moment, Spock had known since the beginning, had been inevitable . . . and necessary.

Watching the door, Marlena maintained a serene yet defiant cast to her features that was almost Vulcan in its reserve. It moved Spock's human half deeply, and he could not remain silent. "Though I have rarely expressed it, Marlena, I want you to know . . . that I love you."

"And I love you, Spock," she said, her poise unbroken.

At that, they turned their eyes back to the doors, which heaved and buckled under constant, brutal assault from without.

The doors splintered apart. Regent Gorkon entered the Forum Hall with Legate Renar, the supreme commander of the Cardassian Union. In the wide corridor behind them, the floor was littered with the corpses of Spock's elite Vulcan guards.

Two platoons of foot soldiers—one Cardassian, the other Klingon—followed the officers into the Forum Hall, fanned out, and flanked Spock and Marlena. Gorkon and Renar stopped a few meters in front of the couple.

"Consul Spock," Gorkon bellowed, filling the empty reaches of the hall with his voice. "Your Starfleet is destroyed, your capital occupied, your government fallen. Kneel and surrender."

Evincing neither pride nor despair, Spock replied, "No."

His answer seemed to perplex the Klingon Regent.

"Surrender, Spock," Gorkon demanded. "Kneel before me and I will show mercy to your conquered people."

"I do not believe you," Spock said. "And I do not surrender."

Renar stepped in front of Gorkon and smirked at Spock.

"You're right not to trust him," he said, tilting his head at Gorkon. "There won't be any mercy for your people. I'll see to that." The Cardassian's smirk broadened to a smile, and that erupted into a mocking laugh. "You really are a fool, aren't you? Diplomacy? Disarmament? What were you thinking?"

"I did what was logical and necessary," Spock said.

Spock watched Renar wind up to strike him. He could have caught Renar's hand before the blow landed, twisted his wrist, broken his arm. It was possible that Spock might even have been able to kill Renar before the troops on either side of him shot him down. Instead, he remained still and let Renar backhand him across the face. Spock's lower lip split open on impact. He ignored the throbbing sting and the warm trickle of blood on his chin. It was only pain, a mental illusion.

Seething with contempt, Renar loomed over the Vulcan. "Your people have been the most brutal overlords in the quadrant for nearly a century! Did you really think we'd pass up a chance to destroy the Terran Empire?"

"You have done no such thing," Spock said. "I destroyed the Terran Empire—two years ago, with a single declaration. What you have conquered is the Republic that replaced it."

Gorkon moved forward to stand beside Renar. Looking down at Spock, the Regent appeared bewildered. "You have delivered your people into ruin, Spock. Presided over the end of all you were trusted to defend. Are you so cold-blooded that you feel not a whit of remorse? Not a single pang of guilt for your failure?"

"I regret nothing," Spock said. "I concede no defeat. I admit no failure." He weaved his fingers between Marlena's and clutched her hand tightly.

Legate Renar turned to one of the officers in his platoon. "Start recording this," he said to the man. "I want the entire galaxy to see what happens when fools lead empires." The junior officer activated a scanning device to make an audiovisual recording. Renar looked back at Spock. "Any last words?"

"With the fall of my civilization begins the end of your own. Freedom will overcome. Tyranny cannot prevail."

Renar snorted derisively. "It can if it tries hard enough," he said. "And if people like you lack the will to oppose it." He and Gorkon stepped back. The Cardassian Legate lifted his arm, and then the order was given.

A flash of light was all Spock saw of the killing blow, but in that moment he knew that he had won.

15

An Army of Shadows

For a week since Spock's execution, the skies of Vulcan had been dark with the ships of the enemy.

Klingon and Cardassian troops had come by the thousands to every major city, and had met no resistance in any of them. No violence had hampered the Alliance's efforts to establish total control over the planet. No one had protested when the curfews were imposed, or when the planet's interstellar communications capability was disabled and placed under Klingon control.

On the first day, President Sarek had surrendered immediately and unconditionally. Kang, the new Klingon governor, had responded by cutting off Sarek's head and leaving it with Sarek's body in the main square of ShiKahr.

When a crowd had gathered to claim Sarek's remains, the Cardassians had slaughtered them all in the street, laughing uproariously amid the screeching of their weapons. The new masters of civilization had seemed determined to prove themselves infinitely crueler than their predecessors.

The second day had brought mass executions. Little reason had been given for who was put to death or why. Government bureaucrats. Law enforcement personnel. Clergy and adepts from Mount Seleya. Journalists. Artists. Teachers. Musicians.

Landmarks and symbols had been the victims on the third day. An orbital bombardment had reduced the temple at Mount Seleya to shattered stone and radioactive glass. Lost now were the ancient teachings of Surak, the eons of preserved memory in the Halls of Ancient Thought, the arcane mysteries of *fal-tor-pan* and the *Kolinahr*. The Vulcan Science Academy lay in smoldering ruins. Hundreds of museums, universities, and libraries were demolished, their contents incinerated, their faculties slain.

At dawn on the fourth day in ShiKahr, the Alliance troops had begun dividing the Vulcan population by age and gender, by profession and body type. Parents had found themselves riven from children, siblings had been forced apart, lovers and spouses were torn asunder. By the tens of thousands, the people of Vulcan had been marched into ramshackle internment camps, implanted with biometric transceivers, logged and identified and "processed."

The old and the sick were disposed of on the fifth day.

By the end of the sixth day, the Alliance had determined where all its new, pacifistic slaves would be of the most use throughout their newly expanded empire, and so they had begun the long and continuing process of herding millions of Vulcans onto transport ships. Each man, woman, and child was branded with the mark of a slave, collared, and manacled.

It was sunset in ShiKahr on the seventh day of the new galactic order. Saavik, clothed in dirty civilian garb, marched with plodding steps in a line of prisoners. She was one of ten thousand newly bound slaves being shepherded toward a massive transport ship, which was perched atop the rubble of the city's once-glorious plaza. The line jerked forward, stopping and starting and stopping again. A cluster of Cardassian officers and clerks, working at the bottom of the transport's main ramp, processed a few slaves at a time.

Bitter smoke from nearby burning buildings lingered heavily in the dry, hot air as Saavik neared the front of the line. At its head, the prisoners were funneled to one of ten processing clerks.

She overheard the people ahead of her being questioned by the Cardassian officers.

"Name, city of residence, profession," asked a Cardassian officer. It was always the same question, asked the same way.

"Temok, LalKan, particle physicist," a man answered, then he held out his hand.

A Cardassian clerk scanned it, logged the information from the man's subcutaneous transponder, and confirmed his identity. The Cardassian officer nodded, said, "Research division," then waved the enslaved scientist past him, onto the transport.

"Name, city of residence, profession."

T'Shen, PelHan, engineer. "Construction corps."

Sokol, KorLir, surgeon. "Domestic servant."

Kolok, ShiKahr, architect. "Construction corps."

T'Shya, LorEm, computer programmer. "Research division."

Saavik moved to the front of the line. She listened to the Cardassians talking between themselves, speaking about the Vulcans as if they were deaf or incapable of understanding. "These are the best slaves we've seen in a long time," said one officer. "Sturdy. They'll hold up well on planets like Harkoum."

"The pacifism's my favorite part," another officer said. "Makes them easy to control. Not like the Andorians."

"I heard Gul Merdan's people had to wipe out most of Andoria," a clerk interjected.

The officers nodded, and the one who had spoken first said, "Some people just aren't meant to be slaves." He smirked and nodded at the line of prisoners. "And then there's this filth."

A guard nudged Saavik with the muzzle of his rifle and ushered her toward an open processing desk. Following the example she had observed while waiting her turn, she halted in front of the table, just within arm's reach of the Cardassian officer and his clerk.

"Name, city of residence, profession."

"L'Nesh," she said, using the alias she had been given upon her return to Vulcan two years ago. "ShiKahr, stone mason." She held out her hand and kept it steady as the clerk scanned the chip that other Cardassians had implanted into Saavik's palm.

A soft tone signaled confirmation of Saavik's cover identity.

The officer's face was drawn with boredom as he mumbled, "Domestic servant," and waved Saavik onto the transport.

Continuing past the processing desk, Saavik concealed her amazement that Spock's prediction had proved so accurate. Until this moment, she had continued to harbor doubts that his strategy would work, but now, watching it unfold on such a massive scale, she allowed herself to believe, finally, that he had been right. The Klingons and the Cardassians, like despots everywhere, looked upon slaves and servants as nonentities, as an underclass to be almost universally ignored so long as it remains under control. Lulled by the Vulcans' cultural professions of pacifism and logic, the Klingons and the Cardassians had walked blindly into Spock's trap and fallen prey to the greatest disinformation campaign in galactic history.

Flush with overconfidence after their swift military victory, they were now ushering a hundred million touch-telepath sleeper agents into their homes and halls of power.

This day had been years in the making. The network of Vulcan sleepers had grown slowly at first, as each new recruit had been brought into the fold with extreme caution. But as the network added members, its rate of expansion had accelerated. Spies and turncoats had been exposed and eliminated with prejudice. Only the faithful insurgents remained now, Spock's loyalists . . . and soon they would be ensconced in the First City of Qo'noS, in the Central Command of Cardassia Prime, on the capital ships of the Alliance, in the shadowy redoubts of its secret military research facilities.

Saavik knew that toppling the Alliance—and, one day, the Romulan Star Empire—would not be easy, nor would it be swift. But she was certain now that Spock had been right.

It was inevitable.

Fo Tsrow Eht Sdlrow Htob

Greg Cox

To my parents,
for putting me up while I wrote this story.
And a whole lot more.

1

Dead warriors guarded the entrance to the burial mound. The petrified mummies stood facing each other across the weathered stone archway, clad in the ceremonial garb of Vulcan executioners. Veils masked their skeletal faces. Withered ears tapered to a point. Their bare chests exposed dry brown skin stretched over protruding ribs. Leather nooses hung from the faded blue sashes girding their waists. Each mummy gripped the shaft of an upraised *lirpa,* holding the traditional weapon aloft so that the sharpened blades at the end of the weighted staffs met above the portal.

Luc Picard eyed the shadowy opening with anticipation. It had taken hours to clear away the packed dirt and clay that had concealed the archway, but at last he was ready to explore the ancient tomb itself. Heaps of excavated earth were piled up behind him. Perspiration gleamed on his brow. His coarsely woven shirt and trousers were soaked with sweat. He couldn't complain, though. *All this hard work will be worth it,* he thought, *if I find what I'm looking for.*

He tapped the combadge affixed to his scuffed brown vest. "September 28, 2371 A.C.E.," he dictated to his ship's computer, stubbornly clinging to the old Terran dating system even though all reputable archeologists now used the birth of the Alliance as their chronological touchstone. "I have exposed the entrance to a Sakethan burial mound on New T'Karath. The mound resembles those found on Calder II, which bodes well for this expedition. A preliminary inspection suggests that the tomb has been undisturbed for at least two millennia."

Picard smiled. He had been afraid that another tomb raider might have already beaten him to his prize. *Looks like I'm the first person to visit this site since it was sealed up hundreds of centuries ago.* Although uninhabited now, and under Alliance dominion, New T'Karath had once been home to a small colony of Vulcan dissidents and mystics. *Probably just as well that they died out several generations back, before they lived to see their homeworld laid waste by the old Terran Empire.*

Although eager to step inside the mound, he didn't rush in blindly. Instead he peered suspiciously at the gleaming blades of the *lirpas* as they hung suspended above the threshold. An inscription was carved into the stone archway. Picard thought he got the gist of what the ancient pictographs said, but he pulled out his tricorder just to be sure. The device's built-in automatic translator had been programmed with over a dozen obscure and forgotten Vulcan dialects. He scanned the glyphs with the tricorder.

" 'Go no further,' " it translated, " 'lest Mind and Body part for all time.' "

A death threat, in other words. He nodded gravely. *I figured as much.* He hadn't lasted this long as a treasure hunter without learning to take a few reasonable precautions. Bending over, he extracted a fist-sized rock from the ground and hurled it past the immobile guards into the murky tunnel beyond. The rock clattered to a stop somewhere in the shadows. To Picard's surprise, the raised weapons remained where they were. He arched an eyebrow. Perhaps the armed mummies were purely decorative?

"Not bloody likely," he muttered. He walked over to his backpack, which was propped up against a pile of rubble, and retrieved a miniature antigrav pallet, about the size of a shoebox. Ordinarily, the pallet was used to transport heavy objects, but Picard had a different purpose in mind. "There's more than one way to trigger a trap."

He keyed a negative amount into the pallet's graviton inverter, then gave it a shove toward the marble archway. Momentum carried the floating pallet over the threshold while its antigrav unit projected the weight of an adult humanoid onto the tomb's dusty stone floor.

The razor-sharp *lirpas* came swinging down, slicing the empty pallet in two. Sparks and smoke erupted from the bisected device. Metal components crashed to the ground.

That's more like it, Picard thought. Confident that the archway's ominous threat had now been carried out, he stepped over the lowered blades and ventured into the tunnel. A beam of visible light from his tricorder illuminated the way ahead, revealing a sloping passageway that descended steeply beneath the surface of the planet. He swept the tricorder from side to side, recording visual and spectrographic data for later analysis. He looked forward to examining the scans at leisure . . . after he had found his prize, of course.

His footsteps echoed off the dense limestone walls, which contained enough kelbonite to seriously inhibit any long-range scans or transporters. As a result, Picard had been forced to explore the forgotten tomb in person; he couldn't just beam up the artifact he was looking for, as he had on Calder II. *No matter,* he thought. To be honest, he preferred it this way. He liked getting his hands dirty.

He soon came to a junction of three tunnels, branching out in different directions. *Just as I expected,* he thought. If these catacombs were anything like some of the other tombs he'd encountered before, this was only the beginning of an elaborate maze designed to foil unwanted intruders. An unprepared grave robber could easily end up lost forever in the subterranean labyrinth ahead.

Fortunately, Picard knew what he was doing. Crouching before the triple portal, he carefully brushed away the dust of ages to expose an inscription chiseled into the floor.

" 'As in all things,' " the tricorder translated, " 'let the Mind be your Guide.' "

Picard rose to his feet. The Sakethans, he recalled, had been an ascetic sect that had prized the mind above all things. Their mazes were often based on the distinctive convolutions of the Vulcan cerebral cortex, which they had believed to be the seat of the *katra,* a Vulcan's spiritual essence. The cryptic inscription implied that this maze was no exception.

He called up a diagram of the cortex on the tricorder's display screen. Assuming that the initial corridor represented the brain stem, the diagram suggested that he proceed down the central pathway. Tricorder in hand, he took off down the tunnel, certain that he was heading in the right direction. More junctions followed, and he used the brain map to guide his way through a winding path that continued to slope steadily downward. The deeper he descended, the more the temperature in the tunnels decreased. He shivered from the cold, wishing that he had put on a jacket before entering the tomb. The air was thin and musty, and he was soon breathing hard.

Time for another pick-me-up, he realized. New T'Karath's sparse atmosphere was better suited to Vulcans than Terrans, so he injected himself with a tri-ox compound before continuing his trek through the underground labyrinth. The weight upon his chest lifted and he quickened his pace. By his estimation, he had to be nearing the primary burial chamber at the end of the maze. But would his prize be there as he expected? That was the real question.

The beam from his tricorder shone upon the age-old walls of the catacombs. Recessed niches held a number of *katric* arks, polycrystalline vessels that supposedly held the disembodied souls of departed monks. The presence of the arks provided yet more evidence that this particular burial mound had never been looted, making Picard all the more eager to reach the central crypt.

Rounding a curve, however, he found himself confronted by what appeared to be a dead end. The mummified body of a robed Vulcan monk stood at attention within an upright stone sarcophagus that appeared to have been carved out of the very walls of the cavern. The monk's right palm was held up before him, as though signaling Picard to halt. The mummy's shriveled features bore an inscrutable expression. Dust muted the color of the monk's tangerine robe.

Puzzled, Picard stopped in his tracks. Had he taken a wrong turn somewhere? He consulted his map of the Vulcan cortex, mentally retracing his steps. As nearly as he could tell, he had followed the convolutions exactly. *I can't be mistaken,* he thought. *There has to be a way past this barrier.*

He scanned the sarcophagus blocking his path, but the tricorder's sensors were unable to penetrate the dense limestone. *Damn kelbonite!* He was sorely tempted to blast his way through with his phaser, but the archeologist in him recoiled from the idea of vandalizing the historic site. Putting his tricorder aside for the moment, he ran his fingers around the edges of the sarcophagus, searching for some sort of hidden lever. *Maybe there's a secret passageway,* he speculated, *like the one in those ruins on Camus II.*

Despite his best efforts, though, he was unable to locate any concealed latch or trigger. Frustrated, he stepped back to take another look at the dead monk in its sepulcher. His restless gaze fell upon an inscription above the sarcophagus. He didn't need his tricorder to translate the timeless salutation:

"Live long and prosper."

Another clue? The optimistic greeting seemed singularly out of place in this funereal setting. A thought occurred to Picard, and his keen eyes zeroed in on the mummy's upraised palm. Could it be . . . ?

Approaching the sarcophagus, he reached out and gingerly took hold of the mummy's fingers. As he pushed the third and fourth fingers apart, forming a traditional Vulcan hand sign, he heard a delicate apparatus click at the junction of the two digits. "Eureka," he murmured, grinning. He parted his own fingers in response. "Open sesame."

The rumble of concealed machinery filled the gloomy corridor. Picard backed away from the mummy as the ponderous sound of stone sliding against stone violated the hushed atmosphere. Ancient gears engaged and the entire sarcophagus swung outward, exposing a darkened chamber beyond. Picard retrieved his tricorder and hurried forward, not even waiting for the swinging barrier to come to a complete stop.

I knew it! he thought. *Just like Camus II!*

The spotlight from his tricorder revealed a circular burial chamber at the very center of the maze. Rows of dusty *katric* arks lined the walls while a pair of unlit braziers flanked another upright sarcophagus directly ahead of Picard. The mummified remains of a Vulcan high priestess resided within the polished stone sepulcher. Picard's eyes widened in excitement as he spotted what looked like a carved granite octahedron embedded in the center of the mummy's brow.

That's it, he thought. *It has to be!*

Something glittered dimly above the mummy's head. Lifting the beam of his searchlight, he was momentarily taken aback by a snarling face with six-inch fangs and blazing green eyes. His heart missed a beat before he realized that the face belonged to the head and shoulders of a sculpted marble *sehlat.* The beast's vicious fangs and foreclaws stood guard over the dead priestess. Emerald bloodstones served as the animal's eyes. A final inscription was engraved between the *sehlat*'s paws:

"The guilt of a thief weighs heavy upon the heart."

Maintaining a safe distance from both the mummy and her ursine guardian, he scanned the eight-sided stone die lodged in the priestess's forehead. The degree of terikon particle decay corresponded with the spectral signature he was looking for. *A perfect match,* he thought triumphantly. *That's the real thing.*

The precious artifact called out to him, but Picard resisted the urge to run forward and pluck the relic from the mummy's skull. His own brow furrowed as he pondered the ominous inscription above the sarcophagus, which resisted easy interpretation. Did the moralistic adage contain some hidden message?

A quick scan of the twin braziers assured him that their contents contained no deadly toxins. In deference to the crypt's solemn history, he used his disruptor to light the braziers. Dancing yellow flames cast flickering shadows upon the curved wall of the burial chamber. The scent of incense suffused the air. Picard felt as though he had been transported a hundred years into the past. *Before the fall of Vulcan,* he reflected, *and the rise of the Alliance.*

Deep in thought, he listened to an errant breeze as it whistled through the hushed catacombs outside, while his eyes remained fixed on the tantalizing artifact only a few paces away. He waited several moments before finally striding forward and reaching out for the granite die. *This is too easy,* he thought.

"Not so fast, Picard!" A harsh voice intruded on the scene. "Step away from the mummy!"

Picard spun around to confront a disruptor pistol aimed at his skull. A dwarfish figure, wearing a garish piebald suit, scuttled into the crypt. Elephantine ears framed a leering orange face. Picard recognized him at once.

"Sovak!" he spat. The unscrupulous Ferengi was a long-time rival. Picard scowled contemptuously at the newcomer. "I thought I'd shaken you on Yadalla Prime."

"You should be so lucky!" Sovak's beady black eyes stared down the barrel of his disruptor. His bulbous nose wrinkled disdainfully. "Lose the disruptor."

Picard grudgingly dropped his own weapon on the floor. Keeping the human in his sights, Sovak scurried forward and kicked the discarded disruptor across the room. "Back away from those fires and keep your hands where I can see them," he instructed as he sidled toward the sarcophagus. He chortled with avaricious glee. "Thanks for leading the way, Picard. I could've never made it this far without you!"

"You're welcome," Picard said dryly.

The Ferengi's greedy fingers closed around the treasure in the dead priestess's brow. Before he could wrest it from her skull, however, the *sehlat*'s eyes glowed brightly, targeting Sovak with a pair of brilliant emerald beams. He jerked his hand away from his prize, but it was already too late for him. His flesh sagged downward as though yanked by an intense gravity field. Bones cracked audibly as he crumpled to the floor. Collapsing lungs managed only a single high-pitched squeal before falling silent. Flesh and bone were pulped to jelly. His disruptor imploded. Within seconds, all that remained of Sovak was a flattened puddle of orange goo. The artificial super-gravity had indeed "weighed heavily" upon the thief's heart.

"And thank you," Picard said, lowering his hands. The scheming Ferengi had uncovered the crypt's ultimate deathtrap, just as Picard had anticipated. He recovered his disruptor from the floor and blasted the sculpted *sehlat* right between its luminous eyes. A concealed graviton projector exploded in a shower of sparks.

So much for that, he thought. Taking care not to step in Sovak's liquefied remains, he firmly took hold of the granite die and pulled it free from the mummy's forehead, leaving an empty socket behind. He held the relic before the light of the flickering braziers, admiring the intricate hieroglyphics inscribed upon the artifact. The markings confirmed the object's identity beyond a shadow of a doubt.

"The Stone of Gol," he whispered aloud. Or, to be more exact, a crucial fragment of the legendary Vulcan weapon. According to myth, the fearsome artifact had been destroyed by the gods when the ancient Vulcans first found the way of peace. In fact, Picard had deduced that the Stone had been divided into three interlocking components, which had then been hidden throughout the galaxy. He had tracked down the first piece of the relic on Calder II several months ago. Now only one more fragment remained lost to history, at least for the time being.

Two down, one to go.

He carefully wrapped the die in several layers of cloth and tucked it safely into the pocket of his trousers. *A good day's work,* he concluded. He couldn't wait to examine the Stone back aboard his ship. He took a deep breath of the crypt's pungent incense before heading for the door. *Stargazer* awaited him.

He left the goopy orange residue as a puzzle for the future archeologists.

2

Celtris III was a barren class-M planet located deep in Cardassian space. The Alliance maintained a solitary outpost along the planet's equator. Rumor had it that the Cardies were secretly developing new metagenic weapons at a hidden laboratory somewhere within the sprawling military installation. Picard didn't know anything about that. He didn't want to know.

His ship touched down at a commercial spaceport on the outskirts of the base. The landing was bumpier than he would have liked; *Stargazer* was a run-down, secondhand runabout that had definitely seen better days. Picard scowled as the rough landing jolted his bones. He would have to see about having the thrusters repaired before he embarked on his next expedition.

Times like this he wished that he actually had a crew to see to such matters, but that was just a ridiculous fantasy. *Not in this universe,* he thought sourly. *Stargazer* had a crew of one, and he was lucky to rate that much. Most humans could only dream of being at the helm of their own ship. He glanced around at the modest cockpit. *Such as it is.*

Shutting down all systems to save energy, he tucked the Stone of Gol into a canvas shoulder bag and exited the ship. As always, the oppressive heat of the equatorial base hit him like a solar flare. The temperature was uncomfortably warm by human standards, although ideal for Cardassians. He raised a hand to shield his eyes from the harsh morning sunlight. Sweat began to soak through his clothes.

"You there, Terran! Just who do you think you are?"

The bellicose query came from one of a pair of Klingon guards who appeared to be patrolling the spaceport. The uniformed warriors stomped toward him. An ugly white scar streaked the face of the speaker. His partner was a hulking brute whose cranium was just as bald as Picard's, albeit a good deal craggier.

Picard didn't recognize either guard. *They must be new here.* He wondered whom they had offended to get assigned to Celtris III. Perspiration shone upon the soldiers' bestial features. They looked bored and irritable. A bad combination, especially where Klingons were concerned.

"Can I help you, Officers?" he asked. The strap of his carryall was slung over his shoulders, freeing his hands. A patch on his lapel bore a stylized portrait of Earth, marking him as a Terran. He reached beneath his jacket for his ID. "I have my identification disks right here."

The Klingons invaded his personal space. "Keep your hands where I can see them!" the scarred warrior snarled at Picard, his face only inches from the unarmed human's. His rank breath, which reeked of stale bloodwine and *gagh,* assailed Picard's nostrils. The outnumbered archeologist stepped back, only to bump into the armored form of the bald Klingon directly behind him. The hairless soldier growled in his ear. He roughly shoved Picard forward. The bag bounced against Picard's back, causing Picard to worry about the safety of the artifact therein. Had he wrapped the precious stone in enough padding?

"What's your designation?" the bald warrior demanded, roughly frisking Picard from behind. The human was glad that he had left his weapon back aboard the ship. Alliance soldiers didn't take kindly to armed Terrans walking the streets.

"Lambda," Picard volunteered. His elevated designation entitled him to privileges denied most other Terrans, but did not necessarily spare him from this sort of harassment. "Like I said, I have my identifica—"

"Is that your ship?" the first Klingon interrupted, nodding at *Stargazer.* Drawing a dagger from his belt, he jabbed the tip of the blade into Picard's chest, not quite hard enough to draw blood . . . yet. "What's a *Terran* doing flying a ship like that?" His sneering tone turned "Terran" into the vilest of insults. "Answer me, you cur!"

Picard bit down on his tongue, holding back an angry retort. Even after all these years, he still hated being treated like dirt by the likes of these arrogant barbarians. Still, he knew better than to pick a fight with Klingons. He was all too aware of the knifepoint pressing against his breast, and of the potentially fatal consequences of provoking the guards any further. After all, it wasn't like any Alliance doctor was going to waste an artificial heart on a mere human should the scarred Klingon take it into his lumpy skull to stab him.

"Actually, the ship belongs to my patron," Picard said mildly. Swallowing his pride, he raised his open palms before him. He kept his voice and expression carefully neutral. "Gul Madred."

The Klingon blinked in surprise, caught off guard by the name of the outpost's commander. His partner grunted and backed away from Picard, making him feel a little less trapped. "Khone?" he asked the other Klingon uncertainly.

To Picard's relief, Madred's name seemed to give the two guards pause. "Will you be needing me much longer?" Picard asked, pressing his luck. "The gul is expecting me."

The scarred warrior, Khone, frowned and stepped aside. "All right, Terran. Go about your business." He sullenly thrust his dagger back into his belt. "But watch yourself, Earther. Don't forget your place, or we may just have to remind you . . . the hard way." Glowering darkly, he turned and stalked away from Picard. "Come on, Gwarz!" he called out to his comrade. "I'm sick of breathing this human's stench."

Picard waited until he heard the Klingons' heavy boots recede into the distance before letting out a pent-up breath. Tension drained from his body, although the encounter left a bad taste in his mouth, reminding him of just how low humans ranked in the overall scheme of things. He couldn't complain, though. *That could have gone much worse,* he reminded himself.

"Stupid Klingons!" a new voice piped up. An adolescent human scrambled out from behind one of *Stargazer*'s landing struts. He grinned mischievously at Picard. "Way to go, Luc! You sure showed those slime-devils who was boss."

Picard's mood lifted a little. "Hello, Wesley" he said warmly. He was fond of the scrappy young urchin, whose pluck and entrepreneurial spirit had managed to survive the Alliance's best efforts to crush it. Fascinated with starships and warp technology, he often hung about the spaceport. He had even helped Picard adjust the engines a few times. "I'm not sure that was quite the victory you're making it out to be, but thank you nonetheless."

"Any time a Klingon walks away without one of your vital organs counts as a win in my book," Wesley insisted. A fraying cotton jacket hung in tatters upon the boy's lanky frame. The patches on his soiled trousers had patches. "You heard the one about the Klingon short-order cook?"

"Maybe another time," Picard said. Madred had surely been notified of *Stargazer*'s arrival by now. He fished a handful of coins from his pocket and lobbed them into Wesley's eager hands. "Keep an eye on *Stargazer* for me?"

"You bet!" the teenager enthused. "Just like always!"

Leaving the spaceport behind, Picard walked quickly to Gul Madred's headquarters at the center of the outpost. Arched pylons rose above the forbidding stronghold. A Cardie lieutenant escorted him to an antechamber outside Madred's office. "Wait here," the soldier said curtly. He did not offer Picard a seat. "The gul will be with you at his convenience."

The door to Madred's inner sanctum was slightly ajar. Agonized cries and whimpers escaped the chamber; apparently, the Cardassian commander was interrogating a prisoner. Through the open crack, Picard glimpsed a nude human figure hanging suspended from a pair of steel manacles. A member of the human resistance movement? Picard had heard rumors of Resistance activity in this sector.

A nearby guard watched Picard's face as the nameless prisoner was tortured only a few yards away, but Picard refused to give the smirking soldier the reaction he was surely hoping for. He maintained a stony expression, even as he winced inwardly at the pitiable noises coming from his fellow human. Had the door deliberately been left open for his benefit? Picard wouldn't put it past the spoonheads. Gul Madred loved his mind games.

Finally, after what felt like hours, the brutal session came to an end. Picard watched stoically as two Cardassian soldiers dragged the naked prisoner past him. "Five lights," the man mumbled weakly, only half conscious. "I see *five* lights. . . ."

What's that all about? Picard wondered. He hoped he never found out.

"Come in, Luc," Gul Madred called from his office. "I'm ready for you now."

Pushing the tortured man from his mind, Picard entered the chamber. The bare steel walls gave the room a forbidding feel. Yellow sunlight, filtered through translucent crystal windows, failed to relieve the gloomy atmosphere. The hanging manacles had mercifully been retracted into the ceiling, yet the prisoner's gasps and moans still echoed within Picard's skull. A single drop of human blood glistened upon the floor.

"Welcome back, Luc." Gul Madred sat behind a large obsidian desk, beneath an array of unlit spotlights. The Cardassian's phlegmatic tone belied the hospitality of his greeting. Time and responsibility had weathered his reptilian features. "I trust you have something for me."

"Indeed." Picard extracted the Stone from his carryall and laid it atop Madred's desk. "Another fragment of the fabled Stone of Gol, just as I promised."

Madred examined the relic. "So I see. An excellent addition to my collection." A scaly finger traced the glyphs carved upon the Stone. "From the so-called Time of Awakening, over four thousand years ago."

Two thousand, Picard thought irritably. Although Madred fancied himself quite the scholar, Picard secretly considered the

Cardie no more than an archeological dilettante. Still, as he depended on the gul to subsidize his expeditions, he declined to correct his patron. Dealing with Madred was the price he paid to continue his work. He regretted having to hand over the artifact to Madred, as he had the Sword of Kahless, the Orb of Prophecy, and so many others, but at least he'd had the opportunity to examine and catalog the Stone fragment extensively before it disappeared into Madred's private collection. Picard's workstation back aboard *Stargazer* was currently buried beneath copious notes and diagrams.

"I'd guard that carefully," he advised Madred. "According to legend, the intact Stone of Gol was a weapon of considerable power." The location of the third and final component remained a mystery, but it couldn't hurt to keep the other two pieces safely under lock and key, just in case. "Some scholars believe that the device was actually a powerful psionic resonator that amplified a Vulcan's natural telepathic abilities to a lethal degree."

"Superstitious nonsense." Madred dismissed Picard's concerns with a wave of his hand. He placed the Stone down on his desk, next to the authentic Veltan sex idol he used as a paperweight. "Cardassian science has conclusively proven that the Vulcans' vaunted 'powers of the mind' amount to little more than cheap parlor tricks. The Alliance has nothing to fear from primitive myths and propaganda."

Picard bit down on his lip. Experience had taught him that there was nothing to be gained by challenging the Alliance's revisionist approach to history. "It was only a theory."

"Of course," Madred said affably. "Don't be too embarrassed, Luc. It's hardly your fault that your own ignorant species never saw past the Vulcans' smoke and mirrors." He poured himself a cup of steaming fish juice from a thermos on his desk. "Now then, what do you have in mind for your next expedition?"

Picard stepped forward eagerly. This was the part of the meeting he had been waiting for, the part that made all the rest worthwhile. "I have a lead—a strong one—on the location of a genuine

Native American colony on an unnamed planet somewhere in Sector V-17. According to reliable reports, the people on this planet still live much as the ancient Mohicans did on Earth over eight centuries ago." He didn't bother to conceal the excitement in his voice. There was so much that could be learned from such an isolated community, if it truly existed. "We could be talking about living history here."

"I see." Madred sounded underwhelmed. "And would these hypothetical throwbacks have produced any valuable artwork or jewelry? Are they likely to possess any artifacts of historic importance?"

"Well, that depends on how you define importance," Picard hedged. If only he could convince Gul Madred of the magnitude of such a discovery! "Just observing their way of life could be of incalculable value in illuminating the past, not only of the human race, but of other early tribal cultures."

Madred shook his head. "I sincerely doubt that there is anything of value to be learned from some debased remnant of *Terran* civilization." He sighed wearily. "Luc, Luc, we've had this conversation before. Nobody's interested in the failed history of your undistinguished breed. The Vulcans, at least, gave birth to the Romulan Star Empire, but the human race has left no legacy worth noting. And I certainly do not employ you to go digging through the dirt for crude beads and stone knives." Picard started to object, but Madred raised his hand to forestall any further discussion. "I admire your persistence, but better that you focus your energies on recovering legitimate archeological treasures." He fondled the Stone on his desk. "Like, perhaps, the third component of this intriguing little item?"

Picard's shoulders sagged in defeat. *I should have known better than to raise my hopes,* he thought bitterly. Madred had never shown any interest in the history of mankind and its short-lived Empire. *I was wasting my breath.*

"I'll get right on that," he acquiesced. "Let me get back to my research."

"That's the spirit, Luc," Madred said. The Stone of Gol component disappeared into a drawer beneath the polished black desktop. "Make it so."

Picard's mood was dark as he trudged back to the spaceport. This was hardly the first time that Gul Madred had shot down Picard's own archeological agenda. The acquisitive Cardassian had also consistently refused to sponsor any investigation into the theories of the late Richard Galen, Picard's deceased mentor. Although entirely self-educated and lacking any academic standing within the Alliance, Galen had known more about galactic history than any expert Picard had ever met, human or otherwise. Buried anger simmered deep inside him as he recalled how Galen had been executed years ago because of his "seditious" theory that the Cardassians and the Klingons shared a common genetic heritage with the human race. Part of Picard had never forgiven the Alliance for Galen's death . . . and for the way they had stonewalled any further research in that direction.

No wonder Madred vetoed the Mohican expedition, he thought. *I was a fool to ever think he would do otherwise.*

No overbearing Klingons accosted him upon his return to *Stargazer,* for which Picard was grateful. Wesley, who was camped out in front of the ship, sprang to his feet as he approached. "Everything's just the way you left it, Luc," he proclaimed loudly. "Nobody's going to mess with *Stargazer* while I'm around."

"Thanks for looking after her for me." Picard tossed the teenager another coin, as was their tradition. "Now go find yourself something to eat . . . and don't spend it all on Thalian chocolate."

Wesley licked his lips. "Chocolate. What a great idea!" He scurried away before Picard could lecture him on the importance of proper nutrition. He winked impishly at the older man. "See you later, Luc!"

"*Au revoir,* you scamp." Picard smiled and shook his head as the urchin disappeared into the dusty streets beyond the spaceport.

Life couldn't be easy for the orphaned lad; like so many children of the street, he didn't even know who his father was. Yet Wesley never seemed to let his impoverished existence weigh down his spirits. Picard envied his exuberance. *I could do worse than follow his example.*

He was surprised to find the lights on inside *Stargazer.* He frowned, certain that he had powered down the vessel before setting out earlier. His eyes searched the central cabin, which served as both his living quarters and office. Nothing appeared to be amiss, but he warily retrieved his disruptor pistol from a concealed compartment beneath a counter. Weapon in hand, he stalked through the cabin, on guard against any possible intruder. He glanced at his workstation over by the starboard bulkhead. Star charts and data padds still littered the desktop. Ship's life support provided relief from the torrid heat outside. Wadded sheets lay in a heap atop his empty bunk.

A loose tile squeaked behind him and he whirled around, his finger tightening on the trigger of his weapon. Before he fired, however, a familiar figure emerged from the rear cargo compartment. His eyes widened as he recognized the slender brunette standing in the doorway.

"Really, Jean-Luc," Vash chided him. "Is that any way to greet the love of your life?"

"*Former* love," he corrected her. "Your idea, as I recall." He relaxed his trigger finger, but did not lower the weapon. "How did you get past Wesley?"

"He's a teenage boy," she said with a shrug. "I bribed him. How else?" A two-piece khaki jumpsuit clung to her athletic physique. "Plus, I convinced him that you wouldn't be too upset to find an attractive woman waiting for you." She struck a vampish pose. "There may have also been just the tiniest bit of Vulcan massage involved."

Picard remembered Vash's nimble fingers. Poor Wesley never stood a chance. "Robbing the cradle are we now?"

"Beats robbing tombs," she shot back. Chestnut eyes flashed

defiantly, not at all intimidated by the weapon aimed at her head. "I assume you're still plundering the galaxy for your Cardie masters?"

"I am conducting important archeological research under the best terms I can manage, given the harsh realities of the universe we live in." He bristled at her accusation. "What about you?" he challenged her. "Are you still risking your life in some quixotic attempt to overthrow the Alliance?"

"The Resistance is this galaxy's last hope for freedom," she declared passionately. "You'd know that if you weren't too busy collaborating with the enemy." Her harsh words seemed to catch her by surprise, and she took a deep breath to calm herself. When she spoke again, her husky voice sounded more tired than angry. "Please, Jean-Luc, let's not have the same old fight all over again." Plaintive eyes entreated him. "Put down that disruptor."

Picard had to admit that she had a point. He was disappointed at how quickly they had fallen back into the same ugly argument. It hadn't always been that way, he remembered. He and Vash had once traveled the galaxy together, before splitting up over politics. Sometimes he almost convinced himself that he didn't miss her.

He lowered the disruptor and tucked it into his belt. "Hello, Vash," he said softly. "What brings you my way after all this time?"

"Can't a girl just drop in on her ex for old times' sake?"

I doubt it, he thought, but didn't feel like pressing the issue just yet. Vash would surely make her true intentions known when the time came. "I suppose." He gestured at a nearby seat. "Make yourself at home. More so than you already have, that is."

"Thank you, Jean-Luc." She was the only person who ever called him by his full name. Ignoring the proffered chair, she sat down on the edge of his bunk instead. "I don't mind if I do."

Her eyes surveyed the cluttered cabin, lingering on the handwritten notes strewn about his workspace. "You look like you've been keeping busy."

"Collaborating is a full-time occupation," he said dryly. He didn't ask her how she had been occupying her time lately. The less he knew about her subversive activities, the better for both of them. "Pardon the mess. I wasn't expecting company."

Wesley owes me a coin, he thought. *Some watchdog he turned out to be.*

She smoothed out the crumpled sheets beneath her. "You don't need to clean up for me," she teased him. "I already know what a terrible housekeeper you are." Her gaze drifted to a star chart affixed to the port bulkhead. "So, have you made any progress on the Iconian front?"

"That's still a tough nut to crack," he admitted, "but I've been working on a new approach." He didn't volunteer the details; why share his secrets with the Resistance? "Nothing I'm ready to discuss yet, though."

Vash took the hint and changed the subject. She nodded at an old-fashioned bottle of wine carefully stored upon a nearby shelf. A miniature stasis field protected the glass bottle from breakage. "I see you still haven't opened the '47."

"I'm saving it for a special occasion," he insisted. A recurring pang stabbed at his heart. As far as he knew, the fragile bottle contained the last surviving sample of Château Picard in existence. His family's ancestral vineyards had been long ago confiscated by the Alliance. An ore-processing plant now occupied the once-green farmlands. His brother's bones were buried somewhere beneath the plant. Stubborn to the last, Robert had foolishly tried to defend the winery against the occupying forces. Picard had never been able to find out what had become of his brother's wife and child. Doubtless they had ended up dead or enslaved.

The solitary bottle was all that remained of his family's heritage.

Vash knew all this, of course. He half expected her to launch into another spirited call to arms against the Alliance, but instead she merely eyed him sadly, sharing his pain. "Maybe someday you'll have something to celebrate," she whispered.

"Perhaps." He made an effort to shake off the melancholy

coming over him, if only for his visitor's sake. "We can only hope."

She patted the edge of the bunk, inviting him to join her. Her voice took on a more playful tone. "Speaking of celebrations, remember the time we 'christened' this ship right after we moved in?"

"How could I forget?" The memories stirred his senses, especially with Vash's long legs stretched out in front of him. "As I recall, we did quite a thorough job of it, from the cockpit to the cargo hold." He sat down beside her, acutely aware of her lithe body next to his. Proximity alarms went off in his head. "So, are you . . . seeing . . . anyone these days? Aside from Wesley, I mean."

"What can I say?" she joked. "His ragged attire drove me wild." She eyed him slyly. "What about you? I hope I'm not cramping your style by showing up without notice. You sure you aren't expecting any special visitor this afternoon?"

"Hardly." He had not exactly been celibate since she had left him, yet his occasional liaisons had been fleeting and superficial. No woman, of whatever species, had ever filled the hole that Vash had left in his life. "I had only long hours of diligent study in front of me."

"Well then, thank goodness I came along to rescue you." Turning toward him, she reached out and wrapped her arms around him. His mouth found hers, and he savored the intoxicating taste of her lips. He inhaled her familiar fragrance. The gravitational tug of her presence was irresistible.

This is a mistake, Picard thought, even as she pulled him down onto the unmade bed. Her hands deftly undid his belt and tossed his disruptor aside. It clanked harmlessly to the floor. Picard barely noticed.

His modest bunk was not large, but it was large enough. . . .

"Why are you *really* here?" he asked her afterward.

"There's someone I want you to meet."

★ ★ ★

The squalid tavern had been set up inside an abandoned dilithium refinery, and most of its furnishings looked as if they had been salvaged from a junkyard. Empty valves and conduits ran across the ceiling. The corroded steel walls were patched with crumbling thermoconcrete. A ceiling fan, constructed from a discarded turbine, fought a losing battle against the muggy atmosphere. Metal grates covered the floor, providing a degree of traction despite the spilled drinks and puddles of spit. A homemade still chugged behind the bar, dispensing a crude alcoholic concoction that bore little resemblance to the exquisite vintages once produced by Château Picard. Metal crates and barrels served as tables. Portable lights glowed feebly atop the tables.

The clientele consisted mostly of human laborers, trying to get drunk as cheaply and efficiently as possible on the bar's dubious spirits. A handful of Andorians, Tellarites, Bolians, Deltans, and other subject races were mixed in with the humans. The scruffy-looking patrons huddled around the makeshift tables, muttering among themselves. Mandatory patches on their soiled coveralls identified their planets of origin. Klingons and Cardassians were conspicuously absent; the elite of the Alliance wouldn't be caught dead in a place like this.

Picard wondered what he was doing here. Against his better judgment, he let Vash lead him to a murky corner far from the front entrance, where an elderly stranger was seated behind an upright steel drum that, according to a faded Klingon label, had once held biomimetic waste. Vash slid in beside the man and waited for Picard to join them. Three tarnished tin mugs rested atop the lid of the barrel.

"Jean-Luc Picard, meet Noonien Soong."

He peered across the table at perhaps the oldest human he had ever met. Deep wrinkles creased Soong's face. Age spots peppered sere brown skin that reminded Picard of crinkled papyrus. A worn burlap overcoat was draped over his hunched shoulders. Wisps of thin white hair clung to his cranium. Under Alliance rule, the average life expectancy for humans had been declining for years, but Soong had to be in his eighties at least. Picard was impressed despite himself.

"Pleased to meet you," Soong said in a dry croak of a voice. "I took the liberty of ordering our drinks, such as they are." Alert gray eyes belied his obvious age and infirmity. "The lovely Vash speaks highly of you."

"Does she now?" Picard arched his eyebrow.

The dim lighting made it hard to tell if she was blushing. "Soong is a genius," she explained, ignoring Picard's teasing query. "Comparable to Daystrom or Cochrane." She glanced around to make sure that no one was listening; Gul Madred was not above employing human informers. "The Alliance enslaved him for decades, forcing him to employ his brilliance on their behalf, but the Resistance helped him go underground a few weeks back."

"I see," Picard said. He noticed that Soong did not object to Vash's extravagant praise; perhaps he also considered himself the equal of humanity's greatest minds. "And do you share the Resistance's revolutionary ambitions?"

The old man chuckled quietly. "To tell you the truth, I've always been more interested in science than politics." Taking a sip from his cup, he grimaced at the taste. "I just got frustrated that my Alliance supervisors wouldn't let me pursue my lifelong interest in artificial life-forms. They wanted me to concentrate on new automated weapons systems instead." He shook his head in disgust. "What an appalling waste of my intellect!"

Picard sympathized, but remained wary. "What does this have to do with me?"

"I'm glad you asked that." Soong leaned forward eagerly. He grinned at Picard. "Have you ever heard of the Borg?"

"The who?" The name meant nothing to Picard.

Soong couldn't wait to explain. "I've recently uncovered evidence of a possibly cybernetic species known only as the Borg, who are mentioned in historical documents relating to the mysterious extinction of the El-Aurian civilization over a hundred years ago. Vash tells me that you have a well-deserved reputation for finding things that no one else can. I want you to help me track down these Borg and make contact with them." His eyes gleamed at the prospect. "Think of it, Picard: a sentient life-form more artificial than organic. I've always dreamed of encountering such a being. It would be the ultimate vindication of my theories about the possibility of genuine positronic intelligence."

"And that's not all, Jean-Luc," Vash added. "If these Borg are as advanced as Soong believes, they could prove to be a valuable ally against the Alliance." She searched his face, looking for a spark of interest. "If that doesn't matter to you, consider the archeological implications. The Borg could be responsible for the collapse of any number of bygone alien civilizations, like the Tkon Empire, the Taguans, or the ancient Iconians. Remember how we used to speculate about what really happened to all those extinct cultures? The Borg might be the answer to some of history's most tantalizing riddles."

Picard was tempted. The galaxy was indeed littered with the remains of lost civilizations whose demises remained obscure. The idea that these Borg creatures might have played some part in their downfall intrigued him. Ultimately, though, he knew he had to say no. He had a workable arrangement going with Madred. He couldn't risk getting involved with the Resistance, and a fugitive scientist, just to chase after some cryptic alien myth.

"I'm sorry," he said. "I can't help you."

"Jean-Luc!" Vash blurted in dismay. "Don't you get it? The Borg may be our best chance to overthrow the Alliance once and for all. As a human being, how can you not care about that?" She reached across the table to grip his arm. "We need you, Jean-Luc. Humanity needs you!"

Here we go again, he thought glumly. Why couldn't Vash see that the Resistance was just a useless pipe dream? Why did she insist on throwing her life away for the sake of a doomed crusade? The Alliance was too powerful to be brought down, not in their lifetimes.

These Borg were just another false hope that was going to get plenty of naïve, well-intentioned people killed. *Leave me out of it.*

"You've got the wrong man," he told her. "I have my own work to see to."

The look of disappointment on her face seared him like a disruptor beam, but he hid his pain behind a rigid expression. Removing her hand from his arm, he rose to go. There was no point in prolonging this encounter any longer. He should never have let her bring him here.

"Good-bye, Vash." Clearly, he would be sleeping alone tonight. He gulped down the contents of his mug. "Good luck with—"

A loud crash interrupted him. Spinning around, he saw a cadre of mixed Klingon and Cardassian soldiers kick open the front door of the tavern. Armed with both disruptor rifles and truncheons, they poured into the crowded watering hole. Startled customers cried out in alarm and jumped to their feet. Several bolted for the back exit, only to be met by yet more soldiers invading from the rear. A desperate Betazoid tried to dash past the intruders, but was struck to the floor by a Klingon's heavy truncheon. The soldiers drove the frightened laborers back with the muzzles of their rifles.

It's a raid! Picard realized. *Of all nights for us to come here . . . !*

"Stay where you are, scum!" a Cardie officer shouted over the chaos. "We have reason to believe that this stinking cesspool harbors known terrorists and their sympathizers. You are all assumed guilty until proven otherwise." Whimpers of fear arose from the bar's more timid patrons. "No one is leaving here until they have been thoroughly interrogated."

Picard shot a worried look at Vash and Soong. Thanks to his connection to Madred, he might be able to come out of this fiasco with nothing more than a few bruises, but his companions were another story. He didn't want to think about what the Alliance might do to Vash if they found out about her links to the Resistance—or even if they didn't. "We have to get you out of here!" he whispered urgently.

But how? The hostile soldiers were already fanning out through the tavern, roughly herding the customers into the middle of the old refinery. Muscular Klingons shoved the junkyard furniture aside to create a holding area for the prisoners. Cups and pitchers clattered onto the floor. The smell of spilled alcohol filled the chamber. Picard looked in vain for an escape route.

"The barrel!" Soong croaked. He and Vash had both lurched to their feet. The old man threw his weight against the sturdy metal drum, but the table didn't budge. "Beneath the barrel!"

Vash added her strength to Soong's. The bottom of the drum scraped against the floor as they pushed the barrel to one side, exposing a sealed metal hatch. Hope surged inside Picard. Maybe there was still a chance to get away, provided they moved quickly enough.

"You there!" A Cardassian soldier, flanked by two scowling Klingons, marched toward them. He squinted suspiciously. "What are you doing?" He waved his rifle at the three humans. "Get over here with the rest of the prisoners!"

Picard glanced up at the ceiling fan. The spinning turbine was directly above the Cardie and his comrades. Snatching his disruptor from beneath his vest, he fired at the motor connecting the fan to the ceiling. The crimson beam lit up the gloomy tavern even as the dislodged fan plummeted down onto the advancing soldiers. Cries of pain and fury escaped the startled warriors, punctuated by a loud metallic crash. Sparks flew where the spinning blade scraped against the floor grates. The Klingons' purple blood spread out from beneath the crushed soldiers, mixing with the dark red blood of the wounded Cardie. The remaining soldiers shouted in confusion.

"What the—?" the Cardassian officer exclaimed. "Terran bastards!"

Taking advantage of the distraction, frantic prisoners tried to make a break for it. Scuffles broke out as the reckless men and women clashed with their captors. Klingons growled and Cardassians cursed, suddenly finding themselves with a riot on their hands. The customers fought back with whatever was handy, from bare fists to homemade shanks. The tavern's owner cowered behind his bar. Disruptor blasts added to the tumult. A stray shot blew up the still, sending bodies flying into the air. Shrapnel tore into the combatants, injuring both soldiers and slaves alike. Flames licked at the splattered spirits. Smoke filled the air.

That bought us a few moments, Picard thought.

Behind him, Vash dropped to her knees and tried to open the circular hatch. Rusted metal resisted her efforts. "Get back!" he told her, turning his disruptor on the stubborn steel barrier. Vash scrambled out of the way, and he used the weapon's maximum setting to disintegrate the hatch, which dissolved in a nimbus of radiant red energy. Picard glimpsed the top of some sort of access shaft. "After you!"

"Hurry!" she urged Soong as she helped the old man into the open shaft. As soon as his wispy white hair disappeared from view, she clambered down after him. "Come on, Jean-Luc! Stick with us!"

A disruptor blast tore apart a hanging pipe only a few inches from his skull. Ducking his head, Picard decided that he had outworn his welcome here. "Get that hairless Terran!" the Cardassian officer bellowed at her troops. Her dark hair and armor were singed from the explosion. "Don't let him get away!"

More blasts targeted Picard, who fired back to cover his exit. He dove headfirst through the gap in the floor, hoping that there wasn't too big a drop in store. Stale air, redolent of toxic chemicals, rushed past his face as he plunged down the open shaft. His right hand held on tightly to the grip of his disruptor.

This could be another rough landing. . . .

He splashed down into a layer of thick, black sludge. The noxious gook cushioned his fall somewhat, although the impact still knocked the wind out of him. Anxious hands grabbed onto him as Vash tugged him to his feet. "Thank God!" she gasped. "You made it!"

So far, Picard thought. Light from above revealed what appeared to be some sort of old drainage tunnel, dating back to the refinery's original installation. Voles scurried along the fringes of the sludge, which was nearly waist-deep in places. He wrinkled his nose at the caustic stench. Something long and sinuous swam past his leg.

Angry voices sounded high above them. Disruptors' blasts fired down the two-hundred-meter-high shaft, scorching the surface of the sludge. Picard spotted a ladder running up the side of the shaft and vaporized it with his phaser. He wondered how far the soldiers would go to capture a trio of anonymous Terrans. *Not too far,* he hoped. They were going to be busy enough trying to bring things under control upstairs.

Maybe.

"Keep moving," he told the others. Wading through the viscous goo, they hurried down the tunnel. Picard guarded the rear, disruptor in hand, while Soong led the way, assisted by Vash. There was a limit, alas, to just how quickly the frail old man could travel. Picard was half tempted to throw Soong over his shoulder and carry him the rest of the way. He prayed it wouldn't come to that.

"This way," Soong instructed. "There's an outlet up ahead."

The farther they got from the shaft, the darker the tunnel became. Picard produced a handheld spotlight from his belt. He swept the beam over the gaping passageway before them. "How did you know about this tunnel?" he asked Soong.

"I accessed the original blueprints before the meeting," the scientist explained. He snickered beneath his breath. "Call me paranoid, but I always like to have an escape route available. How do you think I got away from the Alliance in the first place?"

"Paranoia works for me," Picard grunted, not about to look a gift horse in the mouth. "Especially where the Alliance is concerned." He listened carefully, but did not hear any sounds of pursuit behind him. Apparently the soldiers had better things to do than trudge through contaminated filth in search of the fugitives. He glanced down at the black sludge coating every inch of his clothes and skin. For all he knew, the slimy refuse was taking years off his life.

His soaked garments weighed him down as he wearily sloshed down the tunnel. He felt like Jean Valjean escaping through the sewers of Paris in *Les Misérables.* The Alliance had banned Hugo's work, along with many other "decadent" examples of human art and literature, but Picard had once perused a black-market Romulan translation. He couldn't help remembering that Jean Valjean had died in the end.

"Ah, here we are!" Soong announced at last. The seemingly endless tunnel finally opened up onto a dry riverbed outside the colony. Dried sludge coated the rocky floor of the gully. Flecks of unprocessed dilithium glittered amid the sticky black residue. Soong dropped onto a couch-sized boulder to rest his aged bones. Vash sagged against the rock as well, breathing hard. Sludge oozed down her arms and legs. Although less drenched than Picard, she was still smeared with goo.

"Thanks for your help, Jean-Luc," she said, wiping her hands off on the arid slope of the gully. Her voice was less scornful than before. "We wouldn't have gotten out of there without you."

Picard wasn't interested in her thanks. Now that they were no longer in immediate peril, he was free to express his anger at being dragged into this situation to begin with. "You see!" he said acidly. Thrusting his disruptor back into his belt, he stripped off his shirt and vest and tossed the sodden bundle at her feet. "*This* is why I wanted nothing to do with your precious Resistance."

She flinched at his words, then her face settled into a look of mournful resignation. "Very well," she said. "I won't bother you again." She sounded as if she were presiding over the funeral of the man she had once known. "You've made your feelings quite clear. About everything."

Merde, he thought. This was not how he wanted to end things, especially after their reunion in *Stargazer*'s bunk, but he had learned a long time ago that the universe couldn't care less about what he wanted.

He took a moment to catch his breath, then climbed up and out of the riverbed. The armories and barracks of the outpost rose before him, roughly a kilometer to the north. A barren wasteland stretched out interminably behind him. "Can you make it back to your rebel lair on your own?" he asked Vash brusquely. No doubt the Resistance had some cramped basement she and Soong could retreat to.

"Yes, Jean-Luc." The coldness in her voice approached absolute zero. "You needn't trouble yourself anymore on our account."

"Fine." He set off toward the spaceport. He had a long walk ahead of him.

"Picard! Wait!" Soong called out. "It's not too late. We can still go looking for the Borg. It's the chance of a lifetime!"

He kept on walking.

3

By the time he got back to the spaceport, it was well past midnight. The lights of the outpost washed out the stars overhead. Tendrils of thick gray smoke rose from the slums of the human quarter, presumably from the burning tavern. Picard himself presented a pathetic sight; although he had wiped off most of the clinging sludge with a rag, his boots and trousers were still caked with filth. Dirty and half-naked, he looked more like a homeless indigent than a space-faring archeologist. "Go sleep it off!" a Cardie patrolman hissed at him as Picard staggered by. "Worthless Terran trash!"

His feet squished with every step, and he let out a sigh of relief as he spied *Stargazer* parked upon the tarmac right where he'd left her. For a moment, he wondered if Vash had made it to safety yet. *That's no longer my concern,* he reminded himself. All he craved right now was a quick sonic shower, a few hours of sleep, and a chance to forget that the last solar day had ever happened.

Let the Resistance look after her and Soong.

As he neared his ship, however, he saw that the main airlock was already open. "What the devil?" His eyes widened as he spotted a diminutive figure sprawled at the foot of the gangplank. Adrenaline shot through his veins, overcoming his exhaustion. He hurried forward to find Wesley lying in a puddle of his own blood. Picard saw at once that the young Terran had been beaten within an inch of his life. His right eye was swollen shut. A flattened nose, split lip, and torn ear added to the damage. Fractured limbs jutted at unnatural angles.

"Wesley!"

The boy struggled to lift his head. "I tried to stop them, Luc. . . ." He coughed up a mouthful of blood and broken teeth. "I tried . . ."

Them?

For a few tense heartbeats, Picard feared that the Alliance's security forces had already uncovered his role in this evening's debacle. He flirted with the idea of fleeing back into the night. He had contacts who might be able to arrange transport off-planet, but he was reluctant to leave all his notes and research behind. Guttural laughter escaped the interior of the ship, and Picard suddenly had a pretty good idea whom he was dealing with here. His momentary relief was dispelled by the sound of rampant breakage accompanying the harsh laughter.

What the hell are they up to?

Pausing only long enough to make Wesley slightly more comfortable, Picard charged up the gangplank into *Stargazer.* Just as he feared, he found a pair of Klingon guards ransacking the ship. He recognized them immediately as the same guards who had bullied him several hours ago. They stomped through the main cabin, carelessly rifling through Picard's meager possessions. Precious books and mementos littered the floor. A few minor relics and artifacts, too mundane to warrant inclusion in Gul Madred's collection, lay in pieces upon the scuffed metal tiles. Picard winced at the sight of a twenty-first-century Risan fertility idol splintering beneath the heel of one of the Klingon's boots. A miniature Kurlan statuette had already been crushed into powder. Grimy footprints spoiled an authentic Mintakan tapestry.

"Stop that!" he demanded, losing his temper. "What is the meaning of this?"

"Look, Gwarz!" the scarred Klingon brayed drunkenly. Picard recalled that his name was Khone. "The 'captain' has returned to his ship."

"About time!" the bald guard said. He laughed at Picard's bedraggled appearance. "What's the matter, Terran? Lose your shirt in a game of *dom-jot*?" He tore the Iconian star charts down from the wall, then tossed them aside. "Guess this isn't your night!"

Picard struggled to contain himself. "What is this all about?"

"Nothing much," Khone answered, unimpressed by Picard's indignant tone. He lumbered toward Picard, his unsteady gait hinting at excessive consumption of bloodwine. "My partner and I figure we're entitled to an extra 'docking fee' for letting this broken-down garbage scow stink up the landing field." He barked in Picard's face, spraying him with spittle. "Unless you have a problem with that."

Picard's fingers itched to grab the disruptor hidden in his boot, but they wisely stayed where they were. Not even Madred would be able to protect him if he pulled a weapon on soldiers of the Alliance. The altercation at the tavern was one thing; if he was lucky, nobody had gotten a good look at his face during the raid and ensuing riot. He judged it unlikely that he would be identified. That wouldn't be the case if he was caught defending *Stargazer* from these warriors.

"No," Picard muttered.

"No what?" Khone pressed. "Speak up, Terran!"

Picard's jaw tightened. "No. I don't have a problem."

"I didn't think so," Khone said, sneering contemptuously. He shoved Picard in the chest, then went back to looting the cabin. His fists clenched at his sides, Picard watched in impotent fury as Gwarz trashed his notes on the New T'Karath expedition. An angry vein pulsed in his temple.

"What's this offal?" the bald Klingon groused, sweeping the accumulated padds and isolinear rods onto the floor. He stalked away from the workstation, trampling the fruits of Picard's labors under his feet. "I should have known we wouldn't find anything worth taking on this miserable ship."

His piggish gaze fell upon the antique wine bottle resting on its shelf. "Hold on a moment," he corrected himself. He reeled across the cabin. "Now we're getting somewhere!"

Picard's heart sank. *No,* he thought. *Anything but that.*

Gwarz reached for the bottle. A flash of blue energy crackled as the stasis field repelled his fingers. *"Gre'thor!"* he swore angrily and smashed the compact field projector with his fist. The field flickered weakly before evaporating. "That's more like it!" Snatching the bottle from the shelf, he yanked out the cork with his teeth.

"Wait!" Picard protested. That single bottle meant more to him than all the age-old relics littering the floor. "Please! You don't want that, believe me."

"Shut your mouth, Terran!" Without even bothering to sniff the exquisite bouquet, he guzzled from the bottle. Château Picard dribbled down his chin. "Hah!" he laughed. "It's not blood-wine, but it will do."

He handed the bottle over to Khone, who took a gulp. Making a face, he spit the precious vintage onto the floor. "Terran swill!" he declared in disgust, shaking his head at his partner. "How can you swallow that bilge?" He wiped the taste from his lips with the back of his hand. "I swear, you've got worse taste in drinks than a Vulcan!"

"Eh, issh not so bad," Gwarz slurred. Reclaiming the bottle, he finished off the wine. Picard felt sick as he watched the last few drops of his family's legacy drip from the Klingon's matted beard—2347 had been a particularly good year. . . .

Gwarz belched and tossed the emptied bottle over his shoulder. It shattered at Picard's feet. He stared murderously at the broken shards. Given half a chance, he would have gladly slit the Klingons' throats with the jagged glass.

And then gone to work on the rest of the Alliance. . . .

"I've done what I can for him," the crone said. "The rest is up to time and fate." She coolly appraised her patient. "He's young, though. Given time to heal, maybe he won't end up *too* badly crippled."

Wesley groaned atop the dingy sheets. Splints bound up his fractured limbs. Crude herbal poultices coated his wounds. No respectable Cardassian physician would bother with a penniless Terran urchin, of course, so the best Picard had been able to do for

Wesley was to buy the boy a cot in a seedy flophouse and secure the services of an unlicensed human healer named "Momma" Pulaski. He frowned at the woman's bleak diagnosis.

"Here," he said, handing the haggard medicine woman several *leks* in currency. Gul Madred would never notice the expense, which Picard intended to bury amid his usual expenditures. "This should be enough for his bed and care, for as long as he needs them both."

The crone's eyes lit up at the sight of the coins. "More than enough," she agreed, greedily tucking the coins into the folds of her blood-speckled apron. 'I'll look after him as though he were my own flesh and blood."

"See that you do," Picard admonished her. Returning his attention to the injured boy, he leaned over the cot and spoke gently. "I have to go away for a time, Wesley. There's something important I have to do. But this woman will make sure you get everything you need to recover."

"Including Thalian chocolate?" He grinned weakly. "Don't worry about me, Luc. I'll be all right." He tried to sit up, but his battered body refused to cooperate. He grimaced in pain. "Sorry I didn't do a better job guarding *Stargazer* for you. I'd offer you a refund, 'cept I already spent your money."

"That won't be necessary," Picard assured him. His expression darkened. "It wasn't your fault."

But I know whose fault it was. A volcanic fury seethed inside him as he gazed down at the wreck the Klingons had made of his friend. He silently cursed the brutal regime that let such crimes go unpunished on a daily basis. *And I know what I have to do.* Before the day was out, he intended to get word to Vash that he'd changed his mind. If there was even a chance that the Borg could bring down the Alliance, he was going to find them.

Or die trying.

"You're quite certain about this, Luc?"

"Well, the evidence is encouraging," Picard lied. He spread out

an intimidating assortment of star charts, transit logs, and doc-
tored archeological surveys atop Gul Madred's desk. "The third
and final segment of the Stone of Gol used to reside in a museum
on Vulcan itself, but was supposedly smuggled off-planet right
before the Terran invasion. These records give me strong reason
to believe that the fragment ended up in an obscure Vulcan
monastery on P'Jem. The sanctuary was destroyed decades ago,
of course, but it's possible that the final piece of the Stone is still
buried somewhere beneath the ruins."

It was a total fabrication, of course. In order to search for the
Borg, Picard needed his patron to authorize another expedition
into deep space. Once he was safely away from Celtris III, with
sufficient funds to subsidize his search, he would be free to pursue his real objective.

No matter where it takes me.

If fortune was with him, he would return to Celtris III in the
forefront of an unstoppable Borg invasion force, with the Resistance providing support on the ground. If he failed, and the Borg
proved to be more myth than machine, he could always claim
that his quest for the missing Stone of Gol segment had turned
out to be a wild-goose chase. Madred would be displeased, but
not lethally so; even the merciless Cardassian understood that
there were no guarantees in archeology.

But would Madred fall for the hoax? Picard tried not to let his
anxiety show as he tensely watched the commander examine the
fabricated evidence. A cold sweat glued his shirt to his back. The
consequences, should Madred catch on that he was attempting to
dupe him, would be severe. Picard imagined himself hanging
from the cruel administrator's ceiling. For once he was grateful
that Madred was nowhere near the scholar he thought he was.
"Finding the third segment will be quite a coup," Picard pointed
out. "Romulan historians will be literally green with envy."

Madred smiled coldly at the prospect. "Very well, Luc," he
said finally. "You've convinced me. How soon can you embark on
the expedition?"

"I just need to take on the necessary provisions." Picard suppressed a sigh of relief. Moving with deliberate casualness, he reclaimed the various documents from the desk and headed toward the exit. He wanted to get clear of the office before Madred had a chance to change his mind. "I should be able to depart within forty-eight hours at the most."

Depending on how long it takes to smuggle Soong onto Stargazer.

He had almost made it to the door when Madred spoke up. "Just a moment, Luc." Something in his tone sent a chill down Picard's spine. "You are not dismissed yet. There's another matter I wish to discuss with you."

Picard turned around reluctantly, resisting an urge to run for his life. "Yes?"

"There was an unfortunate incident at a Terran saloon a few nights ago. During a routine security check, a trio of unidentified Terrans launched an unprovoked attack on Alliance soldiers before cowardly escaping into the night. Unfortunately, the officers involved were only able to provide vague descriptions of the perpetrators." He eyed Picard suspiciously. "You wouldn't know anything about this disturbance, would you, Luc?"

Picard swallowed hard. Just how much did Madred already know about the raid on the tavern? Was this some sort of trap? "I'm afraid not," Picard said, hoping to brazen it out. "I don't make it a habit to frequent such establishments."

"Of course not," Madred said smoothly. "You're too smart for that. I know you would *never* be so foolhardy as to do anything that might embarrass me. After all, I should hate to lose your valuable services." It was hard to miss the veiled warning in his words. "That's all, Luc. You may go now. Good hunting." He cracked open a boiled taspar egg and jabbed a fork into the feathered embryo inside. "I'll clear a space in my collection for the rest of the Stone."

Picard hurried out of the office. He felt as though he had just been granted a stay of execution.

The sooner he left Celtris III, the better.

4

The outpost was located on the Romulan side of the Neutral Zone, at the very edge of the disputed boundary between the Alliance and the Romulan Empire. Despite its official status as a science station, only a fool could fail to realize that the outpost's true purpose was to spy on the Alliance from across the border. The Romulans had maintained a wary guard against the Alliance for decades, and vice versa. The precise nature of the outpost had become academic, however.

The Tranome Sar Science Station no longer existed.

Picard and Soong stood on the lip of an enormous crater, looking down at the lifeless cavity where the Romulan base had once been. Nothing remained of the colony except for a gaping wound in the surface of the planet, several kilometers in diameter. The sloping walls of the crater, which descended deep into the bedrock, were shockingly smooth. It was as if the entire outpost, buildings and all, had been scooped up and carried away.

By the Borg?

"This matches the historical accounts of the Borg's attack on the El-Aurian homeworld, over one hundred years ago," Picard observed. Records of that attack, which had taken place after the end of the old Terran Empire, were sparse and incomplete, but he felt confident that they were on the right track. "I've read fragmentary reports of whole cities being whisked into space by an implacable foe."

Contemplating the vast crater before him, he struggled to imagine how such a feat was even possible. Whoever did this obviously possessed technology far beyond that of either the Alliance or the Romulans. From the looks of things, not a single inhabitant of the colony had survived the assault. Picard didn't know whether to be encouraged or alarmed by this awe-inspiring evidence of the Borg's power.

Maybe a little bit of both.

"Astounding, isn't it, Picard?" Soong did not seem to share Picard's reservations. The aged scientist was clearly thrilled by their discovery. Intellectual excitement animated his wizened face. "The Borg must be incredibly more advanced than we are, just as I would expect them to be." He gestured at the yawning crater. "This just goes to prove what can be accomplished when organic intelligence is enhanced by cybernetic means." His gaze turned heavenward. "I can scarcely wait to meet them!"

The passion in the old man's voice disturbed Picard. He had no love for the Romulans, who had not lifted a finger while the Alliance enslaved their Vulcan kinsmen, but Soong's jubilation struck Picard as somewhat unseemly in the presence of such appalling devastation. By his estimates, at least five hundred Romulans had died here.

Not that Soong seemed to care.

"Where does it come from?" Picard asked. "This . . . fascination . . . with artificial life-forms?" In the interest of tact, he avoided the word "obsession."

Soong chuckled hoarsely. "Sort of a family tradition, you might say. One of my ancestors, a contemporary of the famous Jonathan Archer, laid the groundwork for future endeavors in the field, before he was executed by the first Empress Sato as a danger to the Terran Empire." He shook his head sadly. "A woefully short-sighted decision, which stalled progress for generations—and may have contributed to the demise of the Empire. Who knows? With an army of intelligent androids on our side, humanity might have been able to repel the Alliance."

"Perhaps," Picard admitted. "But what about the threat posed by the androids themselves? Aren't you afraid that any truly sentient robots might eventually turn on their creators, as they did on Exo III?" Most archeologists now accepted that a flourishing humanoid civilization on that planet had been exterminated by self-aware androids of its own creation. Picard had personally inspected the ruins, searching for yet more treasures for Gul Madred. "Exo III is nothing but a graveyard now."

Soong snorted impatiently. "That was a freak event, obviously caused by a fatal flaw in the androids' programming. And I could prove it, too, if James Kirk hadn't destroyed the last surviving android nearly a hundred years ago. Another bad decision that deprived Terran science of vital information."

"Maybe Kirk made the right call," Picard suggested. "He usually knew what he was doing." Indeed, the fall of the Terran Empire had begun the day Kirk was betrayed by his treacherous first officer, Spock, who had eventually set the Empire on the road to ruin. As a historian, Picard often wondered what might have been had Spock been assassinated instead. "If not for Kirk, we might be ruled by androids now, instead of by the Alliance."

"And would that be so bad?" Soong challenged him. "Like my visionary forebear, I firmly believe that cybernetic intelligence is the next big breakthrough in evolution, and the only logical development where the future of sentient thought is concerned." He tapped his skull. "Plain old gray matter is on its way out."

I'm not sure I like the sound of that, Picard thought. He was tired of debating the old man, though, so he kept his doubts to himself. Not for the first time, he wished that Vash could have joined them on this leg of the expedition; unfortunately, Resistance business had delayed her departure from Celtris III. Picard hoped that she could rendezvous with them soon.

Soong scanned the crater with a customized tricorder. "Hmm, I'm detecting some interesting magnetic resonance traces, which don't correspond to any technology I'm familiar with. The Borg's unique signature, perhaps?" He looked up from his readings. "So where to now, Picard?"

"That depends," Picard said. "My contacts on this side of the border have passed on rumors of similar attacks on other outposts in this region. If we can confirm these reports, perhaps by scanning for those resonance traces you just mentioned, we might be able to extrapolate where the Borg will strike next."

"And get there in time to make contact with them!" Soong's eyes gleamed with anticipation. "I like the way you think, Picard!"

Picard wished he possessed the scientist's enthusiasm. On impulse, he tossed a rock into the crater. It took an unnervingly long time to hit the bottom.

Did they really want to meet the creatures that did this?

The caves beneath Celtris III reminded Vash of the underground temples on Ktaria VII. She and Jean-Luc had once spent a glorious weekend exploring those catacombs while assembling a substantial collection of antique burial stones. Alas, she was not looking for anything old and precious tonight; instead, she was hunting for something new and terribly dangerous.

"I am detecting definite subspace signals," Selar reported, sweeping the area with her tricorder. "Readings are consistent with theta band emissions."

"Guess there's some truth to those rumors after all." Vash trusted the Vulcan scientist's judgment. Selar was no Noonien Soong, but she knew her stuff. As a bonus, she was also an excellent combat medic. "I knew the spoonheads were up to something nasty."

"What about life signs?" Bagro grumbled. The Tellarite demolitions expert grunted beneath the weight of his camouflaged backpack. "That's what you should be scanning for. The Cardies will have our hides if they catch us down here."

Selar arched an eyebrow. "The only life-forms in this vicinity are Celtran sand-bats and assorted varieties of invertebrates." A stolen Alliance medkit was strapped over her shoulder. "I doubt that they will pose a significant threat to your safety."

"Are you questioning my courage?" Bagro said, bristling. He

snorted aggressively through his snout. A thick yellow beard wreathed his face. "I won't stand for—"

"Quiet, both of you," Vash ordered. Vulcans and Tellarites typically got along like oil and water; she briefly questioned her wisdom in assigning them both to her team. There was no way around it, though. She needed their respective talents to complete this mission, especially if they found what they were looking for.

The three-person team was investigating unconfirmed reports that the Alliance was developing metagenic weapons in an underground installation beneath Gul Madred's headquarters. Such bioweapons, which used genetically engineered viruses to destroy all forms of DNA, were theoretically capable of killing an entire ecosystem in a matter of days. They were strictly banned by a treaty between the Alliance and the Romulan Star Empire, but Vash wouldn't put it past the Cardassians to be working on them just the same. Ultimately, the weapons could be used to eradicate all life on any planet, moon, or space station liberated by the Resistance.

Spoonheaded slime! Her blood boiled at the very thought. It would be just like the Cardies and their Klingon buddies to wipe out any biosphere that wasn't under their despotic control. She couldn't let that happen. If the rumored facility existed, they had to destroy it. That's where Bagro came in. Tellarites loved blowing things up.

"Theta radiation bursts of this nature are often associated with the production of metagenic weapons," Selar reported. "By compressing the detection band, I have been able to obtain a directional fix." She gestured toward a cleft in a cave wall. Inky blackness concealed what lay beyond the opening.

"Lead the way," Vash instructed.

Marching single file, they trekked through a maze of subterranean tunnels and grottoes. Stalactites hung like dragon's teeth above their heads. Calcite formations encrusted the walls. Vash heard moisture dripping somewhere in the background. Blind, colorless grubs scuttled away from the glare of her searchlight, which cast ominous shadows upon the uneven path before them. Camouflage garb helped the team blend into the scenery. Insulated soles muffled their footsteps. Compared to the arid surface of the planet, the caves were very chilly. Vash found herself walking briskly just to stay warm. The tunnels smelled of bat piss and guano.

Bagro soon lagged behind the two women. Huffing and puffing, the out-of-shape Tellarite dragged his feet, while continuing to look about nervously. The porcine alien was obviously reluctant to proceed.

"Get a move on," Vash urged him. "That secret lab isn't going to be there forever."

"You're not the one carrying a homemade bomb on his back," he protested. "I'm walking slowly on purpose!"

Vash heard a squeal of anxiety in his voice. Beneath his bluster, Bagro was probably more frightened than he cared to admit. She recalled that his entire herd had been butchered by Alliance soldiers when he was just a piglet. Small wonder he got the willies infiltrating enemy territory.

Good thing I know how to handle him.

"Is that my problem?" she barked at him, mostly to ease his nerves. A boisterous argument would do more to reassure a Tellarite than any soothing words she might utter; the belligerent attitude was just what he needed to feel at home. "More walking and less whining, mister!"

"You're just lucky I don't turn around and leave the both of you to get killed on your own!" Bagro grumbled back at her. Sounding in slightly better spirits, he quickened his pace to catch up with the two women. His rotund belly jiggled as he trotted after them. "I'd like to see you blow up that nest of vipers without me!"

Selar sighed loudly, no doubt finding the heated exchange distasteful. "May I suggest that you both lower your voices. Unless I'm mistaken, this was supposed to be a *covert* mission."

Not a bad idea, Vash conceded, even though they were still at least a kilometer away from the alleged location of the underground facility. The party silently made their way through the shadowy labyrinth until they came to a narrow ledge running along the edge of a deep abyss. Sheer limestone walls descended sharply for hundreds of meters. Shining her light into the chasm, Vash glimpsed a forest of stalagmites jutting up from the floor of the pit. Rocky points waited to impale any clumsy spelunker.

"Watch your step," she warned the others.

Consulting her tricorder, Selar confirmed that the theta band emissions were coming from the other side of the ledge.

All right then, Vash decided. She nodded at Selar.

One by one, they inched across the ledge, which was no more than thirty centimeters wide at most. Vash pressed her back firmly against the steep cave wall behind her, feeling the cold of the buried stone seep into her bones. Selar led the way, while Bagro brought up the rear, with Vash edging along between them. The Vulcan woman moved at a steady, deliberate pace; if the vertiginous drop concerned her, Selar's stoic features betrayed no discomfort, only an intense degree of concentration. Bagro had needed to remove his backpack to fit onto the ledge. He clutched the parcel against his chest and muttered grumpily into his beard. Vash just tried to avoid looking down.

Times like this, she thought, *I wish humans were descended from mountain goats instead of primates.*

She was about halfway across the ledge when a wobbly patch of rock gave way beneath her feet. Loose gravel clattered down the side of the abyss as she suddenly felt nothing but empty air below her. Gravity seized her and she dropped like a stone. A mental image of herself, skewered upon the vicious stalagmites, flashed across her mind. She yelped out loud.

"Got you!" A three-fingered hand grabbed onto her wrist, halting her free fall. The sudden stop wrenched her arm, but that was infinitely better than the alternative. Her body twisted in his grip and she slammed face-first into the wall of the crevasse. Wincing, she looked up to see Bagro holding on to her with one arm while clutching his backpack with the other. Ivory tusks pro-truded from his lower lip as he strained to support her weight. "Thank fortune you Terran females are so bony!"

Vash's free hand and feet scrabbled against the cliff face, franti-cally seeking purchase. She gripped her searchlight between her teeth, while her legs dangled precariously above the waiting pit.

"Allow me," Selar volunteered. Crouching down, she took hold of Vash's right arm and helped Bagro pull their human com-panion back up toward the ledge. Vash gratefully threw her el-bows over the edge of the crumbling rock shelf and laboriously hauled herself up to a sitting position on the ledge. Her heart rac-ing, she leaned back against the cave wall and took a moment to catch her breath. Adrenaline coursed through her veins. Her mouth felt as dry as Vulcan's Forge. Selar handed her a bootleg water-pack and she sucked it dry in a couple of gulps.

"Thanks for the quick reflexes," she gasped to her comrades, after her heart and lungs had calmed down a bit. She closed her eyes, but still saw the sharpened stalagmites jabbing up at her. "I almost saved the Alliance the cost of a disruptor blast."

"Didn't have much choice," Bagro said gruffly. He peeked into his knapsack to make sure his explosives were still intact. "The Resistance frowns on operatives losing their cell leaders. You're the only ones who actually know what's going on!"

"Indeed," Selar concurred. "It was the only logical choice of action." She rose to her feet beside Vash. "I fear, however, that a more controlled descent is unavoidable." She shone a beam of light on the stretch of ledge still before them. Vash saw that at least four meters of ledge had crumbled away entirely, making the way impassable.

Great, she thought wryly. Leaning forward, she peered down into the yawning chasm that had almost claimed her life. Unset-tled scree continued to rattle at the bottom of the pit. *One way or another, it looks like we're taking the direct route down.*

She detached a set of fusing pitons from her belt, as well as a coil of sturdy de-cel line. Climbing carefully to her feet, she placed the business end of a piton against the hard granite wall behind her. The push of a button ignited a momentary blue flare and a loud whoosh as the metallic spike fused with the wall on a molecular level. She tugged on the piton just to make sure it was secure.

It didn't budge.

Good, she thought. The Resistance often had to scrounge for its arms and equipment, which could be of highly variable quality. *Not another dud.*

While Selar and Bagro donned their rappelling harnesses, Vash affixed one end of her cable to the piton, then tossed the rest of the coil over the edge of the precipice. She clipped the line to her own harness. "Control your speed," she warned the others, "and watch out for those stalagmites at the bottom."

"Don't worry," Bagro assured her. "I'm not planning to end up a shish kebab today." He tested the sturdy monofilament line, assuring himself that it would support his weight. "Meet you down below."

Vash was glad to discover that the bomb expert was not subject to acrophobia. Nodding at her team, she eased herself backward and over the edge. The soles of her hiking boots rebounded against solid rock as she deftly rappelled down the side of the cliff face. The sensation reminded her once again of that spelunking expedition with Jean-Luc. Feeling the cable slide between her fingers, she couldn't help wondering what Jean-Luc and Soong were up to right now. And wishing he were here.

Have they tracked down the Borg yet? Are they safe?

She touched down on the floor of the chasm and unclipped the line from her harness. Selar and Bagro soon joined her in what appeared to be a vaulted chamber at the base of the cliff. A rustling noise, coming from high above their heads, briefly puzzled Vash until her searchlight exposed an enormous nest of Celtran bats hanging upside down from the ceiling. There appeared to be dozens of the insect-eating mammals, their leathery yellow wings folded about them. High-pitched chirps objected to the glare from her searchbeam, so she quickly lowered the light.

Big deal, she thought. *I'll take bats over Cardassians any day.*

A quick sweep of the searchlight revealed that the spacious chamber branched out into a number of available shafts and tunnels. Vash looked at Selar.

The other woman checked her tricorder. "This way," she said, indicating an opening a few meters ahead. It looked like a tight fit, but Vash figured they could all squeeze through, including Bagro. "The theta emissions are growing stronger. I believe we are nearing our destination."

"Music to my ears." Vash drew her phaser. "Let's do this."

They wriggled through the cleft, discovering another warren of tunnels on the other side. Now that they were getting close to the supposed site of the underground lab, Vash kept the search beam lowered toward their feet to avoid alerting any lurking guards. She wished that they could do without the light entirely, but, this far beneath the surface, the only alternative was total darkness. Not even night-vision goggles would do them much good down here. She made a mental note to try to get the Resistance some of those new full-spectrum visors. . . .

Selar stopped and extended her arm, blocking the other two rebels. She cocked her head to one side and cupped a hand around an elegantly tapered ear. Vash couldn't hear anything, but then again, she didn't have a Vulcan's hypersensitive hearing. "Someone's ahead," Selar whispered.

Bagro sniffed the air. "Smells like a Cardassian."

Vash took their word for it. She repressed a twinge of envy; it was unpatriotic, but sometimes having merely human DNA was a pain. *No wonder our empire fell,* she thought. *Almost every other sentient species in the galaxy has extra abilities, and lives longer to boot.* Maybe the notorious Khan Noonien Singh had been right after all. *Would the Alliance have conquered us if we hadn't banned human genetic augmentation?*

She wondered what Jean-Luc would think of that question.

Clicking off her flashlight, she gulped involuntarily as utter blackness enveloped them. Vash couldn't even see the proverbial hand in front of her face, let alone her fellow freedom fighters. It was like staring into a black hole—not a single photon of light escaped the darkness. She laid a hand on Selar's shoulder, counting on the Vulcan's tricorder and superior hearing to guide them the rest of the way. Bagro shuffled closely behind them.

They crept stealthily through the dark. After a few minutes of squinting uselessly into the blackness, Vash spotted a glimmer of light up ahead. The lambent glow appeared to be coming from just around the corner of an upcoming intersection. *This must be it,* she guessed. *The illegal bioweapons facility.*

Her heart pounded as she squeezed past Selar for a better look. Peering around the corner of a rocky partition, she spotted a solitary Cardassian soldier pacing back and forth in front of a closed metal hatch built into a solid stone wall. Plasma lights were mounted on the ceiling above him. A disruptor rifle leaned against the sentry's shoulder. His booted footsteps beat like a metronome against the floor. He hummed a militant Cardassian marching song that quickly grated on Vash's nerves. He looked and sounded bored.

Perhaps we can remedy that, Vash thought. She raised her disruptor.

"Wait," Selar whispered softly into her ear. She placed a restraining hand upon Vash's arm. "The energy discharge might trigger an alarm." She slipped quietly around her leader and handed Vash her tricorder. "Permit me to deal with this obstacle."

Vash nodded.

Selar waited until the unwary soldier's back was turned before creeping up on the guard as silently as a Romulan shadow assassin. Vash covered her with the disruptor just in case, but she needn't have bothered. Before the nameless Cardassian knew what was happening, Selar came up behind him and applied pressure to a specific portion of the guard's throat. His eyes rolled back in his skull. His body went limp.

She took hold of the unconscious guard and quietly lowered him to the ground. Vash and Bagro came around the corner to join her.

"A nerve pinch?" Vash teased the other woman. Breaking his neck would have been just as easy. "Getting soft in your old age?"

Selar was unrepentant. "Not at all," she said, nudging the spoonhead's slumbering form with the toe of her boot. "There may be some use to keeping him alive." She knelt to search her victim's body. "The logic is irrefutable."

History had it that the Vulcans had once been pacifists, but that was a long time ago. Life was cheaper these days.

"Works for me," Vash said. She confiscated the man's rifle and slung it over her shoulder. A good Resistance fighter never let a working weapon go to waste. "But kinder than he deserved."

She glanced around, taking stock of their situation. Columns of hardened calcite supported the curved ceiling of a cylindrical tunnel that extended past the metal hatch in two directions. Smooth, polished walls suggested that the tunnel had been artificially widened at some point, perhaps by an enslaved Horta. She searched the corners for security cameras, but no visible lenses looked back at her.

Just the same, she didn't want to waste any more time here than they had to. Who knew when the unlucky guard's replacement was due, or whether he was expected to check in with his superiors at regular intervals? Vash inspected the gleaming silver hatch, suspecting that what they were looking for was on the other side. There was no obvious handle, but a touch-sensitive keypad was embedded in the stone wall beside the door. A combination lock?

"Any code or key on him?" she asked Selar.

The Vulcan's fingers probed the guard's armor. "Negative."

"Damn," Vash muttered. Selar and her clever tricorder could probably bypass the code in time, but that would be tempting fate. Besides, what if any attempt to hack into the lock set off some sort of alarm? *We could use Jean-Luc here,* she thought. *He was always good at cryptology.* "Any ideas?"

"I could always try to blow it up," Bagro volunteered. He shrugged off his backpack.

"That may not be necessary," Selar announced soberly.

Something in her tone caught Vash's attention. She eyed the kneeling Vulcan uneasily. "What do you have in mind?"

"An eel interrogation," Selar proposed. She extracted a small plastic vial from a pouch on her camo suit. A slick black organism oozed inside the vial. "Fortunately, I came prepared."

Vash repressed a shudder at the sight of the creature. "I don't know. That's a pretty evil thing to do to anyone, even a Cardassian."

"It is distasteful," Selar conceded. If Vash didn't know better, she'd have sworn that she heard a genuine note of remorse in the other woman's voice. "But I believe that it is our best recourse at this point." Her eyes held a determined glint. "The Alliance cannot be allowed to develop metagenic weapons with impunity."

Without waiting for Vash's assent, she applied pressure to a nerve cluster at the base of the Cardie's neck. He instantly regained consciousness, looking about him in surprise as he jumped to his feet. The guard reached for his rifle, only to find Vash aiming it at his skull.

"Don't move," she warned him. "I voted to kill you in the first place."

He clenched his fists, seething with indignation. "Rebel scum. You don't belong here."

"Tell me something I don't know," Vash replied. Maybe they wouldn't need to resort to the eel after all. The Cardassian guard didn't know it, but this might be his lucky day. "What's the code for the door?"

He spat at her feet. "You won't get anything from me. I'll die first."

No, Vash thought. *But you might wish you had.*

They couldn't afford to waste any more time. "He's all yours," she told Selar.

And may history forgive us.

"Hold him," the Vulcan instructed Bagro. "He may struggle."

"You think?" the Tellarite said sarcastically. He got behind the

Cardie and twisted the guard's arms behind his back. Wincing in pain, the soldier squirmed in Bagro's grasp, but could not break free. "I'd be climbing the walls by now, and not in a good way."

The Cardie gulped. Apprehension started to undermine his arrogance. "What's happening?" he asked nervously. "What are you going to do?"

Vash didn't bother to explain. She just kept the gun pointed at his head. Selar stepped toward the guard, holding the vial in her fingers. The Cardie's slate-colored eyes widened in fright as he spotted the loathsome creature inside the vial. "Is that . . . ?" The dreadful truth sunk in. "No! You can't . . . I'm begging you . . . !"

He thrashed frantically, desperate to get away. Bagro grunted as he strained to hold on to the panicked soldier. Vash figured he could use a little help.

She fired a warning shot into the wall behind the prisoner. An intensely bright disruptor blast seared the solid stone . . . and reminded the Cardie just how weak his position was.

"No more of that." She gave him one more chance at avoiding what Selar had in store for him. "The code?"

The guard wavered, torn between his duty and his terror. Sweat seeped from beneath his scales. His face twitched as he wrestled with what a Cardassian might consider a conscience. His anguished gaze never left the vial in Selar's hand, and the ghastly organism inside. For a second, Vash thought he was going to spill the beans, but then his strict military training reasserted itself. He bit down on his lip to keep from talking. His stubbornness would cost him dearly.

"Do it," she told Selar. *Let's get this over with.*

The Vulcan uncapped the vial and tipped it onto the Cardassian's neck. A slimy black larva, about two centimeters in length, dropped onto the guard's neck, eliciting a shudder that shook the doomed soldier from head to toe. Squeezing his eyes shut, he looked away from the thing on his neck, unable to bear the sight of it oozing across his flesh. Tears streaked his scaly face.

And the worst was still to come. . . .

The fearsome Ceti eels had been discovered on a barren planet in the Mutara Sector. The Alliance had attempted to set up a prison camp there before discovering that Ceti Alpha V was not entirely uninhabited. Dozens of prisoners, as well as several guards and the warden, had perished before someone finally trapped a specimen of their killer.

"Ugh!" Bagro exclaimed. His snout wrinkled in disgust as he pulled his head away from the creature climbing his prisoner's throat. "I can't believe we're actually doing this!"

He gave us no choice, Vash thought.

The parasitic organisms were actually mollusks, not eels, but in their larval forms they resembled small black eels and so the designation had stuck. Officially, the Alliance had declared the planet off-limits and the species exterminated, but in reality the black market supported a thriving trade in the disgusting larvae, due to the eels' unique effect on the humanoid nervous system. They were particularly popular among slavers and assassins.

Vash watched in horrified fascination as the slimy larva wriggled up the Cardie's segmented throat, leaving a trail of mucus behind it. The creature disappeared in the right ear of the guard, who convulsed in pain as the eel burrowed its way into his brain, wrapping itself around his cerebral cortex. He started to scream, but Selar clamped her hand down over his mouth, muffling his agonized cry. Dark blood trickled from the punctured ear.

"How soon will it take effect?" Vash asked Selar, feeling sick to her stomach. She had heard about this process, of course, but she had never actually witnessed it with her own eyes before. Her hand instinctively covered her own ear. She had no doubt that the eel would be playing a starring role in her nightmares for weeks to come.

"That depends on the species of the host," Selar explained. With her free hand, she tucked the empty vial back into the pouch on her suit. "It should not be long."

The Vulcan's predictions were as accurate as ever. Within moments, the Cardassian's writhing body ceased its futile struggle. His arms drooped limply and his face went slack. Glassy eyes possessed all the animation of a Klingon mind-sifter casualty. Selar cautiously removed her hand from the man's mouth, but the guard did not cry out. His jaw sagged open. A thin thread of drool dripped from the corner of his mouth.

"I believe he is ready," Selar announced. She nodded at Bagro. "You may release him."

The Tellarite gratefully let go of the prisoner. He backed away from the Cardassian, putting plenty of floor space between himself and the eel's new host. "By the Holy Trough," he murmured in a hushed tone. Stubby fingers traced a Tellarite religious symbol in the air. "This is an abomination!"

Vash didn't argue the point. But it was one she was willing to take advantage of for the sake of the Resistance. Lowering her rifle, she walked right up to the lobotomized guard. "The code!" she demanded, getting down to business. "What is the code?"

As the survivors of the prison camp had eventually discovered, humanoids whose brains were infected by a larval eel soon became highly suggestible, lacking any will of their own. It was this peculiar side effect that had made the eels so sought after by the more unscrupulous inhabitants of the galaxy. Vash had heard rumors of secret Alliance nurseries where the mind-controlling eels were bred in mass quantities. . . .

"Code?" the soldier echoed. He sounded confused and disoriented, as if he barely knew his own name. A chill wormed down Vash's spine as she pondered whether, on some level, the infected prisoner knew what was happening to him. She hoped not, for his sake. "But . . . the code is secret . . . top secret. . . ."

Was it possible that the sentry hadn't even known the code to the door he was guarding? Had they committed this unspeakable atrocity for no purpose?

No. Vash wouldn't let that be true. She glanced hurriedly at the insignia on the guard's uniform. "Lieutenant!" she barked, doing her best impression of an impatient Cardassian commander. She shouted in the man's face. "Stand and report. The entrance code . . . now!"

He snapped to attention. The classified info spilled haltingly from his lips: "Security code . . . trimega . . . zero . . . one . . . zero . . . two . . . delta . . . four. . . ."

"Is that it?" Vash made him repeat the code one more time before committing it to memory. *That's enough,* she decided. *I'm ending this now.* "That's enough, Selar. You know what to do."

"Indeed." The Vulcan reached out for the Cardassian's neck once more. Betraying a touch of squeamishness, her skilled fingers carefully avoided the mucus trail left by the eel's passage. The entranced guard offered no resistance as she firmly gripped his throat and twisted her wrist just so. His neck snapped with an audible crack.

Tal-shaya, Vash observed, nodding in recognition. The technique had once been considered a merciful form of execution on ancient Vulcan, and was currently enjoying a comeback among the Resistance's Vulcan operatives. Vash admired its efficiency . . . and relative painlessness.

There was no known cure for a Ceti eel infestation. The uncooperative guard had been a dead man from the moment the parasite had first entered his ear canal. Selar's death grip had spared him from progressive brain damage, dementia, and death.

He owes her one.

Once again, Selar lowered her victim to the ground, this time for good. Anxious to put this sickening experience behind her, Vash turned and walked toward the sealed door. *Let's see if all that was worth it.*

"Watch out!" Bagro shouted fearfully. He almost tripped over his own bomb in his haste to get away from the soldier's body. Genuine terror raised his voice several octaves. "It's loose!"

Vash glanced back at the corpse on the floor. Something stirred beneath his head and she watched, nauseated, as the eel larva abandoned its lifeless host. Bloody mucus coated the parasite as it slid out of the guard's ear onto the floor of the cavern. It oozed across the ground in search of a fresh brain to inhabit.

Forget that, she thought. "Stand back." She blasted the eel with the guard's own rifle. It burst into flame, dissolving into a puddle of steaming protoplasm. She gagged on the smell.

Bagro let out a gasp of relief, then glared at Selar. "Where in slop did you get that vile thing anyway?"

"I have my sources," she replied cryptically.

"Where?" he accused her. "The Black Sty of Acherron?"

Vash called the discussion short. "We can compare shopping tips later. Right now we still have a job to do."

She entered the code into the keypad by the door. *Trimega zero one zero two delta four.* Holding her breath, she stepped back to see what happened next.

"Code received," a computerized voice announced. Concealed mechanisms engaged, and the thick steel hatch swung outward, revealing a lighted chamber beyond. "Access granted."

Gripping her newly acquired disruptor rifle, Vash stepped quickly through the doorway. "Nobody move!" she ordered anyone who might be inside the chamber, but her warning was greeted only by a series of electronic beeps. Looking around, she instantly determined that the vault was empty except for a single device resting in the center of the room. Blinking lights accompanied the beeps emanating from the machine, which was in the form of a vertical cylinder about a meter in height.

She gazed about in confusion at the bare white walls surrounding her. This was it? The modest chamber looked like nothing she had expected. Where were the teams of evil biochemists at work? Where were the test tubes and beakers and chromosome splicers, not to mention the brewing vats of genocidal terror? What sort of underground germ warfare plant was this?

Bagro followed her into the chamber, carrying his volatile knapsack in front of him. His ruddy face looked just as baffled as hers. "I don't get it." He scratched his thick beard in confusion as Selar entered after him. "Are we in the right place?"

Good question, Vash thought. A dreadful suspicion dawned within her. Raising the tricorder, she scanned the blinking steel cylinder. Sure enough, the device was emitting the subspace signals that had lured them here, but there wasn't a hint of metagenic research to be seen. She pressed a power switch on the cylinder, and the incriminating theta band emissions vanished without a trace.

There could be only one explanation.

"It's a trap!" she blurted.

And we walked right into it!

Without warning, the steel hatch slammed shut behind them, trapping them inside. A hissing sound alerted Vash to another threat, and she looked up to see thick white fumes entering the chamber via vents in the ceiling. She felt a numbing sensation at the back of her throat and recognized the narcotizing effect of anesthezine gas.

The cowardly spoonheads were trying to drug them.

"Cover your mouths and noses! Try not to inhale the fumes!" She tugged the collar of her camo suit up over the bottom half of her face. Such measures would only buy them a few extra moments of consciousness, she knew; they had to get out of there fast. Setting the disruptor rifle on maximum power, she took aim at the closed hatchway and pulled the trigger.

An incandescent purple beam struck the steel door head-on, then ricocheted back into the chamber. Vash and her teammates dived out of the way as the reflected disruptor blast hit the decoy theta band emitter, which was instantly vaporized. Vash felt a momentary burst of heat against her skin.

So much for that idea, she realized. Obviously, the gleaming door was shielded by some kind of ablative coating. The gleaming metal wasn't even scorched.

By now, the anesthezine vapors were rapidly filling up the chamber. Vash heard Selar and Bagro coughing and choking behind her. The burly Tellarite was tottering unsteadily upon his feet, while Selar, supporting herself against the rear wall, was already sliding down toward the floor.

Vash knew how they felt. She was starting to feel pretty woozy herself. Her vision blurred before her. Her legs felt like over-cooked Argelian pasta.

Don't cave in, she told herself vehemently. *That's just what the Cardies want.*

Her bleary eyes zeroed in on the backpack in Bagro's hands. Without pausing to consider the consequences, she staggered toward him and wrenched the bundle away from him. A few wobbly steps carried her over to the exit, where she wedged the pack up against the base of the hatch. "Take cover!" she hollered through the fabric over her mouth. She backed away from the door as far as she could go. Unslinging the rifle once more, she fixed the pack in the weapon's sights.

Here's hoping Bagro whipped up one hell of a bomb.

"Fire in the hole!" She turned her face away from her target and fired the disruptor.

A deafening explosion knocked her off her feet. Tumbling across the floor, she rolled herself up into a ball and covered her ears with her hands. The force of the explosion brutally threw her against a wall. The jarring impact bulldozed the breath from her lungs. She felt as if she'd been hit by a runaway shuttlecraft.

"Vash!" Rough hands shook her to see if she was still alive. She heard Bagro panting in her ear. "Vash, can you hear me?"

"Barely," she croaked. Her head and ears were still ringing from the thunderous detonation. She wanted to curl up and sleep until the twenty-fifth century, but knew that wasn't really an option. *Where are those old-fashioned cryo-suspension tubes now that I need them?* Bagro helped her climb painfully to her feet, and she turned to inspect her handiwork.

The blast had nearly torn the steel hatch off its hinges. The anesthezine escaped through the open gap, making it easier to breathe. As her head began to clear, she wiped the soot from her face and nodded at the doorway. Every bone and muscle in her body ached, and she knew that she was going to be black and blue tomorrow, assuming she survived the next few hours. "Get a move on!" she ordered. There was no way that the bad guys weren't coming for them, especially after that explosion. "Run for it!"

Ducking beneath the awkwardly hanging door, they rushed into the tunnel outside. A disruptor blast tore into a stone column only a few centimeters from Vash's head, peppering her face with bits of powdered granite. A mixed band of Klingon and Cardassian soldiers came storming down the corridor toward them. Searchlights were mounted to the barrels of their rifles.

"Weapons on stun!" a scaly Cardassian glinn shouted at the warriors. "The gul wants them alive!"

Vash was less picky. Taking refuge behind the chipped stone column, she fired back at the soldiers. Her rifle was definitely *not* set on stun. The glinn fell over backward, a smoking hole in his chest. Vash smiled wolfishly.

One down.

A full-fledged firefight erupted in the subterranean intersection. The air hummed with the sizzle of opposing disruptor beams, even as the last wisps of anesthezine dispersed through the adjacent tunnels and shafts. Hiding behind a nearby wall, Bagro and Selar added their fire to their leader's, temporarily holding the Alliance troops at bay.

"Come and get us, you tuskless butchers!" Bagro bellowed. His disruptor blasts fired wildly at their foes. "You face a true son of Tellar this day. You'll never take me alive!"

Cool under fire, Selar picked out her targets with more precision. "That is undeniably an outcome to be avoided," she observed.

Vash admired their spirit, but knew they couldn't hold out for long. She heard the pounding boots of more guards coming their way. They had to make a break for it now, before they were hopelessly surrounded and outnumbered. She signaled the others to go first, then let loose a massive barrage of disruptor beams to cover their retreat.

"Go!"

The two rebels sprinted from their refuge toward the outer

tunnels. Bagro galloped with surprising speed, but Selar, weakened by the gas, moved a trifle too slowly. A Klingon beam winged her in the leg and she crumpled to the ground. Bagro heard her cry out in pain. He swore and turned around to retrieve her. The bulky Tellarite scooped Selar up and heaved her over his shoulder before resuming his dash for safety. Red and purple beams zipped past him, missing him and Selar by mere centimeters.

He disappeared into a murky side tunnel. Vash took a deep breath, committed her body and soul to the inscrutable gods of probability, and launched herself after him. She fired back over her shoulder at the pursuing guards. A Klingon warrior, of Amazonian proportions, hit the dirt. Running soldiers tripped over her fallen body, slowing their progress. Vash extended her lead by a couple of meters and darted into the same tunnel as her friends.

She switched on the searchlight attached to her own rifle. The sudden illumination showed her Bagro up ahead, with Selar still slung over his shoulder. The wounded Vulcan watched the Tellarite's back, aiming her disruptor back the way they had come. Recognizing Vash behind them, she wisely refrained from firing.

"Keep going!" Vash shouted. "Don't wait for me!" Gaining on the encumbered Tellarite, she had caught up with them just as they emerged from the tunnel into yet another confusing intersection. A variety of escape routes presented themselves. "Just pick one and run." Vile threats and racing footsteps echoed from the tunnel behind them. "They're right on our tail!"

Then, unexpectedly, their enemies were in front of them as well. Rifles blazing, two more guards burst from an archway several meters ahead of them. Before any of the rebels could react, a disruptor beam stunned Bagro, who collapsed in a heap on the floor, taking Selar with him. The woman's weapon went flying from her hand.

"Bagro!" Vash nailed the Tellarite's attacker with a purple beam right between his eyes, but the second guard took shelter behind a fountain-sized stalagmite. *Think you're safe now?* she thought vindictively. Lifting her gaze, she fired her rifle at a corresponding stalactite directly above the hidden guard. The blast dislodged the jagged stone spear, which plunged down onto the soldier. A geyser of dark Cardassian blood sprayed up from behind the stalagmite.

Think again.

Over on the floor of the intersection, Selar struggled to untangle herself from Bagro's limp body. The smell of charred Vulcan flesh wafted from the ugly green disruptor burn on her leg. Ignoring her own pain, she checked Bagro's pulse.

"Is he still alive?" Vash called out. She nervously eyed the mouth of the tunnel they had just left. The other guards sounded as if they'd be here at any moment.

"Yes," Selar reported, "but that doesn't matter." She gave Vash a piercing look. "You must eliminate us before you complete your escape."

"What?" Vash knew what the other woman meant, but she didn't want to admit it. "Are you insane?"

"It is the only way," Selar said calmly. "For all our sakes, you cannot allow us to be interrogated by the Alliance." She might have been talking about deleting an inconvenient computer file for all the emotion she displayed. "The needs of the Resistance outweigh any personal considerations."

The disruptor rifle in Vash's arms suddenly weighed a ton. "I can't," she insisted. "Don't ask me to do it." A narrow side tunnel beckoned to her, but she couldn't bring herself to leave her fellow freedom fighters behind, alive or otherwise. "I signed up to kill our enemies, not my allies!"

Selar shook her head in disappointment. "Terrans! You weren't so softhearted when your ancestors conquered my people." She crawled toward her lost disruptor, dragging her injured leg behind her. She left a trail of glistening green blood in her wake. Her fingers groped for the weapon, which lay amid a pile of rubble just beyond her reach. "Flee then. I'll attend to matters myself."

Inching forward, her fingers finally fell upon the disruptor's outer casing.

A crimson beam struck from the darkness, stunning her before she could kill either Bagro or herself. Selar's head dropped onto the floor of the cavern.

Another beam slammed into the ground at Vash's feet. An explosion of rock fragments drove her back into the nearest open tunnel. Cursing herself for not being tough enough to do what was necessary, she turned and ran deeper into the unknown passageway. She fired back at the cave entrance, setting off a miniature cave-in that effectively cut her off from her pursuers . . . at least for the moment.

Hot tears streaked her sooty face as she dashed headlong through the never-ending maze of tunnels and grottoes. Her searchlight illuminated the way ahead, alerting her to dangers waiting in her path. She leaped over dangerous chasms and crevasses, while living in fear of finding herself trapped in a dead end. Childhood memories surfaced, bringing echoes of ancient stories that had once made her shiver beneath her covers. She suddenly felt like Becky Thatcher of old Earth, being chased through unmapped caverns by Injun Joe.

If Becky had a disruptor rifle, that is.

Angry shouts and commands, reverberating through the tunnels, confirmed that her enemies were still hunting her. *What?* she thought bitterly. *My friends weren't good enough for you?* As cell leader, she knew her primary responsibility was to avoid being captured herself, but that didn't make leaving the others behind any easier.

She squeezed through a familiar cleft to find herself back in the roomy chamber at the base of the five-hundred-meter drop. Her searchlight found her rappelling cable, still dangling against the face of the underground cliff. Unfortunately, it was of no use to her now. She couldn't possibly scale the sheer rock face quickly enough. Chances were, she'd get caught halfway up the cliff when her pursuers found her. One quick disruptor blast and she'd find herself impaled on a stalagmite in no time.

Her beam swept the vaulted chamber, looking for a safer way out. After a minute or two, she spotted a small lava tube that appeared to angle up toward the surface of the planet. The mouth of the tube was less than a meter in diameter, but that might be enough to crawl through. *Could be worth a shot.*

She stepped forward to take a closer look, only to be caught off guard as a muscular figure lunged from the shadows and grabbed her from behind. "I got her!" the Klingon shouted, wrapping one arm tightly around her waist. He tore her rifle from her hands, nearly breaking her fingers in the process, and hurled it into an open shaft several paces away. His hot breath blew against the back of her neck. She heard the rifle scrape loudly against the side of the shaft as it plummeted out of sight. Vash fought to free herself, but the Klingon's grip was too strong. He leaned back, lifting her feet off the ground. "Squirm all you like, Terran! You're not going anywhere!"

To hell with the rifle, she thought. Plucking another fusing piton from her belt, she swung it back over her shoulder and into the Klingon's bony forehead. Sparks flared as she triggered the fusing mechanism, welding the spike to the warrior's brow. Howling in torment, he dropped her like a sack of stem bolts. She scrambled away from him before turning around to observe his reaction.

The Klingon reeled about wildly. His fists were wrapped around the piton as he tried and failed to detach the spike from his skull. In his pain and distress, he tumbled over the edge of an open shaft. A second later, Vash heard a grisly splat.

But her troubles weren't over yet. Drawn by the Klingon's shouts and screams, the rest of the guards converged on the grotto. Sizzling beams targeted Vash from all directions, forcing her to duck behind a large rock formation. The blazing rays criss-crossed above her head, making escape impossible. The mouth of the lava tube was only a short dash away, but it might as well have been in the Gamma Quadrant. She'd be stunned senseless a dozen times over before she got even partway there.

Not good, she thought, assessing her chances. Although she had lost the disruptor rifle, she still had her own disruptor, but what good would that do? She was ridiculously outgunned. *This is that nightmare on Penthara IV all over again.* She had been lucky to get out of that ambush in one piece. What were the odds she could pull that off again?

Not very high, she estimated.

A purple disruptor beam came at her from another angle, requiring her to shift position around the rocky outcropping. To her surprise, her right foot landed on something slippery, throwing her off balance. Grabbing onto the rock to steady herself, she looked down at the slimy mess beneath her foot.

Fresh bat droppings. Of course.

Vash remembered the tremendous flock of Celtran bats roosting overhead. A wild idea occurred to her. Reclaiming her weapon from her belt, she fired up at the ceiling. Shattered stalactites rained down on her foes, but that was just the beginning. The concentrated light and heat woke the bats from their slumber . . . and threw them into a panic.

Suddenly, the cavern was alive with dozens of furry bodies flying about frantically. The startled cries of the Alliance soldiers were almost lost amid a cacophony of high-pitched squeaks and the flapping of countless leathery wings. Besieged by the frightened yellow bats, the Cardassian and Klingon warriors swatted at the winged creatures, trying to bat their stinging claws and teeth away from their faces. Colorful obscenities tested the universal translator's capacity for invective.

Almost forgotten amid the chaos, Vash took advantage of the confusion to scurry toward the lava tube. Bats didn't scare her; she had spent too much time poking around in forgotten caves and catacombs with Jean-Luc Picard. Reaching the mouth of the tube, she jumped headfirst into the open tunnel.

The sounds of the crazed bats and soldiers faded into the background as she crawled on her hands and knees up the sloping tube. Pitch blackness surrounded her and she had to feel her way through the cramped tunnel. It was going to be a long, hard up-hill climb, but she didn't care. She couldn't wait to get out of these godforsaken caverns.

If only Selar and Bagro were coming with her . . . !

She hated the idea of leaving her comrades in the hands of the enemy, especially a sadistic bastard like Gul Madred. But all she could do for them now was honor their memory, and devote all her energy to ensuring that their heroism had not been in vain. *You will be avenged,* she promised them silently.

Perhaps when the Borg came.

Practical matters intruded upon her grief. Had any of the soldiers seen her face? She had to assume that the spoonheads would identify her eventually, which meant that she needed to get off Celtris III as soon as possible. *I'd better contact Odan as soon as I reach the surface,* she decided. The crafty Trill owed her a favor.

She tried not to think too hard about the fact that this entire mission had turned out to be a huge error on her part. Two Resistance members had been captured, just to eliminate a top-secret military installation that didn't really exist!

She just hoped that, wherever they were, Jean-Luc and Soong were having better luck than she was.

5

Weeks later, *Stargazer* hid behind a moon as she waited for a Romulan warbird to pass by. The runabout's murky cockpit was lit only by emergency lights; Picard had powered down all but the most essential systems to avoid detection. Hell, he was tempted to turn off the artificial gravity as well. Anything to avoid showing up on the warbird's sensors.

"That ship must be gone by now," Soong insisted. Riding shotgun beside Picard, he fidgeted impatiently in his seat. "We should be on our way."

"Not yet," Picard said, playing it safe. He wasn't taking any chances where the enemy vessel was concerned. The unarmed runabout was no match for the massive warbird. At Gul Madred's insistence, *Stargazer* was equipped with only defensive systems. Unfortunately, there was no way to scan for the other ship's presence without risking exposure. "We wait a while longer."

"But we're going to be too late!" Soong protested. "Again!"

Picard understood the other man's frustration. After finding the same magnetic resonance traces at the other Romulan outposts, they had been trying—and failing—to catch up with the Borg ever since. Here in the Nequencia system, they had arrived mere hours after another attack, only to discover that the Borg had already moved on. *At least we know that we've extrapolated their trajectory correctly,* he thought. *Which means we know where to go next.*

"What about the lovely Vash?" Soong pressed him. Picard had transmitted their future coordinates to Vash right before the warbird had warped onto the scene. "Surely you don't want to keep her waiting?"

"I don't want to end up in a Romulan prison camp either," Picard said gruffly. He was anxious to rendezvous with Vash, but not enough to gamble with their lives. "Or worse."

Had the warbird been responding to a distress call from the doomed colony? By now, its captain and crew must surely have discovered that they were too late to save the outpost. *Another good reason to avoid being caught here,* Picard thought. Never hospitable at the best of times, the Romulans were likely to be on edge after these recent assaults on their bases. He had no desire to attract the attention of a trigger-happy Romulan commander.

Soong muttered unhappily under his breath as Picard waited another two hours before powering up *Stargazer* once more. The lights came back on in the cockpit, and he heard the thrum of the runabout's impulse engines. *Stargazer* crept out from behind the uninhabited moon as Picard cautiously scanned for any sign that the formidable warbird might still be prowling the system. His fingers hovered over the warp controls, ready to go to warp at the first hint of a Romulan energy signature. He held his breath.

Next to him, Soong ceased his grousing. The restless scientist was not so obsessively focused on catching up with the Borg that he didn't appreciate the potential danger. He leaned forward in his seat, peering at the viewscreen. "Olly, olly, oxen free," he chanted, crossing his fingers for luck. "Come out, come out, wherever you are!"

"All clear," Picard said after a moment. He scrutinized the sensor readings just to be sure. "Looks like our green-blooded friends have left Nequencia behind." He wondered how the Imperial Senate back on Romulus was reacting to the news that yet another of their outposts had been wiped out of existence. "I'm guessing that they're hunting for something a whole lot more impressive than one little runabout."

"Then why are we still here?" Soong asked. He drummed his

fingers against the armrests of his seat. "Hit it, Picard. The Borg are waiting for us!"

And so was Vash.

Going to warp, *Stargazer* made a dash for the Neutral Zone. According to their calculations, the Borg's next target was likely to be a Klingon listening post on the other side of the Zone. Unlike the Romulans, the Klingons didn't bother disguising their surveillance stations. Little did they know, however, that a foe even more powerful than the Romulans had their outpost in its sights.

The Alliance was about to meet the Borg head-on.

"Please, I'll tell you anything!"

"Of course you will," Gul Madred said softly.

The prisoner, a foul-smelling Tellarite, lay curled in a fetal position on the cold steel floor of the interrogation chamber. A coarse gray robe barely covered his porcine form. Noxious bodily fluids puddled beneath him as he groaned weakly.

"So you confess to taking part in an unlawful attempt to sabotage this base?" Never mind that the facility he had hoped to destroy did not actually exist. The lure of those fictional metagenic weapons had proven just as irresistible as Madred had hoped. The terrorists had taken the bait like the miserable vermin they were.

"Yes, yes!" the Tellarite exclaimed. Trembling, he rose to his knees. Greasy tears leaked from his piggish eyes. Mucus streamed from his snout. A surgical scar could be glimpsed on a shaved portion of his chest. Dried blood and vomit caked his bristly yellow beard. "I built the bomb myself! Using concentrated trinitrogen chloride from some cleaning solution!"

"See, I knew you could be cooperative," Madred said approvingly. In truth, he was somewhat bored; breaking the Tellarite had posed no challenge at all. He glanced at his notes. "Who is the leader of your Resistance cell?"

The prisoner hesitated, apparently reluctant to implicate his former comrades.

"You disappoint me." Madred sighed. "It seems you have a re-markably short memory." He calmly activated the agonizer implanted in the Tellarite's chest. The prisoner collapsed onto the floor, squealing like a stuck *targ*. His stubby limbs convulsed in agony. Shaking fingers clawed impotently at the scar on his chest.

As always, Madred admired the efficacy of the device. *A human invention,* he recalled. *The Terran Empire's one lasting contribution to galactic civilization.*

He let the Tellarite suffer for a moment or two before turning off the agonizer. "Who is the leader of your Resistance cell?"

"V-Vash," the prisoner gasped. He quivered on the floor, the last vestiges of his recalcitrance completely shattered. In Madred's experience, Tellarites had a usefully low tolerance for pain. "A Terran female named Vash."

That's better, Madred thought. He reviewed the reports on his desk. According to the officer in charge of the operation, a Terran woman had managed to escape when the Tellarite and one other accomplice had been captured. Madred had looked forward to breaking the Vulcan female, but she had cheated him by taking her own life first. The jailkeeper whose sloppiness had allowed the woman to escape justice in such a manner now occupied the Vulcan's former cell.

Madred keyed the name "Vash" into his computer interface, and a grainy photo of a brown-haired human female appeared on his screen, alongside a litany of suspected Resistance activities and contacts. Apparently, this "Vash" was quite the enterprising terrorist. *A pity she got away,* he thought. He made a mental note to circulate her image among his security personnel. Chances were, she had already fled Celtris III, but you never knew. *Perhaps we'll get lucky.*

"Ask him about the scientist," a gruff voice instructed him. A Klingon warrior stood alongside Madred's desk, observing the interrogation. Commander Nu'Daq had recently arrived in search of a wanted fugitive by the name of Soong.

Madred scowled. He rather resented the Klingon's interference, but he had no choice but to tolerate Nu'Daq's presence in the interest of harmonious relations between allies. *So long as this doesn't take too long.* He was determined to finish up this tedious business in time for his daughter's birthday party later this afternoon. Jil Orra would be expecting him, and he didn't want to disappoint her. *Family is important.*

"Very well." He fixed an icy gaze on the prone Tellarite. "What do you know about a Terran named Noonien Soong?"

The agonizer had taught its lesson well; this time there was no hesitation. "That crazy old man?" the Tellarite said, slowly rising to a sitting position. He stared bleakly at his feet. Blood stained his whiskers; apparently he had bitten his tongue during his convulsions. "He was with us for a while, but not anymore. We smuggled him onto a ship weeks ago, hidden inside a cargo container."

Nu'Daq cursed in Klingonese.

"What ship?" Madred demanded.

"*Stargazer!*" the Tellarite volunteered. "A beat-up old runabout named *Stargazer.*"

Madred stiffened in surprise. He struggled to conceal his shock from the Klingon. His gaze drifted guiltily to the ancient Ventanian thimble sitting on his desk, then hastily darted away again. Anger flared brightly behind his veiling expression.

Picard!

"You know this ship?" Nu'Daq asked darkly.

Madred nodded. "And I know how to find it." He summoned his guards via the comm. "Take this creature away," he said, indicating the cowering Tellarite. "See that he's disposed of promptly."

The alien screamed and pleaded for mercy, but Madred wasn't listening. He had more important matters to deal with now.

Forgive me, Jil Orra. It seems I won't be attending your party after all.

"Hurry, Picard!" Soong urged him. "Can't this ship of yours go any faster?"

"I'm going as fast as I dare!" Picard replied. Celestial bodies streaked past the windows at warp speed. *Stargazer*'s overtaxed engines were already close to their limit. The entire ship vibrated alarmingly, sending jarring tremors through his body. He kept his gaze fixed on the viewscreen ahead. "Hold your horses. We're almost there."

He slowed to impulse as they entered the Carraya system. In theory, Vash was supposed to meet them in orbit above the system's fourth planet. He smiled as their sensors detected another vessel directly ahead. He hoped she hadn't been waiting long.

"There she is," he stated as an antique Vulcan shuttle that made *Stargazer* look like the fabled *I.S.S. Enterprise* appeared on the viewscreen. The smaller spacecraft occupied a geostationary orbit above Carraya IV, safely out of sight of the Klingon base on the opposite side of the planet. "Picard to Vash," he hailed her on an encrypted frequency. "Sorry for the delay. We had a close call with a predatory warbird."

He waited for her response.

And waited . . .

"Picard to Vash," he repeated, his smile fading. "Please respond."

Static greeted his hails.

Soong's palsied fingers operated the control panel in front of him. "I'm not detecting any life signs aboard," he reported. "Terran or otherwise."

"What about life support?" Picard asked anxiously.

Soong scrutinized the readings. "All systems seem to be operational, and there's no obvious damage from weapons fire." He turned toward the other man. "I don't think she's aboard, Picard."

Then where the hell was she? Peering at the viewscreen, Picard confirmed with his own eyes that the shuttle's hull appeared both intact and devoid of scorch marks. He couldn't see any obvious reason why Vash would have had to abandon her ship like this. Had the Klingons taken her into custody? Or the

Borg? He stared at Carraya IV. Jungles covered much of the lush green world. Nighttime shrouded the planet's eastern hemisphere, which was currently turned away from the sun. Had Vash beamed down to the surface for some reason?

"We have to find her," he declared. Getting up from his seat, he headed for the transporter at the rear of the main cabin. "You take the helm. I'm going to search her ship for clues." Perhaps she had left a message aboard the shuttle? "Don't go anywhere without me."

"Picard, wait!" Soong spun around in his seat. "I'm picking up a distress call from the Klingon outpost." His eyes were wide with excitement. "The Borg. They're here!"

What? Picard hurried back toward his seat, but Soong was already piloting *Stargazer* around the curvature of the planet to investigate. Carraya IV spun beneath them, daylight spreading across its surface. Picard's jaw dropped as a shocking tableau came into view.

The Klingon base was under attack from a single vessel: a gigantic steel diamond large enough to contain several *Galor*-class warships within its angular walls. Layers of intricate machinery covered the diamond's hull, like ivy overrunning an abandoned temple. Sickly green lights radiated from somewhere deep inside the bizarre vessel, which resembled no starship Picard had ever encountered before. The technology-encrusted faces of the diamond, which had to be at least three thousand meters across, were strangely uniform in design. He could discern no obvious bridge, propulsion units, or hatches.

There was no mistaking the ship's weaponry, however. A crimson beam, emanating from one of the diamond's vertices, strafed the planet below, cutting a circular fissure around the perimeter of the Klingon base. The heavily armed fortress fired back with ground-to-space disruptor cannons, but the powerful beams were unable to penetrate the diamond's shields. Azure energy flashed uselessly against an invisible barrier.

Had the Alliance met its match at last?

Moments later, a pale green tractor beam latched onto the outpost, effortlessly wrenching it from the bedrock and out into orbit. The disruptor cannons fell silent as the base and its inhabitants were suddenly exposed to the icy vacuum of space. Picard wondered if the outpost's inhabitants had time to realize what was happening before their lives were abruptly snuffed out. Had Vash been a prisoner within the base? Picard prayed that his lover was anywhere else right now.

"It's definitely the Borg!" Soong said gleefully. His face bore a rapturous expression, unshaken by the horrific nature of the attack. He was practically bouncing in his seat. "I'm detecting the same magnetic resonance traces as before!"

We did it, Picard thought. *We found the Borg.*

Let's hope we don't live to regret it.

To his relief, their tiny runabout appeared to be beneath the Borg ship's notice. For better or for worse, they had a front-row seat as their elusive quarry proceeded to take apart its prize. Tractor beams held the floating colony in place while incandescent red lasers carved up the murdered outpost like a roasted *targ*. Isolated chunks of hardware were absorbed into the diamond, disappearing into concealed openings in the ship's hull. The Borg were evidently more interested in the base's technology than its inhabitants; Klingon and Cardassian bodies drifted away from the breached outpost as the Borg systematically dissected the various buildings and weapons emplacements. Lasers sliced off disruptor banks and power stations.

"Interesting," Soong observed. "They seem to be collecting samples for examination. Perhaps they're on a scientific mission? Curiosity is one of the hallmarks of an advanced intelligence. One would expect its presence in any truly evolved cybernetic consciousness."

Before Picard could reply, another vessel warped into the system. "Look over there!" he exclaimed, recognizing the newcomer as a Klingon *Vor'cha*-class attack cruiser. The massive ship was many times larger than *Stargazer,* but was dwarfed by the enormous diamond. "Reinforcements from the Alliance!"

The Klingon warship had responded to the attack much faster than had its Romulan counterpart. Picard wondered if the Alliance had been anticipating the Borg's incursion, perhaps from monitoring the attacks on the Romulan outposts? *Maybe we're not the only ones who noticed a pattern at work.*

"My money's still on the Borg," Soong said. "Never bet against an artificial intelligence."

Sounds like words to live by, Picard thought.

Like the Borg ship, the massive attack cruiser ignored *Stargazer,* winging past the runabout to confront the gigantic diamond. Picard eavesdropped electronically on the warship's transmissions.

"Alien vessel!" a deep voice hailed the Borg. *"This is Captain K'muc of the* Imperial Starship Mek'leth*!"* The face of a jowly Klingon warrior appeared on the viewscreen. Fury contorted his whiskered features. *"Your treacherous sneak attack on Alliance territory will not go unavenged. Surrender at once, or be destroyed!"*

Soong snorted in derision. "Empty threats. That thick-headed brute has no idea of what he's dealing with." He consulted the sensor displays. "The Borg are scanning his vessel even as we speak."

I don't know, Picard thought. A Klingon attack cruiser was not to be taken lightly. Would the Borg choose to fight or flee?

Breaking off their dissection of the captured outpost, the Borg responded to the Klingons' hails. *"Your threats are irrelevant,"* said a chorus of robotic voices, speaking in unison. In marked contrast to the bellicose tone of Captain K'muc, the voice(s) of the Borg were utterly devoid of emotion. *"We have analyzed your defensive capabilities. You are unable to withstand us. Prepare to be assimilated into our Collective. Resistance is futile."*

The flat, uninflected statements sent a chill through Picard's blood. Vulcans spoke with more feeling.

"Fascinating," Soong enthused. "It appears that the Borg possess some sort of group mind, linking their collective intelligence into a single unified purpose." He nodded thoughtfully. "That would explain why I can't detect any individual life signs aboard their vessel. It's possible that the Borg don't even exist as individuals. How incredibly efficient!"

And inhuman, Picard thought.

"We'll show you futile!" Captain K'muc barked back. He shook his fist at the faceless voice. *"No one defies the Alliance with impunity. Death is upon you!"*

The Klingon commander wasted no further breath on his enemies. His face disappeared from the viewscreen as he cut off the transmission. The *Mek'leth,* named after a traditional Klingon short sword, launched its attack. Disruptors raked the exposed faces of the huge diamond, but the corrosive beams seemed to have no more effect on the Borg ship than Carraya IV's own defenses had. The diamond wasn't even scratched.

"Resistance is futile," the Borg repeated. *"Your technological and biological distinctiveness will be added to our Collective."*

I don't like the sound of that, Picard thought. *What exactly do they mean?*

On-screen, the Klingon warship had not yet exhausted its arsenal. With the disruptors proving ineffective, the *Mek'leth* fired photon torpedoes at the enemy vessel. The torpedoes exploded against the Borg ship's shields with far more effect than the disruptor beams had. The blinding detonations tore out great chunks of the Borg ship's hull, leaving charred craters in the face of the great diamond. It seemed the Borg could be hurt after all.

"Perhaps the Borg are not as invincible as we believed," Picard said. Vash would be disappointed, if she was still alive, but he had distinctly mixed feelings about this evidence of the Borg's fallibility. The Resistance needed a powerful ally, but maybe not *too* powerful. . . .

Soong scowled at the viewscreen. "We'll see." There was no question whom the old scientist was rooting for in the silent conflict before them. "I wouldn't be surprised if the Borg still have a few good tricks up their sleeve."

No doubt emboldened by his success, the Klingon commander launched another salvo of torpedoes at the Borg. The deadly missiles tore across the void, igniting brilliantly in the air-less dark. Picard leaned forward, anxious to see how badly the torpedoes had damaged the Borg ship, yet when the glare from the explosions faded, he was surprised to discover that the huge diamond had been left unscathed by the second bombardment. If anything, the Borg ship looked less damaged than before.

"Hah!" Soong cackled. "You see, Picard? The Borg have *already* adapted to the Klingons' weapons, and modified their shields ac-cordingly. Their reaction time is astounding! Do you grasp just how quickly they learned to defend themselves from those torpe-does? No mere organic intelligence can adapt that swiftly!" He clapped his hands, applauding the Borg's near-instantaneous learning curve. "And look, the ship is repairing itself as well."

It was true. Before Picard's eyes, the breached areas of the Borg ship's hull were being restored automatically. Severed gird-ers and conduits snaked across the open wounds, forming new connections. White-hot flares fused ruptured steel together. Gray metal plating spread over the newly erected scaffolding like a fresh layer of skin. It was almost as though the ship itself were a living organism, healing at an incredibly accelerated rate.

Picard felt a touch of superstitious dread. A Klingon or Car-dassian ship would have required weeks in spacedock to repair that kind of damage, but the Borg ship looked like it would be as good as new in no time. *What kind of beings are we dealing with here?*

A greenish tractor beam latched onto the *Mek'leth*. Scanning the battle from a safe distance, Picard saw that the beam was rap-idly draining energy from the Klingon ship's deflectors. The *Mek'leth*'s shields were already down fifty-seven percent; at this rate, the Klingons would be defenseless within minutes. A nim-bus of chartreuse energy flickered weakly around the embattled ship.

Had Picard been in K'muc's place, he would have attempted to escape from the fearsome diamond, diverting all of the ship's re-maining resources to its warp drive, but Klingons never ran from a foe. The attack cruiser targeted the source of the tractor beam with a blistering volley of disruptor blasts and photon torpedoes, seemingly throwing everything in its armory up against the Borg, yet all its fire and fury came to naught. Additional tractor beams emanated from the diamond's vertices, catching the warship even more tightly in their snares. Picard doubted that the *Mek'leth* could have retreated even if the Klingons had been willing to sacrifice their barbaric "honor" for safety.

"Their shields are gone," he reported grimly.

Slowly, methodically, the Borg's lasers dismantled the trapped attack cruiser. *Mek'leth's* warp nacelles, battle bridge, and engineering section were surgically removed from the warship before being drawn into the voracious maws of the looming Borg diamond. Glowing plasma and Klingon bodies spilled out into space. Picard wondered if K'muc's corpse was among those floating lifelessly in the vacuum.

"They never stood a chance," he realized. He felt a flicker of sympathy for the outmatched Klingons, then remembered how those two drunken guards had trampled over his work and memories back on Celtris III. He pictured Wesley's broken body, lying in a filthy cot. *Maybe Vash was right,* he thought. As cold-bloodedly ruthless as they appeared to be, perhaps the Borg were just the allies the Terran Resistance needed. Who else could annihilate the Klingons so easily?

"Of course not," Soong said confidently, as though the outcome of the battle had never been in doubt. "The Borg clearly possess superior technology, not to mention the strategic advantage of a collective mind that can make and implement decisions at the speed of thought." He beamed benignly at the floating diamond as it reduced the once-formidable warship to raw material, then went back to "assimilating" the uprooted outpost. "They're everything I dreamed they'd be."

By the time the Borg ship completed its work, all that was left of the former military base was a small cloud of scrap metal and Klingon remains. The Borg ship released the debris from its tractor beam, letting it drift away on the solar winds. At least some of the corpses, Picard guessed, would be caught by the planet's gravity and burn up in reentry. Meanwhile, the metallic diamond floated in orbit above Carraya IV, still and silent. He wondered what it was waiting for.

Us?

Soong grinned at Picard. "So when shall we pay them a visit?"

"I'm not sure this is a good idea."

Picard joined Soong on the small transporter platform at the rear of the cabin. He glanced back over his shoulder at the cockpit. *Stargazer* was locked into a stable orbit less than two kilometers away from the Borg vessel. He couldn't help thinking that was too close for comfort.

"Nonsense," Soong replied. A communicator badge was pinned to the scientist's ragged overcoat, just in case they were separated. "Now's the perfect time to make contact. Sensors indicate that the Borg have lowered their defensive shields now that they've finished assimilating that Klingon settlement. In fact, a decline in their total energy output suggests that the entire ship has gone into some sort of dormant mode. I theorize that the Borg need time to fully absorb the technology and data they harvested from Carraya IV."

Picard nodded. "While they finish 'digesting' their meal, so to speak."

"Precisely," Soong said. "And to fully recover from the battle." He tapped his foot impatiently on the platform. "No doubt this dormant state helps speed up the healing process."

No wonder they haven't responded to our hails, Picard thought. Despite his reservations, he keyed in the coordinates for the Borg vessel, along with the emergency retrieval codes. *This is what we came here for,* he reminded himself. Certainly, there was no denying that the Borg would make a formidable ally against the Alliance. He also hoped to find Vash alive and well within the Borg ship. *Perhaps she's already trying to enlist them in her cause?*

"Let's hope they don't mind us dropping in." He drew his disruptor and assumed a stationary position on the platform. "Transporter, engage."

The familiar tingle of the transporter effect enveloped him, then quickly dissipated as the two men found themselves deep within the vast Borg diamond. Picard gripped his phaser as he swiftly surveyed their surroundings.

Level upon level of metal catwalks extended above and below them. The walkways formed an immense steel lattice that seemed to fill the entirety of the vessel. Amber lights, built into panels above the corridors, provided dim illumination. Circular monitors cast a gangrenous green glow over the scene. The air was uncomfortably warm and humid, not unlike Celtris III. The gravity felt normal.

"Mon dieu!"

Picard started at the sight of a grotesque humanoid standing a few feet away from him. Mottled white flesh, like that of a drowned man, peeked out from beneath overlapping layers of matte-black insulation and artificial prosthetics. Exposed circuitry and cables connected the electrical components that covered the creature's body like barnacles. A telescoping lens jutted from the being's right eye socket. An ugly black headset was implanted in a hairless white cranium. The left arm looked entirely mechanical. An unblinking organic eye stared blankly ahead.

The Borg, I presume.

His body tensed in anticipation of an alarm or attack, and he stepped defensively in front of the old man. A heartbeat passed, yet the Borg did not react to their arrival. The creature stood motionlessly within a recessed metal alcove that faced out onto the walkway, so that its occupant looked like one of those petrified mummies back on New T'Karath, complete with sarcophagus. Stepping backward, Picard saw that the corridor ran past several such niches, each one containing an individual Borg. He gradually lowered his weapon as it became apparent that he and Soong were in no immediate danger. The Borg were indeed in a dormant state, at least for the time being.

"Out of my way, Picard." Soong tottered out from behind the other man to get a closer look. He squinted at the nearest Borg, his face only centimeters away from the humanoid's pallid countenance. "Exquisite," he murmured to himself, sounding almost as though he were having a religious experience. "Most exquisite." He peered at a blinking ceramic component embedded in the Borg's right temple. "Some sort of cortical node? Or perhaps a sensory input processor?"

The enthralled scientist was speaking in tongues as far as Picard was concerned. While his companion spewed technobabble, he glanced around at the Borg's sprawling habitat. Equipment racks and power couplings filled the spaces between the individual alcoves. Glowing green disks, located above the Borg's heads, seemed to monitor their vital signs. The circular displays looked incongruously like haloes, although the cybernetic humanoids bore little resemblance to any angels Picard was familiar with. More like drones in a beehive.

He was struck by the relentless uniformity of it all. Earlier scans had failed to locate any discernible command area, engineering section, or living quarters. Now his own eyes confirmed that the ship's interior was bizarrely decentralized. He had chosen their landing coordinates more or less at random, but apparently that hadn't made any difference. One location was as good as any other.

"I'm going to look around," he informed Soong. Unlike the scientist, he was more interested in finding out if Vash was aboard, than examining the Borg. His boots resounded against the metal walkway as he walked farther down the corridor. Retrieving a tricorder from his belt, he scanned for life signs, but the results came up negative.

Damn, he thought. *Where are you, Vash?* He was tempted to call out her name, but found himself reluctant to disturb the sepulchral hush of the slumbering Borg vessel. Perhaps she was down on the planet instead? He tried not to think about the possibility that she might have died along with the Klingons, but ghastly images of her graceful body being sliced apart by lasers intruded upon his consciousness nonetheless. *No!* he thought stubbornly. *I'm not giving up on her yet.*

A hissing sound caught his attention, and he rounded a corner to investigate. Vapor gushed from a punctured conduit that appeared to be in the process of repairing itself. Picard scanned the atmosphere, but detected only trace levels of tetryon particles, nothing to really worry about. The temperature registered at exactly 39.1 degrees Celsius. The humidity was 92 percent. He wondered if those numbers would mean anything to Soong.

Another row of inert Borg drones stretched ahead of him. The monotony, as well as conspicuous lack of aesthetics, discouraged Picard. From the look of things, the Borg cared only about function, not form. The Collective's soulless voice echoed in his memory. He gazed into the unseeing eye of the closest Borg; this one looked vaguely Romulan. What if the Borg didn't want to ally with the Resistance? Why should a bunch of unfeeling machines care about the freedom of the human race?

Exploring further, he stumbled onto what appeared to be some sort of highly sophisticated operating room. An elevated metal pallet, large enough to accommodate a standard-sized humanoid, occupied the center of the chamber. An array of gleaming steel probes and surgical instruments resided on a tray next to the pallet. A mobile beam projector was mounted above the platform, perhaps to conduct deep-tissue scans or laser surgery? Picard lifted one of the silver instruments from the tray and tried to guess its purpose. It seemed just the right size and shape to, say, scoop out an eyeball.

He was unpleasantly reminded of Gul Madred's interrogation room. On closer inspection, the sterile compartment struck him as less like a medical facility and more like a torture chamber. The pallet itself was conspicuously missing any cushions or other measures to ensure a patient's comfort. And were those restraints built into the sides of the bed? Glancing around, he didn't see anything that resembled a conventional anesthetic provider. He started to wonder just how voluntary the operations conducted in this chamber were.

A series of metal drawers had been installed along one wall. Picard noticed that the top drawer was slightly ajar. He guessed that it had been shaken loose during the battle with the Klingon battle cruiser. A strip of crumpled turquoise fabric, dangling over the edge of the drawer, caught his eye and he walked over to investigate.

The drawer held scraps of clothing, of varying hues and textures. Sorting through the samples, he identified fragments of Klingon, Cardassian, and Romulan military uniforms, as well as various civilian garments. Bemused by the interspecies rag collection, he was starting to slide the drawer shut when his gaze fell on a solitary shred of fabric peeking out from beneath the other remnants. It was a cheap piece of khaki, the kind Vash had been wearing the night she had surprised him aboard his ship.

He pulled the khaki free from the pile and ran his fingers over it. The texture was just as he remembered it. He raised it to his nostrils. Vash's unmistakable fragrance still clung to the fabric, so distinctive that it stirred more memories and feelings within Picard than even the most celebrated literary madeleine. *She* was *here,* he realized. *She might still be alive.*

But where was she now? Ominously, the edges of the sample had been sliced smoothly, as though by surgical scalpel or laser. Peering intently at the fabric, he discerned a single spot of dried human blood. . . .

Vash!

Tucking the precious evidence into his pocket, he hurried back to Soong. He found the old man standing transfixed in front of an unconscious drone.

"Amazing, aren't they?" Soong declared, before Picard could tell him about the khaki fragment. "There appears to be a degree of specialization differentiating the individual units. No doubt they can also modify themselves as needed." He stroked his chin. "One wonders why they even bother with their organic components."

"I think they're hideous," Picard said bluntly.

Soong sighed. "Your antiquated prejudices blind you, Picard. That's the problem with you archeologists. You're so enamored of the past that you can't see the future even when it's right in front of you." He regarded the Borg with outright awe. "You're looking at the evolution in action: adaptation by cybernetic enhancement. Even beyond their surface implants, I'm detecting sophisticated nanotechnology at a cellular level. They've artificially upgraded their own DNA!"

This dubious accomplishment impressed Soong no end, but left Picard feeling even more apprehensive. His skin crawled as he contemplated the unsettling figure before him. *If this is the future,* he thought, *I'm not sure I want any part of it.*

"I just wish they'd wake up so we can have a decent conversation," Soong complained. "There's so much I want to ask them, and I'm not exactly getting any younger." He stepped forward and prodded the Borg with his finger. "Hello? Can you hear me?" Grabbing the Borg's arm, he tried to tug the drone from its alcove. "Rise and shine!"

"Wait!" Picard said, alarmed. Who knew how the Borg would react to this disturbance? He peeled Soong's fingers away from the Borg's arm and physically dragged him back from the alcove. "Have you lost your mind?"

Soong squirmed in his grasp, but was unable to free himself from the younger man's grip. "Blast it, Picard!" he protested. "Unhand me!"

Not on your life, he thought. He eyed the insensate Borg worriedly, half expecting it to lunge from its niche at any moment. The drone remained stationary, however, and Picard decided that that they were still safe enough. *No thanks to this crazy old man!*

Then he heard the footsteps.

"Someone's coming," he realized. The steady tread of the approaching steps reverberated down the corridor.

"About time," Soong said.

Picard let go of the scientist and drew his disruptor. *I guess this*

Borg isn't done hibernating, he thought, *but others are coming to investigate.* "Looks like you're getting your way, Soong. You'd better hope that the Borg are just as evolved as you think they are."

The clanking footsteps grew louder, along with the whirring of mechanical parts. Picard braced himself for whatever was coming, while Soong quivered in anticipation. "Greetings," the old man called out. Only Picard's firm grip kept him from scampering ahead to meet the aliens. "My name is Noonien Soong. I'm eager to learn from you!"

A trio of monochromatic figures marched into view. Fumes from the ruptured conduit momentarily veiled their appearance, but they quickly emerged from the mist. Picard gasped out loud as he recognized a familiar face behind an array of cybernetic implants.

"Vash!"

His lover's skin was chalky white, and her skull was shaved bare. Fully half her face was covered by wires and circuitry, yet there was no mistaking what remained of her elegant features. A blinking red scanner had replaced her right eye. Gears and servos hummed when she moved. Steel pincers clicked together at the end of a large prosthetic arm.

"Oh my God," Picard exclaimed. "What have they done to you?"

Her single brown eye showed no sign of recognition. Not bothering to reply, she led the other two Borg toward the alcove of the sleeping drone. Her zombie-like gait was nothing like her usual seductive saunter. Thrusting his disruptor into his belt, Picard ran forward and grabbed her by the shoulders. "Answer me!" he demanded as he stared into her mutilated face, searching desperately for the woman she used to be. "Do you know who I am?"

She knocked him aside with a sweep of her artificial arm. The inhuman strength of the blow caught him by surprise; his body slammed into a nearby guardrail, bruising his ribs. A pain-filled grunt escaped his lips.

Vash ignored his distress. Intent on her mission, she inspected the Borg that Soong had accosted moments ago. A probe at the end of her arm fitted into a corresponding slot in the framework of the alcove. Electronic beeps emanated from her headset as she ran some sort of diagnostic on her fellow Borg. The other two drones stood by silently, apparently prepared to render assistance if necessary. Or were they standing guard over the procedure, just in case he or Soong tried to intervene?

Picard's throat tightened. "Vash," he pleaded hoarsely, staggering away from the rail. Had the Borg captured Vash when they'd assimilated the Klingon base, or had she encountered them earlier? "Talk to me, please. Tell me you're still in there somewhere."

"It's too late, Picard." Soong laid a restraining hand upon his shoulder. "She's evolved beyond you." His raspy voice held a tinge of sympathy. "A pity, really, but progress has its costs. Something is always lost with each new breakthrough." He sounded like a professor lecturing a slow-witted student. "You have to look past your broken heart, keep your eye on the larger picture."

"Shut up!" Picard snapped. The old man's insane ramblings meant nothing to him now. All he cared about was getting through to Vash—if there was still something left of her to save. "Listen to me, Vash. Remember who you are." He wrenched his shoulder free from Soong's grasp. "I don't care what these monsters have done to your body. You're still the same person you always were. You're still the woman I love!"

"Please, Picard," Soong exhorted him. "You're embarrassing yourself." He called out to Vash's Borg companions. "Hello? May I have your attention? I'm very interested in learning more about your species' origins."

The silent drones ignored him.

So did Picard.

The beeping ceased and Vash disengaged her arm from the other Borg's alcove. She turned stiffly toward the two men. "Prepare to be assimilated," she announced in a dead voice. "Your biological distinctiveness will be added to our own."

Is that what the Borg had done to Vash? "Assimilated" everything that made her unique? Picard felt sick to his stomach. It occurred to him that they might not have encountered her randomly; it was possible that the Collective was deliberately using Vash to communicate with others of her species, to ease their absorption into the hive mind. *If her presence is supposed to calm us,* he thought bitterly, *then the Borg don't understand us at all.*

Extending her prosthetic arm before her, she approached the men. Her cybernetic companions walked in lockstep behind her. Gleaming probes and pincers spun at the end of the oversized arm. Her leprous complexion looked dry and flaky. An antiseptic odor preceded her, masking her former fragrance. Picard's heart sank. Vash didn't even smell like herself anymore.

"Think, Vash! Remember what's important to you!" He backed away from Vash and the other two Borg, while racking his brain for some way to reach her. Even if she didn't respond to him anymore, he knew what mattered to her more than anything else. "Think of the Resistance!"

"Resistance is futile," she replied.

Picard's last shred of hope evaporated. *There's nothing left,* he realized. *She's gone.* This creature was not Vash; it was an obscene parody of her, a walking desecration of everything she had ever believed in. His face hardened as he drew his disruptor. *I can't let her live like this.*

He squeezed the trigger, and a beam of red-hot energy struck the female Borg squarely in the chest. Sparks erupted from her wire-encrusted torso as she toppled over onto her back, crashing loudly onto the metal grillework. Her limbs twitched, and the pincers of her prosthetic arm clicked together spasmodically before freezing in place. Mechanical servos stopped whirring. Her blinking red eye went dark.

Rest in peace, he thought. *You deserved so much more than this. So much more than I could ever give you.*

"Good Lord, Picard!" Soong exclaimed. He stared in shock at the smoking body of the dead Borg. "What's come over you? That was completely unnecessary!"

Picard shot the scientist a murderous glare. Vash would still be alive if not for Soong's dangerous obsession with the Borg. He was sorely tempted to leave the old man to the Borg's tender mercies, but he wasn't sure he wanted the Borg to assimilate the man's genius. They were lethal enough as is.

The Borg are going to have to do without both of us, he vowed. *At least if I have anything to say about it.*

Provoked by Picard's attack on Vash, the other two Borg went into action. One knelt to retrieve vital components from its fallen comrade, while the other advanced on the two men, picking up where Vash had left off.

"Resistance is futile," it intoned.

We'll see about that, Picard thought. He fired at the Borg, hoping to kill it as easily as he had the Vash-Borg. To his surprise, however, a translucent force shield appeared between the Borg and the beam, blocking the disruptor blast. Picard shifted his aim, but the planar shield moved with him. Try as he might, his beams couldn't get past the Borg's defenses.

"You're wasting your time, Picard." Soong clearly regarded the impenetrable shield as yet more proof of the Borg's manifest superiority. "Don't you see? They've already adapted to your weaponry, just like they did with the Klingons!"

For once, the crazed scientist had a point. The Borg were obviously quick learners. Switching tactics, Picard fired at the walkway beneath the drone's feet instead. The catwalk disappeared in a flash of scarlet energy and the Borg plummeted through the gap, landing on the catwalk below. A metallic clang rang out, loud enough to wake the dead.

More Borg stirred within their alcoves.

"We have to get out of here," Picard stated. The third Borg, having finished with its salvage job on Vash's remains, stomped toward them. A force field bridged the yawning gap in the walkway, and Picard knew better than to try the same trick again. He reached for his communicator badge, to trigger the emergency beam-out, but Soong grabbed onto his arm, yanking it away from his chest. "Let go of me, you lunatic!"

"No!" the scientist shouted. "Not yet! We can still make contact with them, learn where they came from." Picard tried to shake off the old man, but Soong clung to him with frantic determination. "We can't leave yet. I have too many questions!"

"Damn your questions!" Picard finally yanked his arm free, but Soong's delay had cost him precious seconds. The third Borg was almost upon them, less than a meter away. Picard recoiled from the drone's outstretched pincers. He couldn't imagine a worse fate than being transformed the way Vash had been. Being tortured to death by Gul Madred sounded like a mercy by comparison. "I won't become one of these . . . things!"

Spotting a plasma conduit on the wall between two alcoves, he blasted it with his phaser. Superheated vapor jetted from the wreckage, momentarily slowing the Borg's advance. "Time to go," Picard said. He tapped his combadge. "Emergency Code Waterl—."

"Speak for yourself, Picard!" Soong interrupted. The scientist snatched his own combadge from his overcoat and flung it at the floor. It clattered against the walkway before falling through the metal grating. Soong smirked victoriously at Picard. "I'm not going anywhere!"

You senile maniac! Picard thought angrily. *Stargazer*'s transporter would not be able to lock onto Soong without the combadge, and there was no time to transmit revised coordinates to the runabout's computer. Even as he hesitated, Picard saw more Borg emerging from their alcoves all along the corridor. They had him hemmed in in both directions, with nowhere to go except back to his ship. If he stayed any longer, he risked ending up like Vash: a soulless cog in the Borg machine.

There was no way around it. He had to leave Soong behind.

"Emergency Code Waterloo."

He glared at Soong in disgust as the transporter beam whisked him away.

6

Back aboard *Stargazer*, Picard did not waste a nanosecond mourning Noonien Soong. The old man had made his choice. Now he would have to live with it, for as long as the Borg permitted him to exist as a separate entity. Chances were, he was already regretting his decision.

I should have killed him myself, Picard thought.

He dashed to the cockpit and dropped into the pilot's seat. Terrified that a Borg tractor beam would latch onto the runabout at any moment, he hurriedly fired up the warp engine. Going to warp inside a solar system was chancy, but, given a choice, he would rather slam into an asteroid at lightspeed than let the Borg get their pincers on him. More than just his life was in jeopardy; his very identity was at stake.

The warp drive engaged, hurling him out of the Carraya system. Stars streaked by as the sudden acceleration slammed him into the back of his seat, decrepit inertial dampers notwithstanding. Picard poured on the speed, not easing up on the throttle until he was dozens of light-years away from the ill-fated system. Long-range sensors scanned the empty space behind him. To his relief, the Borg ship was not in pursuit. Apparently, the Borg did not consider him worth chasing.

He had never been so glad to be insignificant.

His racing heartbeat gradually slowed down. Adrenaline drained from his bloodstream as he sagged within his seat. "My God," he murmured as the enormity of the situation sank in.

Vash was dead, but that was only the beginning. The Borg

were coming, threatening the entire Alpha and Beta Quadrants with a nightmare beyond imagining. Picard staggered back into his cabin and poured himself a stiff drink. The cheap rotgut was no Château Picard, but it helped to steady his nerves. He tossed his disruptor onto his cot. He wondered if he would ever be able to fire the weapon again without remembering how he had used it to destroy the unholy abomination that the Borg had made of Vash. Her ghastly visage haunted his memory. A snatch of poetry, from a forgotten Terran wordsmith, flashed through his brain:

> *The nightmare Life-in-Death was she,*
> *Who thicks man's blood with cold.*

He realized now that the Borg would be a thousand times worse for humanity than the Alliance had ever been. At least under the Klingons and the Cardassians, humans still had their own minds and individuality, not to mention hope of a better future somewhere down the road. The Borg, on the other hand, were the worst of both worlds, combining the ruthless efficiency of machines with the territorial aggressiveness of history's most predatory empires. Gul Madred was Father Christmas by comparison.

But what could one powerless human do to halt the invasion? Picard wasn't sure that the Alliance could stop the Borg's relentless advance even if they heeded his warnings, which was unlikely. He was just a lowly Terran, after all. Picard doubted that even Gul Madred would take him seriously. The Alliance was too confident of its power. The Borg were going to roll right over them.

It's up to me, he thought grimly. If he was smart, he would take off for the Gamma Quadrant and never look back; he might well live out the rest of his life before the Borg caught up with him.

But what about the rest of humanity? And the Vulcans and the Andorians and the rest of the Alliance's subject populations? He thought of all the rich and fascinating cultures that had developed in the cosmos over the last five billion years. All that history would amount to nothing if the Borg had their way. From what he'd seen, they had no use for art or philosophy. All they cared about was technology.

Escape is not an option, he decided. After spending his entire career trying to uncover the secrets of the past, he couldn't just stand by and let the Borg bulldoze over all that history—even if that meant saving the Alliance. *That's not who I am, not who Vash wanted me to be.*

Fortunately, he also had a plan. . . .

Stargazer sped through the Neutral Zone toward an uncharted planet located perilously close to the Romulan border. Picard had long suspected the nameless planet of being Iconia, the near-mythical homeworld of the long-lost and incredibly advanced Iconian civilization. Often referred to in ancient texts as the Demons of Air and Darkness, the Iconians were known to have possessed technology far beyond that of any present interstellar civilization. Perhaps even beyond the Borg?

We can only hope, Picard thought. The bitter irony that he was now risking everything to save the very same Alliance that had oppressed his people for generations was not lost on him. Somehow he doubted that Gul Madred and his brutal regime would appreciate his efforts, even if, against all odds, he succeeded in repelling the Borg. The Alliance would never admit to being saved by a mere Terran, no matter what happened next. The best Picard could hope for was life as a fugitive. *But this isn't just about me. Not anymore.*

The runabout slowed to impulse as it entered the Yelm system. Iconia appeared upon the viewscreen: a rocky brown planet that looked extremely inhospitable to most life-forms. Its ravaged surface still bore the scars of the cataclysmic orbital bombardment that had destroyed the Iconians over two hundred thousand years ago, when their fearful neighbors had joined forces to exterminate the dreaded "Demons" once and for all. Long-range scans detected the ruins of bygone cities, monuments, and palaces. Wispy white clouds drifted across the planet's atmosphere. No life signs registered anywhere on the murdered world.

Picard approached Iconia cautiously. He had longed to explore the planet for years, ever since finding an artifact on Decius III that had pointed him in the right direction, but that was easier said than done. Although long extinct, the Iconians had left potent defenses, as other would-be treasure hunters had learned the hard way. Despite the urgency of his mission, Picard didn't intend to waste his life fruitlessly. He had spent years planning an attempt at Iconia. He wasn't going to rush things now.

Easy does it, he thought. *Stargazer* slowed to one-quarter impulse power, just beyond range of the planet's automated defenses. Picard increased the magnification on the viewscreen, zeroing in on a demolished installation in the mountains of the smaller continent. He kept a wary eye on the ruins as he ran through his preparations, making sure that all the necessary systems were in working order. Much to his relief, nothing stirred within the craggy brown mountains. Scanners detected no unusual energy build-ups. *So far, so good. . . .*

A proximity alarm went off, signaling that another vessel had entered the system. The image on the viewscreen was replaced by the sight of an enormous green starship, many hundred times the size of the runabout. A pointed beak identified it as a *D'deridex*-class Romulan warbird. Picard hastily raised his shields, for what little good that would do. *Stargazer*'s paltry defenses would be of little use against the powerful warship.

I was afraid of this, he thought. One couldn't enter the Neutral Zone without risking just such an encounter, and he had been pushing his luck for some time now. Was this the same warbird he and Soong had narrowly evaded back in the Nequencia system? *Possibly.*

He half expected the warbird to blow him to atoms without further ado, but the starship hailed him instead. Picard gratefully accepted the transmission.

"Attention, unauthorized vessel." A Romulan officer appeared on the viewscreen. Suspicious black eyes peered out from beneath his prominent brow. A black velvet stole was draped over one shoulder of his pleated silver uniform. The man's tone was far from welcoming. *"This is Commander Tebok of the* Imperial Warship Gath'thong. *Identity yourself at once."*

Picard replied to the hail. Perhaps he could still talk his way out of this situation? Certainly, the unarmed runabout posed little threat to the Romulans.

"My name is Galen," he lied. "Forgive my incursion. I'm simply conducting a routine scientific survey of this system." The less he said of his true mission, the better; why let the Iconian's vaunted technology fall into the hands of hostile Romulans? "I meant no harm."

"Your presence in the Neutral Zone, particularly this close to Romulan space, represents a serious violation of treaty," Tebok said sternly. No doubt his sensors had already determined that *Stargazer* was unarmed. *"Acts of espionage will not be tolerated. Prepare to be boarded."*

"Wait!" Picard protested. He couldn't possibly mount a defense against the Borg from inside a Romulan prison camp. "This is all a terrible misunderstanding. I'm an explorer, not a spy!"

"That is for us to determine," Tebok stated. *"This is not a negotiation. Lower your shields or be destroyed."* A warning blast from the *Gath'thong's* disruptors shook the tiny runabout. *Stargazer's* shields lost power by thirty-five percent. *"You will not receive a second warning."*

The Romulan commander curtly cut off the transmission. The emerald warbird loomed menacingly on the viewscreen. Picard could see no alternative to surrender. He reluctantly shut down his shields, wondering whether he should attempt to explain to Tebok about the Borg. The Romulans' remote outposts had already suffered at the hands of the cybernetic invader. Perhaps he could convince them to take his story seriously? As far as he knew, the paranoid Romulans didn't discriminate against Terrans; they distrusted all other species equally.

The Borg don't discriminate either, he reflected. *Which makes them everyone's enemy.*

The *Gath'thong* lowered its own shields in preparation for beaming over the boarding party. This presented no tactical advantage to Picard. Even if *Stargazer* had been equipped with disruptor banks, he doubted that he could have made a dent against the colossal warbird. Bracing himself for the Romulans' arrival, he spun around in his chair. A low-pitched whine started up at the rear of the main cabin. The shimmer of a transporter beam began to materialize inside the runabout. Picard put aside his disruptor and raised his hands. He hoped the centurions wouldn't rough him up too much. That would just complicate things.

Without warning, a Cardassian warship uncloaked behind the *Gath'thong.* "What the devil?" Picard exclaimed. The newcomer unleashed a devastating salvo of disruptors and photon torpedoes against the unshielded warbird. A blinding glare filled the viewscreen, causing Picard to throw up a hand before his eyes as the Romulan starship exploded into pieces. A white-hot ball of blazing plasma engulfed the wreckage. A shock wave sent *Stargazer* tumbling backward through the vacuum, throwing Picard from his seat. He slammed against the starboard bulkhead before landing in a heap on the floor. Bits of burning debris bounced off the runabout's hull. Metallic clangs echoed through the cockpit. He tasted blood.

Where did that Cardie ship come from? Picard thought anxiously. *And what the hell is it doing here?*

Bruised and bleeding, he jumped to his feet and staggered toward the controls. Automated systems quickly stabilized the runabout's flight path, halting its out-of-control somersaulting through space. Grabbing onto the pilot's seat to steady himself, he rapidly raised what remained of the ship's shields. The alarming echoes faded as the restored deflectors diverted shrapnel away from *Stargazer*'s hull. Picard dropped into his seat and wiped the blood away from a split lip. Crimson traces smeared the back of his hand. His brain feverishly tried to catch up with events.

The *Gath'thong* was gone. Commander Tebok and his entire crew were dead, mercilessly slaughtered by the Cardassian vessel's sneak attack. Picard glanced back at the rear of the cabin. The nascent shimmer had dissipated entirely, suggesting that the warbird's transporter room had been destroyed before the transmission had been completed. The boarding party's atoms must have been scattered throughout the sector.

At least they died quickly, he thought. *All the Romulans did.*

Their destroyer took the warbird's place on the viewscreen: a *Galor*-class warship, among the most powerful in the Alliance fleet. Pale orange plating armored the imposing vessel from prow to stern. Although slightly smaller than the warbird it had just destroyed, the Cardassian ship was still a giant compared to the humble runabout. The vessel's name, *Hebitia,* was inscribed in Cardassian on the ship's wedge-shaped prow, and it owed its cloaking technology to the spoonheads' Klingon allies. Picard wondered what an Alliance ship was doing so near the Romulan border. He doubted that it had come all this way just to lend him a hand.

To the contrary, I expect.

Matters became somewhat clearer when a hail from the warship forced itself upon his viewscreen. Gul Madred glowered balefully from the captain's seat of the other vessel. A scowling Klingon, whom Picard didn't recognize, stood at Madred's shoulder, his beefy arms crossed in front of his chest. Had it been the Klingon's idea to blow the Romulans into spacedust? There was no love lost between their respective empires, especially after the Klingons betrayed the Romulans at Khitomer twenty years ago.

"Hello, Luc," Madred said coldly. *"You're a long way from P'Jem."*

How much did he know? "I can explain," Picard began. "I uncovered a new lead underneath that old Vulcan monastery. . . ."

"Don't bother," Madred said, holding up his hand to forestall any further attempts at prevarication. *"Your subversive activities have already come to light."* He shook his head. *"Whatever were you thinking, Luc? I had thought you smarter than this."* His saturnine features bore testament to his extreme displeasure. Simmering resent-

ment suffused his voice. *"Fortunately, I had the foresight to plant a tracking device upon* Stargazer *years ago, when we first began our association. I must admit I never expected to find you this far into the Neutral Zone. Is there a rebel base down on that wretched planet ahead?"*

So that's how he found me here, Picard thought. He should have suspected that there was a tracking device aboard the runabout. Since when would a Cardassian let a Terran loose in the cosmos without a leash of some sort? But there was no point crying over spilled *kanar.* There were vastly more important issues at stake here. *I don't have time for this.*

"Listen to me, Madred," Picard pleaded. "The entire Alliance is in danger. An alien species called the Borg is intent on invading this region of the galaxy. They're incredibly powerful and impossible to negotiate with. If we don't work together, the Borg will sweep over your empire like a horde of locusts!"

Madred smirked mirthlessly. *"More of your primitive myths and legends, Luc? Spare me your pitiful attempts at obfuscation. I erred in trusting you as much as I did."* His pitiless gray eyes shot daggers at Picard. *"Rest assured that I shall not make that mistake again."*

The Klingon laughed boisterously in the background, eliciting a venomous look from Madred. Picard grasped that the Cardassian commander had been deeply embarrassed by the exposure of Picard's extracurricular involvement with the Resistance. He could expect no mercy at the gul's hands.

"You don't understand," Picard insisted. "This is bigger than just you and me. The Borg want to assimilate us all, turn us into soulless, mechanized creatures like themselves." Vash's transformed visage flashed behind his eyes. "For God's sake, Madred. Think of your family, your daughter. Do you want her to be conquered by the Borg? They'll steal her very *self* from her. Believe me, I've seen it with my own eyes. They're relentless!"

"That's enough," Madred barked, losing his composure. *"Never speak of my family again, or I'll have your tongue surgically removed. You'll have to scribble your confession with bloody stumps before I'm done with you."* He took a deep breath to calm himself. *"Or you can coop-*

erate fully and perhaps earn a relatively painless execution. Where is the rebel leader named Vash? And the fugitive, Noonien Soong?"

Picard didn't know whether to laugh or cry. "Vash is dead, and Soong might as well be."

"You truly expect me to believe that?" Madred snarled.

"Not really," Picard said. He was wasting his breath. Madred was too angry at being made a fool of to listen to anything Picard had to say. *I have to get away from him before I find myself in an interrogation chamber aboard that warship.* A desperate strategy occurred to him. There was no way *Stargazer* could outrun the *Hebitia* for long, but maybe it didn't have to. . . .

Cutting off the transmission, he accelerated toward Iconia at nearly full impulse power. His fingers danced over the helm controls, taking evasive action as the *Hebitia* pursued the fleeing runabout. *Stargazer* zigzagged through space, veering sharply at random intervals in order to keep the Cardassian vessel from locking onto the smaller ship with its disruptors. Violet beams sliced through the void. A lucky shot strafed *Stargazer*'s port nacelle. Bright blue flashes of Cerenkov radiation flared wherever a deadly beam intersected with the runabout's weakening shields. Warning lights blinked on *Stargazer*'s control panel. Violent energy discharges jarred the cockpit.

Picard executed a hard right turn, yanking the endangered nacelle away from the disruptor blasts. The move pushed the inertial dampers to their limit, throwing him hard to one side. Diagnostic readings indicated that the deflectors were down another twelve percent. *No photon torpedoes yet,* he noted, thanking providence for small favors. Madred seemed to be targeting the warp nacelles instead. *Guess he's determined to take me alive.*

A second blast tagged the starboard nacelle. Sparks erupted from the console in front of Picard as the energy surge caused a system overload. Smoke rose from the helm controls, along with the acrid smell of burnt circuitry. His face and eyebrows slightly singed by the sparks, Picard threw himself into the copilot's seat and diverted helm control to the auxiliary backup system. He tried to check on shield status, but the diagnostic display had gone blank. No matter; he knew *Stargazer* couldn't take many more hits like that.

The desolate brown surface of Iconia grew steadily larger on the viewscreen, until it fairly filled the monitor before him. *Almost there,* he thought. His gaze stayed fixed on one particular mountain range, where all his hopes resided. Evasive maneuvers helped the runabout dodge the ceaseless disruptor beams. *Just a few more kilometers . . .*

Gul Madred forced his way back onto the viewscreen. *"That's right, Luc. Lead me right to your rebel friends' hiding place on that clan-forsaken planet."* He leered in anticipation. *"I can't wait to make their acquaintance."*

Stabbing at the console with his fingertip, Picard killed the visual but kept open an audio line to the *Hebitia*. "Come and get me!" he taunted Madred, luring him in. He stabbed at the Cardassian's wounded pride like an ancient Terran picador tormenting an enraged bull. The runabout cruised into orbit around Iconia, with the *Hebitia* hot on its tail. *Here goes nothing,* he thought. Would his reckless ploy pay off?

As if in answer to his unspoken prayers, a bright light suddenly flared amid the rocky peaks of the southern mountain range. *Yes!* Picard thought jubilantly. The late great Terran pirate, Black Jack Crusher, had reported an identical flare during his ill-fated attempt to plunder Iconia twelve years ago. Picard had spent hours poring over Crusher's log, along with the accounts of the few survivors. He had also tracked down fragmentary records of earlier, even more disastrous expeditions. Unlike Madred, he had done his homework. He knew what the flare meant . . . and what was coming next.

"Battle stations!" Madred shouted. Evidently his people had detected the activity on the planet's surface as well. *"Alpha alert!"*

Only seconds after its launch, the Iconian probe entered orbit between *Stargazer* and the *Hebitia*. The artificial construct took the form of a glowing blue sphere, roughly six hundred meters in diameter. Coruscating bolts of energy circled the globe.

"Damn you, Picard!" Madred cursed him. *"What are you and your filthy insurgents up to? How dare they fire upon a ship of the Alliance?"*

Madred obviously believed the sphere to be some new Resistance weapon.

He should be so lucky, Picard thought.

"Quick, Madred!" he urged his enemy. "Destroy that probe before it's too late!"

"I'll do nothing of the sort!" the Cardassian shot back. *"How foolish do you think I am, to fall for your trickery yet again? You Terran scum speak the truth only under torture. Otherwise, you lie as readily as you breathe!"*

Picard repressed a smile. Clearly, Cardassian children's literature contained no equivalent to Brer Rabbit and the briar patch. . . .

Too bad for them. They should never have suppressed Terran culture.

As he had hoped, the probe focused on the larger vessel first. If Picard's theories were correct, the automated sentry was scanning the *Hebitia* at this very moment. But that wasn't all it was doing; the seemingly harmless scan was also infecting the Cardassian warship with an incredibly sophisticated computer virus that would spread like a contagion throughout the entire ship, causing escalating breakdowns in every vital system, from life-support to propulsion. In the past, every ship that had ever encountered an Iconian probe had been destroyed by some sort of catastrophic malfunction. A warp core explosion had torn apart Black Jack Crusher's cruiser, the *Bonny Beverly*. Life-support failures, unplanned decompressions, and other fatal errors had doomed prior vessels, and Picard had every reason to expect that the *Hebitia* would soon suffer the same fate.

The trick was going to be staying alive long enough for the virus to take effect.

Time to stall, Picard thought. At the same time, he shut down *Stargazer*'s linked computer network, switching to manual control.

He hailed the other ship. "What's the matter, Madred? Don't you recognize that probe? I thought you were a scholar and historian?"

The Cardassian's face reappeared upon the screen. *"Explain yourself, Luc!"* he demanded. Behind him, the Klingon was bellowing orders at subordinates. *"What is that thing out there?"*

"You're the one with the priceless collection of ancient artifacts," Picard said mockingly. "You figure it out."

Madred's face purpled beneath his scales. *"I'll get my answers from you, Luc. One way or another."*

"Try and catch me," Picard challenged him. The runabout pushed its impulse engines to the breaking point as it zoomed above Iconia, clinging to the planet's orbit as though hoping to place the dense rotundity of the world between itself and the pursuing warship. The strain on the engines set the cockpit rattling around Picard; he could feel the vibration in his bones. The tips of the warp nacelles began to glow ominously, hinting at a risky FTL departure. In fact, he had no intention of fleeing the system. He just needed to give the Iconian computer virus time to work its high-tech magic.

"Don't think that you can escape me, Luc," Madred threatened him. *"You're only delaying the inevita—"* He looked up in surprise as the overhead lighting aboard his bridge flickered unexpectedly. Early evidence of the virus's progress through the *Hebitia*'s systems? *"Halt that ship!"* Madred barked. *"Don't let him get away!"*

Stargazer's warp core was located along the top of the runabout, with the deuterium tank located at one end and the antideuterium at the other. Picard gulped as he felt a disruptor burst strike the roof of his ship. *"Warning,"* a computerized voice announced. *"Warp containment field failing. Estimate total containment collapse in eleven-point-three-zero seconds."*

"Damn!" Picard cursed. With only heartbeats to spare, he ejected the warp core before the entire runabout could be destroyed in the imminent matter/antimatter explosion. Was it too much to hope that the detonation would take out the Cardassian battleship instead?

A disruptor blast from the *Hebitia* quickly squelched that feeble hope. The beam ignited the warp core well ahead of the larger ship's path. Protected by its formidable shields, the starship cruised unscathed past the explosion, even as a tremendous shock wave buffeted *Stargazer,* jarring Picard in his seat.

So much for my warp drive, he realized. The runabout wouldn't be exiting this system any time soon, at least not via a working warp core. And even his impulse engines were starting to falter. Propulsion came and went in hiccups as *Stargazer* jerked forward erratically, gradually slowing to less than one-half impulse power. Picard reluctantly eased up on the engines to avoid burning them out completely. The runabout listed to one side, suggesting that the port engine was all but shot. Picard had to reduce power to the starboard engine to compensate. At this rate, he'd be dead in space in no time.

But the *Hebitia* appeared to be having problems of its own. Chaos spread on the starship's bridge, visible on the screen before Picard's eyes. The lights above the command area dimmed once more. Electronic snow blurred Madred's image. A data padd floated across the screen as the ship's artificial gravity failed. A pair of turbolift doors behaved like chattering teeth, opening and closing at a rapid pace. Agitated voices babbled in the background. The Klingon instinctively drew his disruptor pistol, but the weapon was of no use against the invisible foe sabotaging their ship.

"What's happening?" Madred snapped irritably. He had to grab onto the armrests of his seat to keep from drifting upward. Static distorted his voice. *"Somebody fix this before I have you all charged with criminal incompetence!"*

Picard was impressed by the speed with which the Iconian virus was undermining the *Hebitia*'s operations. Cardassian computer systems seemed to be exceptionally vulnerable to the insidious virus, which was tearing through the ship's computer firewalls and antivirus protections as though they barely existed. No surprise there; compared to the immeasurably advanced Iconian program, twenty-fourth-century software was like a child's early attempt at finger painting. Modern security measures were hopelessly outmatched.

It's only a matter of time now, Picard thought.

"It's that accursed probe!" Madred realized belatedly. His face livid, he yelled at an off-screen tactical officer. *"Destroy it at once."*

Told you so, Picard gloated silently. *You should have listened to me.*

"Disruptor controls not responding!" a panicky voice reported. *"I'm completely locked out!"*

"Then use the torpedoes, you fool!" Madred shrieked. His cool, condescending manner had disintegrated entirely. The imperious gul was exposed as what he truly was: a small, pitiable man who hid his lack of character behind the trappings of authority. *"Do I have to think of everything myself?"*

"Launching torpedoes," his underling reported. *"Targeting . . . wait! Something's wrong! The torpedoes didn't launch!"*

A series of violent explosions tore apart the *Hebitia* as the armed torpedoes went off inside their own launch tubes. Gul Madred, the unnamed Klingon, and everyone else aboard the starship perished instantly as the *Hebitia*'s own warp core detonated spectacularly. Jagged pieces of scorched duranium rained down on Iconia, contaminating the two-hundred-thousand-year-old ruins on the planet's surface. Picard mentally apologized to his fellow archeologists.

Beyond that, he had no regrets.

But what about the probe itself? Picard scanned for the glowing orb, hoping that it had not been consumed by the conflagration. He breathed a sigh of relief as the radiant blue sphere appeared on the viewscreen. Thankfully, Madred had not managed to destroy the probe with his torpedoes, which meant that Picard didn't have to wait for another probe to be launched from the Iconian base.

This one will do just fine, he thought.

The probe hovered in space not far from the site of the *Hebitia*'s fiery demise. Picard guessed that he had only a few moments before the probe turned its attention to the runabout. Moving quickly, he snagged the probe in a stasis beam. Heavy layers of kelbonite shielding guarded *Stargazer*'s computer core, but he kept the runabout on manual control just to be safe. "Got you!" he muttered. Now he just needed to get the captured probe to where it was needed, without a warp drive or any other computerized propulsion system.

As was so often the case, the answer lay in the distant past. Rising from his seat, he pulled down a lever embedded in the ceiling of the cockpit. Outside the ship, metal panels slid away, releasing an array of delicate solar sails from concealed compartments built into the runabout's hull. The filmy golden sails unfolded both above and below the tiny vessel, swelling and rippling beneath the subtle pressure of the tachyon eddies swirling across the void. The reflective sails resembled the wings of some alien butterfly, with a smaller jib sail sprouting between them like antennae.

Over eight centuries ago, the ancient Bajorans had employed similar sails to explore vast reaches of interstellar space, even reaching Cardassia Prime many light-years away. Alliance propagandists regularly trumpeted this accomplishment as proof of the historic bond between Bajor and Cardassia. Picard had chosen to focus instead on the solar sails as an elegant way of bypassing the Iconian computer virus.

His original plan had been to use the solar sails to reach the surface of Iconia, where he'd hoped to explore the tantalizing ruins dotting the planet. His priorities had changed, however, so instead he tacked against the astral winds, charting a course back toward Alliance space. His tractor beam dragged the Iconian probe behind him.

To cut down on his mass, he jettisoned the useless warp nacelles. They'd cost a pretty penny to replace someday, but he couldn't afford to worry about that now. A subatomic stream of faster-than-light particles swept *Stargazer* forward at an ever accelerating rate. He caught a powerful eddy just outside the Iconian system, and soon the runabout was sailing through space at nearly warp six. Picard searched the runabout for more nonessentials to jettison. A spare deuterium injector, a secondhand environmental suit, three bars of gold-pressed latinum (courtesy of Gul Madred), a chest of contraband Denevan crystals (ditto), a defective flow regulator, a supply of Alliance-issue water packs, drained neodymium power cells, and a case of Ktarian merlot were all beamed out into space, just to increase his speed. All that mattered was whether he could get the ship going fast enough to make a difference.

He had an appointment with the Borg.

Stargazer's walls had nearly been stripped bare by the time he intercepted the Borg. Tracking the relentless invader had proved no challenge at all. The Borg diamond was making a beeline for the Klingon homeworld, leaving a trail of devastated colonies and bases behind it. Beta Thoridar, Khitomer, and Morska had all fallen before the Borg's ceaseless onslaught. Picard just had to follow the distress signals:

"Mayday! Mayday! W'Nakki Central—the entire city—was just yanked into space. Survivors require immediate assistance. Please respond!"

Picard regretted that he could not pause to offer succor to the shell-shocked victims. Until the Borg were stopped, no one in the Alliance was safe.

I've got enough on my plate already, he thought. *Those poor souls are going to have to fend for themselves.*

Sailing toward Qo'noS, he encountered a flood of refugee ships heading in the opposite direction. All manner of freighters, shuttles, scout ships, and other transports were taking part in a frantic exodus from the Borg's path of destruction. Abandoning the Beta Quadrant altogether, the frightened civilians warped past *Stargazer* as they raced toward Cardassian space. Picard felt like a Terran salmon swimming upstream.

"You're going the wrong way, you damn fool!" a Bajoran vedek hailed him from a fleeing *Antares*-class carrier. Picard glimpsed a cargo bay full of weeping orphans behind her. *"The Day of Reckoning is upon us. Save yourself if you can!"*

Picard appreciated the warning, even if he had to ignore it. "Thanks," he said gruffly, "but I know what I'm doing."

I hope.

"Then may the Prophets preserve you," the vedek said. Picard was aware that some of her order ran an "underground spaceway" that helped smuggle Terran slaves to freedom outside the Alliance. *"And shield you from damnation."*

Her distraught face blinked off the screen. The orphan ship vanished into the distance.

"You, too," Picard muttered. He had never been a religious man, but he accepted the vedek's blessing without complaint. Against the Borg, he was going to need all the help he could get.

By all indications, the Alliance was making its stand in the Kowletz system, near Rura Penthe. The frozen prison planet was known throughout the galaxy as "the alien's graveyard." Countless rebels and dissidents had met their end on that frigid planetoid. Would it now become the site of the Alliance's demise as well? There would be a certain poetic justice in that.

A full-scale battle was already under way as *Stargazer* glided into the system. Picard was impressed despite himself at the massive armada aligned against the oncoming Borg diamond. Klingon birds-of-prey and battle cruisers, Cardassian warships, Bajoran assault vessels, and even a few Ferengi marauders swarmed around the gigantic diamond like angry wasps, strafing the Borg ship's hull with phasers and photon torpedoes. Fiery explosions blossomed against the diamond's technology-encrusted faces, but did not appear to be inflicting any significant damage. Ruptured bulkheads repaired themselves with unnerving speed. Force fields deflected disruptor beams of varying hues and intensity. Lethal pyrotechnics lit up the darkness.

No Romulan ships, Picard noted. The Star Empire was letting the Alliance take on their common enemy alone. *That could be a tragically shortsighted decision.*

He saw at once that the battle was going badly for the Alliance. Although severely outnumbered, the Borg ship was cutting a deadly swath through the assembled fleet. Incandescent ruby beams targeted the attacking starships with merciless efficiency. Not a single shot was wasted; every beam struck home. The searing lasers punched straight through the shields of both Cardassian and Klingon warships. Superheated plasma gushed from gaping wounds in the ships' fragile hulls. Picard watched in horror as an unlucky marauder was split right down the middle, spilling a crew of murdered Ferengi into the vacuum of space. *The Divine Treasury just got a little more crowded,* Picard thought. *It's going to be a seller's market at the Celestial Auction.*

His comm system picked up snippets of agitated voices:

". . . situation urgent. Require immediate reinforcements!"

"Casualties at ninety percent, deflectors off-line!"

"Rotarran is gone! Repeat, Rotarran *is gone. . . ."*

". . . this is Glinn Telle, assuming command. Request fresh instructions. . . ."

"Who is in charge here? We need a new strategy!"

". . . shields failing . . . multiple hull breaches on levels delta through . . ."

"Execute attack sequence thirty-seven-zee . . . now, damnit!"

". . . it's firing again . . . attempting to eva—"

"Somebody stop these honorless baktags!*"*

"Fire at will!"

Picard eyed the savage fireworks warily. He hadn't come all this way just to get caught in a cross fire. His sails flapped wildly as he tacked to windward. He skirted around the edges of the conflict, trying to get as close to the Borg ship as he dared. Wrecked starships, in varying stages of obliteration, cluttered the battlefield. Well-acquainted with the Alliance's forces, as every savvy Terran needed to be, Picard recognized several of the derelict vessels. The *B'Moth,* the *Groumall,* the *Vor'nak,* the *Ya'Vang,* the *Akorem,* the *Reklar,* and numerous other warships drifted like flotsam across the smoky void. A Bajoran assault vessel, spewing sparks from its tail section, crashed into the arctic wastes of Rura Penthe, raising a cloud of snow and ice within the planetoid's atmosphere. Seconds later, Picard had to tack sharply to the left to avoid colliding with a spinning fragment of charred tritanium. The jagged shard, which was at least twice the length of *Stargazer,* went whirling off into space.

Viewing the massacre, Picard had profoundly mixed feelings. If there was any justice, those two brutal guards from Celtris III had been aboard one of those ravaged battle cruisers. He was almost tempted to let the Borg reach Qo'noS, just to see the Klingon Empire brought to ruin. This was Vash's most fervent dream come to life: the Alliance routed at last.

Too bad that dream was also a nightmare.

"Resistance is futile." The Borg broke into the fleet's babel of frenzied communications. *"Lower your shields and surrender your vessels. We will assimilate your technology and biological distinctiveness. Your constituent species will adapt to serve us."*

The voice of the Borg sounded different, as though it was emanating from a single throat instead of the usual faceless multitude. It took Picard a moment to place the dull, uninflected tones.

Soong?

"The Klingon Empire will never surrender!" a guttural voice bellowed angrily. Picard traced the transmission to a battle-scarred bird-of-prey. The winged vessel swooped past the Borg diamond, unleashing a volley of photon torpedoes—to no avail. *"We will die with honor first! So says Kang!"*

His spoonheaded allies responded differently. *"Alliance forces,"* a cooler voice addressed the surviving combatants. *"This is Gul Trepar. Pull back at once."* A battered Cardassian warship turned away from the fray, leading a retreat toward the Alpha Quadrant . . . and Cardassia Prime. *"Regroup at the rendezvous point."*

Cardassian pragmatism won out over Klingon honor as the Cardassian and Bajoran vessels abandoned the fight, leaving only a handful of Klingon ships to carry on the battle against the Borg. *"Cowards! Traitors!"* Kang railed at his departing allies. His bird-of-prey took potshots at the fleeing armada. *"Your souls will swelter on the Barge of the Dead!"*

Picard had to smile at the disarray. If the Alliance survived the next few hours, there would be some serious fence-mending to be done between the Cardassians and the Klingons. The High Council would demand that heads roll. Literally.

But first he had to save the Alliance.

"Klingon vessels," he broadcast, announcing his presence. "This is Agent Galen on a classified mission for the Obsidian Order." The truth would have taken far longer to explain. "Do not fire upon me while I take action against the Borg."

He held his breath, waiting for the Klingons' response.

"*Understood,*" Kang said. The grizzled face of an elderly Klingon warrior appeared on the viewscreen. A disheveled gray mane hinted that the veteran soldier was at least one hundred years old, while his face was clean-shaven, unusual for a warrior. Seemingly oblivious to the jagged gash upon his ridged brown, he scrutinized Picard. If he wondered why any human would be working for the Cardassian secret police, he clearly had more pressing matters on his mind. *"All forces, hold your fire!"* He nodded gravely at Picard. *"Do what you can, Terran. At this point, I'd accept help from an army of tribbles."*

Likewise, Picard thought, relieved that he didn't have to worry about friendly fire for the moment. For a Klingon, Kang seemed eminently sensible. On Picard's viewscreen, the surviving birds-of-prey and battle cruisers pulled back to allow *Stargazer* a clear path at the Borg diamond. Picard took a deep breath before committing himself. There was no turning back now. It was time to cross the Rubicon . . . and hope for the best.

Towing the captured probe behind her, *Stargazer* sailed toward the oncoming Borg ship. Compared to the looming steel edifice, as well as the lurking Klingon warships, the compact runabout was easily the least intimidating vessel in the entire system. *Good,* Picard thought. *Let them underestimate me.*

His approach, however, did not go unnoticed. The Borg ship's menacing image vanished from the screen, replaced by a color-less, black-and-white figure. Picard blinked in surprise, barely recognizing the man in front of him.

"Soong?"

"I am Locutus of Borg," the figure corrected him. Like Vash before him, the aged scientist had obviously been assimilated into the Borg Collective. A black ceramic implant, connected by cables to corresponding units on the figure's torso, covered the left half of Soong's face. A red laser sensor augmented his human senses. The old man's wrinkled complexion was as pale and brittle as bleached papyrus. Layers of circuitry and black insulation had replaced his ratty attire. "Locutus" stared blankly ahead, his fixed gaze completely devoid of Noonien Soong's impishness and intellectual enthusiasm. He spoke in a lifeless monotone. *"You are the specimen designated Picard. Prepare to be assimilated."*

Picard felt as though someone had just walked across his grave. "Like hell!" he snarled.

"Your objections are irrelevant," Locutus declared. *"This unit retains the memory of your species' oppression under the Alliance. Your bondage is now at an end. All assimilated species are equal in the Collective."* Behind the transformed scientist, rows of inert Borg drones seemed to stretch backward into infinity. Many of them appeared to be Klingon or Romulan in origin. *"We are the future."*

Is this supposed to tempt me? Picard wondered. One look at the hideous thing that Noonien Soong had become was enough to convince him that the Borg had to be stopped at any cost. Soong might have been a dangerous maniac, but Picard wouldn't wish his ghastly fate on anyone. Not even the Alliance.

"Sorry," he replied. "Meet the past."

Stargazer swung about by one hundred and eighty degrees, turning her stern toward the Borg ship. Picard reversed the tractor beam holding onto the Iconian probe and sent the glowing blue orb spinning toward the enormous steel diamond. Killing the tractor beam, he let momentum carry the probe onward.

Now to see if the Borg took the bait. . . .

Picard leaned forward hopefully as the Borg ship scanned the probe with a shimmering sensor beam. Just as he'd hoped, the Borg had been unable to resist the lure of Iconia's exotic technology. In theory, the age-old computer virus was infecting the Collective at this very moment.

"Targeted artifact does not correspond with this sector's current state of technological progress," Locutus observed. His robotic voice acquired a hint of curiosity. He fixed his unblinking gaze on Picard. *"Explain anomaly at once."*

"Figure it out yourself," the human answered.

Having delivered the virus, there was nothing more for Picard to do here. *Time for a strategic withdrawal,* he concluded. Reactivating his computer system, he fired up the impulse engines and headed away from the towering Borg vessel, which was altogether too close for comfort. *Stargazer* had traveled less than a kilometer, however, before a Borg tractor beam grabbed onto the speeding runabout. Picard was thrown forward in his seat as *Stargazer*'s headlong flight for freedom came to an abrupt halt. A moment later, he felt his ship being dragged backward toward the waiting diamond.

"Escape is impossible," Locutus informed him. *"Assimilation is inevitable."*

We'll see about that, Picard thought stubbornly. He urgently worked the control panel as he turned both the impulse engines and the solar sails to the vital task of breaking free from the tractor beam's vigorous grip. Subatomic winds blew against the sails, causing them to billow outward, while the impulse engines hummed loudly in his ears. Picard diverted every kilojoule of available power to his dual propulsion systems, even as he pined for his dearly departed warp drive.

It wasn't enough. Even at full impulse power, the best he could do was retard *Stargazer*'s steady, inexorable progress toward the Borg ship. Aft sensors revealed a circular maw opening in one face of the enormous diamond, ready to swallow the runabout whole. Pulled in two directions, delicate solar sails were torn apart, the gossamer wings shredding under the pressure. Filmy gold ribbons fluttered around the runabout's hull. The mast of the jib sail toppled over, crashing against the roof of the cockpit with a resounding bang. Picard anxiously checked the navigational display. According to the readout, the Borg ship was only seven hundred meters away and closing.

"Lower your shields," Locutus intoned. *"Prepare to be assimilated."*

Never!

"Computer, initiate self-destruct sequence," Picard instructed. He had been prepared for this moment ever since he had escaped the Borg's inhuman clutches the first time. Better instant annihilation than a living death among the Collective. *Hang on, Vash. I'll be with you shortly.*

"Self-destruct sequence activated," Stargazer confirmed. Its computerized voice sounded more human than Locutus. *"Fifteen seconds and counting."*

Locutus waited patiently upon the screen. *"Pre-prepare for assim-assim . . ."*

Wait. What was that? Picard's ears perked up as he heard Locutus stumble over his words. Could the Iconian virus be taking effect already? If so, Picard realized, it would still be too late for him.

"Nine seconds and counting," the computer announced. "Eight . . ."

The Borg ship was only five hundred meters away.

At least I got to see the virus take root, Picard mused. He could die happy, knowing that he had struck his blow against the Borg . . . and drawn blood. *Too bad I won't be around for the final act.*

"Ramming speed!" Kang's exultant voice erupted from the comm as his damaged bird-of-prey came swooping down between Stargazer and the Borg diamond. Picard realized that the Klingons were buying him time, perhaps not realizing that he had already completed his mission. *"For the Empire!"*

The winged warship crashed into the source of the Borg's tractor beam. A blazing fireball consumed the emitter, releasing Stargazer. The runabout surged forward on impulse power as Picard realized, to his amazement, that he owed his life to the courage of a Klingon commander. *What universe is this?* he thought, dumbfounded by this unexpected turn of events. *Surely not the one I know.*

"Computer, cancel self-destruct sequence!"

"Affirmative," Stargazer replied. *"Sequence halted at two-point-six-eight seconds."*

Picard wiped the sweat from his brow. That had been a close one.

Pouring on the speed, he flew *Stargazer* away from the Borg ship as fast as he could manage. He half expected another tractor beam to seize him at any minute, but it appeared that the Collective had bigger fish to fry. On-screen, Locutus looked like he'd seen better days. His right eye twitched erratically. The miniature laser affixed to his temple shorted out. Subtle tremors shook his body. A grimace twisted his features. Greasy black drool spilled down his chin.

"I am Locutus, Locutus, Locutus," he stammered like a broken holoprogram. Behind him, the other drones staggered from their respective sarcophagi, lurching about in a state of obvious confusion. They collided into each other, their bionic limbs beyond their control. Diagnostic panels exploded above their heads. White-hot sparks spewed onto the catwalk below. The murky corridors filled with thick black smoke. *"A-a-alien data rejecting a-assimilation. Systemic p-purge failing . . ."*

For once, the Borg's collective consciousness seemed to be working against them, as the Iconian virus attacked every drone and system simultaneously. The sickly green glow radiating from within the Borg ship flickered and turned an ugly shade of mauve. Jets of superheated plasma vented from the intricate scaffolding covering the diamond's exterior. Concealed hatches opened at random. The entire ship began to tumble end over end. Even its astounding regenerative capacity was affected by the virus; shapeless, disorganized metal structures spread across the surface of the diamond like cancer. Borg efficiency, it seemed, was no match for the almost-preternaturally advanced technology of the ancient Iconians. The entire Collective was on the verge of a fatal cybernetic crash.

"Warning, warning!" Locutus blurted. His body jerked as though gripped by an epileptic seizure. Bloodshot eyes rolled wildly in their sockets. Tendrils of white smoke rose from the circuitry embedded in his pasty flesh. His prosthetic arm semaphored at his side, smashing into nearby equipment racks. Telescoping pincers scraped against the face of the communications console. *"Central plexus, plexus . . . corrupted."* A greenish froth sprayed from his lips. Watery eyes rolled upward until only the whites could be seen. *"P-polarizing generators losing field integrity . . . exponential collapse . . . Tra- transwarp coils . . . critical malfunction imminent . . ."*

A laser beam lashed out, destroying the probe. Significantly, it took the beam emitter two tries before it hit its target. The glowing azure globe exploded in a starburst of radiating sparks.

But the poison had already been swallowed.

7

Deep in the bowels of his mechanical hive, shielded by over-lapping layers of multigenerative security grids, the Borg king detected a disturbance spreading through the Collective, interfering with the proper operation of the ship. Ego buffers protected the king from the alien pathogen, which was rapidly overcoming the various measures installed to protect the ship's systems from contamination. The king noted that the mysterious pathogen had already infected the vinculum linking the vessel's various drones and unimatrixes. *Interesting,* he mused.

His cranium and spinal column resided in a dimly lit chamber at the heart of the Borg diamond. Blinking steel vertebrae were plugged directly into the central plexus that connected this soli-tary vessel with the rest of the Collective throughout the galaxy. The king's pale flesh glistened damply upon a humanoid visage. Thick black cables flowed from the neural transponders embed-ded in the back of his head. Holographic screens floated before his shrewd black eyes. The displays charted the progress of the pathogen as it worked its way through drones and apparatus alike. A separate screen preserved the image of the luminous blue orb that had carried the virus.

Where did you come from? the king wondered, more intrigued than alarmed by this unexpected development. The cybernetic language that composed the pathogen did not correspond with the technology of any species that the Borg had yet encountered in their mission to share their perfection with lesser beings. Cer-tainly, it had not originated with the Klingons, the Romulans, the

Cardassians, or any of the other primitive life-forms they had assimilated in this region. The very existence of the orb presented a provocative riddle that could not be left unsolved.

But not today. The safety of the larger Collective dictated that the pathogen not be allowed to spread beyond this vessel. The king had already blocked access to the central plexus from all input except his own, but he knew that was only a temporary solution at best; at the rate that the pathogen was propagating itself throughout the ship's neural networks, he estimated that the plexus would be corrupted in a matter of minutes. The only way to ensure that the virus did not infect the rest of the Collective was to destroy this ship immediately.

That this expedient would result in the termination of his corporeal form was of little consequence. Backup copies of his individual consciousness would be transmitted via a subspace carrier wave back to Unimatrix One up until the last nanosecond before termination. A new physicality awaited him.

Perhaps a female this time.

It was vital that his experiences in this sector be preserved. The loss of a single expeditionary diamond was a small price to pay for the discovery of this wondrous new technology. Assimilating this region, and locating the origin of the pathogen, had just become his top priority.

We will return, he resolved. A holographic display screen flickered momentarily, indicating that the virus was progressing even faster than he had anticipated. He immediately shut down the infected vinculum and willed the ship to commence the self-destruct sequence.

Then he began planning the next invasion. . . .

"Picard? Is that you?"

The quizzical tone caught Picard's attention. Locutus's eyes came back into focus and he looked around in confusion. The ashen face displayed genuine distress, and Picard realized that Soong's original personality had somehow reasserted himself, if only for the moment. The mutilated scientist gazed with bulging eyes at his own rampaging metal arm. Human fingers explored his transformed countenance. Palsied twitches continued to afflict his face and body. *"Oh my lord,"* he murmured. *"What did they do to me?"* Guilt filled his voice as he perhaps recalled the atrocities he had overseen as Locutus. *"What in heaven's name have I done . . . ?"*

The idea that some trace of Soong had still been present within his transfigured flesh appalled Picard. He doubted that this ill-timed return to individuality constituted any sort of mercy. Soong might have been better off before, when he couldn't appreciate what he had lost. *Thank God I killed Vash when I had the chance!*

"Picard?" the old man addressed him plaintively. He slumped against the Borg communications console, trying and failing to control the tremors shaking his mechanized frame. Gripping the prosthetic arm with his free hand, he put all his weight into trying to hold down the bucking artificial limb. A single tear streaked his cheek. His voice was hoarse with emotion. *"I was so wrong. Believe me, Picard, I never meant for . . ."*

Before he could complete the sentence, a convulsive shudder passed through his entire body. His posture stiffened, and the light fled from his eyes.

"I am Locutus of B-Borg," he stuttered. Facial tics confirmed that the virus was still rewriting his neural software. Equally stricken drones flailed about in the background. He slurred his words. Static fuzz interfered with the transmission. *"Resistance is futile, futile, futile. . . ."*

"Vive la Résistance," Picard replied.

Seconds later, the Borg diamond exploded from within. Picard had no idea how a transwarp engine worked, but powerful forces had obviously been employed. Unleashed by the cascading system failures, the violent energies tore through the cancer-ridden hull of the immense ship. Chunks of distorted mechanical tumors blew apart in all directions. Purple flames erupted from the ship's core. Deprived of its structural integrity, the entire diamond split into billions of smoking fragments. For a second, Picard thought he could see Vash's face in the glowing debris.

I did it! Picard rejoiced. *I destroyed the Borg!*

An irresistible shock wave hurled *Stargazer* away from the wreckage.

Afterward, Picard managed to salvage a workable warp core from one of the many lifeless hulks littering the system. The space around Rura Penthe had become a cosmic junkyard with spare parts free for the taking, as long as one didn't mind scouring through the gory remains of hundreds of Alliance soldiers. *An enterprising Ferengi could do well here,* Picard reflected.

For himself, he had bigger ambitions.

A few Klingon ships remained in the vicinity. In appreciation of his key role in the Borg's defeat, they left him more or less alone. Maybe there was something to this whole Klingon "honor" business after all? Just the same, Picard was glad that the Borg had managed to destroy the probe before their ultimate demise. He wouldn't want the Iconian's miraculous technology to fall into the hands of the Alliance.

It took him nearly a solar day to retrofit the warp engine from a trashed Bajoran scout ship into *Stargazer,* but at last he was able to leave the forlorn battlefield under his own power. Distant constellations stretched like taffy upon the viewscreen as he exited the Kowletz system at warp speed.

Besides a new engine, he had also found a new purpose in life. He had learned enough about the Borg to know that they were not the sort to be turned away by a single defeat. If anything, today's success could very well increase their curiosity about this corner of the galaxy. *They'll be back,* he figured, *and that probe trick isn't likely to work a second time. They'll adapt and try again.*

Picard intended to be ready for them. There was a big universe out there, with over six billion years of sentient history to explore. Who knew what forgotten secrets and weapons a resourceful tomb raider might be able to track down.

Taking care to steer clear of the fleeing Cardassian armada, he set course for Risa. The legendary pleasure planet was now the exclusive playground of the Alliance's elite, but Picard had a few ideas about how he might be able to poke around undetected.

Vash had once mentioned something called the *Tox Uthat*. . . .

Acknowledgments

Age of the Empress

We offer our heartfelt thanks to editor Margaret Clark at Pocket Books for asking us to participate in this project. It was an unexpected invitation and one we were thrilled to receive.

We also wish to thank Mike Sussman, the leader of this little expedition back to the Mirror Universe. Even though *Age of the Empress* is very much Mike's story, he welcomed us with open arms and called on us to invest ourselves in the project as though it was our own from the beginning. It was terrific fun from start to finish.

Of course, our acknowledgments are never complete until we thank our wives, Michi and Michelle. As always, their support is unwavering, their tolerance for our antics eternal. Ladies, what we do, we could not do without you.

(Yes, we'll get the trash out as soon as we're done here. Promise!)

The Sorrows of Empire

My first and deepest thanks, as ever, belong to my beloved wife, Kara. Her encouragement and support make my labors both bearable and worthwhile.

This book marks my first time working directly with editor Margaret Clark. It was she who called me out of the blue one day and asked if I would write the story of Emperor Spock for her just-approved Mirror Universe project. Knowing a tremendous honor and opportunity when it comes knocking, I said "yes."

Keith R.A. DeCandido, as always, was a great help during the conceptual stages of this tale, and his devotion to teamwork and collaboration led him to send me pages from his Mirror Universe *Voyager* book that dovetailed with my own story. For being a good friend and a good creative partner, I tip my hat to you, sir.

Pocket Books editor Marco Palmieri was also greatly helpful in making certain that a number of continuing story threads I wanted to set in motion in this book would be carried forward into the other Mirror Universe projects.

Working on a project like this, I would have been lost without the first-rate reference works of Michael and Denise Okuda (*The Star Trek Encyclopedia, The Star Trek Chronology*) and Geoffrey Mandel (*Star Trek Star Charts*).

And, lest I forget, none of this would exist at all if not for the brilliance of "Mirror, Mirror" scriptwriter Jerome Bixby, and the rest of the cast and crew of the original *Star Trek* television series, including the original "one man with a vision," Gene Roddenberry.

The Worst of Both Worlds
Thanks, most of all, to Margaret Clark for coming up with the basic idea for this story, then trusting me to write it. Also to my friends and family in Seattle, who provided a great deal of logistical support while I was trying to write this in the midst of an extended family reunion.

And particularly to Sumi Lee, for loaning me a VCR on which I could watch various crucial episodes over and over.

About the Authors

MIKE SUSSMAN has written or co-written more than thirty episodes of *Star Trek,* including the two-part *Enterprise* episode "In a Mirror, Darkly," hailed by *The New York Daily News* as "the best hours of *Enterprise* yet." Sussman began his television writing career in earnest when he was hired as a story editor during the seventh season of *Star Trek: Voyager.* In 2001, he was one of the first writers to come aboard the next chapter in the *Star Trek* saga, *Enterprise,* eventually rising to the level of producer. His other scripts include "Twilight," which was broadcast as the "Number 1 Fan Favorite episode" during the final season of *Enterprise.* After leaving *Star Trek,* Sussman worked as a writer and supervising producer on the CBS drama *Threshold.* He lives in Los Angeles and can be visited on the Web at www.mikesussman.net.

DAYTON WARD has been a fan of *Star Trek* since conception (his, not the show's). His professional writing career began with stories selected for each of Pocket Books' first three *Star Trek: Strange New Worlds* anthologies. In addition to the numerous credits he shares with friend and co-writer Kevin Dilmore, Dayton is the author of the *Star Trek* novel *In the Name of Honor* and the science fiction novels *The Last World War* and *The Genesis Protocol* as well as short stories that have appeared in *Kansas City Voices* magazine and the *Star Trek: New Frontier* anthology *No Limits.* Though he currently lives in Kansas City with his wife and daughter, Dayton is a Florida native and still maintains a torrid long-distance romance with his beloved Tampa Bay Buccaneers. Visit him on the Web at www.daytonward.com.

KEVIN DILMORE, for more than eight years, was a contributing writer to *Star Trek Communicator,* penning news stories and personality profiles for the bimonthly publication of the Official *Star Trek* Fan Club. On the storytelling side of things, his story "The Road to Edos" was published as part of the *Star Trek: New Frontier* anthology *No Limits*. With Dayton Ward, his work includes stories for the *Star Trek: Tales of the Dominion War* and *Star Trek: Constellations* anthologies, the *Star Trek: The Next Generation* novels *A Time to Sow* and *A Time to Harvest*, ten installments of the original eBook series *Star Trek: S.C.E.* and *Star Trek: Corps of Engineers*, the first installment of the *Star Trek: Mere Anarchy* mini-series, and the *Star Trek: Vanguard* novel *Summon the Thunder*. A graduate of the University of Kansas, Kevin lives in Prairie Village, Kansas, with his wife, Michelle, and their three daughters, and is a senior writer for Hallmark Cards in Kansas City, Missouri.

DAVID MACK is the author of numerous *Star Trek* novels, including the *USA Today* bestseller *A Time to Heal* and its companion volume, *A Time to Kill*. Mack's other novels include Wolverine: *Road of Bones*; *Star Trek: Deep Space Nine—Warpath*; *Star Trek: Vanguard—Harbinger*, the first volume in a series that he developed with editor Marco Palmieri; *Star Trek: S.C.E.—Wildfire*; and numerous eBooks and short stories.

Before writing books, Mack co-wrote two episodes of *Star Trek: Deep Space Nine*. He co-wrote the episode "Starship Down" with John J. Ordover. Mack and Ordover teamed up again to pen the story treatment for the episode "It's Only a Paper Moon," for which Ronald D. Moore wrote the teleplay.

Among Mack's upcoming projects are another installment in the *Star Trek: Vanguard* saga and a number of original novels.

An avid fan of the Canadian progressive-rock trio Rush, Mack has been to all of the band's concert tours since 1982.

Mack currently resides in New York City with his wife, Kara. Learn more about him and his work on his official Web site: www.infinitydog.com.

GREG COX is the *New York Times* bestselling author of numerous *Star Trek* books and short stories, including *To Reign in Hell, The Eugenics Wars, The Q Continuum, The Black Shore*, and *Assignment: Eternity*. His short fiction can be found in *Star Trek: The Amazing Stories, Enterprise Logs*, and *Tales of the Dominion War*.

In addition, he has written books and stories based on such popular series as *Alias, Batman, Buffy the Vampire Slayer, Daredevil, Farscape, Fantastic Four, Infinite Crisis, Iron Man, Roswell, Underworld, Xena*, and *X-Men*.

He lives in Oxford, Pennsylvania.

Cox's offical Web site is www.gregcox-author.com.

Printed in the United States
By Bookmasters